TEN DAYS IN PARADISE

Cindy,
Thanks again for your
interest in reading and
reviewing my novel!
Warm Wishes.
Linda

Linda Abbott

WB
WHITE BIRCH PUBLISHING

www.TenDaysInParadise.com

This is a work of fiction. Names, characters, places and incidents either are the product of the author's imagination or are used fictitiously. Any resemblance to actual persons, living or dead, events, or locales is entirely coincidental.

Copyright © 2013 by Linda Abbott

White Birch Publishing
ISBN 978-0692345504

To Paul and Charlie
for your love and encouragement

A silly idea is current that good people do not know what temptation means. This is an obvious lie. Only those who try to resist temptation know how strong it is . . . A man who gives into temptation after five minutes simply does not know what it would have been like an hour later.

—C. S. Lewis
Mere Christianity

The encounter that would unravel the staid fabric of David Blakemore's middle-age life started innocently enough. Certainly it was ironic that this unexpected twist of fate occurred on the first day of his family's long-awaited vacation. In deference to an urgent plea from his wife, he'd gone on a mission to find a cache of beach toys for their children, Ethan, Emma, and Colin. Marianne wanted an immediate inventory so she knew what to buy from the pricey tourist shops when she went into town. The fact that their children, ages six, four and two years old, typically refused to go along with any adult-inspired recreational activity simply did not occur to her. His wife had an agenda and today's agenda was the acquisition of a full set of brightly colored plastic pails, shovels and castle shapes.

The incandescent sunlight darkened as if on a dimmer switch as he entered the garage, a concrete structure supporting the large oceanfront condo building. He headed to the storage locker where the owners kept their beach paraphernalia. It was cool down here, and it felt good on his perspiring forehead. As he turned the corner into a narrow cinder block hallway lit by a dingy lightbulb, he was startled by the presence of another person. In the next second he recognized her. It was the woman he'd seen at the pool this morning.

He had first noticed her while playing with Ethan and Emma in the tropical lagoon-style pool. Alone in a sea of couples and

3

families, oblivious to everyone around her, she wore a ruby red swimsuit that fit like a leather glove on her slender figure. She had been reading a hardcover book, occasionally lifting her head to take in the postcard view, a glimmering ribbon of white sand beach under a dome of sapphire sky. The Paradise Resort and Spa certainly was everything the brochure promised and then some. Though he wasn't the kind of guy who made a habit of looking at other women, his gaze kept returning to her.

There was no avoiding her in the dank corridor. She stood in front of the storage unit opposite his, turning the key in the rusty deadbolt lock, trying without success to unlock the door. Dressed simply in a pale yellow cotton shirt and denim shorts, there was nothing overtly provocative about her appearance. A cascade of sable-colored hair framed a delicate face on which the most prominent feature were luminous hazel eyes. She was exceptionally pretty. He saw the glint of an emerald-cut diamond wedding ring on her left hand. Her voice, smooth like pancake syrup, interrupted his thoughts.

"Excuse me," she said, still twisting the key, "do you know if there is a trick to opening these doors? I'm not having any luck with this."

"Here let me try it," he said, moving toward her. She handed him the key, her fingers lightly brushing his, her proximity in equal measure intoxicating and overwhelming. Her hair carried the fresh scent of grapefruit, a scent that was clean and enticing and reminded him of long ago warm summer nights and the fervent ache of adolescence. His heartbeat quickened, and an unexpected blast of desire surged through him. He hoped this was not noticeable, and wondered what was behind the razor's edge intensity of his reaction. Not enough sex? Was he losing it? Was this the start of a mid-life crisis, something that he had witnessed in his older friends? Too much sun?

"Thank you so much. If you can't get it I'll just call the office, but I want to be sure because they already think I'm an idiot because I couldn't figure out how to work the bath tub," she said. "It was so embarrassing, turns out you have to *pull* the knob instead of *turning* it."

Glad for the task at hand, he carefully inserted the key into the deadbolt lock, slowly turned it, and then repeated the motion in the doorknob keyhole. "Here you go—problem solved."

She looked relieved and smiled at him, thrusting him deeper into his attraction to her. "You're a godsend, thanks again for your help."

His mind raced to find a way to prolong the encounter. Common sense told him to say "you're welcome" and leave before he did something stupid. He was, after all, a happily married man, right? It seemed incomprehensible that a perfect stranger could have this visceral of an effect on him, that this day that had started so uneventfully had taken this unanticipated turn, that the seemingly innocuous task of finding pails and shovels for his children had put him in harm's way. It made him think of small towns and tornadoes that strike without warning in the middle of the night.

She headed into the darkened tomb-like storage room and he seized the opportunity. "Let me hold the door for you."

She slipped inside, deftly navigating the mélange of beach toys, chairs, fishing poles and assorted beach gear. "So what is it you hope to find in here?" he asked, peering into the dark space.

"A bike. The people I'm renting from offer it with the condo."

It was resting against the back wall of the cinder block prison. She grabbed the handlebars, flipped up the kickstand and wheeled out a woman's no-frills standard-issue bicycle— large padded seat, thick tires, no hand breaks or gears and a wire basket. "You have no idea of how relieved I am that you're here. I'm terribly claustrophobic . . . I can just imagine that door swinging shut and getting locked in there for days!"

"A terrible way to spend a vacation at the beach," he joked, the flirtation in his voice effortless. The thought of her being afraid made him want to protect her.

"Have you been on the bike path yet?" he asked.

"This is my first day out. A couple of years ago we came here on a day trip and rode all over the island. How about yourself?"

"Not yet. My kids are too young to ride so I haven't been out yet." His choice of the "I" pronoun instead of "we" came naturally.

It was a good segue into the question he really wanted to ask. The mere fact that she was wearing a wedding ring didn't mean she was happily-ever-after married. Could be separated or on her way to divorce. He took in a deep breath, shifting his weight from one leg to the other. "Are you here with your family?"

"Actually, I'm here alone, a first for me. My husband and son—he's fifteen—are at home. I decided to take a vacation by myself, actually a much needed break from raising a teenager. Fifteen is a delightful age," she said, a lilt of unmistakable sarcasm in her voice.

"Yes, so I've heard. My best friend's kids are teenagers and they're giving him a run for his money. His solution is to drink heavily and play a lot of golf," he said.

She laughed. "How long are you going to be here?"

"Ten days. It's our first real vacation in a long time. We're having a family reunion to celebrate my parents' fiftieth wedding anniversary."

"What a great idea—your parents must be so happy," she said, her eyes engulfing him. *If she weren't so damn beautiful, I could relax, he thought.* He caught himself as his eyes drifted to the curve of her breasts pressed against soft cotton.

"You know, we're having a barbecue later this week. Very informal, you're welcome to join us. Does one get lonely taking a vacation alone?"

"I haven't been here long enough to answer that," she said, again that easy laugh like wind chimes on a breezy day. "Thanks for the invitation, who knows maybe our paths will cross again. Well, I'd better be going. Isn't this just the most incredible place?"

A final smile, and she turned and walked away with the bike. She was halfway across the parking lot when he realized that he didn't even get her name.

"David, will you take Ethan down to the pool to look for his Spiderman sunglasses? I think he left them by the slide."

Standing in the kitchen of their luxurious $3,000-a-week oceanfront condo, Marianne spoke as she wiped her hands on a crumpled kitchen towel. Dressed in a forest-green Nike T-shirt and khaki shorts, her long blonde tresses bound in a hastily-arranged scrunchie ponytail, she had just finished making a snack for Colin, who insisted on Cheerios and marshmallows every day before his nap. His mother, as in all things with the children, was only too happy to oblige this ritual that she had created and assiduously nurtured. In the sumptuous living room, Emma pulled at the hem of her lilac sundress, oblivious to her new surroundings, happily watching a *Sponge Bob* DVD. Sponge Bob and Patrick were a big part of Emma's life these days. She too was scheduled for a nap, or at least some quiet time. High strung by nature and given to tantrums, Emma needed her rest.

The condo, immaculate when they had arrived, was now a cluttered swamp of children's toys, clothes, DVDs and video games. Juice boxes and sippy cups were lined up on the glass coffee table, and Emma's twin Bitty Babies were "sleeping" on the leather sofa. The dolls' pink diaper bag sat nearby, next to a fresh Juicy Juice stain on the almond-colored carpet.

Still unnerved from the garage encounter, David was only too happy to oblige his wife's request. He needed a few minutes to regain his composure.

"C'mon Ethan, let's go find those sunglasses."

Ethan, wearing Spiderman swim trunks and a Lord of the Rings T-shirt, played his negotiating card. "Okay, but will you let me go down the slide?"

"Sure pal. You can go down the slide as many times as you want."

The words were no sooner out of David's mouth when he realized his mistake. Like the Energizer Bunny with a new nine-volt battery, Emma was instantly activated. "Daddy Daddy take me to the slide too. I want to go down the slide too. Please Daddy PULL-EASE . . ."

"Emma, we'll go down the slide later after you have your nappy." The kids had been at the pool all morning.

"No Daddy I don't want my nappy. Daddy PULL-EASE take me—I wanna go down the slide will you take me? I wanna go down the slide!" Emma's near platinum ringlet curls bounced in cadence with her words as she ran to her father, clinging to his leg, her slate-blue eyes fixed with determination.

David didn't want this trip to look for sunglasses to turn into an hour of watching Emma go down the slide. Especially when they were all going to dinner tonight and Emma would turn into Sleepwalker Zombie Child in the restaurant, which would in turn ruin his parents' dinner.

"Look Emma, I promise I'll take you later. But first you have to take your nappy."

"Honey," Marianne intoned from kitchen, "why don't you just take her? She doesn't understand why Ethan gets to go and she doesn't." While she spoke, Colin decided he'd had enough of his snack, picked up his plastic Bob the Builder bowl, turned it upside down and put it on his head, saying "ma ma ma ma" in rising decibel intensity. A fountain of miniature marshmallows and Cheerios splashed onto his wispy blond hair and shoulders, and then splattered on the floor. Marianne watched in quiet amusement and calmly picked up the bowl. "All done sweetie?"

she asked, taking him out of the high chair.

David, used to doing Marianne's bidding where the children were concerned, for some reason didn't want to comply with any more of her demands today. He was also slightly annoyed to see the floor of their $3,000-a-week condo covered with Cheerios and marshmallows. At least they were dry.

"Let me explain it to her. Listen Emma, you need your sleepy time so tonight we can go out to a nice dinner with Grandma and Grandpa. And then later we'll go down the slide."

"I wanna go down the slide now I don't wanna take my nappy," Emma protested loudly. Eyes filling with tears, she started to cry.

Marianne stood in the kitchen doorway, a look of reproach in her eyes. David knew the look well. This wasn't worth an argument.

"All right. Enough of this. C'mon let's go. Emma, you can go down the slide three times then it's back here for your nappy. Do you understand?"

"Five times, Daddy. I want to go down the slide five times, okay Daddy?" Emma asked, her tears having miraculously vanished.

Frustrated and desperate to buy a ticket out of this confrontation, he agreed. Marianne handed him two beach towels and went to retrieve Emma's swimsuit.

"She'll be fine," Marianne said, "and don't worry about your parents. They just need to relax more where the kids are concerned."

David held his tongue. His parents' parenting methods and Marianne's were light-years apart, but there was no sense getting into that now.

After making sure she had a bottle of water, the bike lock, sunglasses and the condo key, Ellen Bennett set out to explore the island. A whisper of ocean breeze felt like silk on her sun-warmed face. The bike path curved through a dense jungle of tropical trees, shrubs and sprawling bouquets of fuchsia-colored bougainvillea. Riding away from the shore, a cathedral of Australian pines shaded the path, offering a respite from the afternoon sun that had warmed the day to a balmy eighty-four degrees. In a word, she thought, heavenly.

She remembered her trip to Sanibel several years earlier; she and Jeremy and Andrew had rented bicycles and had ridden all over the island. They watched dolphins swimming, marveled at the plethora of shells on the beach, and stuffed their pockets until they were full of gems. They stopped at a rustic bar and grill and had fried grouper sandwiches for lunch. It was a golden memory now tucked into one of her meticulously organized vacation scrapbooks; had it only been three years ago that they had been so happy? She pushed the thought aside. None of that mattered now. This was her day—it was as if the good Lord had smiled on her and given her a gift. She pedaled, breathed deeply, and happily realized she had not felt this exuberant in a long time. She was free, her liberation a long time coming.

The bike path led westward, toward Sunset Beach. Across the street stood a magnificent row of beachfront condos, one more opulent than the next, properties that commanded the kinds of prices only the very wealthy could afford. *Private Property* signs staked out in lovely flowerbeds warned the uninvited to stay out. A shiny black jaguar, driven by an elegant looking older woman, silently passed her and turned into one of the gated entrances. Ellen pondered the realities of such a lifestyle. Was it as wonderful as it looked from the outside, living in a million dollar oceanfront condo, flying first class, going to spas and dining in five-star restaurants? Did the "haves" of Sanibel and elsewhere, born into wealth and privilege, realize their good fortune? Or were their lives mired in the same unpleasant realities of the human condition that faced people regardless of income level?

Ellen understood that she led a life that by many would be viewed as privileged and perhaps the same questions could be asked of her. True she was here off-season when the prices bore some resemblance to sanity, but there were plenty of poor souls on the planet who would never visit a place like this, or even know it existed. Yet she envied the people who owned a slice of this paradise, not so much for their money, but for their proximity to the ocean, which in recent years had become her passion: the soothing rhythm of the gentle surf, boundless cerulean skies and perpetual ballet of shorebirds dancing at the water's edge. It was the one place she could walk and pray and actually *feel* her connection to all of creation.

It was the pull of the ocean that had brought her here, at least that's what she had told everyone. What she had not revealed, and what most people would have had difficulty believing, was that her picture-perfect life was coming apart at the seams. Her husband was mired in a depression from which he couldn't seem to escape and their relationship with Andrew had deteriorated into an endless series of confrontations that destroyed the harmony they once took for granted. Ever since Andrew hit the teenage years, he'd been on a pedal-to-the-metal collision course with trouble—at home, at school and most recently with his high school basketball team. His grades were suffering, and teachers complained that he wasn't engaged in the classroom. Ellen and

Jeremy didn't like what they saw but had no idea how to stop it. It hadn't been this way with Steven, Jeremy's son from his first marriage, who was fourteen when they got married. Remarkably, Steven defied the conventional wisdom that a child of divorce could certainly be expected to test the limits of parental and academic discipline. Steven had cruised through high school with a 4.0 grade point average, graduated magna cum laude from Dartmouth and now held a lucrative job as an investment banker in London, where he lived with his girlfriend and an extremely indulged bichon frise.

Steven's success only amplified Andrew's struggles, and made Ellen feel like a failure as a mother. Once treasured, the relationship she had with her fifteen-year-old son was now in tatters. Right now, the only thing that interested Andrew was skateboarding, heavy metal bands and "hot" girls. He was angry a lot, and she was the recipient of much of his rage. She told herself this was normal adolescent behavior that would pass. Jeremy was very much an advocate of this theory, but after a while she began to seriously doubt its validity and came to see it as an excuse for deplorable behavior. No matter what she did, no matter how hard she tried to avoid conflict, the arguments were frequent and awful. She didn't understand how all the love she had poured into him could have produced his contempt for her, and she didn't know how to fix it. The reality of their stormy relationship was at times unbearable, and that, in a nutshell, is why she was here.

"Shut the fuck up," he had hissed at her from across the dinner table one night, his disrespect chilling her to the bone. This particular night the remark was so uncalled for, so out of line, that she left the dinner table and cried for an hour in bed. After she pulled herself together, she spent the next two hours online, finding her escape in a plane ticket to Florida and an oceanfront condo rental. It was ironic, that Andrew's tirades had unwittingly given her the determination to embark on this adventure. *Justice prevails.*

The bike path turned into the business district, taking her

past quaint shops and food vendors with names like Norm's Old Fashioned Hot Dogs. Suddenly running toward her was a deeply-tanned and fit thirty-something guy who looked like he ran every day. Which brought to mind the man in the garage whose GQ looks and personal charisma had registered a 6.0 on the encounters-with-strangers Richter scale. She didn't know his name, but surely she would see him again at Paradise. And he *did* invite her to the barbecue, which had surprised her. She couldn't imagine showing up and meeting his family. "Hi, I'm the married woman vacationing alone down the way." She'd be as welcome as a child with strep throat at a daycare center. Was he merely being kind to invite her, or perhaps he was nervous or . . . could it be that he found her attractive?

Now the path cut through a thick jungle of foliage. As she pedaled through the tunnel of greenery, she felt a tiny prick of anxiety. Alone in this beautiful place, she suddenly felt vulnerable to forces she did not fully understand.

An hour later, Ellen turned into the public beach access parking lot. It was six thirty, fifteen minutes until sunset, an event celebrated by islanders with the kind of reverence once bestowed on ancient pagan rituals. She fished the bike lock from her beach bag and wove it through the spokes of the wheels and then onto the steel rack. She grabbed her camera. A well-trodden wooden bridge, beaten by the sun and in dire need of a coat of stain, led to the beach. *No Parking* signs were posted everywhere, leaving her to wonder what people did with their cars here.

A group of beachgoers wearing sun visors and clutching digital cameras had gathered along the shore, determined to capture the mystical moment when the ball of sun vanished into the horizon. Some sat on blankets with picnic baskets and bottles of wine. Ellen kept walking to find a wide open shot and uninhabited photo of what was to come. Then she waited.

Over the next few minutes the heavens erupted. A fiery

blitzkrieg of scarlet, violet and amber illumined and electrified the pewter canvas of endless sky. Squadrons of pelicans flew over cobalt-darkened waters more ominous than inviting in the fading light. Shorebirds flitted to and fro in a prism of golden light on velvet sand. Over the years, Ellen had taken hundreds of pictures at sunset, transfixed by the subliminal show of nature. It was not uncommon for her to stand in awe until the very last speck of daylight had disappeared; she had seen sunsets so breathtakingly beautiful that a more powerful argument for God could not be made.

Standing there, she was overcome by a sense of joy and exhilaration.

The white-sand beach, as wide as an expressway, stretched for miles in both directions. Off in the distance she could see more than a dozen people standing in a tight circle at the water's edge. Curious, she started to move toward them. Squinting against the sun's dying light, she was surprised to see that they were in formal attire, men in dark suits and women in little black cocktail dresses and heels, the latter being no small feat on the sand. Puzzled, she scanned the crowd. In their midst, two people, a bride and groom.

Stunningly beautiful, the bride wore an ivory satin tea-length dress with a plunging back that showed off her tan, her hair done in an elegant chignon seemingly impervious to ocean breezes. The groom had that just-graduated-from-Harvard-Law look to him, the kind of young man that every mother wants for her daughter and seldom gets. Set back about a hundred yards from the beach stood an enormous stone building, banked with floor-to-ceiling Gothic windows that framed the magnificent ocean view.

A small group of casually dressed older women stood at a respectful distance watching the oceanside nuptials. Ellen joined them, exchanging knowing smiles with the women, who looked to be mostly in their sixties. "It's so romantic," one of them said quietly, her eyes hidden behind tortoise-colored Dior sunglasses. In her hand was a mesh bag stuffed with seashells.

"Brings back memories, doesn't it?" said another.

"Yes," said Ellen, nodding in agreement. The bride's eyes, brimming with loving adoration, were fixed on the groom's as he slipped the ring on her finger. It was a lovely moment, and the women breathed it in deeply, wanting to savor it and carry it home like the shells in their bags. Etched in the fine lines of their sixty-something faces was a wistful nostalgia, a longing for days past, and Ellen imagined, indelible memories of first loves. The years had passed but desire had not, its smoldering embers rekindled by this storybook bride and groom. Age robs women of many things, their looks, their children, the firmness of their flesh, but the one thing that age does not rob women of is this enduring desire for romantic love. It was something that Ellen herself had not comprehended as a younger woman, but at forty-five she understood it well.

A large flock of herring gulls circled overhead. The bride and groom exchanged their wedding vows and kissed after the minister pronounced them man and wife.

"I don't know why anyone would want to live on an island," George grumbled, his rugged looks and working class demeanor an unorthodox match for the Laura Ashley floral print chair on which he sat across the room from his wife of fifty years. "There's only one road in and one road out. And people pay a million dollars for these places. It's nuts."

Unlike Judy, who could adjust to new surroundings in the time it took to close her suitcase, George wasn't thrilled about being "stuck" on Sanibel for ten days. He shifted his weight, trying to get comfortable in a chair that had not been designed for comfort. "What are we going to do here for two weeks, watch those little rug rats try to drown each other in the pool?"

"George, calm down," Judy said with well-honed patience, checking her stylish new haircut in the mirror over the sofa. "First of all, those so-called 'little rug rats' are your grandchildren and you know how much you love them. You'll have a great time here, just wait and see. It's a beautiful place, we can go for walks on the beach and you can go golfing and deep-sea fishing."

Wearing a tropical shirt, tan shorts and his "Master Bait Fish & Tackle" hat that he had picked up many years ago on a family vacation, George was not to be humored. "Last time I went deep-sea fishing I threw up like Mount Vesuvius."

"That was years ago. You went lots of times and enjoyed it, remember when you and David caught so many fish they filled a laundry basket. C'mon, let's be positive about this. It's the first time we've all been together in years. I think it's wonderful that the kids wanted to do this for us. You should be happy they care. You know, Muriel and Tom barely get a Christmas card from Ronny and Pete," said Judy of their longtime friends and neighbors.

"A blessing in disguise from those two low-life drug addicts. Probably they don't even know it's Christmas. And if they did, they'd break into their own house and steal the gifts."

Judy simply didn't want to deal with George's negativity today. Not when the sun was flooding the room in buoyant light and the rolling waves proffered a constancy of soothing sound that to her ears were a panacea for anything that ailed her, mentally or physically. At the moment that included George's complaining.

"Muriel said they both went into treatment and are doing much better now," Judy said, reciting what Muriel had told her and what she had found hard to believe. Ronny and Pete had been trouble for as long as she could remember. Judy had spent the better part of her kids' teenage years keeping them away from the pair as much as possible while Muriel had spent most of her life in denial.

Judy looked contentedly around the elegantly appointed condo. *No matter what, I'm going to enjoy myself on this vacation.* She desperately wanted to park the worries of recent months back at home. No doubt they would be waiting there for her when she returned. Snapping her attention back to the present, walked over to the closet and took out a claret-colored sleeveless silk dress and perfectly matched low-heeled sandals. She was looking forward to dinner at Tommy D's Seafood Grille, one of the best restaurants on the island. She liked her dress more than she remembered, it really was striking. Perfect for her figure. At seventy, Judy was still an attractive woman with an impeccable sense of style.

"C'mon George. Let's take a walk before we have to get ready to go," she said.

"All right," George said, "under one condition that we stop and get a cold one on the way back."

"Deal," said Judy, grabbing her camera and keys. Unlike her husband, she couldn't wait to explore her new surroundings.

November on Sanibel was a quiet time. The hordes of upscale transients were gone, thankfully, the island having purged itself of another summer tourist season. Now came the true denizens, the Fortune 500 CEOs, successful entrepreneurs, wealthy investment bankers and other "winners of life's lottery" as some politicians were fond of calling them. They arrived at their multimillion dollar oceanfront villas and luxury yachts from places like New York, Boston and Chicago to avoid the brutality of freezing cold temps and the endless dreary gray days of winter. They came with wives, children, nannies and occasionally a mistress.

The paradigm of island demographics had shifted markedly in recent years. Today's new residents were younger and much wealthier. So much money had arrived on the island, in fact, that real estate prices had skyrocketed, triggering constant chatter and speculation among the locals. "Did you hear Tom and Sally got a *million dollars* for their cottage?" said one incredulous old-timer to another at the Coffee Cup Diner, a place locals met for breakfast and feasted on gossip.

There was a downside to this new prosperity: many of the year-round retirees who bought charming cottages in the 1970s and 1980s could no longer afford the property taxes and were forced to sell. Living in paradise wasn't cheap. Some locals even stayed with relatives during prime season and rented out their homes to pay their taxes. Even in this bastion of wealth and exclusivity, there were "haves" and "have-nots" and an uneasy truce was in effect. The old-timers resented the New Money and the wretched excess it had come to symbolize. After all, who really needed an 8,000 square foot Italianate villa?

NOVEMBER WAS BECCA JONES favorite time of year. She didn't have to wait two hours for a table at Anthony's and the nightmare of summer traffic had eased, making it much easier to get to the mainland, to Fort Myers with its twenty-plex cinemas and sprawling outlet malls. The upscale ambience of Sanibel was the antithesis of the rabid commercialism of Fort Myers, where scantily clad spring breakers had elevated binge drinking and wet T-shirt contests to high art. It was only a six dollar toll and a short ride across the causeway bridge, but it might as well have been another planet for the cultural and socioeconomic differences.

Becca parked her car behind The Palms Courtyard Shoppes, an eclectic mix of high end boutiques and restaurants on the edge of Sanibel's downtown business district. Though she'd been here more than two years now, she had not lost one iota of appreciation for the island's extraordinary beauty, absorbing it with renewed pleasure as she walked through the lush gardenscape. A profusion of palm fronds floated like umbrellas over the sturdy cedar benches along the brick path. In front of Aunt Betty's Tasty Ice Cream Cones, a group of children gathered in front of Rafael, a brightly-plumed South American parrot that delighted passersby with his constant chatter. Aunt Betty's, currently managed by a young woman from the Ukraine named Natasha, sold eight dollar waffle cones topped with enormous scoops of ice cream in sixteen flavors. Designer-clad moms sporting Prada handbags and daughters in sprayed-on denim shorts and clingy Abercrombie T-shirts sat on benches texting their friends.

She had traveled far from her former life, the one she lived before the merger that had cut her umbilical cord from the corporate world. She could have looked for a position with another pharmaceutical company, but at thirty-four she decided it was time for an adventure. Relying on a nice severance package, her plan was to spend a few months on Sanibel, and then return to her life in Connecticut. After a few weeks of doing absolutely nothing except soaking up the sun on the beach and marveling at the serenity and beauty of her new environment, she took a part-time job as a hostess at Andy's Steak House. Soon after she met Michael Thompson, drop-dead gorgeous and dining alone. He asked for her phone number, took her to dinner and then to bed. He was passionate, worldly, incredibly intelligent and emotionally aloof. Though she told herself the attraction was mostly physical, she fell in love with him on their first date.

It wasn't long before Michael offered her a job managing his upscale boutique at The Palms. Michael learned the business of selling outrageously priced goods from his mother, who owned a successful shop in the Hamptons, but his true passion was painting.

Becca's sense of style and unflagging work ethic helped make the boutique one of the hottest shops on Sanibel but luck and timing played a role as well. The Big Money that had invaded the island brought with it an insatiable appetite for big-ticket designer dresses, handbags, shoes and other extravagances. They renamed the shop Over the Rainbow to reflect Becca's shrewd marketing strategy of selling $600 dresses and sweaters in a rainbow of pastel colors with lovely leather handbags and shoes to match. The formula worked brilliantly; at times the well-heeled clientele were almost giddy over the striking palette of lavender, lemon chiffon, mint green and soft peach. No loud colors or bright floral beachwear here. Rainbow was elegant, sheik, expensive and a huge success.

She hoped that Michael eventually would want to get married, but reality kept intruding on her dream. She often thought he suffered from bipolar disorder. At times he was wonderful, but more often he descended into a Hades underworld of dark moods, staying away sometimes for days at a time in his artist studio. He wasn't the kind of man who said "I love you," though she felt he did. Yet she loved him deeply, imperfections and all.

Lately she had the gnawing feeling there was something wrong, an undercurrent of tension and distance had surfaced that she could not dismiss. She was afraid to broach the subject of their future for fear that he would see her as a clinging, needy girlfriend instead of the free spirit she tried so hard to be. Truth be told, her resentment was building in perfect tandem with the clichéd ticking of her biological clock. Facing her thirty-fifth birthday, she was shocked to find the idea of having a child was very much on her mind.

Where this would all lead was anybody's guess but clearly the idea of fatherhood wasn't keeping Michael up at night. All this uncertainty was unsettling. Grateful for the distraction of her job, she purged these thoughts from her mind as she arrived at the boutique.

Inside the dimly lit interior of Tommy D's Seafood Grille, a cluster of sixty-something couples congregated at the bar, exchanging stories and gossip. A large, boisterous man could be heard telling a long-winded story about the sand trap at the seventh hole at the Harbor View Golf Club. The well-coiffed women exchanged stories about their families, shopping and in particular, the new designer outlet mall in Fort Myers. The rhythm of conversation ebbed and flowed through the restaurant, at times laughter ringing out. A modern day fresco of the good life, the retired denizens of Sanibel were enjoying the fruits of their labors, having liberated themselves from the burdens and responsibilities of their professional lives as CEOs, lawyers, corporate VPs and the like.

Rarely was there an evening when the bar wasn't full at Tommy D's, which was, in the minds of tourists and locals, without question the best restaurant on the island, the signature dish a fourteen-ounce lobster tail and mouthwatering eight-ounce certified black angus filet. David was glad they had gotten there early. He had met his parents at the restaurant, sparing them the ride over in the rented SUV with Ethan and the unpredictable Miss Emma. Colin, clutching his blankie and looking like a war refugee, had been deposited at the resort's pricey Kid's Club, this after a long battle with Marianne who had objected to leaving him behind.

Tonight was one of the few times this week he and his parents would be alone, relatively speaking. Over the next few days the rest of the family would begin to arrive: his sister, Julia, who had planned the trip, with her husband Richard and daughters Nicole and Rachel, various aunts and uncles and family friends. The festivities kicked off with the hotel luau on Friday night, followed by the anniversary party on Saturday night.

The hostess, a tall and slim attractive older woman wearing black polyester slacks and a red silk blouse, led them to a table in front of a large window overlooking a courtyard garden. David eyed the table and decided to put his parents next to the window, so he and Marianne could be a buffer between them and the kids.

"Can you bring a booster chair?" Marianne inquired of the hostess, who dutifully went to find one. Emma said loudly, "I don't want a booster. I'm a big girl."

"Unfortunately not big enough for this table. Be a good girl and maybe you can color Grandma a picture," David cajoled her in an attempt to shut down the nascent protest. Without the booster, Emma could barely see over the table, her chin touching the edge.

"Daddy," she said, rejecting his offer with steely determination, "I don't wanna booster chair. I'm a big girl."

"Emma . . ." David started.

"Booster chairs are for *babies*. I'm not a baby."

"Emma," David said sternly yet with a pleading look in his eyes. But he was interrupted before he could finish.

"Emma, honey" said Marianne in a conspiratorial tone, leaning in to her daughter, "if you sit in the booster chair you can get a hot fudge sundae for dessert."

"Can I get chocolate sprinkles on it?" Emma shot back. Ethan, realizing he might be missing out on something, jumped in. "Can I get ice cream too with chocolate sprinkles?"

"I'm not sure if they have chocolate sprinkles, but if they do you can have them," Marianne promised.

Problem solved, crisis averted. Marianne started digging in Emma's backpack for crayons and other things to keep the kids busy, while David turned his attention to his parents. Judy, looking much younger than her seventy years in the candlelight, radiated enthusiasm for her new surroundings. "It smells incredible in here. Everyone says this is the best restaurant on the island."

They ordered drinks, merlot for the women, kiddie cocktails for Emma and Ethan with two extra cherries, and Heinekens for David and his father, who was being more quiet than usual.

Before David could even speak, Judy looked at all of them with genuine happiness in her eyes and lifted her glass. "We're so happy you're here with us," she beamed. "This was the greatest anniversary present anyone could ever ask for. Thank you so much for being part of it."

David smiled. That was one of the things he truly loved about his mother. She was so easy to please. Never asked for much but had given so much in return. It had been that way his entire life. David held up his glass, "To the best parents ever."

"To family," Judy added as they clinked their glasses.

Conversation drifted to plans for the week ahead, the party, and whether they should go deep sea fishing tomorrow or the next day. When there was a bit of a lull in the conversation Marianne jumped in. "Did David tell you my news?"

Judy, immediately thinking her daughter-in-law was pregnant again, took a generous swallow of merlot. "What news, David?" she said, looking quizzically at him. George was preoccupied with the menu, trying to decide between the eighteen-ounce T-bone and the BBQ ribs. The children were intent on coloring.

"My friend Adelle—you remember you met her at Ethan's birthday party last year—is opening a preschool and she asked me to help get it started. It won't be full time or anything, she's just asked me to do some planning and initial groundwork for this new center. I'm so excited because it will be a perfect environment for Emma until she goes to kindergarten."

"Congratulations," said Judy, smiling at her daughter-in-law, intrigued because unlike Julia, Marianne was a devout stay-at-home mom. Though Marianne had been a kindergarten teacher when they first got married, once the children were born she quit her job and happily announced that she wouldn't be going back. "It sounds exciting to be in on the ground floor of something new."

"It is," Marianne said, her pale blue eyes widening. "It's not only new, it's revolutionary in terms of curriculum. Adelle is a pioneer. She is developing a curriculum to cater to the needs of children like Emma, Indigo children."

David took a swig of his beer and wished his wife would have stopped before that last detail.

He saw his father ever so slightly raise an eyebrow over the top of the menu.

"Indigo children?" Judy said. "I'm not sure I know what that is."

"Are they blue like smurfs?" George quipped. Marianne ignored him.

"There's a new book out—I'll let you borrow mine—that examines a new generation of children the author calls Indigo children. This is truly groundbreaking research. There are literally thousands of Indigos out there, and I believe Emma is one of them. Few people understand what these kids are all about. They have special needs and don't thrive in traditional settings."

Marianne lowered her voice, and moved her head closer to Judy's. "I told you what a problem Emma is having in her nursery school class. As an Indigo, it's hard for her to cope with the rigid structure of the classroom. Unfortunately, her teacher isn't interested in finding ways to help her."

"Really," Judy mustered, trying to look interested. George's head was deep in the menu. David felt like going to the restroom, or actually wished the kids would interrupt. But for the moment, Ethan and Emma were busy finishing their pictures.

"Adelle has gone to several seminars on this, and has consulted with the author and other experts. This could be really big. For years, we've been herding our children into cookie-cutter nursery schools, regardless of their individual needs. Indigo schools will help us reach these kids, and provide a nurturing environment where they can thrive and their differentness can be respected, not punished."

David watched his mother try to politely respond to what he knew she thought was utter nonsense. "Why do you think Emma is one of these children?" Judy asked.

"Emma could be a poster child for Indigo children," Marianne said, with conviction Judy found vaguely disconcerting. "Indigos come into the world with a feeling of royalty, they don't respond to guilt-trip discipline, they're not shy about letting others know what they need and they simply will not do certain things. They have a deep need to be creatively engaged . . . they have so much to offer. That's Emma to a T."

"Sounds to me like a bunch of spoiled brats who need a good swift smack on the ass," interjected George, unable to be silent any more.

"George," Judy implored in a tone that both admonished him but at the same time tried to make light of his comment. She added, "Watch what you say in front of the children." But it was too late because their highly specialized internal radar detectors that pick up on things adults say that they should not hear had been activated. Upon hearing the word "ass" they erupted into giggles. Ethan, eyes shining with delight, started chanting: "Grandpa said ass. Grandpa said ass." Emma chimed in, and momentarily the people at the next tables were staring at them.

"Shhh," said David. "Ethan, Emma. Stop it right now! NOW!

Marianne, shooting George a look of reproach, said, "I think you can find better words to use in front of the children."

Judy wasn't surprised at George's comment, he had little patience for Marianne's theories about childrearing, but usually he had the sense not to make remarks like that in front of her. He had been so cranky lately, and her patience was running thin.

George turned his attention back to the menu. Thankfully the waitress appeared and the tension of the moment passed. Marianne asked for more time to discuss the menu choices with

Ethan and Emma.

"Why don't we just get them the kid's meal," David said.

"Emma told me this afternoon that she wants to try lobster," Marianne said. "So I thought we would get a tail for her and Ethan to share."

"I don't want lobster. I want steak like Daddy." Ethan said, starting to play with the saltshakers on the table.

David looked at his wife and children. A lobster and steak, *yeah sure why not.* Why not spend an extra seventy-five dollars on two kids that would take two bites of food and then ask for dessert. He didn't normally lose his temper with Marianne, but this was ridiculous. But in the name of harmony and his mother's happiness, he relented.

A few moments later, the waitress reappeared. They ordered, and went on to other, safer topics, leaving the Indigo children behind in their conversational wake.

The next morning, David woke up in a state of mild confusion, realizing he wasn't at home in his own bed as he opened his eyes and took in the new surroundings. The room was flooded with light unlike his bedroom at home, and the gentle rhythm of the surf could be heard through the sliding glass doors that opened to the lanai.

His next immediate sensation was one of raw physical desire. Marianne lay next to him, still sleeping. Maybe that's all he needed, to have sex with his wife so he could stop thinking about the woman he met yesterday and had spent his last waking moments thinking about last night.

He reached over for Marianne, aware of the futility of his gesture. Ever since she had children, and especially now that the kids were older, Marianne had difficulty divorcing her "mother" self from her sexual self. Over the past several years, the number of times they made love had dwindled from almost every night in the early days of their marriage to about once every two or three weeks, for David a notch above sexual starvation but enough to keep him going. Sex just wasn't a huge part of his life now, and he had learned to cope with this fact like many of his friends had, who sometimes would either joke or lament over this state of affairs, usually after one too many beers. He always found such admissions embarrassing, and a little depressing, but he tried not to dwell on such things. After all the kids and his career dominated their lives, and it was hard to find the time and opportunity.

He remembered how it had been in the beginning, the excitement and lusty passion, lounging in bed for hours on Sunday mornings or other times when she would seduce him out of the blue. He missed that, and right now he missed it very much. He also missed the old Marianne, the Marianne who liked sex as much as he did, who used to make him feel like he could conquer the world.

He touched her hair, she was still asleep or possibly faking it. He moved closer to her, wrapping his body around her in the spoons position, rubbing himself against her, the power of his arousal taking hold of him.

"Good morning," he said softly into her ear. "Are you awake?"

She murmured something unintelligible. David had the crazy thought that if he started the process while she was still waking up, he may achieve the mission. He put his arms around her and caressed her breasts. Her once svelte figure had given way to a larger less shapely form of a woman who had given birth to three children, yet this morning none of that mattered.

"Hey, come over here by me," he whispered, his whole body in motion, his hands gently moving over her.

"David, what are you doing?" Marianne said sleepily.

"I need you."

Marianne, tangled hair falling over one side of her face, pulled away from his grasp. "David, the children are right on the other side of that wall."

"We'll be very very quiet," he whispered. "They'll never hear a thing." He kissed the back of her neck.

"David, no. Emma could wake up and walk in here any minute."

"We could lock the door," he said, but realized his arguments were in vain. He stopped caressing her and pulled away. She couldn't cope or didn't care what he needed. The window closed, the opportunity vanished like early morning fog in the first rays of sunshine. It made him angry. Couldn't she just this one time put his needs first?

He got out of bed and walked into the bathroom, closed the door and turned on the shower. There was one way to relieve this powerful urge. Warm water pelting his body, it took less than sixty seconds for the relief to come. The whole time he was in the shower, his mind was not on the reluctant Marianne, but on the ruby red bathing suit and the incredibly sexy woman it clung to.

Afterward, as he shaved and got dressed, he vowed that he would put this wild fantasy out of his head. Instead, he would devote all his energies to his kids and having a vacation they would remember for years to come. That was the right thing to do and he always did the right thing.

MARIANNE'S CELL PHONE RANG just as they were finishing breakfast. The kids had nibbled at pancakes and turkey bacon, and Colin was chugging on his bottle. She answered it, and David could hear the tense voice of her sister Susan amplified by the phone.

Susan had called to tell Marianne that their father had been taken to the hospital for severe chest pains. Though his condition was stable, they were monitoring him closely and doing tests. Marianne's parents lived about 120 miles away on the mainland, in an active-adult community in Bradenton, Florida.

Marianne paced back and forth, gleaning the sketchy details from her distraught sister. Ethan and Emma wandered away from the kitchen table to play video games.

"Let me call you back. I need to talk to David."

Instinctively David knew she would want to leave; she could no more stay here during a family crisis than drop one of the children into the deep end of the pool.

"Look," he said, "why don't you just go, leave the kids here with me. Or we can all go. It's up to you. My parents will understand whatever you decide."

"I don't know . . . Julia has been planning this so long, and how will you take care of the kids and Josh and Kaitlin will be so disappointed if I show up without them." Josh and Kaitlin were Susan's children, who adored Ethan, Emma and Colin. Given all that was going on, David wondered why this was even a consideration, but said nothing.

She turned to David, her eyes filled with apprehension and worry. "Why did this have to happen? My father is too young to have a heart attack. He's only sixty-eight."

"Look, don't think the worst. He'll be fine," he said, with more conviction than he actually possessed. "He's very healthy, and the good news is that he's already at the hospital where he can get the care he needs. Why don't you just go? I don't want you to stay here and worry about him and I'm perfectly capable of taking care of the kids. Mom will help if I get in over my head," he said, smiling to ease the tension.

"This is going to sound a little crazy," she said, "but I would really like to take the kids. It's not that far and I think it would do my mother good."

"Then we'll all go."

"No, you can't leave your parents, that's not right. I'll go and take the kids."

"Are you sure you're up to that?"

"Yes, I just need to be there right now. Maybe I can come back tomorrow if he's okay."

"You're sure?"

"Yes," she said emphatically. "Why don't you take the kids down to the beach, wear them out a bit, I'll pack and get some lunch ready and then we'll leave."

Twenty minutes later, after gathering the beach towels, swim vests, applying SPF 50 sunscreen on squirming Colin and Emma and Ethan, grabbing bottles of water, visors and various pails and shovels, David was on his way. It had taken some coaxing, but he got them to turn off their video games without too much fuss. If left unattended, he thought, his kids would spend their entire childhoods zapping space aliens, fighting bad guys, and, with the arrival of their latest prize, learning magic tricks to earn points at Hogwarts.

*   *   *

It was the time of morning when the sun danced on the waves like a dazzling diamond necklace, the mirrored brilliance of the light blinding. The tide was going out, leaving a fresh harvest of shells—scallops, conch and a plethora of horseshoe crabs that reminded him of miniature World War II German tanks—along the water's frothy edge. On the beach, people were engaged in a myriad of activities, some soaking up the sun, others peering into the shallow tide waters looking for treasure, others jogging or walking with hand weights. Only two beach chairs in a long row of about thirty were unclaimed. With the temperature an idyllic eighty-five degrees and a gentle whiff of a breeze, David couldn't help but wonder why anyone lived in the Midwest.

After getting the kids situated with pails and shovels, he grabbed one of the last chairs, brushed off the sand and settled back to watch the kids. The beach toys were still new to them, so he knew he had a few minutes of peace before he would have to get up, either to chase Colin or referee a dispute between Emma and Ethan. He kept a close eye on Colin just in case he lost interest in castle building. Wearing a bulky swim diaper under his swim trunks and a bright red Harry Potter T-shirt, Colin busied himself scooping up sand in a large shovel and carrying it over to the castle site, his eyes fixated on the payload, losing most of it en route but he didn't seem to mind.

On the sun-drenched beach, his father-in-law's predicament seemed surreal. He was probably in the emergency room right now, or perhaps they had taken him to a room. He desperately hoped this would turn out to be nothing. Despite his calm façade with Marianne, he was worried. Even a mild heart attack was serious, for most people a life-altering experience physically and emotionally.

The situation also shattered the comfortable illusion that their parents were still years away from dealing with aging-related health issues. Despite their advancing years, there had been no serious medical concerns or imminent threats to their longevity. This perpetuated the myth that he and Marianne were too young to cope with such matters, and they clung to this belief even though several of their friends had been thrust into caregiver roles in what had become an anguished rite of middle-age passage.

It was getting close to noon. The kids and Marianne would be leaving soon. He had been so immersed in the moment he hadn't pondered what that meant. He would be alone—free to do whatever he wanted the rest of the day. *What a concept.* He felt guilty as he realized what a strong appeal this had to him. He rarely got a day by himself, it was either work or kids or both.

Immersed in his thoughts of what to do with his newfound freedom, he almost didn't notice her. She was the length of a football field away from him, coming down the steps to the beach. Why he chose to look up at that moment, he couldn't say. But he did, and she was standing there now, decked out in running attire and a white visor. She looked in both directions and after a moment's hesitation, started walking in the opposite direction. He felt a jab of disappointment.

"Daddy come see our fortwess," Ethan yelled. "It's just like where Harry Potter goes to Hogwarts." David pulled himself out of the chaise lounge, and walked over to examine Ethan's creation. The "fortwess" consisted of three overturned buckets of sand studded with large seashells encircled by a deep trench. "Great job!" David exclaimed. "I think this is the best sand castle I've ever seen! Can I help build another one?

"Yes," said Ethan, pleased. "But it's not a sand castle it's a fortwess. Right Dad?"

"Right Ethan. It's the best fortress I've ever seen."

"I helped too," chimed in Emma, making sure she got her share of the credit.

In the midst of his children smiling broadly and basking in their father's approval, he took a deep breath. He could still see her in the distance. Even in gym shorts, she was stunning. The vow he made in the shower was promptly forgotten.

Judy paused on the outdoor landing of the concrete steps that led to the parking lot, her eyes filled with maternal pride as she watched David coming toward her. It was hardly a secret among her children that David, responsible, caring, a good husband and unfailingly thoughtful on all things concerning his mother, was her favorite. Of course, as all mothers do, she publicly denied this and claimed to love them all equally.

With David and Julia, she felt like she had succeeded in her role as a mother. Not so with Maggie, who had just topped off a seemingly endless string of disappointments by leaving her husband and two sons after declaring she was a lesbian and moving in with her new girlfriend.   Her husband Brian was devastated, and her young sons, Tyler and Brad, unaware, had been told that Mommy was away for a special project for work.

"I don't know what to think," an exasperated Judy had confided to her sister Maureen on a long-distance phone call the week before. "She says she's always been gay and just didn't realize it. I'm upset, but George is furious. I don't think he'll ever get over it. I want her to be happy, but how can I condone what she's done to those adorable little boys and Brian?"

"I still remember when gay meant happy, that's what a dinosaur I am," Maureen chuckled. "Remember the *Gay Divorcee* with Fred Astaire and Ginger Rogers? Takes on a whole new meaning today doesn't it? You know she's the first lesbian

I know, though I think a few of those girls on the swim team in high school were, we just didn't know it back then. Maggie always was a bit of a tomboy, wasn't she? Is she coming to the party?"

"I haven't heard from her so I doubt it," Judy replied. What Judy didn't say but her sister knew full well from experience was that having her wayward daughter at a family party typically involved a degree of risk taking and Judy was not a gambler. Maggie had a drinking problem, and with it a habit of provoking arguments and making others uncomfortable. If there was one thing Judy did not like, it was confrontation, especially at a family party.

"Well at least you've got Julia and David. Two out of three isn't bad," Maureen laughed.

Her daughters couldn't be more different. An over-achiever since preschool, Julia excelled academically, socially and professionally—from prom queen to college valedictorian to becoming the youngest vice president in her firm's history. Though Judy was proud of her daughter's phenomenal success, she worried about the toll it took on her grandchildren, sixteen-year-old Nicole and twelve-year-old Rachel. A cadre of well-educated nannies and au pairs helped fill in for a mom who worked sixteen-hour days and traveled constantly. Julia's husband Richard did not share his wife's devotion to corporate America, and as such played an active role in his daughters' lives.

David's voice behind her interrupted her thoughts. "Hi Mom. We just got a call. Marianne's father is in the hospital. They think that he might have had a heart attack."

"What? Oh my gosh, I'm so sorry . . ."

"Thanks. I was surprised, but then again who isn't—like you ever expect a heart attack. Listen, Marianne is driving up to Bradenton to be with them," he said. "They're keeping Jack in the hospital overnight for tests."

Judy placed her hand over her eyes to shield them from the sun's glare. "You go with her. Your father and I will watch the kids."

"I already suggested that. She wants to go with the kids, and insists I stay here with you."

"She's driving there alone with the kids?" Judy asked, thinking she would rather have a root canal than make a two-hour trip that ended at a hospital emergency room with three young children. As was often the case, she didn't understand the decisions her daughter-in-law made.

"I told her I would go with her, and you could watch the kids, or that I'd stay and call you and Dad in for reinforcements, but you know Marianne," he said, giving her a conspiratorial glance signaling what was unspoken but well understood between mother and son. Judy knew all too well how utterly crazy Marianne could be especially where the children were concerned, yet she kept her opinions to herself. As if reading her mind, he said, "I guess she didn't think we were up to the task."

They laughed. "At my age, I'm not sure I *am* up to the task," she replied. "I do hope Jack is going to be okay. He's way too healthy to have a heart attack. Didn't he run in a marathon last year?"

His mother, wearing a mint green cotton shirt tucked neatly into white Calvin Klein shorts, could easily pass for a woman in her fifties. Her lifelong love of tennis had produced a trim figure.

"Yes he did, he's in great shape, been working out for years," David said, realizing he wanted to change the subject because he didn't want to dwell on the fact that seemingly perfectly healthy people could have heart attacks.

"So do you think Dad's up for some golf this afternoon?" David queried. "Of course that's only if you can bear to be away from him?" Again the smile of coconspirators.

"Oh, I think I can manage . . . somehow," she said, her voice trailing off with feigned uncertainty. "Seriously, that's a great idea. He brought his clubs, schlepped them all the way through the airport complaining loudly, of course. It would do him a world of good to get out on the course with you."

Golf was a special bond between David and his father. Growing up, they had spent many Sunday afternoons at Silver

Lake Country Club. His father, who had played competitively in high school and in college, taught him everything he knew about golf—his swing, his stance, how to line up a putt, the rules of golf etiquette and when to use a seven iron or a nine. David's first golf clubs were a set of used Callaways his father had gleefully snatched up at a garage sale. While David's contemporaries were out getting stoned and listening to Jimmy Hendrix, he thrived in a culture they derided as hopelessly establishment.

Yes, it would be great to spend some quality time with his dad, away from the kids, to have a chance to really visit and talk. Although they saw each other several times a year on visits to his parents' home in Minneapolis or when his parents visited them in Chicago, ever since the kids were born their visits were generally chaotic and there was little time for meaningful conversations.

"I'll go up and see Dad," he said.

Looking over her shoulder to watch her handsome son walking down the corridor, Judy was overjoyed at the thought of having the afternoon to herself.

Hopefully they'd play eighteen.

"Incredible" was the only word to describe it. David and his father had been on some beautiful golf courses, but never one quite like this. As far as the eye could see, a lush carpet of verdant green draped the gentle curves of the earth, the horizon rising up to touch a cloudless blue sky.

"Hope you got a full bag of water balls," said George, staring down at a map of the fairways while they waited for a foursome to tee off at the first hole. He was dressed in a bright red golf shirt, white shorts and a Minnesota Vikings football cap. "Because you're gonna need 'em. Look at the fifth hole!"

"Yeah, and I brought some extra for you," David shot back. "How much you want to wager on this game? The usual?"

"No I think we should raise 'em. Twenty bucks. Payable in cash or cocktails."

"You're on."

It had been a long time since they had been out together like this, and it felt good. He wondered why it had been so long since the last time they had played golf. Ever since his kids were born, it seemed his life was stuck on fast forward. Summer mysteriously morphed into fall, fall into Christmas and another year flew by and then another so fast it was scary.

"I was reading this article on the plane," David said. "Do you know what Arnold Palmer said about golf?"

"What? That it made him incredibly rich?" said George,

taking a practice swing with his favorite wood.

"He said the toughest six inches in the game of golf is between a player's ears. That ninety percent of golf is mental. It's all in your head."

"He never saw my chip shot," George replied, looking down the 325-yard fairway, seeing that the foursome was finally on the green. "Okay, we better go."

George planted a bright yellow tee under his ball. He fired off his first shot, straight and high, more than 250 yards, landing in the middle of the fairway. A beauty, just like old times.

AT THE SEVENTH HOLE, they were held up by the foursome again.

Taking a seat on a bench under a shiny-leafed gumbo limbo tree, they took in the panoramic view of the manicured fairways, sculpted greens, and in the distance, the sparkling blue waters of the gulf.

"Hey, I forgot to tell you I saw Kevin the other day," David said. "He said to say hi."

George shifted his eyes from the landscape to David. "Who?"

"Kevin Hammersmith."

His father stared at him blankly, no hint of recognition whatsoever. David, slightly confused at this reaction but eager to spare his father any embarrassment, continued, "Kevin, you know, who worked on the house last summer. Jim and Carol's son."

"Oh yeah, Kevin," George replied, snapping back from the opaque stare, his eyes refocusing on his son again. "What's he up to?"

"He's starting his own remodeling business. He's such a great kid, I'm going to try to help him out if I can. You know Jim and Carol have been having a rough time of it. Carol had breast cancer and Jim lost his health insurance when the plant closed."

George had taken a liking to Kevin, a serious young man who showed up for work every day before seven o'clock. It had been right after George had sold his plumbing business and retired.

At the time, David remembered thinking what a godsend it was to have Kevin around to keep Dad company.

David's phone rang. He normally didn't take his cell phone with him on the golf course, but was anxious about Marianne. "Hello."

"Hi. I just got in and everything is fine," Marianne said. "The kids were great and Dad is okay. They're going to keep him overnight and probably let him go home in the morning."

"That's great. Do you think you'll come back then?"

"I'm not sure. Ethan and Emma are dying to see their cousins. I told them we'll go over there as soon as we leave the hospital. What are you doing?"

"Golfing with Dad. We're on the seventh hole waiting for four putzers to get on the green."

"Sounds like fun," she said. "Listen, I've gotta run, the kids are antsy and I promised to take them to TCBY. I'll talk to you tomorrow."

He said goodbye and clicked off the call. The foursome finally was out of the way. David walked to the golf cart to get a club, his father right behind him. Focus. That's all he needed to do. If only golf—or life for that matter—were that simple.

E llen scrutinized her magnified reflection in her Lady Clairol makeup mirror that she had lugged halfway across the country in her bulging suitcase. She had used this kind of mirror since she had first applied Maybelline mascara and lipstick at age thirteen. As a teenager she had been intrigued by the mirror's three light settings—daytime, office and evening. Over the years, "evening's" soft glow had come to be the kindest, much like a candlelit restaurant was the best friend of a woman over forty. Though Ellen at forty-five frequently was told she looked ten years younger than her age, there were subtle signs of aging that she preferred not to think about.

She tried to concentrate on the task at hand but her nervous system was on overdrive. It was almost as if after living in a cave for twenty years she were going out on a date. *As if . . .* she *was.* Who was she kidding? She had run into him while walking back from the beach. He had been at the pool with two older people she assumed were his parents. They appeared to be having a good time, relaxing over a late afternoon cocktail. His mother was attractive. She wondered where his wife and kids were.

Standing on the brick path that curved through the spongy grass, they finally exchanged introductions. In the bright sunlight, she had a much better look at his features, a strong jaw, prominent cheekbones and eyes so intensely brown they could be chocolate. The smooth planes of his face bore no sign of lines or wrinkles, though his thick crop of chestnut hair was faintly tinged with gray. She had the feeling that this was a man who had gotten more attractive with age.

They spoke for a few minutes, just the usual chit-chat of two people on vacation, weather, restaurants, things to do on the island. He explained that his wife Marianne had to leave to attend to a family emergency, that her father had suffered a mild heart attack, but seemed to be okay. He told her that he was really looking forward to exploring the bike paths tomorrow. Then, out of the blue, like a small sparrow alighting on a tree branch, the invitation appeared. He said he knew of an incredible Italian restaurant on Captiva, would she like to join him for dinner there?

He carried it off with great aplomb, his tone and manner were one of "this is totally above board, we're just two people having a casual dinner together" and not one of seduction. Still, she was flummoxed. She had certainly not expected this. Her first inclination was to create an excuse but there wasn't one— she was alone on an island with no family, friends or obligations. No reason except one she could not readily disclose—yes, *I'd love to go to dinner with you but I'm afraid something could happen because I'm very vulnerable right now.* The seconds ticked inexorably by as she ran through the pros and cons. He did not seem like a womanizer, a breed of man she detested. It was possible, she had to admit, that he was merely being friendly and wanted some companionship for dinner. Plus, how often did she get a chance to do something spontaneous? Adventure and spontaneity were largely MIA in her life. This was a chance to do something about it. *What harm is there with having dinner with a fellow traveler?*

So she had said yes.

She fished through her makeup case for her Estee Lauder coral lipstick. It was a perfect match to the dress she planned to wear, the dress she had almost left at home. At the last minute, she had attempted to lighten the load in her suitcase, deciding it wasn't necessary to bring half of her extensive wardrobe for a ten-day trip. What would she need a dress for, she had mused, but for some reason she had brought it anyway. A new Rebecca Lavelle pale peach chiffon sundress, it was simple yet elegant, sexy but not revealing, very feminine—her best look. Ellen never had been one to flaunt cleavage; true, many men were turned on by that but they were mostly Neanderthals—not the kind of men she found attractive. For Ellen, desire started in the brain. It was a man's intellect and more importantly the degree of challenge he presented to her that she was drawn to. *Like a moth to the flame.*

They had agreed to meet out in the parking lot near the back of her condo building at seven o'clock. She wondered if he had told his parents of his dinner plans, or his wife. Ellen was glad she had talked to her husband this morning so he would not be calling tonight. Plus she could always use the excuse that she missed the call. The cell signal on the island was erratic; making and receiving calls was an ongoing problem.

She went through the last-minute checks. Lipstick, brush, wallet and keys. She gave herself one more appraisal in the mirror and liked what she saw. She turned the lights off, and closed the door firmly behind her.

THE RESTAURANT WAS EVERYTHING he had promised. A carnival of hibiscus, periwinkle and jasmine spilled out of the gardens that lined the entryway. Bella Napoli's exterior resembled a residence, a white cape cod accented with robin's egg blue shutters and matching door. Flower boxes filled with cascading purple and pink petunias bedecked the windows.

Inside the main dining room were a dozen tables topped with crisp white table cloths, gleaming crystal and a galaxy of tea light candles that emanated a golden glow. Large picture windows looked out over the lawn, past the narrow road to the sand-swept beach. Reproductions of famous French impressionist paintings, including Renoir's *Bal au Moulin de la Galette* and *The Luncheon of the Boating Party*, hung on opposite walls. She loved both paintings, the faces of the crowd and picnickers at the shore conveyed a joie de vivre that transcended the ages. Beethoven's *Eroica Symphony*, playing quietly in the background, reflected the ebullient mood on the canvas. The waiters, young men wearing starched white shirts, black vests and ties, were the embodiment of refined elegance.

The maître d' arranged for their waiter to take them immediately to their table. Ellen sat down on the red velvet-backed chair, unfolded her napkin in her lap and absorbed her surroundings.

"Wow. This is incredible. I had no idea." Wanting to keep things on a light note, Ellen did what she always did to combat nervousness, resorted to humor. Leaning forward, she said in a hushed voice. "So what do you like on your pizza?"

"How presumptuous of you," he said, flashing an engaging mile. "I'll be having the meatball sandwich, easy on the red sauce, with a bottle of their finest Mogen David."

He looked terrific in his burgundy Ralph Lauren shirt and beige slacks. He must work out, she thought, to stay so fit.

"Ahh, Mogen David," she said. "An excellent choice."

"Without question. Full-bodied, yet dense and unrefined. I saw it in *Wine Spectator*, which of course I subscribe to, being the wine connoisseur that I pretend to be."

Ellen laughed. Bantering came easily to them, and Ellen's initial nervousness receded. She picked up the wine list. Incredibly detailed, a brief description followed every wine selection—some running into hundreds of dollars a bottle.

"Here we go," she said. "The R.J. Gordon 2001 special selection cabernet sauvignon from Napa Valley. Exactly what I've been looking for. Aromas of ripe vanilla, black currants— oh I do love those black currants—cherries, roasted coffee beans and exotic spice . . ."

"Exotic Spice . . . isn't she married to David Beckham?" David interjected.

"No, that would be Posh, not to be confused with Baby. Though you'd think it would have been Sporty. Exotic Spice," she grinned, shaking her head in faux admonishment.

The waiter, who introduced himself as Matthew, came to take their drink order. David ordered a bottle of the Napa Valley cabernet. "Does that suit your palate madam?" he asked, as the waiter walked away.

"Fine, as long as you promise to leave the Spice Girls out of it. I must confess I was never into them, although my son once spent twenty dollars at a carnival to win one of their cheesy posters which, by the way, we recently sold at our garage sale for exactly one dollar."

She was amazed how the conversation just flowed. They had so much to share, each of them a blank slate to the other. They talked about their jobs and families, though the latter seemed a bit odd, especially the random mention of their spouses while they were having dinner in this incredibly romantic restaurant. The cabernet had a calming effect, and she was relaxed and happy to be out in the world, conversing with an extremely attractive man who was her intellectual equal.

She learned he was the chief financial officer for a medical software company that had seen business and revenues skyrocket in recent years. Ten years ago the firm had been started in the owner's basement on a credit card and a dream. Since then, it had built a reputation for cutting edge innovation, attracting some of the best software developers in the industry.

"So we're about to leave the dark ages of paper medical records and not a moment too soon," he said, grinning. "It's amazing that we have the most sophisticated machines on the planet that can see into every part of the human anatomy, but the most crucial information about our health is in dog-eared files schlepped around the hospital by an army of clerks."

He exuded a passion for his career; there was an intensity in his manner when he spoke about it though he was not at all overbearing. He looked at her intently whenever he spoke.

"The good news is the business is growing like crazy and the bad news is that the firm is taking over my life. Every day I say I'm going to be home by five and most days I'm not home until seven, and sometimes later. I'm not complaining, I just walk around in a perpetual cloud of guilt over not seeing my family. Thank goodness Marianne doesn't want a career outside the home or I'm not sure what we would do."

He put his wine glass down and looked at her. "I'm sorry. I seem to be monopolizing the conversation."

"Not at all. It's good to hear about someone else's problems because then I don't have to think about my own." She kept her tone lighthearted.

"What problems could you possibly have? You jet off to an island paradise to spend a week by yourself . . ."

"You'd be surprised."

"Surprise me," he said.

She took a slow sip of wine and shook her head. "To quote a famously tired cliché, 'let's not go there.' Let's just say that if I knew being a mom would be this hard I'm not sure I would have signed up for active duty. That's why I'm here," she said, pausing to look at him directly. "I needed time to get away, sort things out. Two days into this little experiment, I can honestly say this is one of the best things I've ever done for myself."

She lifted her glass. "To life."

"To life." A pause. "And meeting you." His eyes were riveted on hers.

Ellen blushed, and hoped it didn't show. It was the first serious indication that the platonic dinner with a fellow traveler was anything but.

DINNER WAS EXTRAORDINARY. She ordered the seafood linguine, laced in a wonderful white wine sauce and topped with fresh braised scallops and shrimp. They decided they could not possibly each order a dessert, so they shared a tiramisu and ordered decaf coffees. By that time, she was feeling slightly flushed, a little giddy and in dire need of some fresh air thanks to two large glasses of ninety-dollar-a-bottle cabernet.

As if reading her mind, he said, "Do you want to go down

by the water? Get some fresh air? Walk off some of the 5,000 calories we've just consumed?"

"Yes. Don't remind me. I'll have to walk ten miles tomorrow to pay for this."

While waiting for the waiter to bring the check, David regaled her with a story about one of his college buddies who recently came to visit. "It's amazing. He hasn't changed at all. He lives in his parents' basement, smokes dope, parties all weekend and works part-time at a video store. He can't get a real job because he refuses to stop smoking pot and everybody drug tests. The funny thing is that he seems happy, doesn't seem to have a care in the world. We're all thinking, *Joey, time to grow up.*"

"He fell asleep, well, actually passed out on our living room floor. So the next morning Emma is watching Sponge Bob and he's red-eyed, hung-over, and he says to me, 'Does she always get up this early?' And I inform him it's eleven o'clock."

They were both laughing as the waiter delivered the check in an impressive leather-bound portfolio. David paid the bill, firmly rejecting her offer to pay half.

"My treat. You saved me from a frozen pizza and getting caught up on my email," he said.

Elizabeth Taylor's house at 202 Azalea Lane had been built in the late 1950s, a decade before the bridge to the mainland had been constructed. The tidy home the color of lemons sat on a winding street in a picturesque subdivision of similar homes. Fiery pink bougainvillea shadowed the entrance, amethyst dahlias lined the front walkway and the perennial garden overflowed its boundaries. Seventy-six year-old Ms. Taylor, who hailed not from Hollywood but from Barrington, Illinois treasured every moment she had in her garden, never having lost her keen Midwestern appreciation for being able to tend to her flowers in mid-January. Thanks to Southeast Florida's endless growing season, her garden boasted vivid colors all year—Indian red garden mums, hot pink sweet william, golden coreopsis and blazing orange day lilies. Every day for at least an hour, she tended, cultivated, weeded, pruned and nurtured. Peace and tranquility were found in abundance here, and she thrived amid the splendors of her patch of heaven.

In what was her nightly ritual, Liz had just finished watching the eleven o'clock news. A small woman with a sturdy build without any hint of the osteoporosis that afflicted so many of her friends, Liz padded across the linoleum floor to put out some milk for Kitty, her twelve-year-old cat. Kitty had been abandoned in a restaurant parking lot as a kitten and had been with Liz since the day she found her there. "Hey Miss Kitty," she said. "You want some milk?" she said affectionately. When she placed the bowl on the floor, the cat looked up at her with her adorable little feline face. "Yes you are a spoiled rotten kitty" Liz said as if speaking to a baby.

She wished she could forget about tomorrow morning. It was a pivotal day for the congregation of Grace Chapel and she was dreading it. There was no putting it off any longer, she had to inform the congregation about the news that had arrived ten days ago in a letter FedExed to her from Gregory Foster, CEO of Linton Industries. Foster owned the chapel and the stately Georgian mansion next door that had once belonged to Winifred Hunter, a wealthy heiress and blue blood descendant of Old Money who had spent winters on the island and eventually established a permanent residence there.

Officially, Liz was the church secretary and editor of *Chapel Chimes*, the monthly newsletter, but in reality, she managed everything that had to do with keeping the chapel up and running except for the sermons, which were handled by Pastor Roberts, a retired minister from North Dakota. Before his arrival, the non-denominational congregation had played host to a steady stream of visiting pastors, prompting one old-timer to quote Forrest Gump, "It's like a box of chocolates, you never know which one you're gonna git." If a visiting pastor ever got off the beaten path of mainstream Christian theology or used the pulpit to promote political views, they weren't invited back. Liz was a hardliner on this, if people wanted to support abortion, fight abortion, outlaw gambling, legalize gambling, condemn the president, support the president, there were better places to do it other than Grace Chapel during Sunday morning worship.

It was a small fellowship of believers, about fifty or so regulars plus the occasional drop-ins. But the people who gathered there Sunday mornings were family to Liz and to each other, and they would not take the news well. Many of them were older, like herself, and had been on Sanibel ever since they retired: Myrtle and Ronnie Dalton, Millie and George Hempstead, Edward and Margaret Campbell, Muriel and Larry

Stanke and Ruby Meyers, who made her laugh more than anyone she'd ever met. Over the years, there had been many others, dear friends who came every week and visitors she would see only a few times a year.

She poured herself a glass of water, turned off the kitchen light and went into her bedroom. An entire wall of shelves bursting with books represented a phantasmagoria of interests: Tolstoy's *War and Peace* leaning on Jane Austen's *Emma* next to Daphne du Maurier's *Rebecca*. Biographies, mysteries, religion, classics, travel, politics—the books were her passion and lifelong companions, in them she found adventure and escape, truth and wisdom, faith and redemption. Though her children would plead with her to donate some of her surplus to the library, she couldn't bear to part with any of them.

Tonight she was too tired to read. She turned off the lights except for the small lamp on her nightstand. She said her prayers, singling out every one of her children and their families for mention, and thanked God for the abundance of blessings in her life. "And give me strength to get through tomorrow."

She turned the light off and closed her eyes, forcing tomorrow's announcement out of her mind. Her thoughts eventually drifted to Harold before she fell asleep. It had been that way for several months now.

O utside, the air was still warm with the faint whisper of a silky breeze. Ellen had been surprised that evening temperatures here were still in the seventies. Vistas of stars sparkled brilliantly against an inky sky, a ribbon of moonlight shimmered on the ocean before them. David led the way on the narrow footpath to the beach. Quickly realizing the perils of walking on the sand in dress sandals, Ellen slipped them off and hid them behind a large rock.

"Good thing you hid them," he said, clearly amused. "You can't be too careful in this neighborhood."

"You may laugh, but I'm not taking any chances with my new sandals."

Talking to him was easy and comfortable. He made her laugh, and she felt exhilarated. People who had been married for twenty years didn't often get to feel this. To a great extent, her life was spent in a pleasurable yet monotonous routine of family, career and responsibility. The things that made the heart pound—a lustful gaze from across the room, a lingering touch, a flirtatious encounter with a handsome stranger—those were the joys of a young woman, and as such, were mostly tucked away in her past. But here she was, walking along the beach on a moonlit night with a man who changed the fundamental equation of her life, even if momentarily, and it thrilled and scared her at the same time.

He had not made any inappropriate moves. For that she was grateful because she didn't know how to respond. She was also a little confused. *Maybe he is just a flirt and the attraction she felt was one-sided.* Yet her basic female instincts told her otherwise. The truth lay beneath his charming and poised demeanor and she wondered, would the truth emerge, or would the evening end as casually as it started? That was the $64,000 question.

"So tell me about the anniversary party," she said.

"It's going to be quite the celebration. Everyone is coming, aunts, uncles, cousins . . . Think of it as *Golden Girls* meets *Friends*," he laughed. "Aunt Gertrude is coming with Aunt Eunice, they're sisters, both in their eighties, who bicker like teenagers and have a vodka tonic every day at five o'clock. Oh and they just retired after teaching Sunday school for fifty years. Aunt Gertrude's claim to fame is being mugged years ago in Central Park and actually getting her handbag back after persuading the mugger to turn his life over to Christ. She claims he left his life of petty crime and sends her a Christmas card every year," he said, pausing to take in her are-you-kidding-me look. "I swear to god I'm not making this up." The memory made him smile, and he looked incredibly handsome, dark hair tousled in the wind, piercing eyes summoning her in a way she could not explain.

They talked about how much they loved the ocean, and why it was that they spent precious little time there. How life always seemed to move too fast without enough time for the things they really enjoyed or wanted to do. He told her that he wanted to hike the Grand Canyon, and camp out at the bottom along the shores of the snaking Colorado River. But now that they had the kids, that trip seemed very far into the future. Ellen told him of her restlessness with her career.

"I just have this nagging question . . . like what I'm going to do with the rest of my life," she smiled. "Some days I get so bored with my job . . . I can do it in my sleep. You're fortunate to have a career and a job that you love."

"Well, let's not get carried away," he said. "True, I'm fortunate in that I'm part of a company that actually does make a difference in people's lives. But in the past couple of years, my job has become so much more demanding and there's a lot more stress and big decisions and no end in sight. In the beginning it was just me and a dozen tech geeks with a good idea to digitize medical records and change the world. Did I mention the venture capitalists?" he said, smiling. "But despite all that, it's hard to imagine walking away, especially now when we're really on the verge of becoming a huge success. But enough of that, what about you?"

"Good question. It's funny, ten years ago I would have killed for this job, and now I feel completely different. It was such a big deal then being named VP of marketing and now it's just not that important," Ellen said. "There's so many other things I'd like to do."

"Like . . ."

"If only I knew. Something that contributes in some way, has meaning. Not that marketing ten thousand dollar stainless refrigerators leaves me feeling unfulfilled," she said wryly, looking up at him and smiling. "But when I think about what a change would mean in terms of completely reordering my life priorities, well, it's easier just to slug it out and go to work every day."

"Wait a minute—don't downplay those stainless refrigerators, I've got one in my kitchen." He paused. "Okay, seriously, I know, at our age, you start thinking, if not now when?" The thing that scares me the most is how everything seems to be moving on fast-forward. It's like the minute you have kids the clock starts whirring around on hyper speed. I look at my mom and dad, they're in great shape, healthy, it's hard to believe they've been married fifty years."

"Are they still in love?" Ellen asked, the words out before she realized it was a very personal question.

"Very much so. Always have been," David responded, and in his voice was a note of solemnity and, Ellen thought, wistfulness.

*   *   *

They walked for a while in silence, listening to the foamy punches of the ebbing tide and watching the waves spill onto the flat sand then recede. A white hexagon-shaped wooden gazebo sat at the edge of a row of billowy pine trees that bordered the beach. David saw it and started walking toward it. Ellen had never been on this stretch of beach before, she imagined how perfect of a spot this would be to visit during the day. A great place to read a book, relax or enjoy the incredible view.

"I'm going to have to come back here this week, this is lovely," she said.

David sat down on the bench that lined the sides of the gazebo. Lattice-work panels on the back offered seclusion from the distant lights of homes on the beach. He rested his elbows on his knees, looking straight ahead as if intently studying the incoming tide. She sat next to him but at a careful distance. His ebullient mood seemed to have changed, like the fizzle going out of a glass of champagne. After a long moment, he turned to face her, his face shadowed and beautiful. Another long silence.

"Time out, he said quietly. "I have a confession to make."

She wasn't prepared for this. Until now she had been floating along on a nice little red wine buzz, enjoying herself immensely, but the next words out his mouth could hurtle this encounter from misdemeanor flirtation to felony adultery. Her ego demanded that he be attracted to her, but up until now the situation was not real. She was married, she loved her husband, but at the moment, none of that seemed to matter. A door was opening and she was powerless to close it. *Play with fire, you get burned*, rang in her head.

She took a desperate stab to keep it light. "Please don't tell me you stole the flatware from that nice Italian family."

"No. I gave up stealing years ago," he replied with mock earnestness. Then silence. She cast her eyes downward.

"Look at me," he said, quietly insistent, his face only inches from hers. She could not escape the strong gravitational pull he seemed to be exerting over her, bringing to mind a long-ago science lesson that never had any relevance in her life until now: gravity is a universal force of nature that is strongest when two objects are closest . . . it is an attractive force between all matter.

"I shouldn't have brought you here tonight," he said. "I told myself that it was okay because we were just having dinner together and what's the harm in that. And now I'm here with you and I'm a little overwhelmed . . . and have been all evening."

Ellen sat in stunned silence, mind reeling. It was as if every decision she had ever made in her life now rested on the decision she had to make in the next thirty seconds.

"I don't know what to say . . . except I understand your dilemma," she said, surprised at how unwittingly her voice had shifted to one of shared intimacy. His eyes, locked on hers, penetrated her being. He came closer. Her heart pounded.

"Ever since I saw you at the pool, I haven't been able to stop thinking about you. Okay, I know that sounds like some incredibly inept pickup line but it's *true*. I don't cheat on my wife. I don't chase other women," he said, evincing a disarming smile. "This has never happened to me before," He shook his head as in disbelief of the bewildering predicament that had been thrust upon him.

Gulls flocked at the water's edge on the darkened tapestry of the shoreline.

"Do you have any idea how beautiful you are . . . I fell asleep last night thinking about you." He came even closer, and she knew he was going to kiss her.

The culmination of his words, the wine and luxuriant ocean breeze created in Ellen an unparalleled sensation of arcing desire. Clearly she was not herself, her entire nervous system electrified by the presence of this man so close to her, this man who thought she was beautiful, who was smitten with longing *for her*. The air she breathed was redolent with his cologne. Her control evaporated. Could it be this easy to commit adultery . . . like someone pushing you over a cliff when you're not looking?

Before he could finish speaking she placed her hand on the

soft clean-shaven skin of his cheek and lifted her face to his. It was the invitation he had been waiting for; he pulled her toward him and kissed her long and hard, his arms quickly around her in a tight embrace. Consumed with desire, she kissed him back, falling into an impassioned abyss where the world around her ceased to exist. She felt an incredible high like a blast of cocaine. Right and wrong vanished, nothing else mattered.

He ran his hand through her hair, gently stroking it away from her face, and kissed her again fervently. Their bodies touched and rubbed and clung to each other, he pulled her up so she was sitting on his lap, his muscular arms cradled her and held her there.

Finally he spoke, quietly, into her tousled hair. "You know what I think. I think you cast a spell on me."

The encounter left her breathless. Had his cell phone not rung that very second, she didn't know what might have happened next.

I nside the luxurious dining room of the stately summer home
of corporate titan Gregory Foster, dessert was being served.
It was nine o'clock, the guests just having finished off a main
course of wild Alaskan king salmon with baby carrots and
roasted potatoes. Two antique candelabras infused the room
with an amber glow that hovered like fog around the guests,
who were comfortably seated in burgundy velvet chairs around a
cherry wood table.

The uniformed server, a young woman with a crisp
professional demeanor, was on loan for the evening from Chez
Maison, the island's most sought-after caterer. She had returned
to the dining room to announce the dessert menu: chocolate
mousse napoleon, crème brulee, or strawberries Romanoff—a
something for everyone fanfare of culinary delight. The $2,500
tab for dinner for eight (tip and wine included) was chump
change for Foster, who was on the fast track to become one of
the wealthiest men in America.

The newly minted Mrs. Jennifer Foster sat at the head of
the table opposite her husband of four months, exuberant with
the thought that the dinner party was going exceedingly well,
considering the circumstances.

Of the three couples invited for dinner, two of them, the Griffins
and the Michaelsons, had been longtime friends of the first Mrs.
Foster, whose twenty-year marriage had crumbled like a Vegas

casino slated for demolition upon the arrival of her husband's new executive assistant, Jennifer Graystone. Poor Mrs. Foster never had a chance, up against a husband with a raging mid-life crisis and a new assistant with a body like Penelope Cruz. Gregory Foster's close friends and business associates had hoped that he would eventually come to his senses and not sacrifice two decades of marriage to a woman he obviously loved, the mother of his three children, for a living and breathing Barbie doll young enough to be his daughter. But he did not come to his senses and now with Jennifer, who had lived and dreamed of this day, he had the quintessential trophy wife.

From time to time Foster gazed affectionately at his beautiful wife, who wore a silky black-and-white halter dress that clung to her body like saran wrap. It showed off her incredible figure to maximum advantage without being vulgar. Jennifer's youth and enormous sex appeal were no match for any woman in the room and rarely were.

If tonight's guests didn't like her it wasn't obvious, but of course they were smarter than that. The Griffins and Michaelsons may not have looked kindly on the brutal dumping of their dear friend Evelyn but there were other matters at hand, like the business relationships they had and desperately wanted to maintain with Gregory, president and CEO of Linton Industries Inc., a global automotive parts manufacturer. Wayne Griffin III did lucrative legal work for the firm, and Charles Michaelson was a self-described corporate "change" consultant. In the case of Linton Industries "change" meant slashing operating costs, closing American plants and opening new ones in China. Six-hundred US employees had just been laid off as a result, and Michaelson had gotten a $100,000 bonus for a job well done.

Gregory relished his role as host, more now than ever with a gorgeous young woman at his side.

"So as I was saying, we really love this old place, but it's seen better days, and the house is in need of major repairs. But who needs the headache and expense of remodeling—why throw good money after bad? So we're going to tear this place down and start over from scratch. Jennifer already has had some preliminary plans drawn up. Well, you should see what she's come up with, I don't think I can afford to leave her alone with the architect!" Gregory bellowed in Citizen Kane mode from the head of the table, a man used to having people hang on his every word. He wasn't handsome; he had the look of an overfed commissar in a soviet republic, but what he lacked in looks he made up in unerring business acumen. The Chinese venture promised to produce even bigger returns: the automotive parts manufactured in the U.S. could be produced in China for a fraction of the cost.

"Tell us about your plans, Jennifer," asked Mrs. Michaelson as if reading invisible cue cards.

Jennifer looked deferentially at her husband and smiled. "Well, first of all it's not that big, but we do need to make room for guests so Gregory's kids can come and visit, and I want him to have a nice office so he can work here more often in the winter instead of having to go back to Chicago all the time."

If anyone thought the comment about Gregory's children was peculiar given the fact they were no longer speaking to their father, it went unsaid. Furious over the way Gregory had dumped their mother, his two grown sons and daughter refused to attend their wedding or have anything to do with them. Jennifer and Gregory, eager to avoid the embarrassment of their absence, canceled their plans for a formal wedding at the Ritz Carlton in Chicago and instead took the corporate jet to Maui and got married there.

"My dear wife," he looked fondly at Jennifer, "thinks she needs to apologize for life's little extravagances, like building the most fantastic mansion on Sanibel. We deserve it darling. That's what all the hard work is about, having the things you want." His eyes lingered on her in a way that suggested he wasn't just talking about real estate.

"I'm so excited," Jennifer said, looking radiantly beautiful in the candlelight, her jade eyes reflecting the glow. "Gregory is leaving me in charge of the entire project. Talk about trust! Can you imagine—the architect, contractors, designers, I can't wait to get started." And that was the fact of the matter for more reasons than they would ever know.

After dessert, they retired to the formal living room, where an expanse of French doors opened up to a flagstone terrace overlooking the darkened ocean. After a brief disappearance Gregory returned with a scroll of architectural drawings. He unfurled the plans on the gleaming glass coffee table, his guests crowding around him to get a look.

The first drawing revealed an immense French country chateau. The intricately designed gabled roof, turrets and paned windows gave the structure a fairy tale-like quality, kind of like Jennifer's marriage, Mrs. Michaelson silently sniffed. If Gregory's ex caught wind of this she would be livid, especially in light of the acrimonious divorce settlement.

"This is it," said Gregory proudly. "We're having this designed by J.C. Dawson, he's simply the best in the business and certainly understands our needs and the challenge of an oceanfront property."

Upon closer examination, the guests saw that Gregory intended to build an eight thousand square foot mansion. The Michaelsons and the Griffins, certainly not people who lived frugally but who did know what things cost, gaped at the size and scope of it all. It would cost a small fortune.

The drawings showed more than a dozen rooms. A massive foyer flanked by a dramatically curved staircase led into a thirty-by-thirty foot two-story living room with a wall of glass at one end to invite the ocean in. Upstairs, the master bedroom suite encompassed an enormous bedroom and bathroom, spacious his-and-her walk-in closets, a study and a sitting room in front of large windows. In the bathroom, the oversized Jacuzzi tub floated on a marble pedestal surrounded by Greek columns.

"See this," said Gregory excitedly, pausing momentarily to take a sip of his Johnny Walker Blue Label scotch on the rocks. "Look down here. This is where we're going to have a small elevator that runs from the garage to the master closet so we never have to carry our luggage. And here," he said, pointing to an oddly shaped room he called the elliptical dining room, "this door leads directly to the wine cellar below! Can you believe it, this guy Dawson thinks of everything. His newest creation is a Venetian palazzo he built in San Diego, and it was just on *Good Morning USA*."

If the guests were surprised that a man of the caliber of Gregory Foster, builder of fortunes, architect of global change, would be impressed by anything on *Good Morning USA*, it went unsaid.

"This is quite impressive, Gregory, though the city fathers won't be thrilled to see you coming," said William Barnsworth, who had just built an opulent home on the island, but nothing like this and not near the ocean where zoning was a certain nightmare. Do you have enough property to build this without a variance?"

"Absolutely. My planners assured me this is doable, but our church friends next door will have to relocate. I'm certainly not going to lose any sleep over that. It's time those proselytizing poachers found a new home. It's been two years since I bought this estate and I've been more than kind to let them use the property for this long."

"This will be stunning when it's done," chimed in Mrs. Michaelson. "Jennifer, I have the most divine designer for you to work with if you're interested. Gabrielle Adams, she's local but her work is simply marvelous. She is a fierce advocate of color, none of this beige on cream on eggshell for her. She did my son's penthouse and it's breathtaking. You must come see it sometime."

"I'll keep that in mind," Jennifer reassured her.

After a while, the conversation moved on to the comings and goings of their rich friends and business associates, one of whom had fallen from grace in a stock options scandal and lost his vacation villa, wife and mistress in the process.

At about eleven o'clock, the guests took their leave and Jennifer, after having closed the front door, slipped off her Italian designer mules and sighed happily. The evening had exceeded expectations and Gregory was pleased, she could tell. She wanted him to know that she could thrive in her new role of society hostess and win the respect of his well-heeled and privileged friends. This was her job now, and she took it seriously.

Coming up behind her, he put his hands around her slender waist. "You're magnificent . . . do you know I think I'm the luckiest man alive," he said, as his hands slid up under the sides of her dress to her breasts. Even though they'd been together for more than a year now, his desire for her had not diminished, and in fact had intensified now that he had discovered a wonder drug that produced erections on demand.

Though she had no interest in sex right now, or for that matter at any time with him, she let her body meld into his, and sighed softly, letting him think this was the most pleasurable thing in the world. After kissing her, he picked her up, walked down the dimly lit hallway to the bedroom, where he deposited her on the puffy clouds of a luxuriant down comforter.

"I need a minute," she said, knowing that at that moment she could have anything she wanted. "I'll be right back and then we can pick up where we left off."

She hated the thought of compromising her dress, so she slipped into her dressing room and gently hung it on one of the satin-covered hangers. From her collection of lingerie that she had acquired since becoming Mrs. Foster, she reached for a lavender stretch lace chemise. Sheer and incredibly sexy, it was a gift but it was not from Gregory. She studied her reflection in the floor-to-ceiling mirror. Her breasts, upgraded by the plastic surgeon from a *B* to a *C* cup, looked fantastic. *Gregory would be pleased, who wouldn't be?* She reached into a tiny drawer and withdrew a small vial. In less than thirty seconds, she snorted two tiny silver spoonfuls of cocaine. She got closer to the mirror, checked for any signs of white powder under her nose and returned to Gregory, who had taken off his trousers and was lying on their king-size bed propped up by a tumble of pillows.

She spent the next hour giving pleasure to a man forty years her senior until he was completely spent. But the entire time her mind was elsewhere, notably on the much-younger man who had given her this lovely lavender chemise, and of her hope that tomorrow, with a little luck, he would be back in her bed.

The onset of moral amnesia is fast and furious, but Ellen discovered there's nothing like a ringing cell phone to jolt the victim back to reality. Startled, she lurched out of his embrace.

David fished the phone out of his pocket, flipped it open, unleashing a band of blue light over his flushed cheek. "Hello."

He was silent for a moment, then said, "Mom, wait a minute—calm down. Where'd he go?"

Ellen could only hear half of the conversation but clearly something was wrong. She quietly got up and walked to the other side of the gazebo to give him at least the semblance of privacy. The breeze had picked up, the surf was getting louder.

"No, I can be there in twenty minutes or so. I just got done with dinner." Appearing eager to change the subject of his whereabouts, he said, "How long has he been gone?"

After telling his mother not to worry again, he hung up. Ellen returned to sit next to him on the bench. Slightly chilled, she drew her sweater around her.

"What happened?"

"My father went out for a walk to pick up a few things at the grocery store and hasn't come back yet and it's been two hours. My mother's worried that something has happened. This is so unlike her to call about something like this . . . I wonder where he is. Maybe he just stopped to have a beer somewhere."

"Well, we better get going," Ellen said, feeling slightly orbital as though she was emerging from a dream sequence.

"Yes, in a minute though. I don't think I can go anywhere right now. Look what you've done to me." He gestured to his slightly disheveled appearance, and ran his hands through his hair in an attempt to straighten it.

"Done to *you*," she said, eyes sparkling, full of mischief. "I think you're mistaken, look at me." She smoothed her hair and straightened her dress. She paused. "Are you worried?"

"I don't know. I'm starting to think I'm in the Twilight Zone. First Marianne's father, then you somehow cast a spell on me and lured me here and now my father's missing. Maybe he was bewitched—do you have a twin sister somewhere here on the island?"

"Lured you here," she started to protest, but he reached over and put his arms around her, making her heart pound again.

"I think it's a good thing she called, or I might have ravaged you right here on this bench," he said softly into her ear, and then kissed her passionately. "Seriously, though," he looked at her, his eyes unsure, yet trusting, "I don't know what just happened here but promise me this isn't goodbye."

Ellen knew at that moment she was at a door that should remain firmly closed. She hesitated, but couldn't bring herself to say no. "Okay."

"I suppose we'd better get going. I'm not sure what I should do," he said.

"You can borrow my bike," she offered. "It's locked at the bike rack and I know the combination. Maybe someone at the resort has a flashlight."

He kissed her again, then looked at her for a long moment, no words needed to acknowledge the megawatt synergy between them that defied intellect, reason and logic. "What am I going to do with you?" he said.

They left the gazebo, and walked back to the restaurant, reclaiming Ellen's sandals on the way. Ellen dropped him off at the entrance to Paradise, just in case his mother was waiting anxiously in the parking lot. No need to explain why he was with another woman—no that would not do.

IN A MATTER OF FIFTEEN MINUTES, David tried to calm his mother, borrowed a flashlight from the front-desk staff, unlocked Ellen's bike from the rack and started pedaling briskly down the path that his father would have taken to the store. Thank goodness for a full moon, its luminosity streaming down on the path before him, making a mockery of the tiny beam emanating from the small flashlight he'd placed in the basket. It was only in the tunnels of thick foliage when the moonlight disappeared did he feel like a blind man.

He didn't know what to expect, maybe this was a stupid exercise—what were the odds that he would find his father wandering around on this path in the darkness? And if he did a new fear materialized, the fear being what if something had happened to his father, what if he had a heart attack . . . what were the odds that his father and Marianne's would have a heart attack on the same day? *No way, get a grip*, he told himself.

He cursed the situation, wondering whether he should immediately abandon this plan and get back in the car. No, that would be the next step, first he had to check this out. He grew alarmed even thinking of next steps and would that mean— the police? *Stay positive*, he chided himself. *This is probably nothing but a huge misunderstanding.* He concentrated on pedaling briskly.

The only benefit of the tense situation at hand was that he had momentarily forgotten what had just transpired on the beach. The memory was like the aftershock of an earthquake. What on earth am I doing? *I just cheated on my wife! And the worst thing is that the part of me that feels bad is overwhelmed by the part of me that wants Ellen.*

Della's Market was less than a mile away from Paradise. Soon the path widened and he could see the road, he must be getting close.

Is this how it happens? Is this why so many people get

divorced? One day you're on vacation with your family, the next you're infatuated with another woman . . . Where is my loyalty to Marianne? Because if I'm really a happily married man then why did I end up making out with another woman on the beach and getting more turned on than I have been in years. If I had my way it would not have stopped there. He marveled at the timing of his mother's phone call. Weird. Almost like someone had been watching out for him.

Della's came into view. The entrance to the upscale supermarket was on the second floor. He parked the bike and bounded up the stairs. Once inside, he offered a brief description of his father to a young woman with an eyebrow and nose piercing at the check-out counter. She didn't recall seeing anyone who fit his description.

His first mission accomplished, David had no idea where to go next. He assessed his options. A few doors down he could see a sign for The Blue Heron, a restaurant and bar. The two businesses immediately to his left were dark. He paced back and forth in front of his bike. Where on earth could he be? Bars? Restaurants? The ideas shot back and forth in his head like errant bullets in a firing range. Suddenly, the ringing of his cell phone pierced the silence. It was his mother.

"David, he's here, he's fine. He just got confused and turned around and ended up on the west end of the beach near the Breakwater Hotel. A young man who works there drove him home. I'm so sorry you had to go out on this chase. Do you want me to come pick you up in the car?" Judy asked.

"No, I'm fine. Thank goodness. I'll have a much better ride back knowing he's okay. I went to the grocery store and I really didn't know what to do next."

"David, I'm really sorry I had to involve you in this."

"Mom, not a problem. I'm just glad he's home. I'll be there in a few minutes."

David flipped his phone closed. His father, lost? A wrong turn and he ended up at the Breakwater Hotel? His father never got lost, he had an innate sense of direction. Something wasn't right, he could feel it in his gut. And then he remembered the conversation on the golf course and the blank look on his father's face at the mention of Kevin Hammersmith. A sense of foreboding came over him.

He got back on the bike and pedaled hard, trying to tire himself out because fatigue seemed a welcome refuge right now.

"**D**ad, what happened?"

Looking tired, his father sat at the kitchen table, drinking a glass of apple juice Judy had poured for him.

"Nothing happened except for your mother's highly over-active imagination. I was out walking and somehow took a wrong turn," said George. "Then your mother decided to put out an APB for me and get all worried and call you. Tomorrow my picture will be on milk cartons with an eight hundred number asking 'have you seen this man?'"

David was glad to see his father's sense of humor was intact.

"George, I had good reason to worry. You were gone for more than two hours and it was dark," said Judy, still visibly shaken from the night's ordeal. David asked her if she wanted a glass of wine.

"No thank you I'm afraid I won't sleep."

That makes two of us, David thought, *though for entirely different reasons.*

"What your mother doesn't understand is that I'm a grown man and can take care of myself, just as I've done every day since I was in third grade," he said, pushing back his chair from the table. "Now that you've called off the dogs, my dear, I'm going to bed." George walked toward the double doors of the master suite. "Good night, and stop worrying about me."

David couldn't help noticing that his father, despite his

seventy one years, still was a remarkably fit man, standing six foot one with an age-defying physique. His vigorous demeanor clearly was at odds with this strange episode of his getting lost.

David turned his attention to his mother, the fluorescent kitchen light unforgiving on her face, accentuating the fine lines around her eyes, making her look drawn and tired.

"Mom, everything is all right. A bit of a scare but that's all. He's fine. Look at him, he's the picture of health, strong as a bull," he said.

She was silent.

"C'mon, don't let this upset you. You know, it's been a long day, you should probably go to bed. You'll wake up tomorrow in this beautiful place and put this all behind you."

Judy looked at him, as if trying to decide whether or not to speak. Her instinct to protect her son was strong, but she was tired and rattled.

"He didn't know the name of the resort," she said, her voice a whisper.

"What?"

"He didn't know where he was staying. The young man from the hotel who drove him home pulled me aside and told me that he was a little disoriented when they found him walking up to the hotel. They asked him where he was going and he didn't know. They named off a bunch of places, finally mentioned Paradise. He remembered then."

"He didn't remember where we were staying? That's strange, Mom . . . was he drinking? Is that it? Has he been hitting the scotch?

"David, at this point I would be happy to think it was scotch, but it wasn't. He was sober as a judge when he left here."

Her eyes avoided his as she stared intently at the cluster of delicate burgundy roses that served as the centerpiece on the glass tabletop. He had the sense that she was struggling with something only known to her. The moments passed; the muted sound of the surf through closed windows the only sound.

"David, there's something I've been meaning to talk to you

about. I was going to mention it a few weeks ago but then I decided to wait until after the party. But I can't keep it to myself anymore."

She paused, took a breath, and then charged ahead.

"I'm really worried about your father. He hasn't been himself lately. The past few months he's had these bouts of depression and he's cranky a lot. Some days he doesn't want to do anything. He goes downstairs and watches TV—you know that's not like him—and sometimes I'll go down there and find him just staring off into space. And reading, you know how he loves to read, well I haven't seen him with a book in months. He seems to be losing interest in things that once made him happy and I don't know what to do."

David took a moment to reflect. "What do you think it is?"

"I don't know. I keep hoping it just goes away because I don't want to have to think about what it could be."

There was a long period of silence. Judy's eyes remained fixed on the flowers, her voice low and stressed. "What if it's Alzheimer's?"

David's brain, tired and mentally exhausted, found it difficult to comprehend her words. *What on earth was going on with his life?* He wished more than anything he could simply turn back the clock to last week, when he eagerly awaited his vacation, when his life was simple, when he was blissfully free of this nascent worry about his father and before he met a woman that rocked the foundation of his marriage.

The look on his mother's face was one of fear mingled with sadness. He knew how difficult this was for her and how scared she was. His mother had many qualities, but facing life-threatening adversity was not one of them. It wasn't her fault that fate had neglected to deliver tragedy to her door step, that her immediate family had so far escaped the devastation of cancer, car accidents, terminal illness and the like. Over the years this distance made her increasingly uneasy, like someone standing in a bakery line waiting for her number to be called.

"Mary's mother suffered for *seven years* before she died," his mother whispered. "It robbed her of everything." Judy's only connection with the dreaded disease was from visiting her friend Mary's mother who lived in a nursing home on a special floor for Alzheimer's patients. The place was clean, the nurses friendly and capable, but the residents were in varying degrees out of their minds. Some screamed for no reason, others sat in chairs parked in front of the TV with vacant stares. Judy was terribly depressed that anyone would have to spend their final years in such a place, and on one visit had burst into tears as soon as the elevator doors closed to take her down to the lobby.

"David, I cannot even bear to think that your father could . . ."

He went to the other side of the table, pulled up the chair next to hers and put his arm around his mother, who suddenly seemed vulnerable and in need of protection.

"C'mon Mom, don't think the worse just because a few weird things have happened. People get crabby when they get old. They get depressed. And maybe sometimes they get lost."

"I hope and pray you're right," she said, hugging him back, putting her head on his shoulder. "I'm really sorry to burden you with this. This has been on my mind for a while."

David knew he had to get his mother to bed. It was futile to discuss this further given the events of the day. "Mom, we're both exhausted. We need sleep. Remember what you used to always tell me, 'things will look better in the morning.' Are you going to be okay? I can stay here if you want."

"I'll be okay and you're right I am exhausted. Go home and enjoy your solitude. You don't have any kids to wake you up in the morning."

"Promise me you will stop thinking the worst."

"I'll try. Thank you for being here for me. I love you honey."

"I love you too Mom, and don't worry everything will be okay."

He was a little disappointed she didn't take him up on his offer to stay. It was safe here, and sleeping on the sofa bed would eliminate the temptation to go knocking on Ellen's door in the middle of the night.

73

E llen knew it would be a sleepless night. Her emotions whipsawed between euphoria and agonizing guilt, and her body felt like she had taken a handful of amphetamines. Over and over, she replayed the scene in her mind . . . the star swept night, the way he looked at her, the feeling of his arms around her. She had been right all along about his intentions; her self-esteem soared. The fact that she could still, at her age, incite this degree of arousal in a man could only be viewed as a personal triumph.

No, she would never get to sleep tonight without help. Making matters worse was the question of whether he would come back. He knew where she was. She needed to make a decision. If he knocked on that door and she opened it, it was all over. The remaining hours of the night loomed like a minefield ablaze with temptation. Right now, she still had a chance to extricate herself from what had been an unprecedented lapse of moral sanity.

She went to her makeup bag and took out a sleeping pill. She walked into the kitchen, poured a glass of water, and gulped it down. She thought about sitting out on the lanai waiting for the pill to kick in, but what if David came by the front of the building. It would look like an invitation. She closed the room-darkening drapes that lined the long wall of windows and curled up on the sofa. The talking heads on cable news were arguing about the war in Iraq, but her thoughts were elsewhere.

What is this force and why is it so hard to subdue? Why is it that we encounter scores of people in our lifetimes—friends, neighbors, coworkers—without incident but suddenly one day a spark is ignited.

She considered herself a woman of faith, and wondered why faith wasn't a shield from incendiary desire. God had created all things good, she had been taught, so what of this? Or was it blasphemy to blame God for her own weakness? She was disappointed in herself, and disappointed that faith in God in and of itself was not an insurance policy from the lusts and passions of the world.

Popular culture and bestselling books trumpeted the belief that spouses cheat when something is lacking in their marriage. No doubt that was often the case, but surely it didn't explain a social landscape littered with stories of men leaving their wives of twenty-five years for women young enough to be their daughters or married women taking up with some guy they met in a bar after work. And what of this chance encounter that had turned her life upside down? She didn't ask for it, it just happened. Could it be that many affairs were merely the perfect storm of fate, desire and opportunity?

A lot of people, like her friend Susan, were in deep denial. "Dennis would *never* cheat on me," Susan pronounced unequivocally at a soccer game upon learning that a neighbor, by all accounts a good husband and father, had left his wife for another woman. Ellen wondered *how she could be so sure?* What if an attractive young receptionist set her sights on Dennis at the office Christmas party after a few cocktails? Was he bullet-proof? Was anyone?

Whatever the cause, the collateral damage was staggering. Marriages ended, parents were forced to make difficult choices about their children, and families were left to pick up the pieces. She had seen enough in her life to know that high-octane sexual liaisons rarely resulted in lifelong happiness and in fact caused misery for all involved. She knew all this intellectually, but there was David's face, smiling at her from across the table, lifting his wine glass to hers . . . was it possible to fall in love with someone over dinner?

She desperately wanted him to come back, she could still smell his cologne on her face. When if ever would she have the chance to experience the passion that had taken grip of her being? She was not getting any younger. It was as if it were two in the morning and the bartender was saying "last call." She knew it was irrational but one of her deepest fears was that no one would want her in another five or ten years. The gig was about up. And this, for a woman, is a profoundly depressing thought.

No good can come of this, her conscience fought back, repeating a maxim she invoked frequently with her son. Her husband didn't deserve this, despite their problems. He had been distant and depressed, he had infuriated her with his unwillingness to tackle his problems. But could she betray him in this manner? A lifetime of guilt for a night of pleasure?

Tired of the news, she channel surfed looking for something—anything—to divert her attention. She settled on an old *Andy Griffith* rerun, the one where Opie breaks the neighbor's window. Life was so simple then, the show always gave her comfort.

Thirty minutes later, the pill kicked in and she went to bed. Sleep eventually came, but it was not restful.

Maggie sat down at her computer, knowing that even a momentary delay could cause her to abandon her plan. She typed in cheap airfares, searching for the best deal from Dulles to Fort Myers.

A slew of flight options appeared. She clicked on the first and cheapest one, a $209 round-trip ticket with a connection in Atlanta. The layover was only an hour. *Damn*, another excuse rendered useless.

For days now, she had been fighting a thunderstorm of guilt over her decision to essentially boycott her parents' fiftieth anniversary. No one expected her to come, and she was still angry enough to stay home. Ever since her marriage had gone into self-destruct mode, her relationship with her family had crashed. Her parents accused her of putting her own needs over those of her children and husband. *Screw them*, she told herself over and over. *Whose life was it anyway?* She couldn't help the fact that her marriage was a bust, that she married a man and then fell in love with a woman, a woman who gave her life meaning and substance and a sexual gratification that had been MIA in her marriage and for that matter in her life. What did they know about anything anyway? Her parents had spent their entire adult lives chasing the American dream in the hallowed canyons of White Bread Suburbia. They didn't understand her growing up and they certainly didn't understand her now.

Yet family was family, and she couldn't ignore the mounting guilt as the celebration drew closer. On one hand, she believed that she was doing her family a favor by not showing up, that her absence would remove the tension that her mere presence would generate. On the other, she didn't want to solidify the breach that existed between her and her parents, the certain result of not showing up for their fiftieth anniversary party. It was the ultimate fuck you, like writing it in concrete. Maybe this *was* an opportunity to try and set things right. Or at least get them moving in the right direction. There would be a lot of people there, and it wouldn't be as awkward as going to see them alone.

She wondered how they would react to her coming. Her mother would be civil, that much she could count on because her mother was not someone who liked to air the family's dirty laundry in public. Her father would grunt hello and basically ignore her. She would probably get into it with Julia because her older sister couldn't keep her opinions to herself. Maggie once respected Julia's accomplishments, an MBA from Northwestern and a six-figure salary by the time she was thirty. But in recent years Maggie's indoctrination into class warfare had the unfortunate consequence of turning Julia into the enemy. Julia was a "have" and Maggie was a vociferous advocate for the "have-nots." Their relationship had degenerated into a microcosm of the venomous political bipolarism that divided the nation.

It was fitting with Julia at the helm of party planning that they were going to Sanibel, *Island of the Haves.* Her sister had sold her soul for a fat cat salary and a million in stock options. Julia worked for a global discount retailer worshipped on Wall Street and reviled by unions and social justice advocates. Her company was setting new lows in the industry for providing inadequate health insurance to its employees, and its voracious appetite for cheap goods was fueling the trend to outsource manufacturing jobs to China. Yet by the world's standards, Julia was a success, and the world's standards were her parent's standards.

She stared for what seemed like minutes at the *Buy Now* button on the screen.

Sasha walked into the room while Maggie pondered her decision. Dressed in Blue Cult jeans and a washed-out GAP T-shirt, wearing no makeup, jet-black hair in a tangle, she was still incredibly beautiful. Maggie's gaze lingered on her statuesque lover, wondering why it took her so many years to acknowledge the reality of her sexuality. "What are you doing?" Sasha asked, standing behind her, placing her hands on Maggie's tense shoulders.

"I'm caving and about to make the worst decision of my life," said Maggie, trying to make light of the situation. "I can't bear the guilt of not going to my parents' anniversary, so I'm one click away from a ticket to disaster."

"Do you want me to go? Moral support?" Sasha asked, her voice just a decibel above a whisper, as she lightly massaged Maggie's neck and shoulders.

"You're so sweet to offer, but no, this is something I've got to do on my own."

Maggie clicked on the *Buy Now* button and took her credit card out of her wallet. Sasha continued to create tingling sensations on her neck with the feathery touch of her soft finger tips. She filled in the requisite information and a few seconds later had an email confirmation.

The online purchase completed, Maggie stood up, gently pulled Sasha toward her and kissed her sensuously on the mouth. Suddenly the anniversary party and reality of dealing with her parents were the furthest thing from her mind.

E llen woke up in the dense brain fog of a sleeping pill. Sunlight streamed in through the bedroom windows; she felt vaguely numb to her senses. It took only a minute or two before her consciousness was jolted to the reality that last night had not been a dream. She had to get out of here. What if he came back?

It was nine o'clock. She would go get a coffee and take a long walk on the beach. Nothing cleared her head like strong coffee and ocean air. She put on some lipstick, and threw on some shorts and a T-shirt.

Like a refugee fleeing from some unseen evil, she left Paradise, sunglasses on, eyes straight ahead. The caffeine had kicked in, and she walked briskly as if she had a destination in mind. She did not. Twenty minutes later she was well on her way, another glorious day, sunny, warm, calm waters and a cloudless crystal blue sky.

She marveled at the frenetic pace of avian activity around her. At the water's edge, dozens of ring-billed gulls frolicked in mid-air then gracefully swooped down for a soft landing on the tawny brown sand. She walked amid platoons of white-breasted soldiers with black wingtips, standing at attention as if awaiting orders from their commander. Suddenly, the signal came, and she found herself in the midst of dozens of fluttering wings as the entire platoon became airborne. Soon they were high above her, an exhilarating sight.

Her mind was a jumble of thoughts. How did it come to this? Walking on a beach a thousand miles away from home, alone, unable to stop thinking about David and what had happened in the gazebo. Like a drug addict, she wanted more. It used to be that way with Jeremy, but not lately. The emotional baggage of the past few years had piled up like trash during a garbage strike. Resentment had become a growth industry in her marriage and nothing she did seemed to make things better. Her successful career and enthusiasm for life in general had combined to somehow become a liability in their relationship. "I didn't marry frickin' wonder woman," he yelled at her one day during an insanely ridiculous argument over household chores. Jeremy needed someone to lash out at, and Ellen often felt as if it wouldn't have mattered who he was married to, they would have suffered a similar fate.

She was attracted to David because he was incredibly sexy and handsome but it was more than that. He was confident, witty, successful, intelligent, engaging and genuinely interested in her. To be lavished with this much attention at this particular time in her life was a powerful brew. And best of all there was no emotional baggage, no resentment, no bitterness of things gone wrong.

Deep in thought, she continued walking until suddenly she realized she had never walked this far down the beach. The luxurious condo buildings had given way to imposing homes with impeccably landscaped lawns. Admiring a lovely garden, she heard the strains of music, what sounded like a church organ. How odd.

The sound seemed to be coming from a two-story Georgian-style mansion, whose French doors opened to a large terrace. Apparently someone was playing a CD. But the closer she got, she realized it actually was an organ. It wasn't coming from the house but from a building next door partially screened by a wall of lofty pine trees.

Moving closer, she could hear it clearly now, it was "Beautiful

Savior," one of her favorite hymns. People were singing. Intrigued, she made her way through the feathery pines branches and over the soft carpet of needles. On the other side, she found herself staring at a shining white clapboard structure with a small unadorned steeple. Curiously, she walked around it to find the entrance. The words "Grace Chapel" were scripted in royal blue and curved over the old wooden door, which made a loud creaking sound as she opened it. She slipped inside, and quietly took a seat in the last row of pews.

THE STURDY WOODEN PEWS WERE NEARLY FULL. Most of the congregants were older, many looked to be retirement age. It reminded her of her congregation back home, where, ever mindful of the fact that without new blood they were destined to extinction, they had launched an aggressive campaign to attract younger people. The unadorned simplicity of this seaside chapel stood in stark contrast to Trinity and its soaring cantilevered ceilings, stained glass windows and sanctuary that seated one thousand people. Here the walls were painted blue green, and two ceiling fans hummed as they sucked in ocean air from casement windows. On the altar, a gleaming bronze cross hung on the wall between two large windows, through which the morning sunlight streamed with the brilliance of an effervescent crystal, almost blinding. The view of the ocean was breathtakingly beautiful, and Ellen was not the first visitor to be awed by it.

The pastor, who looked to be in his seventies, wore a white vestment. Lively and intelligent eyes dominated his face; funny, Ellen thought, you could actually see the goodness in some people. He climbed the two steps to the austere wooden pulpit and announced the Gospel, Matthew chapter 14, then read:

During the fourth watch of the night, Jesus went out to them, walking on the lake. When the disciples saw him walking on the lake, they were terrified . . . But Jesus immediately said to them: "Take courage! It is I. Don't be afraid."

"Lord if it's you," Peter replied, "tell me to come to you on the water."

"Come," he said. Then Peter got down out of the boat, walked on the water and came toward Jesus. But when he saw the wind, he was afraid and, beginning to sink, cried out, "Lord, save me!"

Immediately Jesus reached out his hand and caught him. "You of little faith," he said, "why did you doubt?" And when they climbed into the boat, the wind died down. Then those who were in the boat worshiped him, saying "Truly you are the Son of God."

A blanket of anticipatory silence descended on the sanctuary. The pastor used the long pause to good effect.

"Today I'd like to start with a question: How many of you would have gotten out of the boat to walk to Jesus? Let's see a show of hands," said Pastor Roberts. "C'mon now, don't be shy." Less than a third of the parishioners raised their hands, and the pastor smiled. "Not bad. I've been asking that question for years, and I never get more than a few hands, and even then I'm not sure they're telling the truth." Laughter bubbled up from the congregation.

"Seriously though, today's Gospel reminds us that despite extraordinary advances in science, literature, the arts, people of faith really haven't changed much in two thousand years. Like the disciples, we genuinely want to follow Christ. But when the storms come our faith is shaken. Matthew writes of a real storm, with wind and lightning and rain, but the storms we face are different. It might be illness, a broken relationship, the loss of a loved one, addiction, the list goes on and on. Sometimes these storms burst into our lives with little or no warning, and we're afraid, sometimes terrified. So the question this Gospel lesson raises is this: Are we, as Christians, going to live lives dominated by fear or by faith?"

Ellen, drawn to his quiet yet resonant voice, found it a calming elixir for jarred nerves, the result of too much coffee, a sleeping pill and a highly charged adulterous encounter.

"One of my favorite professors at seminary used to say 'a strong faith is a challenged faith.' For many of us, it's not until we're in the eye of one of these storms that we can, through the power of the Holy Spirit, vanquish our fear and renew our faith. That's the moment we get out of the boat and realize, like Peter, that only Christ can save us. It's when we're willing to take that leap into the unknown that we truly begin to understand this mystery of our faith, and how much God loves us."

For Ellen his words rang true. She was a believer but not a walker on water. Despite her faith and outwardly confident demeanor, she battled fear more than she cared to admit. She knew how utterly senseless this was but had never been able to conquer it.

The pastor stopped for a moment, took a sip of water from a small glass, then set it down under the lectern. "Fear not, the Lord tells us. I want you take a moment and think about how different your life would be if you were never afraid. If you weren't afraid of getting cancer, or afraid of dying or something bad that could happen in the future. My mother used to say fear is the devil's playground. It takes hold of us, robs us of hope and leads us away from God. When I was a young pastor in North Carolina, one of the parishioners was a very wealthy woman who had always wanted to travel the world and see all the great cathedrals of Europe. But she never saw them because the thought of getting on an airplane terrified her. Before she died, she told me how much she regretted never having done so. She had tricked herself into thinking she was 'safe' when in fact she had squandered a marvelous opportunity to grow in faith."

"In Matthew's vivid account, Peter starts to sink. What does Jesus do? He reaches out his hand to save him, just as he reaches out to save us. Even when our faith is weak, even when the storms of this life threaten to overpower us. If you leave here today with nothing else, remember this: nothing can ever separate you from the love of God. As Christians, we can count on his unwavering love in the good times, the bad times—all the time. God will never leave us."

His words lifted her, and unleashed a cloudburst of emotion. The storms in her life *had* overwhelmed her, and she had been trying to go it alone. She felt a rush of joyful exuberance, and said a silent prayer of thanks.

COLLECTING THE OFFERING were two ushers dressed in their Sunday-best suits who looked to be in their early seventies. Ellen fished two loose dollar bills out of her pocket—all the money she had on her—to put in the plate as it came by. The usher closest to her, a broad-shouldered man who looked like he once played linebacker for his college football team, cast her a genuinely warm and welcoming smile. He was wearing a burgundy shirt and a black tie.

In the front of the chapel, a woman placed a silver tray filled with miniature glasses of wine on the altar. There would be communion. If there was one thing that Ellen could always count on, it was the sustaining power of the bread and wine.

After a brief liturgy, the ushers guided the congregants to form a line for communion on the outside aisles, starting at the first pew. Ellen watched as an elderly woman wearing a dusty blue dress from a bygone era tried to pull herself up by grabbing the pew in front of her. Her shoulders significantly stooped from osteoporosis, she looked to be well into her eighties. After several failed attempts, she was finally able to maneuver herself out of the pew, though she seemed unsteady on her feet.

Ellen watched the scene unfold, knowing how fearful older people are of falling, and how far that short distance from the pew to the communion rail must have looked to her. But the usher in the burgundy shirt saw the woman's hesitation and quickly walked over to her. His eyes radiant with kindness, he reached out and took the woman's arm, and helped her walk up to the communion rail, steadying her as she knelt down. Ellen could hear the gentle murmur of "the body of Christ given for you" as the pastor distributed wafers to the kneeling parishioners. After the woman received communion, the usher helped her up and led her back to her pew, gently patting her on the shoulder, in the way mothers comfort their children. The woman looked up at him with a beatific smile, her eyes brimming with gratitude.

The music, the compassion, the living spiritual tableau unfolding before her touched her deeply. Her eyes misted. She felt as if she had just witnessed the grace of God in this little chapel. She savored the moment, and was inspired by it.

David was in major meltdown. He had hardly gotten any sleep, having lain awake for hours after he left his parents, fighting the temptation to return to Ellen and pick up where they left off. Temptation as he had never experienced it in all the years of his marriage had loomed right before him, just a short walk across the courtyard. The digital clock by his bed beamed 10:32 a.m.

Now, with the sun like an oven in the room, it was all too much for his mind to process. He was a wreck, his nerves shot. He didn't want to see his mother because he was afraid she would suspect something was up. Last night she was preoccupied, in the clear light of day she might sense something was wrong.

He wondered where in the hell Marianne and the kids were and when they were coming back. Would any of this have happened if she hadn't left him alone? Ever since he was little, when things didn't go as planned, his mother offered up her tried-and-true maxim, "everything happens for a reason." But what was the reason for this?

He propped the extra bed pillows under his head on the king-size bed. He needed to rest though he had only been up a few minutes. The rhythmic churning of the waves did not sooth him, and instead symbolized his intense emotional upheaval. Under the veneer of guilt was an unsettling realization he had dead bolted in the attic of his conscience. To think of it would give it life and betray his marriage. But he couldn't stop the taunting voice in his head.

So you think you've got the perfect life. Great kids, great wife and mother, awesome house and a big bank account. Yeah right. Just one tiny little crack in the china, you're not even sure you're in love with your wife anymore. You won't admit you're unhappy because what good would it do. What are you going to do, divorce her? Leave your children?

The realization left him numb.

The truth was that ever since the children were born, he *had* slowly become emotionally and physically estranged from his wife, who had inexorably metamorphosed into a New Age mommy machine. The Marianne he had fallen in love was not the Marianne of today. That Marianne had been a spirited, incredibly sexy twenty-year-old woman who could not wait to start her career as a teacher, a woman who shared his ambitions and dreams. Or so he thought. But that all began to change and in profound ways when Ethan was born, and even more so after Emma. At first he was thrilled with Marianne's passion for motherhood. But in the months and years that followed, the lives of their children became Marianne's chief raison d'être, a near-obsession that drove every major and minor decision in their lives. Daily life was a never-ending thread of conversations on how to deal with Ethan's bed-wetting, Emma's tantrums or Colin's crying. She had become so damn *boring* and she didn't even realize it. And downright weird with all the crap she read in childrearing books that she took as gospel.

Like the last time they had seen Rob and Valerie, college friends who now lived in Boston. His parents agreed to take the kids so they could have a weekend away. He had really been looking forward to seeing Rob and Valerie without the kids because it was impossible to have any meaningful conversation with a six-, four- and a two-year-old around. Rob and Valerie were one of those rare couples who actively decided not to have children, and David felt it was unfair to subject them to the bedlam of his family life for three days.

Even with the kids away it was impossible for Marianne to turn off the mommy switch. That night, over a $100 bottle of wine in a five-star seafood restaurant, Marianne couldn't wait to tell everyone about a new parenting book she had just devoured. Marianne bought parenting books the way some women buy lipsticks.

"Of course, Dr. Bob recommends it," she said brightly, as if this mere fact were an endorsement from the Vatican. "This book is a huge best seller, all the moms from playgroup are raving about it." David looked over at her, thinking how remarkable it was that someone who looked essentially the same as she did ten years ago could have morphed into such a different human being. *Invasion of the Body Snatchers*? Did someone leave a New Age Mommy pod and take the real Marianne to outer space?

"David, you *have* to find the time to read this," she said. "It's about learning to control tantrums, and lord knows, we've had a lot of experience with that in our house, especially with Emma." Rob and Valerie knew all too well the problems with Emma, which is why David had arranged the weekend sans children in the first place.

"I'm trying an entirely new approach with Colin," Marianne said, in between nibbling on a wheat cracker and sipping a glass of pinot grigio. "The theory is that toddlers are basically primitive thinkers like cavemen. To deal with them effectively we need to learn to speak their language. Oh, it's not complicated or anything. It's just using the same words they do, but repeating them slowly, using your body language to empathize with their needs."

Rob, a devilish grin on his still youthful face, gazed hungrily at Valerie and grabbed her by the hair. "Ugh. Me take 'em woman back to cave."

"Very funny," Marianne replied, not amused. "Seriously, I've been doing this all week with Colin and it seems to be working. According to the author, Colin is moving out of—now don't laugh—the charming chimp phase and into the little tike Neanderthal stage."

"And so is his father, except he's taller," said Rob, triggering a wave of laughter from Valerie and David.

Valerie, who had grown up one of eight children, couldn't stop giggling. "Yeah, we had some of that caveman stuff going on when I was growing up. You take Billy's ball, BAM you get hit on the head!"

David couldn't resist. "How 'bout I skip the book and watch the Flintstones?"

They all cracked up at that, except Marianne, whose smile was fixed in place to mask her irritation. She always seemed the odd person out where the four of them were concerned, especially lately.

"Maybe you should call him Bam Bam," Valerie giggled, feeling bad for Marianne but unable to stop herself. The wine and talk of cavemen made them silly. Valerie, Rob and David started singing *The Flintstone's* theme song. Marianne tried to hide her annoyance with their ridicule of what she viewed as a groundbreaking parenting tool, one she took very seriously, like she did with everything concerning the children.

And that was just the point, David thought. The needs and concerns of Ethan, Emma and Colin dominated her life and left little room for anything else. David felt terrible even having these thoughts, goodness knows Marianne was a terrific mother and he could never stay at home and deal with one child let alone three. But in her zeal to be the perfect mother, Marianne had enmeshed herself into the lives of her children to the point of obsession. David didn't share her passion for child rearing. He'd grown up on the "children are to be seen and not heard" philosophy.

If he were really honest with himself, he would have to admit he had never settled comfortably into the role of being a father. It was just too much. God forbid Marianne or his mother ever hear him say that. But that's what he felt. Two had been more than enough, and then along came Colin. Not that he didn't want his youngest son, of course he loved his son, it was just that he had other things he wanted to do with his time. He resolved the conflict by pouring himself into his job, with the ready excuse of his corporate responsibilities, which were substantial given his firm's meteoric growth. But in reality he was merely avoiding the reality of his chaotic family life. He had outsourced parenting to Marianne in the same way corporations outsource call centers to India. Was it any wonder she took it so seriously?

He knew deep down that he had the better end of the deal. Go to work, do what you love, come home and help out in the evenings and weekends when you could. He was a CFO, everyone understood his career priorities. Funny how different it was for his sister Julia, an outsourcing pioneer who had divested her parenting responsibilities to a long line of well-educated au pairs and nannies. Not that Julia ever lost any sleep over it, but she had taken a lot of crap over the years from family and friends who believed she was doing her children a huge disservice. Even David, who admired his sister's phenomenal success, questioned the amount of time she spent traveling. But no such issues were ever raised about him. Despite the progress of women, it was still very much a man's world.

His cell phone rang. He grabbed it from the nightstand and answered it. It was Marianne.

"Hi honey, Emma wants to say hi to you. She misses you very much and she wants to tell you all about her cousins."

A drumbeat of guilt pounded in his head. "Okay, put her on," he said with forced enthusiasm, desperate to hide the fact that anything was wrong.

L iz stood before the congregation at the end of the service to do the announcements, pushing her short crop of salt-and-pepper hair back from her face. Every week she mentioned upcoming events like Pot Luck Bible Study or Miriam's Circle just in case people hadn't read their *Chapel Chimes* newsletter.

Glorious sunlight washed the room in an incandescent glow. The news would be a terrible blow to the small congregation. Pastor Roberts, recently widowed and still fragile with grief, hadn't taken the news well. "Isn't there something we can do?" he asked. "The chapel has been here for years. Aren't we a landmark or an historic building?"

Liz explained that legally and literally the chapel stood on sand. Mrs. Hunter died before ever drawing up any legal documents that would have created a perpetual easement or subdivided the land. And even if they did want to fight it, they were up against a wealthy and powerful man. Liz didn't know the intimate details of Foster's business empire, but knew he was worth millions and could deploy a cadre of $500-an-hour attorneys with one phone call—no match for a small band of church-going senior citizens

Her heart beating faster than usual, she looked out at her friends and members of the congregation who had come to mean so much to her over the years. Myrtle and Ronnie Dalton, Muriel and Larry Stanke, Ruby Meyers and Betty Jo Lewis in their usual places in the front row of pews, and in the back, Bernice and Wally Borchard were seated next to Ruthie Watson, a widow in her eighties determined to stay in her island home until "the Lord comes to get me" as she was fond of saying.

And then there was her dear friend Harold. Seated alone in the pew, as had been the case for several months, Harold's still handsome face was lined with worry. His wife, Lucille, was dying of cancer and could no longer leave the house. It was the final chapter in a battle that had been playing out for five years now. Sunday mornings were the only times he ever left her.

"Do you think she'll be all right," he would ask Liz, seeking reassurance for the guilt he felt for leaving her even for an hour.

"Harold, the best thing you can do for her is recharge your spirits," Liz would say.

Liz put down her half-moon alabaster reading glasses as she finished the announcements.

"And there's something else that I need to share with you today, and unfortunately it's not good news," she said. "Two weeks ago I received a letter from Gregory Foster, who as you know owns this chapel and the land underneath it. I'll get straight to the point. Mr. Foster has informed us that Grace Chapel will have to be torn down to make way for his new home.

The stir from the pews was palpable.

"Now I wish I could tell you that we have some legal recourse, that we have a legal right to be here, but unfortunately we do not. Winifred Hunter never parceled off this lot when she built the chapel, we don't have an easement and we're not old enough to be historic. I spoke to a colleague of my late husband about this, and he was very clear that Mr. Foster is well within his rights.

"We have ninety days to make arrangements. Mr. Foster said he would allow us to move the chapel to another location. If it's not gone in ninety days, it will be bulldozed along with the house."

A loud gasp came from Betty Jo Lewis, who had worked as a cook for Winifred at a time when the Hunter estate was the epitome of wealth and status on the island. Lewis, one of the first black women to ever find employment on Sanibel, had been devoted to Winifred, and had remained on her staff even into the twilight years when Winifred became ill and a virtual shut-in.

"Why they gonna tear down that beautiful house? What's wrong with that man? Has he lost his mind? Rich folks don't make much sense round here these days," lamented Betty Jo, who was eighty-two years old and lived alone in a cozy apartment above Suzy's Seashell shop.

"Don't get me started, Betty Jo, or else we might be here all afternoon," Liz said. "I'm at the pulpit so I really ought to behave myself, but I wish someone could tell me why the Gregory Fosters of this world have to build palaces like European royalty when God has given us this natural paradise on earth to live in and enjoy. I'll never understand why the ocean and spectacular sunsets and bougainvillea in three shades of fuchsia are not enough."

"Amen," said Betty Jo. "Darn people gonna ruin this island. Shame on them."

Winston Holcombe, a retired professor of medieval history at Cambridge, raised his hand tentatively. "Can we ask this Foster chap to reconsider?" he asked.

"Already did," Liz replied. "I couldn't get through to speak directly to him, but I did get through to his assistant and she said it was a done deal. The new house is a wedding gift to his new wife."

Liz asked for a show of hands of people willing to serve on a transition committee to discuss their options. More than ten people offered to be on the committee. They decided to meet on Thursday night.

"I want you all to understand something," Liz said. "We may lose our beautiful view, we might even lose this building, but we're not going to lose our fellowship. If we have to move this congregation into my backyard, then that's what we'll do."

Ellen, struck by their plight, had the seed of an idea. And as it blossomed, she suddenly felt that she had come here for a reason.

* * *

AFTER THE SERVICE WAS OVER, the sanctuary was abuzz with the news and people crowded around Liz and Pastor Roberts. "It's just terrible," said one woman, "how can they tear down this beautiful chapel?"

"I can't imagine not being here on Sunday morning for services," said another parishioner, looking demoralized. Ellen patiently waited her turn. Finally, she saw her opportunity, and walked over and extended her hand.

"Good morning, I'm Ellen Bennett. I just wanted to tell you how much I enjoyed the service today, the music, communion, it was wonderful. I didn't even know this was here until I heard the music from the beach," she said, gesturing with her hands to emphasize "this" meant the chapel. "I hope you don't mind me just dropping in. Normally I dress a little more appropriately for church," she added, smiling.

"Glad to meet you Ellen. I'm Elizabeth Taylor, not the one who married Richard Burton, though I would have if he asked me to," she laughed, warmly grasping Ellen's hand. "I go by Liz. Delighted to have you here. Don't give your clothes a second thought, every so often the Holy Spirit hauls in a beach walker and looks like you're catch of the day."

"I'm *so sorry* to hear the news about the chapel. This is such an incredible place."

"It's a bummer, isn't that what you young people say," said Liz. "It's hard for me to accept the fact that we're going to lose this beautiful chapel because somebody wants to build a house the size of a hockey rink. Now mind you I've got nothing against wealth, my husband ran in those circles, he was an attorney and knew some real movers and shakers. Anyway, ever since Foster bought the property, I've been concerned. We've no legal right to be here, not even an easement. Used to be no one even knew where this island was, but today—well you can sell a garage for a million dollars!"

Ellen moved closer to Liz so the other people around wouldn't hear her speaking.

"Liz, have you ever thought about getting the media out here? You may not have any legal standing but this is a story made for the news. It won't cost anything, and who knows, maybe some publicity might change his mind? What have you got to lose? And even if he doesn't budge, maybe the publicity could help raise money for a new church or to move the chapel."

Liz cocked her head to one side, and looked at her with keen interest. "Well now, far be it from me to be a troublemaker," Liz said, smiling. "Tell you what, why don't you come over to my house this afternoon, say about two o'clock or so and we can talk about this. I like your idea. But I don't know how to go about doing such a thing. I wouldn't even know who to call. But sounds like you do."

Ellen said yes without hesitation. It seemed like a perfect moment for spontaneity. Though it violated her rule of never working on vacation, going to Liz's would be a reprieve from the rest of the afternoon and running into David. The best part of this morning was that she had actually put him out of her mind for a while.

Liz gave Ellen directions from the bike path. "We'll have fresh-baked peach cobbler and coffee," Liz promised, then turned away to talk to an elderly gentleman who had been patiently waiting to get her attention.

Talking on the phone with Emma required the kind of patience RNs employ with dementia patients. Emma would beg Marianne to let her call Daddy but when the opportunity presented itself she would retreat into shyness and refuse to speak, leaving David with no choice but to coax her gently, saying, "Emma, are you there? Emma, honey, if you're not going to talk why don't you give the phone back to Mommy."

Today was one of those days. "Emma, I miss you and I can't wait to see you when you get back."

Silence.

Then he heard the familiar call waiting beep. "Hold on a minute, Emma, I've got another call."

"Hello."

"David. It's me. How's it going?"

It took him a moment to process first the question and then the fact that it was his sister Maggie. On the roster of potential callers today, she was dead last on the list. Maggie had been lying low since deciding not to come down for the anniversary party, a decision he had reluctantly agreed with given the tensions in his family.

"Maggie, what a surprise," he said, cringing at how lame that sounded. "It's going great, blue sky, white sand, incredible beach and eighty degrees. I don't know why anyone lives in Chicago."

"I know. Seems crazy doesn't it, having to stay inside most of the year."

He knew Maggie didn't call to discuss the weather. He asked her to hold for a moment, went back to Emma, and told the silence he would call back.

"So what's up, Maggie? Everything okay?"

"Oh yeah, fine, well as fine as everything can be considering my husband hates my guts now and will probably spend the rest of his life turning my children against me."

Though Maggie's directness and acerbic wit were traits he liked about his sister, he found it a bit disconcerting in light of the gravity of the situation.

"Have you seen the boys?" he asked.

"No, Brian doesn't want them to see me so I'm just giving them time. Hopefully they'll come to understand their mother is not the lesbian version of Cruella de Vil. So here's why I'm calling. I wanted to tell you first so you can tell Mom and Dad. I've booked a flight and I'm coming down. I've thought about this long and hard. This is a once in a lifetime deal. It's not like they're going to live forever. I'm coming down so I'll be there for the party on Friday night. I know I said I wasn't going to come but I cannot NOT be there for this. Please help them understand how important this is to me."

David had not expected this from his prodigal sister. His parents and Julia were still upset with Maggie. To them, it was another sorry chapter of irresponsibility and rebellion not to mention a devastated husband and what this would do to the boys. Although David suspected this would all blow over eventually, the wounds were still fresh.

He took a long breath and weighed his words carefully. "Maggie, are you sure you're up for this? I mean, I'm not sure Mom and Dad are ready to roll out the welcome wagon and crack open a bottle of champagne."

"I'm ready to face the music," she said, "whatever it is. Nothing can be worse than what I've already been though. No one knows what this has been like for me. Everyone thinks I'm a selfish bitch, well let them think that. I've made mistakes,

I'm sorry for them, and I'm moving on with my life. Do I judge *them?* What's my crime, being a lesbian? Would I be getting this treatment if I fell in love with another man? It's bullshit."

David knew there was a certain amount of truth to what his sister was saying, but this was a conversation for another day. Perched on the razor's edge of his own moral dilemma, he wasn't comfortable with any discussion of infidelity at the present moment.

"Are you bringing Sasha?" he asked, praying the answer was no. It was one thing for Maggie to show up at the party, but another for Aunt Gertrude to witness this new chapter in his sister's sexuality. He could just see the scene unfold, *"Did you say thespian, honey? My friend Trudy is a thespian, simply adores the theater, she did the costumes for Desdemona in Othello . . ."*

"No," she said. "Not this time. But please just tell Mom and Dad before I get there. I don't want to *totally* surprise them. Dad could have a heart attack and drop dead and Mom would never forgive me for ruining her party."

"All right," said David, though still a little uneasy about being thrust into this role. "I'll do what I can. Listen I've got to go. Have a safe trip." He clicked off the phone.

Wonderful. A family debacle. What a great anniversary present for his parents.

Ellen couldn't remember the last time she felt as relaxed in someone else's home as she was in Liz's bright and comfy kitchen. They sat at the small kitchen table in front of a sunny window framing a picturesque view of Liz's garden and its fountains of vibrant color. The chrome-plated table and cushy vinyl chairs reminded Ellen of her grandma's house.

Though crowded, Liz's house, with its hanging plants, walls lined with books and abundant daylight, exuded the warmth of its owner. The scent of fresh-brewed coffee filled the air. The exception to this harmony was Miss Kitty, as Liz fondly referred to her, who was perched on top of a bookcase looking suspiciously at their guest, as if furtively plotting her demise.

"So, Ellen, what brings you to Sanibel?" Liz asked, lifting a white Corningware pot to pour the coffee. She set it down on a vintage red-and-white ceramic tile hot plate, the kind Ellen had made for her mother in the fourth grade. Liz's magenta sundress shouted pink and drew a bold contrast against the bright yellow walls.

"A first for me, a vacation by myself," Ellen replied, eager for another blast of caffeine since her morning buzz had long faded. "I love the ocean. I've always wanted to come here and I finally decided it was time. I miss my husband and son," she said more out of guilt than truth, "but I really needed some time alone."

"Good for you! That's what I like to hear. Women in my day,

well they just didn't do things like that, though I did my part to shake things up," Liz said. "You should have seen the looks I got when I went back to school after having my children. Some of those June Cleavers in the neighborhood wanted to drag me before a housewife war crimes tribunal! I've got to hand it to my husband, Edward, he encouraged me all the way and even helped me find a good housekeeper. I don't know what I'd have done if I'd stayed home and watched those little hoodlums all day! Well the girls weren't so bad, but the boys certainly were!"

"How many children do you have?"

"Five. Three boys and two girls. They're all grown and raised, with their own families. I've got seven grandchildren and one on the way.

"You must be so proud," Ellen said. "Do you get to see them often?"

"Not as often as I'd like. But at least once a year they make it down here, and I go to visit them. We email each other a lot though, and they send me lots of pictures. I love email!" Liz said, taking a sip of her coffee.

"It's amazing, isn't it, how technology can actually bring people closer together. I have a friend who lives in California, it's like she's next door. Though the downside to all this communication is that work is only a click away no matter where you are. I vowed not to read my work email this week because I'm afraid I'll get sucked into something back at the office!"

"Wise decision," Liz said, nodding in agreement. "I can't tell you all the people I know who are getting up in years who wished they'd spent more time enjoying life and less time at the office. Life is just too short! My friend Clara's husband worked long days and weekends well into his sixties so he could move into one of those fancy golf communities in Naples. A few months after he finally retired, he had a stroke at the dinner table right as he was passing the mashed potatoes. Such a shame, the closest he got to the golf course was the cemetery down the street."

Intrigued by the folksy wisdom of her hostess, Ellen was curious to know more about her. "When did you lose your husband, Liz?"

"Edward died twenty years ago. He was only sixty-one. A brilliant man, my Edward, but he was an alcoholic and it ruined his health. He was an attorney, a partner in his law firm and very politically connected, on a first-name basis with the governor. We went to parties and entertained wealthy clients . . . well you know things were so different back then. Everybody drank martinis and high balls and got plastered! We all smoked cigarettes too," she said, a mischievous grin animating her face.

"But Edward, dear soul, could never stay away from Mr. Johnny Walker, red, black, or blue. Oh he wasn't a mean drunk or anything, it just eventually got to the point where it was ruining his life. Wouldn't go to AA, was too proud to say 'My name is Edward I'm an alcoholic.' There was one time when I was so hopeful, he'd gone four months without a drink. Then one day I got a call from his law partner, telling me he found Edward passed out in his office after lunch, and that there were bottles stashed in his file cabinets. It was pretty much downhill after that."

"That must have been so hard for you and the kids," Ellen said, choosing her words carefully, not wishing to offend.

"Well I won't say it was a picnic in the park," Liz said, "but somehow we got through it. I had to be strong for the children. I had some wonderful friends, a group of women who used to come over on Tuesday nights for Bible study and prayers. They never knew about Edward's problem, few people did until the end when he got sick. But their prayers and fellowship made all the difference in the world to me."

"How did you wind up living here?" Ellen had to ask.

"Well that's another pot of coffee story, but I'll give you the short version. After Edward died, I had to sell the house—it was a beautiful home with six bedrooms and a pool—to pay off the creditors. It was a shock to find out how little money we had, he had made some bad investments over the years and of course I didn't know a thing about our finances.

"Edward and I had come here on vacation a few times and

we both fell in love with the island, even thought about retiring here someday. So on a whim I decided to take a trip down here, and here I am twenty years later! Best thing I ever did, though I do miss my old friends and being close to my kids. So that's my story. Tell me about yourself, Ellen. Do you work?"

"I think I'm pretty boring compared to you," Ellen said laughing. "I'm the vice president of marketing for an appliance manufacturer. I write ads and develop marketing campaigns to sell outrageously priced refrigerators and stoves. Lately I've been wondering if this is the best use of my God-given talents. There's a lot of other things I could be doing, but . . ." she sighed, "the salary is great, the benefits are good and more important than ever because my husband's company isn't doing too well."

"Sounds like you've got a lot on your plate," Liz said.

"Oh, I haven't even got started yet!" Ellen replied, surprised at how easy it was to talk to a woman she had just met. "Work is work, it's the other stuff that's really hard, like being a mom and having a teenage son who loathes you."

Liz nodded in a gesture of empathy. "Boys. They're the worst. Mine were monsters from the time they could walk and didn't get better until they got married." Her grin was infectious.

Ellen smiled. "You know, Liz, the thing I've never really been able to accept is that I've worked so hard at trying to be a good mom and the results are pitiful," Ellen lamented. "I quit my job to stay home with Andrew until he went to kindergarten. I read to him every night until he was ten. I've driven to soccer games and piano lessons and taken him to church and always taught him about hard work and being a good person. And the result of all this is a surly teenager whose singular passion is to argue with me."

"Well there's certainly no end to the grief a child can cause his mother," Liz said, putting the spoon down on the table after stirring the sugar into her coffee. "And teenagers are the worst of the lot. Their minds just don't work right, it's a fact. I read it in a science book. The first thing you've got to do is not take it personally, even though it's the hardest thing in the world for a mother to do."

"So did your kids ever give you trouble?" Ellen asked. The cat agilely jumped down off the bookcase onto a windowsill, staring as if in a hypnotic trance at a hummingbird hovering at the feeder.

"Did my kids give me trouble?" Liz grinned. "Look up the word "trouble" in the dictionary and you'll see a picture of all of them, let me tell you! My daughter Cynthia went out with a married man when she was sixteen and I almost had to have him put in jail. I caught my son Robert stealing a bottle of whiskey from behind our bar when he was fifteen. You can imagine how I felt about that in light of his father's problem. My son Robert wanted to drop out of college freshman year and become a race car driver—after we paid the tuition! But today they are all normal, well as normal as anyone is," she smiled.

Liz paused a moment, lightly tapping her finger on the table.

"Listen Ellen, take it from someone who's been around the block a few times. It may not happen overnight but your son is going to grow out of this nonsense and be fine. You just have to believe it. I can tell you're a good mother. You've given him a solid foundation and a loving home. You've raised a good kid, only neither one of you knows it yet." She chuckled, shaking her head. "Oh if only I had this much wisdom when my kids were young."

Ellen basked in Liz's approval, wanting desperately to believe her. Other mothers had said similar things, but Liz had a conviction about her that was contagious. Could it be possible that someday she would be reminiscing like Liz, firm in the knowledge that her child was okay and beyond all the dangers of adolescence? It was a hope she wanted very much to cling to.

THE LATE AFTERNOON SUNLIGHT flooded into the kitchen.

"So tell me about the chapel," Ellen said.

"Oh, the chapel," Liz said with a sigh. "It was built by Winifred Hunter in the 1980s. She was a lovely lady, but I suspect had I met her years earlier I might have had a different opinion. You see, Winifred came from a very wealthy family but all that money didn't buy her happiness. She had four husbands and a long line of suitors, including some very unsavory characters that were after her money. She drank and took pills to chase away her demons. Then one year, everything changed when she went on safari to Kenya and met an American missionary named Ernest Hollingway. They fell in love and married. The chapel was his idea, but before it was even finished he became very ill, turns out he had pancreatic cancer and he went quickly. After he died she dedicated the chapel to his memory and found much solace there.

"What a story," said Ellen, pondering the weird trajectory of life that led a profligate heiress to Africa to fall in love with a missionary.

"After I moved here, I started a prayer group. Friends invited friends and the next thing I know we ran out of chairs in my living room! Then Bessie O'Connell suggested we ask Winifred if we could use the chapel. By that time Wini was up in years and very ill. She said yes, thought Ernest would have loved the idea, so we started meeting there. A few years later we had enough people to start Sunday services."

"When Winifred died, she left the estate to her nephew William," Liz continued. "He eventually sold it to Mr. Foster, who was still married to his first wife at the time."

"So Mr. Foster has a new wife and he's building her a dream house. Wasn't that a movie, oh, no, that was Mr. Blanding's dream house." Ellen said, and Liz laughed.

"Evelyn Foster was a good woman, but her husband traded her in for a newer model. Now here I go gossiping again . . . but I heard that his new wife really wants the new house because he made her sign a prenup waiving her right to most of his fortune if they get divorced. The house is a gift to *her*. A big house like that on Sanibel will be worth millions."

"Really. So she gets a big asset to cash in on if the marriage doesn't work out or if she decides she likes the pool boy."

"Yes-sir-ree Bob," said Liz, nodding her head. "That's why I'm not sure there's anything we can do to stop this train from leaving the station."

"Well maybe not, but I still think the public has a right to know the chapel is slated for demolition. Might not change anything, but you never know. We'll need some people willing to be interviewed if the press bites on this story."

"I'll get Ruby. She's not afraid of anyone or anything and will speak her mind," Liz said.

By the time they got done talking and eating the peach cobbler, which was delicious, it was after four o'clock. Ellen started to thank Liz for a delightful afternoon, but Liz would have none of it. "I'm the one who should be thanking you," she insisted. "You're taking time away from your vacation just to help us out."

"Does this mean we're getting out of the boat," Ellen said, referring to this morning's sermon.

"I think that's exactly what it means," Liz replied. "Hope we don't sink!"

The afternoon had been a wonderful diversion. It wasn't until Ellen got back on her bike that she saw David's face again, exactly the way he looked right before he kissed her last night.

Jennifer thought Gregory was never going to leave. It was almost three o'clock, well beyond the time they usually left on Sundays. For the past two hours, he'd been on the phone, first with his broker discussing his investment portfolio and then with his VP of operations about a new problem in their China operation. For once she wished he had a commercial flight to catch, instead of the sleek corporate jet waiting at his beck and call.

They'd decided earlier that he would go back to Chicago alone so she could meet with the architect this week. She was eager to start on the building project, as it represented the major asset in her investment portfolio. It had been Gregory's idea to present her with the house as a wedding present, though she suspected at the time he hadn't realized how lavish of a home they would end up building. Right now, construction costs were about $7 million; her goal was to get it to at least $10 million. This was proving easier than she thought, with the architect highly skilled in spending other people's money to cater to their every extravagant whim.

"I'll miss you honey, but it really is lovely here this week, and you can be back by the weekend," she had said to him that morning, still wearing the lavender chemise that had turned him on so much the night before. He made love to her again before she could escape from their sumptuous king-size bed.

Glancing over at her husband seated on the rose-colored sofa, she realized how well he fit in with his surroundings. The house had not been redecorated in more than twenty years, and Gregory, who didn't spend much time on his appearance, was in dire need of a makeover as well, though she had to admit there wasn't much that could be done with his receding hairline, squinty eyes and paunchy jowls. The only thing women ever found attractive about him was his bank account.

Ten minutes later, he was still on the phone. *When was he going to leave?* It had been weeks since she had seen her lover, who was everything Gregory was not—young, sexy, with a lean hard body that didn't need a blockbuster pharmaceutical drug to perform. The attraction was red hot from the beginning when on their first date they had sex in the back seat of her Cadillac Escalade. At first she had been afraid to bring him to the house, but she decided that it was better here than out in public somewhere.

Her best friend Sara thought she was crazy. "You've got Daddy Warbucks wrapped around your little finger and you're gettin' it on with the island stud muffin?"

"Look, Sara, let's be real here," Jennifer protested. "This is the only way I can survive being married to Gregory. He's good to me, sure, and he's loaded, but I'm way too young and attractive to be saddled with an older man. I mean, look at him, did he want an older woman? Hell no. That's why I'm here."

"Modesty is not your strong suit," said Sara, shaking her head, "and your logic is seriously twisted."

She desperately wanted to see him. What if he couldn't make it? No, of course he would come over, she thought, remembering their last torrid encounter, their passions fueled to greater heights by a gram of cocaine. Thank goodness Gregory had a corporate jet so she didn't have to deal with airport security. She had friends who had been busted for trying to take a joint on vacation.

Those friends were mostly in her past. Her life had changed profoundly during the past year, sometimes she was afraid she would wake up and find out it was all a dream. Jennifer never lacked boyfriends, but at twenty-four she had decided she wanted the kind of financial security only a wealthy husband could deliver. Raised in a blue-collar household, there had never been enough money. Much like a violet craves sunlight, Jennifer had grown up in a state of perpetual want.

Her plan of attack was simple. She quit her job at the bank and signed up with a temporary agency known for placing high-level executive assistants. Smart and beautiful, she had no problem snagging assignments. She went as far to target c-suite executives at blue-chip companies, reading about them online. Older was a prerequisite, because younger men were less likely to leave their wives and young children. Sara, who believed in hard work and wanted nothing more than a good husband and three children, was incredulous to hear of her scheme. "Let me get this straight. You're going to take a job with a temp agency so you can snag a CEO? What kind of dope are you smoking? What makes you think any of these guys are going to want to marry you? Sleep with you, yes. Marry you, no."

But Sara's pessimism proved unfounded. On her third gig she met Foster, who immediately was smitten. She played the innocent virgin and gave him the "I could never sleep with a married man" line and he swallowed it hook line and sinker to the point that she almost felt sorry for him. "It's so ironic," she gleefully told Sara. "Here's a guy whose face is plastered all over business magazines for being the smartest guy in the room and I bagged him in less than three months."

Jennifer did not feel guilty about the family she destroyed, because in her mind it would have been destroyed by someone else anyway. Men like Foster might as well have expiration dates like Butternut bread. They got to a certain age and income level where their egos took over. They wanted to walk into a restaurant and have heads turn at the buxom stiletto-wearing young women on their arms. They wanted to forget they were nearing retirement age, pretend they were thirty again and have sex with someone whose breasts did not sag and whose faces were unlined. They had reached the point in their lucrative careers where no one told them "no." Was it any surprise they wanted new wives?

In Jennifer's world what was really pitiful was to watch the desperate attempts of some of their aging wives to stay young. Some of the prettier ones could pull it off, but most of them just looked ridiculous, wearing revealing clothes designed for twenty-one-year-olds, having Botox treatments that made their faces into expressionless masks and getting collagen injections that created Donald Duck lips.

Finally Gregory was off the phone. "When you talk to the architect, darling, ask him about the wine cellar. He's got it drawn in here but I can't read the dimensions. I don't want this to be some little subterranean dungeon, I want to make sure it's big enough for our collection."

He checked his watch. "I think I'm going to get going. If I leave now, I can get home and catch some of the Bears game."

Delighted, Jennifer walked across the room and put her arms around her husband. "I'm going to miss you so much, honey. Promise me you'll come back Friday no matter what happens this week," she purred.

"Nothing would keep me away," he said softly, before kissing her on the lips.

Ten minutes after he drove away, she reached for her cell phone.

E llen took the first step into the hot tub, the scorching water sending a searing sensation up and down her legs.

Bordered by rugged faux rock outcroppings and lush foliage, the designation of 'hot tub' didn't do justice to this steamy meandering lagoon with its hidden enclaves perfect for romantic interludes.

Ellen inched her way down into the churning incandescent water, her anticipation acute for the relaxation it would provide to her exhausted body. She couldn't remember a time that she had endured a day like this. Just twenty-four hours ago she had been sitting down to dinner wondering if the man across the table found her attractive, tonight she was fighting the impulse to hunt him down and sleep with him. She wondered where he was right now, had his wife returned? She marveled at her ability to ignore the fact that he had a wife and she had a husband, her emotions strangely disconnected like a telephone off the hook.

The peace she found at church this morning was proving elusive. Meeting Liz had provided a great distraction, but now she was back here, alone, desperate to relive those moments on the beach. Like a DVD gone haywire, her mind replayed them over and over again. No amount of self-imposed guilt could stop her endless fantasizing about this man.

Another step, she was in up to her waist, her body finally adjusting to the temperature of the frothy water. Alone except for a young couple, she sat down as far away as possible, not wanting to intrude on their privacy. It was after eight o'clock on Sunday night, most people were still at dinner or had retired for the evening. The enormous pool on the other side of the decorative wrought iron fence was empty. Andrew and Jeremy would love it here, she thought with a shiver of guilt.

Gently she sat down on the bench, hoping it wasn't the kind of rough concrete that snagged $200 swimsuits. She had really splurged on her new suit, a huge improvement over her old one, a faded and stretched out leopard print she had worn for years. The bench was smooth. Closing her eyes, she leaned her head back on the tile and stretched her arms in front of her, letting them float, her relaxation enhanced by the two generous glasses of merlot she had poured herself before leaving the condo. She extended her legs toward the jets, luxuriating in the underwater massage of her tired calf muscles. Heaven. The underwater lights gave the water a bluish glow under the onyx night sky. There was an ever-so-slight chill in the air. "A cold front is moving in this week," said the local weatherman, warning that nighttime temps could dip into the low sixties. She almost laughed out loud at that one. Cold front! Someone should invite him to Philadelphia in January.

She tried to empty her mind of all thoughts but it was impossible. She sank down in the tub, her body bombarded by the underwater jets. Was her obsession with David merely a sexual attraction or was it more? What about him? Was he really who he said he was, a straight arrow who didn't cheat on his wife? And if so, why did he ask her to dinner? Was there such a thing as love at first sight? Don't be ridiculous, she chided herself, that only happens in Danielle Steel novels. The thought was interrupted by the clang of the gate. Instinct told her to open her eyes to see who it was.

She did and she was stunned. Clearly her mind was playing tricks on her. Standing a mere fifteen feet away from her sporting an irresistible grin was David. It was as if he stepped out of her daydream into reality. It simply couldn't be. She closed her eyes and opened them again to make sure he was not a product of her hyper-active imagination. A beach towel draped over his shoulders, he looked every bit the hunk he had the night before except that he looked better without clothes.

"What a surprise, Ms. Bennett," he said, tossing his towel on a nearby lawn chair. "Imagine running into to you here." Something in his tone belied the fact that this was an accidental meeting. *Had he been waiting for her? Followed her here?*

"David," she said, more an exclamation than greeting. "How did you know I was here?"

"What makes you think I knew you were here? But now that I am here do you mind if I join you?" His voice carried a lilt of amusement.

"Not at all," she said. "You might want to come in slowly though, the water is very hot."

"The hotter the better, wouldn't you agree, Ms. Bennett," he said, surprising her with what could only be construed as a double entendre. He started down the steps and stopped abruptly, "Woe, you aren't kiddin'." He winced demonstrably in pain.

"I told you it was hot," she admonished him. It was impossible not to notice his striking physique—lean build, shoulders that were broad but not overbearing—as he stood a tantalizing few feet away from her. *He was gorgeous and he wanted her.* Continuing to ease his body into the swirling water, he waded over and sat down next to her, his proximity unnerving.

"And what's with Ms. Bennett?" she asked with feigned indignation. "I certainly think that after last night we should be on a first name basis."

"True, but I like the sound of it. Has a 1940s movie quality to it, you know, the sultry but capable gal Friday who bedazzles her leading man with great wit and charm. I think I was feeling rather bedazzled last night—"

"Well I think you're confusing eras because 'Ms.' wasn't invented until the seventies. And if you're referring to the movie, I believe it was *His Girl Friday*— though I'm not sure I'm flattered by the comparison to Rosalind Russell." She paused, sinking deeper into steamy waters. "But I suppose if I'm Rosalind, that would make you . . . Cary Grant?" she said, eyes wide open with playful incredulity.

"Well, I'm offended that you find that such a stretch, given my boyishly handsome good looks and debonair manner," he said, intensifying the flirtatious badinage. "But I'll forgive you if we can fast forward to the part where I get to kiss you." He said it without hesitation, his eyes locked on hers, unyielding. It was a joke, or was it?

Flummoxed by his bravado, she wondered whether he had been drinking, although he didn't appear to be intoxicated. This was not the David she'd been with last night. She had no way of knowing that he had been waiting for her to return all day, that in his agitated state of mind he had taken solace in a hearty succession of rum and cokes at the pool bar, and that this had the effect of diminishing his inhibitions. Again she felt powerless to fight the intensity of longing sweeping over her. If she didn't make her move now . . . escape was her only option.

"You know what, Cary," she said, trying to glibly ease her way out of the situation, "I think I need to cool off." Clouds of steam emanated from her body as she abruptly rose, taking a giant step up and out of the whirlpool. Once out of the hot water, the air hit her like a deep freeze. She ran quickly down the brick path that led to the swimming pool on the other side of the jungle of shrubbery. She executed her best high school swimming dive into the deep end of the pool, hoping desperately that the shock to her system would bring her to her senses. It was so cold, what a rush. She swam underwater to the far end, with each stroke wondering what to do next. She surfaced a few feet away from a cove under a waterfall. Before she continued, she looked back just in time to see David dive into the pool. He swam powerfully to her, saw her shivering, and when he reached her he put his arms around her as they floated in the darkness, a wall of cascading water screening them from view.

"Rosalind never did this to Cary," he said. "Do you make a habit of jumping out of hot tubs and into freezing cold swimming pools?"

"I make a habit of running away from danger," she said.

"That's too bad," he said, pulling her closer to him, her body weightless in the shimmering water. She took refuge in him, clasping her arms around his neck and locking her legs tight around his waist. Their bodies entwined, he kissed her passionately, and she responded. He tasted of rum, sweet like butterscotch candy. She kissed him again. Desire took over as if someone punched the accelerator.

"Ms. Bennett, if you do not stop that I will not be responsible for the consequences," he said softly.

"I'm freezing," she said, visibly shivering. "Let's go to my place and have a drink."

"I cannot guarantee your safety if you let me into your room," he said in a soft whisper against her wet hair.

All that mattered to her at that moment was getting warm and to a place where they could be alone. The hell with fidelity. She may never get this chance again.

A few hundred feet away, behind a closed and locked bedroom door, Judy took her old scrapbook out of the bottom of her suitcase, where she had carefully bundled it in a beach towel for protection while traveling. The thought of her most cherished memories being tossed about by some strong-armed dope-smoking baggage handler worried her. Seventy years old, many of the album pages were brittle with age. Her mother had painstakingly identified every photograph depicting the life of her oldest daughter growing up in a small town in rural Iowa, where cornfields stretched on earth as flat as an ironing board. Seeing the familiar script produced a sharp twinge of grief; it had been eight years since her mother had died. She wondered if there would ever be a time she could think about her without an avalanche of sadness.

The first photograph in the book had been taken just days after she was born. Cradling her newborn daughter, her winsome mother looked like she had just discovered the most amazing secret. Turning the pages, she saw herself pushing her doll stroller, finding Easter eggs, blowing out birthday candles, and then, as a young woman dressed in cap and gown, holding her high school diploma. She treasured the pictures, wishing there were more. Like life, there was never enough of it.

It had been several years since she had looked at this particular album, and she had deliberately waited until George had fallen asleep. She opened it to a page she knew well. It was a picture of her wearing a glittery taffeta prom dress, standing next to George's younger brother. She closed her eyes, her memory conjuring up the lovely scent of her orchid wrist corsage that had so beautifully complemented the lavender color of her dress. The picture had been taken on a spring evening, a little more than a year before she got married. *Every picture tells a story, she thought. Except no one knows the story except me.*

It had been relatively easy to hide because Danny had been in her life for such a short time, five weeks, four days and a few hours to be exact. They met at the River West High School senior prom on a night when nervous anticipation hovered over the dance floor like a cloud of gentle rain. She had never believed in love at first sight, despite a steady drumbeat of such fare in Harlequin novels and Hollywood movies. But that was before this arresting young man strode confidently across the gymnasium and asked her to dance. He was very handsome but that alone didn't explain her near intoxicated response. Within moments of taking his hand he made her feel beautiful, desirable, as if she were the only other person in the room.

They both had brought other dates, but that didn't stop them from dancing to the haunting melody of Cole Porter's "What Is This Thing Called Love." Her head on his shoulder, she felt like she had stepped into a golden swirl of a dream sequence. She had cherished this memory for her entire life. She fell in love with him right there on the dance floor under the confetti lights.

Later that night after dropping off his date he came over to her house, pelting small stones at her upstairs window until she sneaked outside. Under the leafy branches of an ancient oak, they kissed with a passion unknown and exhilarating. Over the next few weeks they saw each other whenever they could, spending time in parked cars in out-of-the-way places where they could be alone. Though it was unsuitable conduct for two young people in the 1950s, they made love in the back seat of his Chevy Bel Air.

Then one night fate delivered a devastating blow. Driving home from a track meet, Danny was killed instantly in a head-on collision on a dark highway outside of town. Shell-shocked beyond belief, she attended the funeral in a daze, having to hide the depth of her despair because no one knew they were lovers. It was at the funeral that she got to know Danny's brother George, who had come home on leave from the service. Instantly bonded in grief, the seeds of their relationship were sown. In the early days, it was simply too hard to tell George about Danny. After a while it seemed pointless. What good could come of it, she would ask herself.

She stared down at the picture. In it, Judy stood next to Danny in the center and their dates stood beside them. It was almost as if the photographer realized the two people in the middle of the photo should be together. *My god, he was so handsome.*

She blinked back the tears at the memory that existed only in her heart. She wondered what would have happened if that car hadn't veered across the center line and Danny had not died. Would they have lived happily ever after? Or was theirs the passion of a meteor blazing across the night sky, breathtakingly beautiful but ephemeral, leaving behind only stardust memories in its wake.

In the years after the accident, she had longed to talk to someone about what happened, but could not. Who could be trusted with the knowledge that she had been deeply in love with her husband's brother? She could never, ever take the chance George would find out. If he did, it would seem like they had been living a lie all these years. And she had grown to love George with all her heart.

She forced herself to close the album, and placed it back in the suitcase. There was no point dwelling on the past. She was good at putting things away, back into the closet where they belonged. She was lucky that she found George. He loved her and had been an excellent husband and father. They were here to honor that enduring love and she couldn't let anything interfere with that. Not this photograph, not his ugly moods of late—no, they were here to celebrate and that's what they would do.

But when she went to bed she could not sleep.

Shivering, David and Ellen quickly grabbed their towels, slipped on their sandals and left the pool area. They walked together until they reached his building.

She looked beautiful in the moonlight, even with wet hair and smudged makeup around her eyes. Standing next to her, he felt like a different person. Energized. Alive.

"Are you sure this is okay?" He couldn't believe she had invited him to her place. He had hoped, wished and dreamed about making love to her but had not expected it to come to fruition. The rum and cokes had taken care of any lingering moral qualms he had. Alcohol was good for that.

"Yes."

"I'm going to run upstairs, grab some clothes and I'll be right over."

"Okay. I'm going to jump in the shower," she said. "I'll leave the door open but make sure you don't scare me when you come in."

"Shower sounds good. Meet you there," he teased. He disappeared behind a concrete pillar. She had not expected him to kiss her here because they could be seen from every balcony of the buildings fronting the courtyard.

David took the stairs two at a time until he reached the third floor. He put his key in the door, and pressed down on it to get it open. The salty sea air had a way of making things stick, and this deadbolt was no exception. Once inside he flicked on the hallway light, and headed into the master bedroom to grab a fresh shirt and pants. He would towel off his hair, brush his teeth, splash on a little Ralph Lauren, grab a condom and go. Though he and Marianne rarely used them, he kept one in his overnight bag in case of emergency. This was an emergency.

He saw his cell phone on the dresser, he had forgotten to take it to the pool. It had been a while since he checked his messages. *Damn.* The last thing he needed to hear right now was a message from Emma singing the Sponge Bob song or Ethan telling him about his cousin's awesome baseball card collection. *Damn*, the message icon was lit. He played it.

Hi honey. Just wanted to let you know there's been a change in plans. Susan has to take Josh to the doctor tomorrow. He got hurt at his soccer game and she wants to make sure it's okay. Dad is fine, out of the hospital and back home. I was going to spend the night but Ethan and Emma want to come home tonight because they miss you and Grandma and they want to swim in the hotel pool. So I'm coming back tonight, see you soon.

The time on the message was seven o'clock. If she didn't encounter traffic on Interstate 75 she could be home at any minute.

Shit. How could this be? It was like a conspiracy, last night his mother and now this. He had to tell Ellen, he couldn't have her waiting for him. He wished he had gotten her cell phone number. Damn, that was so stupid of him not to get it. He threw on a shirt and pants, ran a comb through his wet hair. The door slammed behind him, making a loud noise in the empty corridor. The silence was shattered by a shout of unmitigated joy.

"Daddy!"

It was Emma, two floors below, beaming up at her father, blonde curls bouncing in delight. "We're home, Daddy! We're home!"

*   *   *

ELLEN WAS FURIOUS WHEN SHE REALIZED David wasn't coming. At first furious at him, then at herself, then at the situation that she had helped to create with her self-indulgent immorality. It was as if she had developed a split personality, Adulteress Ellen vs. Wife and Mother Ellen. Adulteress Ellen didn't give a rip about the fact that David had a wife and children, a characteristic that in another person would have struck her as despicable. She also didn't give a rip about her own marriage vows. Wife and Mother Ellen wondered whether she was on drugs, so bizarre was her behavior. Wrapping herself around him in the pool? Inviting him to her room? What was she thinking?

She was angry that her beautiful vacation alone had degenerated into this libidinous escapade. Why did this have to happen?

She needed desperately to talk to someone but who? No one. Not even her best friend Amy. Even though she trusted Amy with her life she simply couldn't confide in her about this. Amy, her maid of honor and best friend since fifth grade, thought she had a wonderful marriage, even though lately there had been a few bumps in the road. Amy loved Jeremy. Amy's husband loved Jeremy. Amy could not be told. It was off limits. Period.

This entire escapade had gone too far. *Tomorrow I'm going to wake up and forget about all of this and move on, she told herself. I have no business doing this and is it any surprise that I'm suffering? I'm being punished for cheating on my husband and I deserve it, especially since I had the nerve to show up for communion today.* The fact that she had gone to church this morning made this evening seem a hundred times more shameful.

Where is he? Why didn't he come? She was desperate to know. Would he have deliberately stood her up? Cold feet? Did his wife come home?

It didn't matter. She reached for the bottle of merlot and poured herself a large glass. Tonight she wanted to be knocked out. Completely.

On Tuesday morning, a news van with the giant letters WBAY-TV 14 splashed on its side pulled into the small clearing next to Grace Chapel. A shapely young woman wearing a clingy cream-colored skirt, silk blouse and high-heel sandals climbed out of the news van accompanied by a cameraman who looked like he had slept in his clothes. They made for an interesting couple.

Ellen had survived the emotional fallout from her steamy encounter with David with distraction. Thrusting herself full-throttle into a media blitz to save the chapel, on Monday she drafted a press release with a 24-point boldface headline: "Beloved Seaside Chapel Stands in Path of Bulldozers" with a subhead "Seniors mourn loss of spiritual community" and sent it to the local media. Assignment editors from two local television stations and a radio reporter had already called.

The TV reporter walked up to her. "Hi, I'm Roxanne Howell from TV 14," she said with a sugary trace of a southern accent. "Are you the one in charge here?"

"Well no, but I can take you to the person you want to talk to, Elizabeth Taylor. She's in the chapel. I'll walk over there with you."

"Elizabeth Taylor, hmm, is Richard Burton here too?" she asked, a smile dancing on her lips.

Ellen grinned. "Would you believe Larry Fortensky?"

"I never could figure out why she married him," said Roxanne, shaking her head. "I mean he was good looking but marriage? Anyway, do you know how we can get a hold of this Gregory Foster?" said Howell, taking a small spiral-bound notebook out of her leather satchel. "Now he's the man who owns this property, is that right?"

"That's his house right over there," Ellen said pointing beyond the wall of pines, "but I don't know if he's there. Being as though he's the CEO of a $10 billion dollar company he might have to work today."

"Oh yes, that's right. He runs Linton Industries, the company that laid off all those people," said Roxanne, looking off in the distance as if formulating a thought. "Folks down here, real folks, not the rich ones on this island, are gettin' pretty fired up about all these jobs going to China. After we get done here, maybe we'll head over there and see if anyone's home. I'd like to get a comment from him." She jotted down something in her notebook and flipped it shut.

They walked down the shady path that led to the clearing, where the magnificent vista of chapel, ocean and azure sky came into view. Bouquets of black-eyed Susans crowded the sides of the well-trodden wooden steps.

"This is so beautiful!" said Howell, taking in the view. "Why would anyone want to tear this down?"

Ellen's instincts had been right. Anyone could see how special the chapel was. Even if you weren't religious, there weren't many places like this anywhere.

Ellen ushered them inside, where Liz, Ruby Meyers and Betty Jo Lewis were seated in a back pew. All were prepared to do on-camera interviews. Never one to shun the limelight, Ruby had called Norm at Island Drug and asked him if she could borrow one of the walkers they rent out to the elderly. "I told him to get me some of those hideous black wrap-around glasses like the ones Gladys wore after her cataract surgery," she told Liz. "When the reporters come, I'll stand in front of the chapel and say, 'I'm almost blind, please Mr. Wealthy Businessman, don't take our chapel away,' " Ruby said in a weak quivering voice. Ever since she was a little girl, she had the gift of making people laugh.

Ellen made the introductions.

"Welcome to Grace Chapel," said Liz warmly, who looked very attractive in her short-sleeved calico print dress that had a lace Peter Pan collar. She wore a tiny gold cross around her neck. "Well what do you think?" she said, gesturing to her surroundings.

"This is so beautiful. I can't believe someone wants to tear it down. How long has this chapel been here?"

"Winifred Hunter built it in the 1980s. She dedicated it to the memory of her late husband, Ernest, who died before it was completed."

"How sad," Roxanne said. They talked off-camera for a few minutes while Roxanne jotted down a few notes. She reached in her bag and took out a silver compact to check her hair and shiny pink lipstick. "Okay, let's do the interviews first and then Larry can get some shots outside."

Roxanne clipped a tiny mike to Liz's dress. Her voice deepened as she assumed her on-air persona. "You've been coming here for many years and I understand you work here part-time. How do you feel about plans to tear down this chapel?"

"I'll be honest with you, it breaks my heart," Liz said. "This has been our church for nearly twenty years and we're all going to miss it dearly."

"Are you going to fight to keep it here? Do you have any recourse?"

"Well if you're asking if I'm going to stand in front of a bulldozer the answer is no," Liz said, flashing a big smile. "I gave that up years ago! Seriously, the fact of the matter is that this chapel and the land under it belong to Mr. Foster. As much as we don't want to lose it, we have to be respectful of his right to do what he chooses with his property." She added slyly, "Of course we'd love for him to change his mind."

"Will you try to find another location?" Roxanne asked.

"Not sure what we're going to do at this point. I'm afraid

getting another building would cost a lot of money and we don't have any funds for that."

Ruby volunteered to go next. Clutching the borrowed walker, she laboriously made her way out of the pew to the front of the chapel. Suppressing her laughter, Ellen hoped to have that much spunk when she was Ruby's age.

"Darn this arthritis," Ruby lamented. "It's really acting up today."

"Would you rather sit down?" asked Roxanne sympathetically.

"No I'll be fine. At my age it's not a good idea to sit too long. I might atrophy."

"Ready for a few questions?"

"Sure, fire away. Hope I say something interesting," she deadpanned.

Roxanne pinned the mike on Ruby and signaled to the cameraman to roll.

"How long have you been attending church here?"

"Fifteen years, ever since my husband died. Liz invited me and I've been coming ever since."

"How do you feel about losing your place of worship?"

"Well, I'll tell you what I really think but I'm not sure you'll want to put it on TV," Ruby said. "Don't want to sound a communist but it seems to me some people just have too much darn money, I mean why would you want to tear down a house of worship—and a perfectly fine home—to build another home the size of a roller rink? This little chapel is precious, there's no place like it in the world and I'm sick over losing it."

Ruby paused a minute, her brows furrowed. "Hope I don't sound like some crotchety old lady."

"Not at all," said Roxanne, not wanting to discourage a colorful interview.

"Truth be told, if Winifred Hunter knew what Foster was doing to her beloved chapel, she'd be spinning in her grave." she said.

"Shit!"

"What?"

"There's somebody at the door," Jennifer whispered tersely, pulling away from her lover in one abrupt motion. Clothes were strewn everywhere on the plush royal blue carpet of Gregory Foster's bedroom. A sliver of white powder sat on a small cosmetic mirror on the dresser next to a rolled up a twenty dollar bill.

The brass knocker sounded again, echoing in the chandeliered two-story foyer.

"Don't you hear that? Shit!"

Jennifer was in a panic. Naked in bed with her lover—oh my god—she could be caught and her life as she knew it would be over. The generous line of coke she had just snorted made her heart beat even faster. *Why did I have to be so stupid to bring him here!*

"Don't answer it," he said, trying to pull her back, his muscled physique failing the task. He smiled at her, his shoulder-length ginger blond hair in disarray, masking tawny brown eyes and an irresistible grin.

"What are you crazy?" She glared at him. For the moment, his libidinous appeal had no hold on her.

Jennifer flung herself out of bed and crept to the bedroom window, where diaphanous draperies offered only a thin veil of

126

gauzy protection from the outside world. The entryway was not visible, but she could see the side of the house and beyond to the chapel.

"There are cars parked over by the chapel," she said.

"C'mere, Jen. You can't leave me like this," he protested, coaxing her back to bed.

"What if they see your bike? Where did you park it?"

"Just don't answer the door. What'd ya think . . . they're going to march in here and find us? Get a grip. They'll go away. C'mere and get under the covers, I'll hide you."

The insistent shrill of the doorbell pierced the silent house followed by the brass knocker again.

"Come back here. Please. Look what I have for you, you won't be sorry," he said seductively.

"Excuse me but suddenly I'm not in the mood when my entire life could be going up in flames. You have to get dressed," Jennifer said angrily, while throwing on her clothes.

"Man, I don't understand you," he said. "We've been waiting so long for this."

No longer listening, Jennifer cursed herself for her stupidity and recklessness. It could cost her everything. What would Gregory do if he found out she was having sex with someone else in his own bed. He would surely throw her out and she would have nothing, thanks to the draconian prenuptial agreement she had told him she was happy to sign when nothing could have been further from the truth. To think that she could lose everything she had worked so hard for, that she was so close to getting the house that would be at last the gateway to her financial freedom . . .

"Get up and get dressed," she hissed. "And stay away from the windows."

She had made a huge mistake. All because of her insatiable desire to have sex with a gorgeous and virile man who was everything her husband was not. She silently vowed to never be this stupid again.

*   *   *

"I GUESS NOBODY'S HOME," said Roxanne, stepping back from the stately entrance to the Foster residence, her Ray Ban sunglasses giving her the appearance of a Hollywood starlet. "Okay, well I need to get going. Thanks, Ellen, for putting me on to this story. Here's my card. Call me later and I'll let you know when it's going to air."

Ellen lingered as Roxanne gingerly made her way in high heels through the yard and then to the path that led back to the news van. Nearby, a phalanx of sea gulls had perched in the towering Australian pine trees, as if protecting the chapel fortress. With wingspans of ten feet, the flying battleships were roughly the height of a baseball bat. Ellen could see the lanky branches straining under their weight.

The two-story red brick Georgian bore the stamp of an architectural style that was as common as it was uninspired. Back in Winifred's day the home had been one of the finest on the island, a symbol of elegance and good taste, but the times had changed, and now it exuded an air of faded grandeur. It was easy to understand why a man with Foster's money and ego was eager to tear this house down. It was an embarrassment by today's ostentatious standards.

She wondered where the Fosters were, when they would be back. The windows were open. Perhaps a day trip to Naples? Surely they had been here Sunday when she had first heard the music, which she thought had been coming from the open windows on the terrace.

A symmetry of multi-paned windows accentuated the front of the house, two on either side of the front door and five that ran across the second floor. A side-entry garage with an enormous concrete driveway flanked the main house, its windows in harmony with the others. Flowerbeds thick with desert rose and rain lilies straddled a lovely flagstone path that arced from the front door to the garage parking area, which was shielded from view by a verdant clump of bushes.

Curious to see any signs of life, Ellen followed the path

toward the garage. Rounding the corner she stopped. There was someone here. And that someone had an awesome motorcycle. Emblazoned on the metallic gas tank was the iconic Braxton Firestorm logo. It was a rare, expensive vintage bike, and the reason she knew this was because it had been her husband's lifelong dream to own one.

Puzzled she stared at the motorcycle. Who would go away for the day and leave a bike like that out? It didn't make sense. She stood there for a few minutes, looking up at the second story windows of the house, when she had the strangest feeling she was being watched. It was creepy. Time to leave. She really had no business being here anyway, technically she was trespassing.

A fanciful thought popped into her head. Was it possible that Mrs. Foster was in there with someone other than Mr. Foster? The local tennis pro, the pool boy? She shook her head and smiled at her over-active imagination. She really ought to get started on writing that novel.

Julia Henderson stood behind her desk staring at her BlackBerry. Wearing a sleek Valentino suit that showed off her reedy figure and Bruno Magli low-heeled pumps, she looked every bit the part of a high-powered successful businesswoman. Tall, beautiful and intelligent, she could have stepped out of the pages of *CEO Magazine*.

The device in her hand indicated that she missed five calls during this morning's strategic planning meeting, including one from her daughter and one from David. That's odd, she thought. Why would David be calling her today when she was going to see him Thursday? She wondered what was up. Surveying the mountains of paperwork on her desk and dozens of messages scattered around her phone, it seemed impossible that she would ever get to Sanibel this week.

The time management protocol that ruled her life demanded she assign a lower priority to the personal matter of David's call but curiosity got the better of her. She punched in his number and waited for him to pick up, hoping she wouldn't get his voice mail. She was in luck.

"Hello."

"David, it's Julia. What's up? I got your call, and started to worry. Everything okay there?"

"Everything is fine," he lied convincingly. How different a conversation they would have if he resorted to the truth: *I almost slept with another woman last night and Mom thinks Dad has Alzheimer's. Other than that everything is great.* "The resort is beautiful, the weather is incredible, and Mom and Dad are having a great time—well Mom is having a great time and Dad's doing his usual trying to cope with being away from home routine. But he's fine. You're going to love it here. When do you get in?

"Well if I get a shovel and pitch all this stuff out the window, Thursday afternoon," Julia said, a flash of humor cracking her otherwise tense demeanor. "I'm really buried so I won't be able to talk long."

"Okay let's cut to the chase. Here's the deal," he paused. "Maggie is coming to the party. She called me yesterday and said her conscience wouldn't let her stay home. I haven't told Mom yet. I wanted to tell you first."

"That fucking bitch."

"Now is that any way to talk about your sister?" David couldn't help teasing even though he knew this news would upset her.

"The nerve of her. Her *conscience* won't let her stay away. But apparently her *conscience* doesn't have any problem with her ditching her husband and two sons while she 'finds herself' in Lesbian La La Land." Julia was used to her sister's exploits, but in her mind this latest turn of events was beyond the pale. Maggie had children now but was as irresponsible as ever.

"I know," David said, forcing as much empathy as he could into the two words. "But what was I going to say? 'You can't come.' We always thought there was a chance she would come, well now we know."

"You know the thing that really bothers me about this is how it will affect Mom. Mom hasn't told anyone about this. She's not one to spread our dirty laundry around. What will she tell everyone—she's not bringing Sasha, is she?"

"No. She's coming alone."

"Thank goodness she has a grain of sense."

"Yeah, I don't want Mom to have to deal with this now," David said. "I'll talk to Maggie and see if I can get her to keep a lid on the soap opera of her personal life at least while she's down here. We can deal with the rest later."

"Agreed. And you're the best one to do that because if I get on the phone with her it probably won't end well. I don't want Mom to have to deal with her bullshit during her vacation. She's really gone off the rails this time, leaving those adorable little boys. I feel bad for saying this, but sometimes I cannot believe she's my sister."

"I know, I know. But here's what we have to keep in mind. Like Maggie said, this is a once-in-a-lifetime celebration for Mom and Dad. They're not getting any younger, that's for sure. And she sounded really good on the phone, better than she has in a long time."

"Yeah, well I'm still pissed off. It's about time Maggie realizes that there are consequences to her actions. She expects everyone to say 'oh how wonderful, we're so glad you figured out your life after all these years' and pay no attention to the family she left behind. What's Brian up to anyway?"

"He's devastated, I feel really bad for him. He said he wanted to be here for Mom and Dad but it's better that he stay home with Tyler and Brad. His mother is staying with them for a while to help out."

Julia looked up at the clock again, it was two thirty. "Listen, I've got to go. I think you better tell Mom right away. If this is too upsetting for her and she doesn't want her to come, I'll get on the phone and deal with Maggie. I've got far too much time and effort invested in this party to let Maggie ruin it."

"Okay, sounds good. Have a safe trip. Can't wait to see you and Richard and the girls."

With that, Julia clicked off. She buzzed her assistant, asked her to get her an organic chicken salad and a vanilla latte. She'd need a jolt of caffeine to get through the rest of the afternoon, and then go home and start packing.

For Aaron Becker, general assignment reporter for the *Fort Meyers Herald*, the test of a good story was how fast it transmitted from his brain to his finger tips to his computer keyboard. He could type at speeds of more than ninety words a minute if he had good material.

Wearing his customary uniform of khaki-colored slacks and a casual short-sleeve shirt, his red tie in a lose knot, he groaned upon hearing the assignment from his editor: interview the bingo brigade on Sanibel about some seaside chapel slated for demolition to make way for a McMansion. Not exactly front-page news, especially in Southwest Florida where new mega homes and sprawling retirement communities sprang up like weeds after a spring rain. Last week he had reported on the death of an eighteen-year-old college honor student who was killed when he careened off a tenth-floor balcony after ingesting a lethal cocktail of booze, Ecstasy and cocaine. Now that was the kind of story that built careers, which is what Aaron wanted more than anything since he had landed his first serious job in journalism. Determined to someday see his byline in *USA Today* or the *Wall Street Journal*, for now he had to deal with the old bitties on Sanibel.

He scarfed down a corn dog from the cafeteria, grabbed his notebook, sunglasses and car keys. Once on the causeway, he decided it wasn't a bad gig after all, getting to drive his new jet-black Sebring convertible out to the island. As the metallic blue waters of the Gulf came into view, he realized once again how much he loved living and working in Florida. It sure beat eight months of winter back home in North Dakota.

He found the house number on Azalea Lane and pulled into the gravel driveway. He rang the doorbell and only had to wait a second before the door was opened by an attractive older woman exuding a youthful enthusiasm.

"Well hello there . . . you must be Mr. Becker," Liz said. "I'm Liz Taylor—not the movie star obviously! Oh some people are so disappointed when they find out," she said, a smile lighting up her eyes like Fourth of July fireworks.

"Glad to meet you," he said, extending his hand.

"C'mon in and I'll get you some coffee. You do drink coffee don't you? I'd be lost without it. You know what I'd love to see on this island," she said in a conspiratorial tone, as if she had known him for years. "A Starbucks. You have to promise not to tell a soul because if anyone knew they'd vote me off the island just like they do on those TV shows!"

"Coffee is great, with a little cream or milk if you have it," he said, a little overwhelmed with the sheer force of her personality. "And I love Starbucks too. Your secret is safe with me."

Aaron watched her as she went to the counter to get a cup from the cupboard. Though Liz's face had the telltale signs of aging, with gentle lines around her eyes and mouth, she had the carriage and posture of someone much younger. "First we'll have coffee, then we can go over to the chapel. That will give us some time to chat."

The interview exceeded his expectations. Captivated by her charm, razor-sharp memory and great sense of humor, he soon forgot her age. She told him about Winifred Hunter, who had seen her share of heartache despite enormous wealth and how she had finally found faith, love and happiness.

"After Winifred died, her nephew kept the chapel open and allowed services to continue in accordance with his aunt's wishes," Liz said. "But then the money started to run out for poor

William, so he had to finally sell the estate. Well, it didn't stay on the market long. Gregory Foster found out about it and snapped it right up. He's been good to us but we knew the writing was on the wall when he bought the place. Now you can't write this in your newspaper," she said, eyes sparkling with the promise of a juicy revelation, "but I heard through the grapevine that this new mansion he's building is a wedding gift to his pretty young wife."

"Interesting," Aaron said, thinking he'd stop by the Foster's on his way back to the office. Maybe he could meet the new wife.

Liz offered to drive her own car over to the chapel, so he wouldn't have to double back to her house, but he offered to drive. They parked in the small clearing and walked down the winding path that led to the chapel.

"Wow, what a view, I can see why you don't want to lose this," he said as the chapel came into view.

Liz reached in her handbag for the keys, and opened the heavy mahogany door. In the sanctuary, the afternoon sun created a prism of light on the altar. She told him about her job as the church secretary, writing the *Chapel Chimes* newsletter and overseeing the maintenance.

"Do you go to church, Aaron?" she asked.

"Not recently," he said sheepishly. "Too many late Saturday nights. But I did growing up—every week."

"And I bet you hated getting up every Sunday—my kids sure did! Oh they'd grumble and complain and find all kinds of mysterious ailments to try to stay home. But it was the most important thing we ever did as a family, and certainly the greatest gift my parents ever gave me. Can't imagine where I'd be today without it. Probably sittin' on a bar stool somewhere, engaged in decadent behavior," she said jauntily.

"Now that's a story," Aaron teased.

"I do worry about kids today," she continued. "So many of them haven't even been inside a church. To think that so many children grow up not ever learning about God, well that's a shame," Liz said.

Aaron was silent, and Liz sensed his apprehension. "Now

don't go off and think I'm going to start speaking in tongues or anything," she said, grinning to put him at ease. "I was raised a plain-old Lutheran, we like to sing dirges and have potlucks in the church basement. But from the time I was old enough to put on a choir robe my mother told me how much God loved me and that no matter what, nothing can ever stand in the way of that love. Like the sun, it never goes out. One time my Aunt Tillie said, 'Oh church is nothing but a bunch of hypocrites.' And my mother shot back, 'Dear sister, there's always room for one more.' That always cracked me up! Here's the good news in a nutshell, we're all sinners but God loves us anyway," she said, her face illumined in a shaft of afternoon sunlight.

He met her eyes, smiling. "Well . . . maybe if you were my Sunday school teacher I'd still be going to church."

They talked for a bit more when they arrived back at her house. He told her that he had really enjoyed the afternoon, and that was the shocking truth of the matter. Driving back to the office, Aaron thought about what Liz said about God. He'd grown up in a church where the notion of a loving God had not been on the front burner. The God he'd grown up with was stern and remote, somewhere off in the clouds, hovering over the ancient tribe of Israel, deigning to come down periodically to dictate a new litany of rules or dole out punishments. Over the years God had become so distant and irrelevant that he no longer really thought about God at all. But this woman had been so full of vitality and life, she had him thinking. What if religion really was about grace and not just about sin? What if God didn't require humans to run religious decathlons to get into heaven? This idea gave him a peace of mind he found oddly comforting.

Back in the office, he made a few more calls to flesh out the story. By the time he was done he was quite pleased with his work. So was his editor, who slated it for the much-coveted page one above-the-fold position. The dreaded assignment had certainly exceeded his expectations—in more ways than one. Much to his surprise, his story moved on the national newswire, spreading like a virus into the newsrooms of the nation's largest daily newspapers with millions of readers, including one very pissed off Gregory Foster.

E llen hadn't talked to Jeremy since the day she had arrived on the island. She had emailed him once, letting him know she'd arrived and everything was fine. She had told him part of the reason for this vacation was to have time to think, the implication twofold: she would not be checking in a lot and she was not happy with the way things were in their lives and in their marriage. Of course, he had already known that. The sad part was that he didn't seem to care.

"How can he just sit there day after day and be miserable and do nothing while his life crumbles around him," she lamented to her best friend Amy while they were having dinner last week at Luigi's, their favorite Italian restaurant. "At first I could be understanding, but how long do I have to wait for him to get out of this funk? He hates his job, he hates his boss, but he refuses to do anything about it. It's like his feet are stuck in cement."

"Do you think he's still depressed about his mother's death?" Amy asked, taking a piece of warm Asiago cheese bread from the basket on their table. Delicious aromas emanated from garlic-laced chicken sizzling on the large open grill. They had already consumed a bottle of chianti.

"Yes I do," Ellen replied. "I don't think he ever got over it. I asked him about counseling and he looked at me like I was selling Amway."

"Why can't men deal with their emotions? It's like they're

twelve-year-old boys trapped in the bodies of middle-age men," Amy said.

"Ever since he lost his mother I think he's mad at God. He doesn't really want to come to church with me anymore and when he does he's just going through the motions. I feel so bad because I think his faith could help him in the grieving process. But he just battens down the hatches, won't talk about it, and accuses me of trying to shove my beliefs down his throat. It makes me so angry when all I'm trying to do is help him."

"Have you thought about marriage counseling?" Amy said. "I know it's hard to even contemplate that but maybe you need a third party to sort things out."

"You're right, it's hard to imagine taking that step, but I wouldn't reject it out of hand," Ellen said, with a rueful smile. "I mean what am I going to say, 'hell no, we don't need any help, our lives are just peachy keen right now.' But I'm not sure Jeremy would go for it. He's very stubborn and he doesn't have a high regard for therapists, mostly because he has an aunt who is a shrink who he thinks is a whack-job."

"Well maybe it's not up to him," Amy said gently, "I care about you Ellen, you know I do. And I think you may have to force the issue. How long can you go on like this? It's not good for any of you."

The question of how they had arrived at this unwelcome juncture played on Ellen's mind often, interrupting her concentration at work or while driving or before she drifted off to sleep at night. No matter how hard she tried to get things back on track, everything she did seemed to blow up in her face. She longed for the closeness they once shared.

Things had been so good in the beginning. Despite the fact that Jeremy was divorced and had a teenage son, for the most part their marriage had sailed along on relatively calm seas. They were hard working, successful, free spirited and had a lot of friends. Jeremy's son Steven had been very accepting of her and quickly erased any misgivings she had about being thrust into the role of stepmother, and when Andrew came along they were happier than ever. For years, Ellen thought she had some kind of genetic immunity to the marital problems she saw in other couples. Life was good, Jeremy had a terrific job, they lived in a beautiful house in a great neighborhood and by most accounts, were living the good life.

But those carefree days of untroubled lives began to slip away. The first domino fell on a beautiful summer day when Jeremy's mother called to tell them she had pancreatic cancer. The news hit Jeremy with the force of a boulder dropped from an overpass. The cancer was advanced, she died four months later. An only child, he was devastated by the loss. No matter how much Ellen tried to console him, he couldn't come to terms with his mother's death and he didn't want to talk about it. The following year, the high-flying IT firm he worked for announced it couldn't pay its bills and out the blue, Jeremy's job, fat expense account and six-figure salary evaporated. To make for a perfect trifecta, Andrew hit adolescence, and the school principal starting calling on a regular basis.

Though it all, Ellen tried to be patient. She tried reaching out to Jeremy, but that generally provoked an angry response. She tried ignoring the situation, but that just produced a wider gulf between them.

The problems with Andrew spilled over into their marriage in a tumultuous showdown of recrimination and anger. Ellen fought with Andrew and then she fought with Jeremy about what to do about Andrew. The escalation of arguments and Andrew's constant run-ins with authority placed a serious strain on their marriage. She and Jeremy clashed constantly on how to deal with their son, Ellen having grown up a steady diet of tough love in contrast with Jeremy's predilection to maintain a good relationship with his son at all costs. "It's just a phase," he would say. "What do you expect, he's a teen-age boy." And Ellen would get a sick feeling in the pit of her stomach, because what she saw in her son was not respect for his father, but raw manipulation.

The unpleasant memory snapped her back into the present. Ellen fired up her laptop to check her email. There were several new messages, including a note from the *Fort Myers Herald* reporter telling her the chapel story would run tomorrow. While that was gratifying, she had the sinking feeling that it wouldn't make any difference. Gregory Foster was a rich and powerful man, and he was unlikely to be swayed by some negative publicity, even if it came at an inopportune time for his company.

The next email was from Jeremy. She clicked on it.

Just thought I'd let you know that we both miss you very much. The house is quiet and we're eating pizza every night. Hope you are enjoying yourself and you don't get too lonely. I know how much you love the ocean and how beautiful it must be there. Andrew wants to know if you've seen any dolphins. He also wanted to tell you he got a "B" on his English test yesterday. Write back when you can. Love, Jeremy.

She stared at the screen for almost a minute as the guilt swept over her. They missed her. Her heart surged with affection for both of them. Andrew wanted her to know he did well on a test—a rare occurrence for him and also a sign that he still needed her approval and love.

She relished the moment. Lately, more accurately for a long time now, she had been thinking they really didn't care.

She thought about calling Jeremy, but didn't want to do anything that could spoil the moment. She sent him a note, letting him know she missed them too. She wasn't ready to talk to him yet, no that would have to wait.

L iz placed the crock pot on the counter in Harold's tiny kitchen and plugged the dangling cord into a wall outlet. It was a ritual she had practiced for nearly a year now, bringing in chicken soup, beef stew or sometimes a casserole. Today she had brought a simmering pot roast with baby carrots and red potatoes. In the beginning, the meals she prepared were to nourish Lucille, Harold's wife of forty-five years, but she had lost her appetite weeks ago and hardly ate anything at all now. The poor woman had been fighting ovarian cancer for years and was in the final throes of the devastating battle. In the way that doctors dole out time like playing cards to terminal patients, Lucille had been given six weeks to live. Liz prayed that it would go faster than that. She had seen enough people suffer in her life to understand that no good came from extending the life of a late-stage cancer patient.

Although Harold was still a handsome man, he had a haggard look about him today. Shoulders slumped, his eyes puffy and tomato soup red, he walked like a man who had lost hope. Despite the fact that Lucille's condition required the professional services of a nurse or hospice worker, Harold refused to ask for help. Lucille, who had been a difficult and demanding woman even before she got sick, did not like having "strangers" in her home, and Harold was incapable of overruling her. Liz had held her tongue for weeks, but taking one look at him was enough.

She was going to have to talk to him.

She sat down on the vinyl upholstered chair at the kitchen table, waiting for him to return from the bedroom. It could be five minutes, it could be twenty. Though she used to visit Lucille in her bedroom, she rarely did anymore. Either Lucille was too sick, or just didn't want to see anyone. Harold would make excuses and Liz wouldn't fight it. Liz knew she could be helpful, but refused to inject herself into a place she was not wanted.

That was one reason, but there were others, none of which she liked to examine in the light of day. She tried to ignore these feelings, but they came all the same. She knew a sin when she saw one, and desperately hoped the good Lord would forgive her. The truth of the matter was that she had come to resent Lucille for a myriad of reasons—her tyrannical hold on Harold, her ill temper and for her refusal to ease the burden of caregiving from her husband when anyone could see he was physically and emotionally exhausted. But the worst secret of all that she could barely bring herself to acknowledge was that she resented Lucille for *being married to Harold.*

Years ago, after Edward died, she never thought that she would have these feelings for another man. She had loved Edward with all her heart; in the long span of years since he died, she'd never felt anything but friendship for the men she encountered in her life. And then one day much to her astonishment she realized something had changed, and Harold had become much more than a friend.

When did it happen, Liz wondered, sometimes late at night lying in bed, a sliver of moonlight through the window. Was it the first day she'd brought over supper and his face lit up like a child's on Christmas morning because he was so grateful to have a home-cooked meal . . . or was it watching him on Sunday mornings walk stoically to the communion rail to receive the bread and wine. Had it been during one of their chats at this very kitchen table, when sometimes he'd forget about Lucille and her illness and talk about happier times, fishing trips to Canada, Friday night card games with friends or the summer he helped his brother-in-law coach Little League and they won the state championship. Or had these feelings simply evolved over time, inexorably building until one day like steam in a pressure valve they had to be released. She didn't know when it happened, she just knew with profound clarity that it had and the recognition shocked her. It was *wrong* to have these feelings for a married man, she told herself. But there it was, just the same.

At times, she felt almost giddy upon realizing that life still had surprises in store for her. Despite her guilt, the feeling of falling in love was still the most delicious in the world.

"I think I need to call the doctor," said Harold, blasting Liz out of her daydream.

"What's wrong?" she asked.

"She's still in pain and I gave her all her pills. I don't know what to do." He sat down, resting his face in the cup of his hands in a gesture of fatigue and bewilderment. Liz felt her heart breaking for him. No matter how difficult Lucille had been, no matter how hard it was to deal with this illness, he felt helpless because he couldn't make her better or stop her pain. Overcome with compassion, and deeply ashamed of her true feelings, Liz ditched her romantic fantasies. A woman was suffering in the next room, and somebody had to do something about it.

"Harold. Listen to me. We can get her help. It's time to get hospice in here. I'm not going to take no for an answer. You can't handle this alone. It's not good for you and it's not good for Lucille. She needs someone who can manage the pain. That's what those people do. Trust me on this Harold, it's for the best."

"But she doesn't want hospice."

"Then don't tell her its hospice. Tell her they're just nurses. It doesn't matter. What matters is that she's comfortable and that she's not in pain. You can't keep living like this, Harold. Let me make the call. Let me do this for you."

He sat quietly in his chair, his eyes fixed on some invisible particle on the opposite wall. A tiny tear formed at the outside corner of his eye. His hands now clasped in front of him on the table, he looked like a man struggling to do the right thing but who was too beaten down to take action.

Liz could think of only one thing to do. "Harold, let's pray." She reached for his hand and said a brief prayer. "Lord, comfort Lucille and heal her pain. Give us the wisdom and strength to help her . . ."

Liz hadn't heard the faint voice from the bedroom, but Harold did. He sighed, pushed his chair back from the table and disappeared into the hallway that led to the bedroom. Liz couldn't wait any more. She'd always been a take-charge person and it was time to act. She grabbed the phone book from the pantry. It was time to make the call.

E llen quickly parked her bicycle and ran toward the tram. The four o'clock tour of the J. N. Ding Darling National Wildlife Refuge was scheduled to leave momentarily.

Famous for its migratory bird populations, the six-thousand-acre refuge provided habitat to more than two hundred species of birds. Though she was eager to see the swans, roseate spoonbills and tri-colored herons, she had another agenda: a diversion to purge the memory of her licentious behavior in the pool the other night.

The deeply tanned tour guide sat in the driver's seat. "No need to rush, we won't leave you behind," he said.

"Thanks," she said, climbing the tram's two steps. "Sorry I'm late!"

"We're just about full, but there's a seat in the back."

She looked down the aisle, quickly scanning the crowded rows of bench seats. In the next instant her heart thudded like a jet landing on a runway.

Sitting in one of the last rows was David. Thankfully her sunglasses cloaked the panic in her eyes.

He didn't notice her yet; he was talking to a little girl on his lap who Ellen judged to be about three or four years old. Next to him was an older boy, probably six or seven, who was staring at a hand-held video game. The woman she assumed to be his wife was seated in the row in front of him, holding a small child on her lap who was contentedly munching on crackers out of a plastic baggie. She looked up at Ellen and gestured that there was room next to her.

Can this really be happening? Ellen fought a fierce urge to flee, and desperately tried to ignore the grenade blast in her chest. Her mind careened through the menu of options—leave, run, stay, remain calm. She realized that to exit the tram now would look ridiculous. She needed to stay cool. What if his wife suspected—now that was a totally paranoid thought. Suddenly it occurred to her just how high the stakes were. *This man is married and this is his wife and these are his children.* She took a deep breath to regain her composure.

She walked to the back, caught David's eye ever so briefly, and sat down next to his wife and son in the only remaining seat. Tapping every ounce of courage she could muster, she smiled warmly and said "Hi." Marianne smiled back, and they settled into the anticipatory silence of waiting for the tour to begin.

"Daddy I just killed all the orcs and now I'm going to fight the trolls," Ethan said excitedly.

"Ethan, why don't you put that away for now," David said, with the patina of frustration endemic to parents of Game Boy-addicted children. Ellen marveled at what surely must be nerves of steel. If David was rattled by her presence, he certainly didn't show it. Ellen, on the other hand, caught in a vise of shame and desire, only had to listen to his voice to realize its effect on her.

"Dad, I can't quit now—I've got to kill the trolls."

"Ethan, I'll give you two minutes to finish, then turn it off."

David turned his attention to his daughter. "Emma wants to see the pretty birds, right Emma?"

"I don't wanna see the birds," she said determinedly. "I wanna go back to the hotel and go swimming."

"After we see the birds we'll go back to the hotel and you can swim."

"I wanna go now. I don't like birds."

"Later honey. Now we're going to see beautiful birds just like the ones in your book."

Marianne, who had been fussing with Colin's shirt buttons, looked over at Ellen. "You look familiar. Are you staying at Paradise?"

"Yes—I thought you looked familiar as well. I think I saw you at the pool the other day. My name is Ellen . . . and you are . . ."

"Marianne. And this is Colin, and that's Emma and Ethan and my husband, David," she said, turning around and gesturing behind them. The bizarreness of the encounter reminded Ellen of the scene in *Fatal Attraction* when Michael Douglas comes home to find his one-night stand turned crazed stalker chatting with his wife. Looking up, David managed a distracted smile. Emma asked if she could have a popsicle.

Ellen tried not to stare, but she was intensely interested in this woman who was David's wife. She would have never guessed it in a million years. She had imagined his wife to be a size-six Neiman Marcus fashionista with a trendy salon haircut. The reality was quite a different story. Borderline frumpy, her long blonde hair was tied back in a messy pony tail, errant strands flying all about. She wore an oversize T-shirt, the kind woman wear to hide their weight, real or imagined. Her face was pretty, though a little plain because she wasn't wearing any makeup.

Ellen was surprised at Marianne's appearance, certainly a stark contrast to her sexy, good-looking husband. *No wonder he finds me attractive,* she thought, dejected that this was the competition and in the next second cursing herself for being so mean.

Just as Ellen was groping for some kind of small talk to keep the conversation with Marianne going, the driver grabbed the microphone, introduced himself as Tom and announced they were starting the tour.

THE TRAM ROLLED TO A STOP at its first destination, a cedar-planked boardwalk slicing through a dense mangrove jungle. They were the most unusual trees Ellen had ever seen. In a weird defiance of nature, a chaotic tangle of branches the diameter of a garden hose arched downward into the water. Exploring the boardwalk's exotic vegetation, she kept a careful distance away from David's family. At one point she caught him looking at her and quickly averted her eyes.

The next stop was the mud flats, a mecca for scores of avian species. "We've got wood storks, white ibis, yellow-crowned night herons, anhingas and three kinds of egrets—snowy, great and reddish," Tom said. "Nearly one-third of the entire U.S. population of roseate spoonbills can be found right here in our refuge."

Tom opened the doors and once again the camera-toting passengers formed an orderly line to exit the tram. Ellen waited patiently in the aisle for her turn to escape from the confines of David and his family, trying to ignore the growing unrest from his children who were quickly tiring of the tour. "This is SO BORING Dad. I don't care about stupid birds," Ethan moaned.

"Maybe you'll see an alligator," David cajoled. "C'mon, you two, let's go explore."

"I don't care about alligators. Alligators are stupid. I want my Game Boy. When are we going home?"

"Ethan, you can play your Game Boy anywhere . . . this is something I want you to see. C'mon."

"I don't like alligators," said Emma, seizing the opportunity to join the uprising.

Ellen stepped off the tram, leaving David and his recalcitrant children behind. Before her, the scene looked like a photo spread borrowed from the pages of *National Geographic*. Barely thirty feet away, countless shore birds gathered on the mudflats, feeding, fluttering their wings and sunning themselves. Tour guide Tom provided running commentary. "That one right there is a white pelican. They're huge birds, they've got a nine-foot wing span. Over there, to the right, is a yellow-crowned heron—now that's a rare bird to see even back here."

Ellen chatted with a couple in their fifties, self-described birders, who had traveled all the way from Canada to visit the refuge. The woman's husband had a serious-looking zoom lens on his 35mm Nikon camera, and he had been snapping away since the tour began.

"Oh my gosh—Phillip—look over there. Is that—is that a reddish egret?" the wife said excitedly, grabbing the binoculars from around her neck and raising them to her eyes. "Oh my gosh, Phillip, it *is* a reddish egret—do you see it? I can't believe it! Phillip quick, quick get a picture!"

Ellen wasn't sure which bird she was pointing to, but smiled at the woman's enthusiasm. Each person has their own avian thrill, she mused, and hers was standing only a few feet away: an exquisitely beautiful roseate spoonbill, sporting brilliant flashes of pink and crimson. If this wasn't Florida's state bird, she thought, it should be. Ellen zoomed in with her lens to get as close of a shot as possible.

Suddenly, a child's scream pierced the tranquility of the avian sanctuary. Clearly spooked, a phalanx of birds—ibis, spoonbills and the prized reddish egret—flapped their great wings and took off in spontaneous flight. If anyone had been quick enough, the birds' departure would have created an incredible photo. But the scream had jolted everyone, and the Kodak moment was lost.

It took Ellen only a second to realize the scream had come from little Emma, whose parents, still on the tram, were frantically hovering over her trying to quiet her down. People around her clearly were irritated. "Spoiled brat," one woman snapped. "Too old to be throwing a tantrum," said another. "Children shouldn't be allowed here if they aren't going to behave."

Tense moments passed as the screaming continued. Ellen was torn. She couldn't bear undisciplined children, and had little patience for parents who catered to every whim, want and desire expressed by their offspring. She abhorred the culture that had produced a generation of child worshippers, yet she couldn't help but feel bad for David and his wife, who were now the recipients of a barrage of cold stares and looks of reproach.

Finally, after several minutes that felt like twenty, Emma's tantrums subsided and a grateful tour group resumed its nature watching. As Tom pointed out an osprey nest, Ellen noticed

David walking toward her, looking very annoyed. Ellen moved closer to the circle of birdwatchers, almost as if for protection in case David tried to talk to her. *Surely he wouldn't take that chance now would he?*

Much to her surprise and discomfort, he did. Pretending to look at the osprey nest, he came up beside her and said furtively, "Listen I just want to tell you I'm so sorry about the other night. I couldn't even call because I didn't know your cell . . ."

"I don't think we should be talking right now," Ellen responded tersely.

"Then later." he said. As if looking for another vantage point to view the osprey, he moved away from her. Shaken by his presence, heart pounding, she pretended to be interested in the large predator bird. But her thoughts were a thousand miles away.

"**M**om?"

The voice startled Judy as she sat by the crystalline pool awash in late afternoon sunshine. George was upstairs in the condo taking a nap, and Judy, though ostensibly reading a Barbara Parker romance novel, found herself obsessing about his strange behavior and what she was going to do about it. She kept telling herself that she wasn't going to let this ruin her anniversary celebration, but her restless mind kept returning to the problem, turning it over and over again. Her options were few. Talk to their family doctor, address the issue head-on with George, or yield to the appealing "no need to worry I'm just imagining all this" mantra. No matter how hard she tried, she couldn't convince herself of the latter. She knew the truth, no one knew George better than she did, having lived with him fifty years she knew his likes, dislikes, his sense of humor, the way he would react to just about any situation, how he liked his cocktails in tall glasses and hated the feel of flannel sheets. No, George was changing, he clearly wasn't himself, his mood shifts were becoming more frequent. She had been ignoring it for months and what good had come of that? After the other night she had grown even more concerned, fearing other people would notice something was amiss. George was a good man, a proud man, and having to confront something like this would be devastating.

A shadow loomed over her beach chair. Startled, she looked

up. "Maggie!" she exclaimed. "What a surprise, we weren't expecting you until tomorrow!"

"I know . . . change of plans," said Maggie, a bit breathlessly. She hesitated a moment, then reached down in an awkward motion to hug her mother, who made it easier for her by immediately standing up to hug her back.

Judy's quick movement belied the fact that for months she had been dreading this reunion. She viewed it as an inevitable confrontation and she avoided confrontation the way some women avoid Tupperware parties. Yet to her complete and utter amazement, in the first few seconds of her daughter's warm embrace, she experienced an intense surge of primordial joy that transcended all the anger, all the pain, all the terrible, hurtful things that had been said over the years. This extraordinary phenomenon, unique to long-suffering mothers of rebellious children, came from deep within her soul, appearing like a double rainbow after a violent thunderstorm . . . without reason or advance notice, it was just there.

Maggie looked wonderful. Gone was the gaunt, thin face with earring-studded eyebrows and hot-pink streaked hair, though she was wearing a T-shirt that said "We All Have AIDS," leaving Judy to wonder what on earth that meant. She had gained weight, lost the sallow complexion and looked much healthier. Judy prayed this improvement of her appearance meant she was drug and alcohol free.

"You look wonderful honey. It's so good to see you," Judy said, lingering in her daughter's embrace.

"You're looking pretty good yourself Mom. Prodigal daughter returns home," Maggie said, her lips turned up in a warm smile, the reunion an oasis of calm in a tumultuous history, dating back to teenage rebellion and years of family turmoil. Whereas David and Julia took honors courses and graduated at the top of their classes, Maggie spent her high school years smoking pot, drinking and getting suspended. She barely graduated, then enrolled in Jefferson Community College, where she spent the next year and a half trying to convince her parents she was going to turn things around but never did. It took a while, but finally her parents opted for tough love and pulled the plug on her financial support.

It forced Maggie to finally get a job. She had rejected out of hand a conventional one, the kind where you have to show up every day at eight o'clock in the morning not to mention pass a drug test. She searched for alternatives, eventually taking a job as a union activist after seeing one of those ads in the local newspaper that promises $500-a-week for people who want to make a difference. In the months that followed, she traded her druggie friends for people on the fringe left who educated her on globalization, militant feminism and the inherent evil of American capitalism. The anti-establishment message had strong appeal to her for two reasons. One, she genuinely cared about the poor and social justice, but more importantly, it offered her a comfortable philosophical refuge from accepting responsibility for her shitty life. It wasn't her fault she was a failure, it was *the system*. This drove Judy and George, two solidly middle-class, church-going, America-loving people, crazy.

Her union activism led to a paid position on the campaign staff of U.S. congressional candidate Patricia Moorland. Possessing an innate talent for grass roots organization, Maggie's efforts were widely credited for helping Moorland secure a razor-thin margin of victory. Her reward was a paid position on the congresswoman's legislative staff in DC, where she met Brian Thompson, a lobbyist for the National Education Association. He provided stability and an opportunity for a conventional life together, she offered spontaneity and adventure. After a whirlwind romance, they were married.

Judy was thrilled, but her happiness was short-lived. Despite the fact that Maggie wasted no time in producing two children, it was soon evident that her wild streak was alive and kicking. The demands of motherhood bored her to tears, and by the time her youngest was taking his first steps around the coffee table, she had returned to her hard-partying ways. Brian put up with her erratic behavior; he considered getting a divorce but she would have bouts of sobriety and normalcy that made him think things would eventually work out. But Sasha was the final blow.

"Where's Dad?"

"He's taking a nap. He's been a little out of sorts on this vacation. Not sleeping well, so he gets tired during the day."

"Is he speaking to me?"

"Hmm. Well you know your father . . . I guess we'll just have to see how that plays out. I haven't talked to him about it other than to tell him you were coming."

"C'mon Mom. You know. Is he still angry?"

"Maggie, you know how he feels about all this. Let's take things one day at a time."

"Okay. But sometimes I still feel like a little girl where he's concerned. I'm a thirty-two-year-old woman but I still want him to kiss me on the forehead and say 'I love you honey.'"

"Some things never change," Judy said ruefully, "no matter how old you are. As far as your father is concerned, well, I think it's just going to take some time. You know that all we want is for you to be happy and have a good life. That's all we've ever wanted."

"I know I've caused a lot of pain but no one has suffered more than me, Mom. You can say this has been hard on you, but what do you think it's been like for me? I want you to understand this: I just didn't get up one day and say 'how can I blow up my nuclear family?' It didn't happen like that. It wasn't intentional. And I do need to patch things up with the boys. I know that. Yeah it would have been better if I would have never got married because I'm certainly not cut out to be a conventional wife and mother. I know this is hard for you to understand but I had to come to terms with my sexuality and guess what I'm a lesbian. I'm still dealing with that and I'm not sure how it's all going to work out. But I'm in love with Sasha and I haven't been this happy in a long time. And I quit drinking. I'm going to AA."

Judy couldn't argue with the results. Maggie looked better and sounded better than she had in a long time. Was it possible she had finally found a way out of her self-destructive behavior? Judy had lived on the roller coaster of Maggie's life long enough to know that it was premature to come to any conclusions, but nonetheless hoped that her daughter had finally unearthed the roots of her unhappiness.

"I'm glad you're happy honey—and it shows. Everything will work out in the end, it just takes time. But I've got to warn you, your father has been a little cranky lately, well a lot cranky to be honest and I'm not sure what the problem is. If you get the cold shoulder, it would mean a lot to me if you just tried to ignore him. The only thing I want for my anniversary is for everyone to get along."

"I know Mom. That's the reason why I wasn't going to come, I thought the only way I could ensure peace and harmony was to stay home. But in the end I couldn't go through with it. You and Dad have been married fifty years," she said, a wistful look in her eyes. "This is a big deal. I *needed* to be here. Despite everything I *am* part of this family. I hope everyone understands."

Judy grabbed her hand and gave it a squeeze. "Have you seen David yet?"

"Just got here Mom, I've barely seen the ocean."

"Okay, let's go down by the beach. This place is incredible. Then we'll go see if David and Marianne are back yet. Wait until you see the kids! They're too cute for words."

Maggie and Judy walked past the bikini-clad sun worshippers, some reading books, a few talking on cell phones and others just lounging on the pool deck with its magnificent ocean view. To anyone watching, they were the perfect picture of a mother-daughter relationship.

A lan Bloomfeldt, senior editor for the *National Tribune*, the country's largest daily newspaper, scanned the afternoon offering of national wire stores, his eyes bloodshot from staring at the twenty-inch monitor, his umbilical cord to the twenty-four seven news cycle. Not much here, he thought, perusing at a speed that would leave most readers in the dust, until he saw one datelined Fort Myers, Florida that caught his eye:

ROCKETING REAL ESTATE VALUES CLAIM LATEST VICTIM
BELOVED CHAPEL TO BE BULLDOZED, PARISHIONERS MOURN LOSS
MR. FOSTER BUILDS HIS DREAM HOUSE

He read the first few graphs of the story. Interesting. Mr. Foster was Gregory Foster, CEO of Linton Industries. Foster, high-flying captain of industry, champion of global trade, friend to senators and lobbyists and a man with buckets of cash for favors on the Hill, was in a spat with a bunch of senior citizens over a chapel on his property. Hmm.

"Hey Randy, come over here, you gotta see this," he said to his managing editor, who was making another pot of coffee despite the fact that it was almost five o'clock in the afternoon.

"What'd ya got?"

"Our buddy Gregory Foster of Linton Industries, you know, paradigm of virtue, building plants in China, slashing American jobs, racking up record profits, apparently he's got a bunch of old geezers in Florida upset because he's tearin' down their chapel to build a gigundo mansion. Guy's all class—dumps his wife, lays off half of his workers and for an encore he's bulldozing the geezers' church. Geez some guys just don't know when to quit."

"Yeah, he's a real piece of work. You wanna do something with it?" said Randy, pouring a cup of coffee the color and consistency of motor oil.

"Is the pope catholic? Do ya think I'm gonna let this little gem just sit here? Hell no, let's go for it! Page one news feature, thirty-six point head: American business tycoon bulldozes beloved church, geezers up in arms," Alan chuckled. "It's got everything, greed, religion, old people— let's do it. It'll be a great story, I think I'll tackle this one myself."

"Okay, but keep me posted. I want to make sure we're on solid ground before we start hearing from Foster's lawyers," Randy said.

"No problemo," Alan replied. Late for a meeting, Randy picked up his high-voltage cup of coffee and wandered into the conference room, leaving Alan elated over the prospect of doing a hit piece on one of his least favorite people.

Ever since her sister left, Becca, who had taken a rare day off from managing Over the Rainbow, had been profoundly depressed. Nancy's visit had been unexpected; she had driven over from Naples where she was attending a conference. For the first time in a long time, Nancy was happy, her long-awaited adoption having just been approved. Excitedly she told Becca that she and her husband Jeff would be going to Guatemala in three weeks to meet their daughter. This was the culmination of more than five years of emotionally exhausting efforts to have a baby, first on their own, then with hormonal cocktails and in-vitro procedures which produced only more disappointment and frustration.

It was during her sister's brief visit that Becca realized she could no longer ignore her desire to have a baby. She had examined these feelings carefully, was this merely her biological clock rearing its head, was it a sliver of competition between her and her sister—did she want a baby because Nancy was getting one? But at the end of the day, her sister's visit merely cemented what she knew to be true. She did want a baby, there was no turning back, and she was in no position to even entertain motherhood given the current state of her relationship with Michael. Michael had been so moody lately, and except for some brief encounters at the boutique, she hadn't seen him for days. They hadn't slept together in more than a week, he'd been holed up in his studio working on a new painting, spending nights sleeping on a futon he kept there. Painting always came first. She once loved the fact that he was an artist, in the beginning it ignited the powerful attraction she felt for him; now she resented it. He seemed to think his art gave him a free pass to ignore her, be rude, distant or distracted.

"There's nothing the matter," he insisted. "I'm just working hard to channel my energy onto the canvas. I feel like I've got something really special here, and creatively you have to strike while the iron is hot. You know that."

She had fallen in love with an unapologetic nonconformist, and now she wanted a conventional boyfriend who wanted to have children and get married. Square pegs, round holes don't work, she used to counsel her girlfriends. Why couldn't she take her own advice?

She wished Nancy wouldn't have come so she could continue to ignore the undercurrents of her unmet needs and lingering doubts about her future with Michael. Her "don't rock the boat" strategy was a miserable failure. Relationships cannot be entirely one-sided, and this one was. It was time to put her cards on the table. And that meant having to sum up the courage to walk away, if it came to that. The thought terrified her.

"George, are ya gonna play? What'd ya doin' over there, takin' a nap?" asked Gertrude, seated at the poolside umbrella table with her brother George, sister Eunice and Judy. It was getting close to lunch time, only a handful of people were swimming or sunning, leaving the card players to enjoy their favorite game—five hundred—in blissful surroundings and relative peace and quiet. The midday sun had boosted the mercury to idyllic eighty-two degrees. A gossamer ocean breeze stirred the leafy fronds of the palms overhead, offering a veil of shade over the expansive pool deck. On the beach, scores of royal terns fluttered over the water's edge, waiting for the tide to recede just enough for their long beaks to snap up lunch.

Gertrude impatiently started drumming her fingers on the fiberglass tabletop, making a dull thumping sound. George narrowed his eyes and shot her a look of annoyance. "Keep your shirt on Gertie," he muttered, turning his attention back on his hand. Judy didn't understand what was taking him so long. *Just throw down a card*, she thought. The suit was spades.

"I'm going to go see a man about a horse," George said abruptly. He got up, pushed his chair away from the table, and at a languid pace made his way to the small restroom located in the cabana at the far side of the pool.

"Well someone got up on the wrong side of the bed today," pronounced Eunice, after George was out of earshot, raising an eyebrow and looking from Judy to Gertrude.

Gertrude gestured "who knows" but did not share Eunice's annoyance at his departure. Wearing a floppy grape-colored hat that hid a mass of snowy white hair and protected her lightly wrinkled face from the sun, Gertrude could have passed for Miss Marple at the seashore.

"While we wait for John Wayne, I've got to tell you about what happened to my friend Velma. Judy, you remember Velma, she came down for Thanksgiving last year. Well Velma started seeing this man who lives down the hall, his name is Stanley. He's a widower, handsome, and my heavens, a dead ringer for Tyrone Power. First man she's ever dated since her husband died ten years ago. I never saw her look so happy and who can blame her.

"A few weeks ago, Velma and I went to visit our friend Edith, who lives at Green Acres, that retirement home over by the mall. They were having a Fred Astaire Film Festival and the place was packed! I mean where can you go to see a decent movie these days? We saw *Top Hat* and *Swing Time* and the dancing was so romantic . . . Ginger's dress billowing around her like a cloud and Fred absolutely smitten . . ." she said dreamily before being interrupted by her sister.

"Gertie, can you stick to the story once in your life, we don't have all day," Eunice said. Gertrude rolled her eyes but complied.

"Anyway, Edith told us she'd been seeing someone too, and she couldn't wait to show us a picture of her new beau. So out comes the picture, and suddenly Velma turns as white as chalk. Looks like she's just seen the Blessed Virgin Mary of Fatima. And do you know why? Because she's looking at a picture of Stanley! Turns out Edith is dating Stanley too! A real Don Jawan if you know what I mean." Gertrude said, crossing her arms over her chest, eyebrows arched accusingly.

Looking around her to ensure no one was eavesdropping, she continued. "Apparently Stanley, or should I say Casanova, got *real popular* with the ladies after he got one of those prescriptions for, you know—Excitra I think it's called. Velma had her niece look it up on the Internet, and they found out," she lowered her voice to barely a whisper, "it makes a man hard for a whole day! *Can you imagine!*"

Eunice, who'd spent the better part of the past sixty years trying to keep Gertrude from straying too far from respectable talk at the card, dinner or any other table, sharply reprimanded her sister. "Gertrude, hush!"

Judy smiled. "Did Velma break it off with him?"

"You bet she did," Gertrude said, craning her head closer to Judy's in a this-is-just-between-us-girls secret. "But she said it was the best sex she ever had!" Gertrude's Cheshire grin triggered a chortle from Judy, but not from her sister.

"Gertrude!" Eunice exclaimed, so loudly a young boy going down the steps into the pool looked over at the table thinking someone was yelling at him.

"That's what she said, swear on a stack of Bibles," Gertrude said. "But she couldn't keep going out with him because he said he couldn't be faithful as long as he had those hard-on pills. So now she's back to sewing quilts with the ladies from Lydia's Circle."

"Oh well, better to have loved once than not to have loved at all, isn't that what they say," Judy said airily.

Eunice seized the opportunity to change the subject. "Judy, is something wrong with George? He seems pretty cranky today."

"You're right, he is cranky." Before she could continue, George quietly returned, picked up his cards and finally threw down a club.

Gertrude, his partner, was quick to respond. "George, what in the sam hell are ya doin'? You can't throw a club on a spade unless you're out of spades."

"Stuff it Gert." With that, George tossed his cards down on the table, kicked back his chair, and walked away in a huff.

"What on earth is wrong with him?" Gertrude said.

"I'm sorry, there's really no excuse for his behavior. Please don't take it personally, I think he just needs some rest. He hasn't been sleeping well since we got here. Last night he woke up at three and I'm not sure he ever got back to sleep," Judy lied, so convincingly she almost believed her own words.

"Well I hope he goes in to take a nap and wakes up in a better mood," Gertrude said.

Since they couldn't finish the hand without George, the three women put their cards face up on the table.

"So Gert, what do you have over there?" asked Eunice. "I was trying to figure out who had the Joker."

"Not much, I was relying on my partner to bail me out."

Gertrude leaned over and turned over the cards George had left on the table.

"Well, would ya look at this," she said with a puzzled look on her face.

Judy felt sick. George's discarded hand included two red jacks and the ace of spades.

"What on earth was he thinking," Gertrude said. "Couldn't ask for a better hand. He sat there staring at those cards like he couldn't figure out what to do . . . ."

Judy couldn't bear the charade one more minute. "I'm going to go check on him. I'm so sorry this happened." She grabbed her straw beach bag and walked briskly across the pool deck toward their condo building.

Gertrude looked at her older sister. "What'd ya think Eunice?"

Eunice looked up, worry engraved on her face like an old pocket watch. "I don't know, but something's wrong. George can play five hundred in his sleep."

"**A**manda, get Christine in here. Pronto."

Amanda could hear the frosty impatience in her boss's voice, and knew she had to act quickly or his frustration would soon be directed at her. She punched in the three-digit extension for Christine Warner, vice president of corporate communications for Linton Industries. After getting voice mail, she dialed her cell.

"Christine, Mr. Foster wants you in his office immediately."

"What's up?"

"I don't know."

Christine rarely was summoned in this manner. There was nothing in her perusal of the morning headlines of concern, in fact Linton's stock price was on nice climb as a result of better-than-expected third quarter earnings and a glowing piece in *Investing Today*, the latter the result of months of pitching, background memos, emails, phone calls and finally a much-coveted interview with their financial reporter. She grabbed a legal pad, and walked down the gleaming marble-floored corridor that led to Foster's fiftieth-floor corner office with its walls of glass and sweeping views of the Chicago skyline. Amanda ushered her in. Foster sat behind his desk, his silhouette framed by towering skyscrapers, and in the distance, the steely blue waters of Lake Michigan stretching out to the horizon. Up here, all the chaos, noise and commotion of the city streets below were mystically transformed into a portrait of majestic urban tranquility. Whenever she walked through these doors, Christine always thought of Gershwin's *Rhapsody in Blue*.

"Amanda just got a call from the *National Tribune*," Gregory growled. "Some reporter named Alan somebody is doing a story about my house on Sanibel. Talking about how all the old folks are up in arms because I'm bulldozing their chapel, which by the way is on my property. Can you believe it? Don't these people have anything better to do?"

Christine, a twenty-year veteran of putting out fires at the highest levels of corporate America, shook her head. It was almost comical, some of the things she had to deal with, like the time she had to tap down a juicy story in the gossip columns about her last boss having dinner with an attractive woman presumed to be his mistress on the very night of his twelve-year-old son's stage debut as Peter Pan.

"Did he call for an interview?"

"Yes."

"Are you bulldozing a chapel?"

"Yes, but it's on my land. I've let them use it since I bought the place, but now it's in the way and it has to go."

"Tell me more." Christine immediately knew that this story— as innocuous as it sounded—could have negative implications for Foster and his company's reputation. They were still fighting fires on the China jobs front, if he drew national attention for pissing off a bunch of old people it would not be helpful to their overall PR efforts to improve the company's sagging image. And that was her top priority this year as dictated by her boss, to transform him from a heartless job-killing SOB to a visionary global business leader. She had her work cut out for her, but that's why she got paid the big bucks, last year $200,000 plus a bonus.

"I'm building a big expensive house," he said, his neck straining against the confinement of his Brooks Brothers shirt. "So what? Is this what it's come to in America? A CEO can't build a luxury vacation home because some liberal left-of-Marx reporter is going to nail him to the wall? That's bullshit!" he roared.

"Agreed. So how did the *Tribune* even find out about this?"

"I don't know. This is the first I've heard about it."

"Okay, the first thing I'll do is stall him," she said. "Do not call him back, I will. I want to find out what's out there, and then come up with a plan to deal with this. No comment probably won't kill the story. Alan is a piranha, he's an East Coast liberal who thinks you're the Antichrist for outsourcing in China. What he doesn't understand about the economy would fill the national archives."

"Whatever. I'll be damned if some lefty reporter is going to make an issue out of my personal life. That's off limits."

"Gregory, you are the CEO of a Fortune 500 company. You don't have a personal life. I don't like it but that's the reality. I'll figure something out, just give me an hour or so."

With that Christine walked out of his office, already deep in thought about how to put this fire out before somebody threw more gasoline on it.

M aggie and Julia had made plans to meet up with David at the Ocean View Lounge near the posh hotel lobby. A shimmering water garden and natural stone-edged koi pond greeted visitors, the lush habitat perfectly conveying hotel's paradise theme. Inside the atrium, regal palm trees towered over euro design chairs parked on shiny travertine marble floors. Glass sculptures of exotic birds floated over walkways that led to an indoor utopia of upscale bars, restaurants and boutiques, where well-heeled guests dropped hundreds of dollars on vintage wines and even more on eighteen-carat gold bracelets. The place reeked of opulence.

The sisters chose two high-back leather stools at the immense cherry wood bar that snaked along the length of the room that, true to its name, opened up to a stunning ocean view. People around them would not have guessed the sibling connection. Julia's perfectly coiffed shoulder-length hair framed inquisitive azure eyes the color of which was the product of tinted contact lenses. Her designer lilac cardigan topped white capris, the outfit accessorized with a diamond pendant and earrings. Maggie's Grateful Dead hippie chic stood in stark contrast, her loose fitting sweater and gypsy print skirt were the kind of things college girls buy at flea markets.

Desperate for David to arrive, Julia sought to fill the awkward silence between them in their first encounter since the heated argument they'd had on the phone weeks ago. Though Julia had learned from her mother that Maggie had quit drinking and was trying to put her life back together, that didn't erase her irritation over the fact that her sister was even here. She'd been planning this celebration for months, and she didn't want Maggie to ruin it. Maggie had always been good at blowing things up, the latest victims, her own family.

The last time they spoke, Maggie had called to tell her that she was leaving Brian and moving in with her partner, Sasha. Julia was shocked at Maggie's unspoken expectation that she would receive the news with blithe acceptance. *She was leaving her husband and children for crying out loud.* They had argued vociferously over what Julia called a lifetime of bad choices and had not spoken since.

David had promised to be here when the three of them met. *Where was he?* He was never late, and of all times to be late why today?

The bartender came over to take their drink order, and in deference to her sister's new sobriety Julia ordered a virgin pina colada. Maggie ordered a 7-Up.

"Mom said you're not drinking, are you sure you're okay in here?" said Julia, trying to be nice.

"I'm fine. I really don't even want a drink right now, so it's okay," said Maggie.

"Are you going to AA?"

"Yeah, four or five times a week, 'I'm Maggie and I'm an alcoholic' you know the drill. It's a big help for me. Sasha and I go together."

"Sasha is an alcoholic?" said Julia, carefully sliding the pineapple and cherry off of the green plastic skewer on her drink.

"Yeah. And that's actually a good thing because we both know if we start drinkin' again it'll ruin our lives and our relationship. I know you find this hard to understand Julia, but I really care about her."

The burst of candor flummoxed Julia. She was contemplating a response when Maggie's attention was suddenly riveted on the

42-inch plasma TV that hung on the wall behind the bar.

"I want to see this. It's a new commercial from Sasha's church. Everybody has been talking about it," Maggie said.

Julia looked up at the TV and saw two intimidating macho men acting as bouncers in front of a traditional looking church. An upscale white couple, a man and a woman, breeze past the bouncers. An obvious-looking gay couple gets turned away. So does a young black man. "Step aside please," said the bouncer. The shot switched to a photo of a large group of diverse people with the narrator saying, "Jesus never turned anyone away. Neither do we."

The name of the ad sponsor, the Universal Church of God and Justice, flashed on the screen.

"That's so awesome!" Maggie said, taking a sip of her 7-up and twirling the straw around in the glass. "It's about time somebody gets it right."

"Gets what right?"

"The fact that most churches are full of hypocrites who look down on anyone who doesn't fit the mold."

"I didn't realize you had spent so much time studying religion," Julia said dryly. "In fact I don't recall you ever setting foot in a church after you made your confirmation."

"That's because most traditional churches are sexist, racist and homophobic."

"Really. Racist? What was racist about our church?"

"Were there any black people there?"

"No. Were there any black people in our neighborhood?"

"There were plenty of black people we could have reached out to but our church didn't want to get involved," Maggie said.

"But we did get involved. We raised money every year to send inner-city kids to camp, we raised scholarship funds . . ."

"Did we invite those black kids into our homes for dinner?"

"You know Maggie I really resent the implication that every church is racist and homophobic except of course for the Universal Church of God and Justice, which somehow is a beacon of tolerance in a world of hate. Don't you find that all a little hard to fathom? Or is all it takes for you to embrace a theology is an endorsement of your sexuality? Funny I don't recall reading anything in the Gospels about that."

"For god's sake Julia open your eyes to the world around you. What would you know about discrimination? You're a white, wealthy woman of privilege who has never been on the outside."

"Oh, right, my life has been a veritable smorgasbord of undeserved good fortune because I am as you say a 'woman of privilege.' I didn't work my way up through the ranks, starting at the bottom, no, someone just gave it all to me on a silver platter—is that what you think? Maggie, you know better than to spout that class warfare crap with me. It might work with your unhinged leftist friends but it doesn't work with me. And another thing. You know what I think about that commercial, Maggie? I think it's a cheap shot. It's offensive because it denigrates all religion. That church is painting other religions in a bad light just to promote its own. Are you going to sit there and tell me that's right, that God would endorse such tactics?"

"Do you think it's right for people to hold up signs saying 'God Hates Fags?' Do you think it's right that some stations won't even air that TV ad because it shows gay people? Do you think it's right that right-wing extremists continue to stoke the fires of hatred and pass laws that say we can't get married? And what is *our* church doing about that? Avoiding the issue, I'm sure. It's discrimination plain and simple. Just like it was in South Africa, the civil rights movement and for the Jews in Germany during World War II—"

Maggie's eyes flashed with anger and her voice had risen to the point of drawing attention from two couples seated at a nearby table.

Julia looked at her sister in complete and utter amazement and shook her head in disbelief.

"You know I thought we could have a civil and intelligent conversation, but I see that is impossible now that you've compared yourself to a Jew in Hitler's Germany. You really need to get a grip on reality, Maggie. Look at your life. Is anyone threatening you? Is there a death camp for gays, lesbians and transgenders? You don't even see the privilege that you have living in this country enjoying every freedom ever known to mankind. Oh I suppose that's sexist—excuse me humankind. The problem is that you and your gay friends expect to take two thousand years of tradition and turn it upside down overnight."

Julia knew from a lifetime of heated encounters with her sister that she needed to disengage and walk away. She put down her drink on the bar. "I'm going to the ladies room. I suggest we change the subject when I return or else it will be pointless to even go through the charade that we can have a civilized conversation."

Julia quickly got up and grabbed her purse. Her sister was a certified whack-job. Nothing had changed. She was enmeshed in her victimhood; *that* was her religion and it had been her entire life.

David looked at the digital clock on the microwave and realized he was late. He'd promised his sisters he'd meet them in the Ocean View Lounge at eight o'clock. Although he prided himself on his punctuality, he'd slipped into the treacherous waters of an argument with Marianne and he couldn't wrest himself away.

The children were out of earshot for the moment, pajama-clad Emma watching a *Powerpuff Girls* video in the master bedroom suite, Ethan cross-legged in a video-induced stupor killing orcs on the 50-inch plasma TV in the study. Colin had been tucked into his portable crib for the evening, the infant monitor placed prominently on the granite countertop in the kitchen. The grease-stained cardboard from a cheese pizza lay on the kitchen table, along with a clutter of paper plates, plastic cups and snack wrappers.

"Marianne, tell me something. Do you think it's normal that we can't go on a family outing without a nuclear meltdown from Emma, or for that matter that our son lives in a fantasy world inhabited by orcs and trolls? This is ridiculous. Emma's way too old to be having tantrums, and in case you haven't noticed, they're not getting better—they're getting worse!"

"You know Emma doesn't do well with structure," replied a defiant Marianne, standing under the unforgiving fluorescent light in the kitchen, arms crossed over her chest. Wearing baggy gray sweats and a T-shirt, she looked exhausted.

David lowered his voice to make sure the kids could not hear him. Usually he was able to control his temper, but something inside of him snapped.

"Do you have any idea how embarrassed I was today? Did you see the looks people were giving us? Did you hear them talking about what a brat she was—because I did. And you know what? They're right!"

"This is rich David, really it is. Now let's see, how much time do you spend with your children? A few hours here and there. And this is how you react? What do you think my life is like, do you think it's one big happy-go-lucky picnic? We have children. And children don't always conform to our adult expectations because they are CHILDREN. On top of that Emma is an Indigo—"

"Oh spare me that bullshit, Marianne. You know what I think. I think our children are spoiled rotten. Can't you see the forest through the trees? 'She doesn't like structure,'" he said in a mockingly caustic tone. "Which one of your off-the-wall parenting books did you get that one from? Do you think you're actually helping her by making excuses for her inexcusable behavior?"

"Don't insult me, David. You really have some nerve. I love how you've become the parenting expert in the course of a few days of actually spending quality time with your children. I know my children. I understand their needs. Emma is a spirited child who doesn't internally validate the need to conform; she's an Indigo whether you want to accept that or not. If you feel compelled to play the traditional authoritative Judy-and-George parenting role on her guess what, it's not going to work. Indigos by nature are nonconformists. They resist manipulation."

"Oh I get it. So now discipline is 'manipulation.' You know what? You're starting to frighten me. What is the most important thing a parent can give a child besides love? Discipline so they know where the boundaries are. No Marianne, I don't read parenting books and I don't have to because it's really not that difficult, it's common sense. Don't you see what's happening here? The more you cater to her the worse it gets. This is insanity and it's hurting our daughter."

"What's hurting Emma, Daddy?"

Both of them whirled around at the sound of Ethan's voice. Neither one of them had noticed that he'd taken a break from the game and had wandered into the kitchen.

"Nothing honey," Marianne said, walking over to him and putting her arm around his small shoulders protectively. "What do you need?"

"I wanna a juice box and a cookie."

"Okay sweetie pie, I'll get it for you." Marianne opened the cupboard and pulled out a box of animal crackers.

Regaining his composure, David said flatly, "I promised Julia and Maggie I'd meet them and I'm already late. I have to go." To Ethan he added, "I'll probably be back after you go to bed big guy. Give Daddy a hug."

Ethan dutifully gave his father a hug, blissfully unaware that he had just stumbled into the fault line of his parents' marriage.

D avid, who thought that his day could not possibly get any worse, was not happy to find himself in another battleground when he arrived at the Ocean View Lounge.

Maggie was seated at the bar alone. With her gypsy-like clothing and nature-girl demeanor, she looked like a Greenpeace volunteer who had stumbled unwittingly into a Republican fund-raiser.

"Hi little sister. Where's Julia," he said, greeting her with warm hug.

"She's in the ladies room, I think, or she left . . . I'm not sure. We had an argument."

"You two had an argument. What a surprise," he said with mock seriousness. "Let me guess . . . global warming . . . the war in Iraq . . . outsourcing jobs to China . . . Sasha . . . am I getting warm?"

"Religion."

"Religion?"

"Yes. Julia would rather defend the status quo than acknowledge the fact that most churches are racist and homophobic. She has no understanding of the discrimination that exists in this country because she's a white woman of privilege who lives her life in a bubble of affluence and denial."

"Well, she is a woman can't argue that . . . and please don't throw the ashtray at me for saying this but she's certainly no stranger to the good ol' boy network, which in fact I believe runs her industry. So on this particular issue you two should be comrades in arms for the sisterhood." he said, smiling. His political views were not that different from Julia's, but Maggie tolerated the same beliefs in him that infuriated her in her sister.

"Then she should understand it all the more. Anyway, you know how it is with her, David, she's *so* judgmental, I mean what even gives her the right to be angry at me about the decisions I make in *my life?* Do I get angry at her for the way she lives her life? And her holier-than-thou concern about Tyler and Brad, 'oh how can you do this to the boys,'" Maggie said, mimicking her sister contemptuously. "Isn't it the height of hypocrisy that she criticizes me for leaving them, which by the way is temporary, when for the past ten years her kids have been raised by a bunch of frickin' nannies?"

In the mirrored wall behind the bar, David looked up and saw Julia's svelte reflection walking toward them. He realized that he must assume the role of diplomat in order to not only salvage the evening, but the next several days. Emotionally exhausted and drained, he wondered if he had the strength to negotiate a cease-fire between his sisters. His memory spun back to their childhood, when they would stay up half the night at Aunt Patty's cabin in northern Minnesota, giggling and whispering all night in their bunk beds. He wondered for the hundredth time what on earth happens when people become adults that makes life and their relationships so damn difficult.

"David, you're finally here. I was starting to think you ditched us," said Julia warmly to her brother while assiduously avoiding eye contact with Maggie. They hugged.

"Julia, you look wonderful. So Maggie tells me the two of you are at each other's throats already," he said, hoping a little humor might defuse the tension.

His sisters had no immediate response, both of them still obviously angry but reassessing the situation. They both dearly loved their brother, and knew what he was going to say before the words even came out of his mouth: that there was no point in arguing, if it continued during their vacation it would only upset their mother. David was an easy-going guy, but when it came to protecting his mother, he was unyielding.

"Okay, let's have a truce," said David, seizing the opportunity. "We're here to celebrate Mom and Dad's anniversary. And what's the most important thing that we can do for them? Get along. Be one big happy family. Or at least not kill each other. So let's put aside our differences and concentrate on having a wonderful time. Sound good?" He felt like he was refereeing a spat between Emma and Ethan.

After a few moments, Julia spoke. "Okay. As long as we agree to disagree. Because I'm not buying into that BS that my church is a bunch of homophobes and racists."

"Fine," said Maggie. "You want to act like a real Christian? Try supporting me when I'm trying to straighten out my life and stop criticizing me for leaving the boys for a while when you don't even raise your own kids a bunch of nannies do."

"Oh really. Let's see, so you're comparing my having a successful career with your ditching your family. I don't think having a career is quite in that league. But maybe that's just me. David, what do you think?"

"Oh no, I'm not getting in the ring. Excuse me, but this isn't sounding like harmony. Do we have a deal or not?" David replied, with a hard edge in his voice that both sisters knew meant business.

A quiet "okay" from Maggie was followed by a terse "all right" from Julia.

"We're not going to get this all straightened out tonight, obviously. Maggie you need to understand that this isn't easy for any of us. We're worried about Brian and the boys and just trying to deal with a difficult situation."

"I'd just like people to stop being angry at me," Maggie said quietly, her voice cracking with emotion.

He put his arm around her. "I think you're right about us being more supportive," he said. "I think we need to start acting like a family, for you, for each other and for Mom and Dad."

Maggie's face brightened with his acknowledgment. Smiling, she said, "That's why you're my favorite brother."

"I'm your only brother, but nonetheless honored."

Julia, not as sanguine, remained silent.

David, eager to change the subject, said, "So you think you've got problems? Let me tell you about problems. Emma is the meltdown queen of her nursery school. She had a full-blown knock-down drag-out tantrum at the nature refuge and the entire bus tour wanted to lynch us."

"Not little Emma, little angel Emma would never do that. She's too sweet," said Maggie, who had a special relationship with David's children. They adored her; she was the kind of aunt who got down on the floor and played imaginative games with them for hours. What they didn't know was that her childlike state usually was induced by smoking a joint at ten o'clock in the morning.

"What happened?" Julia asked, taking a sip of her pina colada, her Chanel fire engine red lipstick leaving a crescent moon on the glass.

"Apparently she doesn't share my appreciation for Mother Nature," he laughed. "Everyone was taking pictures of the birds until Emma started screaming and they scattered like buckshot. You should have seen the dirty looks coming our way."

"You're kidding. Did you just die right there?" asked Julia.

"It was awful. We couldn't calm her down. I think she's way too old to be pulling this crap," said David.

"Hmm," said Julia. "What does Marianne say?"

"Marianne doesn't get too upset about it. She thinks it's normal, basically. Especially because she thinks Emma is an Indigo."

"A what?" Julia asked.

"An Indigo. You know Marianne, she buys into all these New Age parenting theories, and the latest one is that there's a new generation of Indigo children who don't conform well to traditional discipline."

"I've read about them," said Maggie. "It's fascinating. Many of these kids are extremely spiritual and some see angels. Some people believe Indigos are old souls returning to earth to usher in a new era of peace and compassion"

"Really? They see angels?" Julia asked.

"Yeah. And some clairvoyants see deep blue auras around their heads," Maggie said.

"Are you serious? People actually say they see blue halos around their heads?" Julia asked, incredulous.

"That's what I read. And a friend of mine was telling me about it, she thinks her son is an Indigo with special powers. She says he healed their cat after the vet said it was hopeless."

"Healed the cat? Okay . . . let me know when we come back to planet earth," Julia said, rolling her eyes. When it came to anything smacking of New Age philosophy, she was a bona fide skeptic.

"Does Marianne actually believe this about Emma?" Julia asked.

"Without a doubt. But she hasn't laid the blue halo thing on me yet," David said.

"Well the only thing that could make this more ridiculous is an appearance of an Indigo child on Oprah. Then half of the mothers in the world will have an excuse for badly behaved children," Julia said.

"Not to change the subject," Julia continued, "but can we get started on this itinerary for the next few days?" She pulled her BlackBerry out of her leather purse. "I've got everything right here, just want to make sure I haven't forgotten anything."

With Julia's meticulous list of arrangements as a guide, the three of them talked about the guests, seating arrangements, dinner and the music selection for the next hour. Though left unspoken, it felt good to be on safer ground. David and Maggie couldn't help but marvel at the boundless energy of their sister, who clearly had left no stone unturned in planning an anniversary party that her parents would remember for years to come.

It wasn't until after dinner that Judy finally got a chance to talk to George about what had been on her mind since their ill-fated card game. Though she tried not to obsess, she could not purge the gnawing anxiety that was threatening to cast a pall over their anniversary celebration.

While George took a late-afternoon nap, she had gone to Sylvia's, a gourmet take-out restaurant, to pick up dinner. After dessert they moved to the comfortable wicker chairs on the lanai, where the lights of the coastline were barely visible against the immense void of nighttime sky. The wind hinted of a storm, and though they could not see the ocean its presence was amplified by the noisy chaos of the surf. Two floors down, the solar lights lining the walkways resembled flames from tiny matches.

"I've been meaning to ask you, why did you get so angry during our card game? I felt bad for Gertrude and Eunice," Judy said quietly. She desperately wanted to avoid getting into an argument, but couldn't let it go.

"I'll patch it up with Gert and Eunie," he said. "I was just tired and had a headache. Think I was out in the sun too long. I know you love it here, but this isn't my kind of place. I'd rather be out fishing up on Black Bear Lake, weeds and all. Remember our trip and all the crappies we caught?"

Judy smiled. It was a treasured memory and not because of crappies. A friend of George's had invited them up for a long weekend of fishing. At the last minute, the friends couldn't make it but insisted Judy and George go anyway. Upon arrival, they were stunned to find out that the "cottage" was an incredible log home with spectacular views and a Jacuzzi on the deck. They ate breakfast on the screened porch overlooking the pristine lake, thrilled to see a bald eagle swooping through the forest of towering pines. They shared a romantic evening, made love and relaxed in the hot tub under the stars afterward.

"Hmm. Is that what you remember about that trip, the crappies you caught?"

"No I seem to remember something else . . . wait a minute, was that you?" he said, teasing.

"George!" she laughed, "of course it was me," she replied with feigned indignation.

"I'm sorry about today, I promise I'll make it up to you," he said. "And as far as my sisters are concerned, well I'll just spring for a couple of vodka tonics until they get soused and forgive me, which at their age won't take long."

Judy was torn about what to do next. It was great to see George be his old self again, and she didn't want to spoil the moment. But she pressed on, though she couldn't bring herself to mention the winning hand he left on the table. Her husband was a proud man and it seemed like a betrayal.

"Honey," she said, tentatively, "it's not just today. Lately I've been a little worried. You just don't seem like yourself . . . I don't just mean here, but back home too. Is anything wrong?"

"Nothing but the aches and pains of old age, which at my age are not to be trifled with. But other than that, sure I'm okay, look at me. Listen, you don't need to worry about me. I'm a big boy, been living without my mother watching over me for fifty years now."

Judy recognized the not-so-subtle hint to drop the subject as if it were a no trespassing sign. That was the problem. An intensely private person, George had difficulty sharing his inner self even with her. If she pursued it he would become angry. As much as she needed to get this out in the open, she didn't want to ruin the evening.

There was silence as they stared at the ominous expanse of blackness.

"George?"

"Yes dear wife."

"Does it feel to you like we've been married for fifty years?"

He took her hand in his.

"Do you want to know the truth? It feels like I've known you all my life, but I can remember the first time I saw you like it was yesterday."

The tenderness in his eyes and voice touched her deeply.

"I remember it too. You were so handsome in your uniform. I barely recognized you because you had changed so much . . . you went into the service a boy and came back a man." The unspoken name of George's deceased brother hung in the air between them. Although Judy had attended the same high school as George, he was a year ahead of her and had joined the Marines right after graduation. They didn't really get to know each other until Danny's funeral, when their mutual grief brought them together.

"You know that was one of the worst days of my life, and then you walked in and everything changed. I don't know what I would have ever done without you," he said.

He wrapped his sturdy fingers around hers and squeezed tightly. "He'd be seventy this year. After all these years I still miss him. It's funny. I can't see him any older than he was the day he died. He's got eternal youth. And me, well I'm just an old man."

"Hardly," Judy smiled, leaning over to kiss him softly on the cheek.

"You know you're still a beautiful woman, as beautiful as the day I met you"

Even though Judy knew it wasn't true, she loved that he had said it. For the moment, not even her worries could eclipse her joy.

David said goodnight to Julia and Maggie shortly after ten. They wanted to get a good night's sleep and he was only too happy to oblige. After they left, he ordered a Tanqueray gin martini and gulped it down. He considered having another, but suddenly felt the urge to be alone, somewhere where he could think. The beach seemed the likely candidate for solace, he was not ready to face Marianne yet. Leaving the lounge, he walked briskly past tight clusters of strikingly affluent hotel guests, who were laughing, talking, sipping cocktails, seemingly enthralled with their carefree lives. He was anything but.

Outside the suffocating opulence of the hotel, the beach was deserted. The wind sliced every which way, blowing gusts of salty sea air at his face and into his eyes and mouth. Bank after bank of impetuous, heaving waves crashed onto the shore, like raging armies of the deep marching in an endless succession.

The dark windswept night mirrored his tumultuous mood, despite the cheery front he'd put on for his sisters. He deserved an Oscar for that one. Grateful for the anonymity offered by the ubiquitous darkness, his emotions thundered across his cerebral landscape like an out-of-control freight train. The thought of her was there again . . . lovely, irresistible and inescapable. As if the physical attraction were not enough, she'd looked so vulnerable yesterday, she was in a sense not much more than a stranger to him yet he was already connected to her in this bizarrely intimate and primordial way. He wanted to protect her as much as he wanted to make love to her.

Even with his wife and children by his side and a wellspring of deep shame over this lustful infatuation, he could not find the discipline to stop himself. His knew that his actions were irrational and indefensible, he understood all this on an intellectual level, but intellect was not in play here, something else was. He wondered if this is what drug addicts felt like, desperate to stay clean but defenseless in the grip of an unyielding force that obliterates reason and caution.

Drowning in this quicksand of immorality, dissolute thoughts crowded his mind. An insidious voice jeered *your entire life is a fraud.* And he was terrified it was true. The scary part was how quickly the façade had fallen away, crashing down like a Jenga tower as the last block is pulled. He wasn't much of a church-goer, but he did believe in God, and had until now taken his marriage vows seriously. It came as a shock to him that when put to the test, he'd failed miserably. What a fool he had been, so proud of the fact that he hadn't gotten caught up in the marital train wrecks that had ensnared some of his friends, successful people who had not succeeded at home.

And what would his parents think to see him struggling with this relentless temptation. If Maggie's disintegrated marriage was a scandal, what was his? Was he one iota less guilty than his sister? He wondered if in fifty years of marriage whether his mother or father had ever encountered someone who had kindled such passion. He couldn't imagine it . . . there had never been even a hint of it. But surely there was no insurance policy against this type of sexual attraction, his mother after all was an attractive woman, even now, and his father had been handsome and charming and they had had a lot of friends their entire lives, other couples. He wondered, then abandoned the thought because it made him profoundly uncomfortable. And in the end it didn't matter, because they had survived. The question was would he.

Ellen. Even her name was lovely. He couldn't stop thinking

about her, his desire for her boundless. Yesterday he'd watched her as she stood on the shore, mesmerized by the graceful curve of her back, the glint of the late afternoon sun dancing on her hair, even at a distance her eyes illumined her entire being. He remembered how she had clung to him in the pool, her wet body pressed against his, trying to warm her as he felt her shivering through the taut fabric of her bathing suit.

Standing on the rich carpet of sand, his self-control crumbled.

And the worst part was she was *here*. Just a few hundred feet away. From where he stood, he could see her condo on the fourth floor, the corner unit. There were dozens of condos at Paradise, but the only one that mattered tonight was hers. The lights were on. She was there, alone.

He knew that he should turn around, go home, and patch things up with Marianne. That was the right thing and he always did the right thing. But that was before he'd come here, to this place so ironically called Paradise, where the little voice telling him to walk away could no longer be heard.

And so in the amount of time it took to blink the spray of salt water out of his eyes, he made his decision.

A stickler for starting meetings on time, Liz was pleased that all her guests had arrived by seven thirty. A lifetime of hosting prayer groups and Bible studies had taught her to take a firm stand on punctuality, because the minute you relax the rules, even the most devout believers would start showing up late.

Crowded into her small living room were Pastor Roberts and the founding members of the chapel: Muriel and Larry Stanke, Myrtle and Ronnie Dalton, Ruby Meyers, Betty Jo Lewis, Millie and George Hempstead, Edward and Margaret Campbell, and Louise Stevenson and her ninety-one-year-old mother, Esther.

Liz had spent the better part of the afternoon getting ready for what was going to be an important meeting, a defining moment, perhaps, in the life of their spiritual community. Though she had initially viewed the chapel's demise as a fait accompli, over the past few days she was coming around to a different view. Ever since meeting Ellen, she'd been energized by all that was happening around her. After the story appeared in the *Fort Myers Herald*, she'd received several phone calls from well-wishers and others wanting to know what they could do to help. And that had got her to thinking.

While everyone was settling in, she brought out a large carafe of decaf coffee and placed it on the 1970s era walnut coffee table, next to a plate of lemon bars and paper napkins. With more than a dozen people, the room was cramped but cozy, with everyone seated in a meandering circle formed by two wing back chairs, a sofa and folding chairs she had brought in for reinforcements.

Muriel Stanke had brought a copy of the *Fort Myers Herald* and held it up as she spoke. "My eyes almost popped out of my head when I got the paper yesterday." said Muriel. "I said to Larry, 'we're front-page news!'"

A murmur of bemused acknowledgment rippled through the room.

"Liz, how did they find out about this?" asked Muriel.

"Well, it just so happens that a young woman showed up on our doorstep Sunday morning who was walking on the beach when she heard her favorite hymn. She was so taken by the service and my announcement that she came up to me afterward to ask if we had ever thought about publicity. So we talked about it, and I decided what have we got to lose? Next thing I know, we're on the eleven o'clock news, and my phone's ringing off the hook!"

"My sister in Naples saw you on the news yesterday," said Millie Hempstead, clearly in awe that someone she knew had been on television.

"We had so much fun," Liz said. "You should have seen Ruby with that walker and those dark glasses. What a con artist you are!" Liz said, looking affectionately at her friend, whose silver-gray hair was pinned up in a loose bun.

"I haven't had that much fun since we drank cosmopolitans at the all night bingo-a-thon for the Arthritis Foundation," Ruby said. "I say if you can't have a little fun at my age why bother getting out of bed in the morning! I did feel a teeny bit bad when my neighbor Ella called. She was all worried and wanted to bring over a casserole because she thought I'd taken a fall. If I would have played my cards right I could have had a meal every night this week!"

Everyone laughed.

"So Liz, you're saying this woman just offered to do this for us . . . why on earth would she care? Does she live here?" asked

Ronnie Dalton.

"No. She's on vacation, and you're right, she has absolutely no reason to care save one. She heard of our plight and was inspired. Coincidence or answer to prayer—you decide," she said, her benevolent smile expressing where she came down on the question.

Retired school teacher Louise Stevenson had a stern look, the kind she used to keep her students in line many years ago.

"Don't you think Mr. Foster is going to get angry about all this hullabaloo," said Louise, who had spent the past ten years taking care of her chronically ill mother. "Do you think he saw the article?"

"Yes he did and in fact I got a call from someone at his company. She made it clear she was calling on his behalf and told me it would be better if we didn't talk to the newspapers about the chapel. I told her not to worry because I had nothing bad to say about Mr. Foster, which is true. Did I say anything bad about Mr. Foster in that article?" she said, eyes full of mischief. "I said he has the legal right to do anything he wants with his property even if it means bulldozing a chapel."

Ronnie, a retired bureaucrat for the federal government who had worked his entire life in comfortable anonymity avoiding anything that smacked of confrontation, said, "Liz, I'm not sure about all this ruckus you're raising, maybe we should keep quiet on this. Foster's been good to us, he's let us use the chapel but more importantly he's a very rich and powerful man. I don't think we should get in his crosshairs."

"We're doing nothing of the sort. We can't help it if the newspaper wants to know what's going on here. And I'm not going to be silent if someone asks me what I think. Never have and there's no reason to start now." she said adamantly, and Ronnie knew he struck out.

"You're absolutely right Liz," Millie Hempstead piped in. "We're not going to kowtow to the likes of Mr. Gregory Foster. We may be up in years but we're not wimps!" A round of spontaneous applause peppered the room.

Exhausted after a full day of outdoor activity, Ellen leaned back in the overstuffed leather chair and stretched her legs out on the ottoman. High energy by nature, she cherished the feeling of physical fatigue because it came so rarely to her.

After dinner, she finally called Jeremy, a call she had been putting off since she had arrived.

"Do you miss me?" he asked.

"Of course I miss you," she said, feeling totally justified in telling him this little white lie.

"Good, because we miss you. This morning Andrew said it doesn't feel right here without you."

Ellen wished that were true, but was skeptical. Jeremy, on the other hand, always wanted to think the best of Andrew, no matter how much reality got in the way.

"Well tell him I said that I miss him too," she said. "So what's going on at home?"

"Not much. Your brother called to ask if we were coming for Thanksgiving, and Amy called to make sure I was doing okay while you were gone. We ended up talking for a while."

It was so like Amy to check in on Jeremy. She had a genuine concern for others, especially those in her tight-knit circle of friends. Ellen treasured this character trait in her best friend, but it was also the reason she could never, ever, confide in her about David. "Did you know Mark's job is on the line?" he said.

"Really? The last time we talked Amy said the new management was going to keep the IT staff after the acquisition."

"Well that was all BS. He'll be lucky to get six weeks severance," Jeremy said.

"That's terrible. I know how much he loves his job. By the way, did you go to that interview?"

"It got canceled at the last minute," he said, abruptly changing the subject. "What did you do today?"

"I was outside most of the day, walking on the beach, looking for shells, riding my bike and then I watched an incredibly beautiful sunset."

"I wish I were there with you."

"No you don't. You'd be bored with all this nature," she said.

They talked a little while more before hanging up. He obviously missed her, and she felt a wave of tenderness toward him, a welcome reprieve from their recent mutual hostility. Surely this was the reason "absence makes the heart grow fonder" was one of the most quoted clichés in the history of the world. It would be so nice to wipe the past away and embrace this rapprochement but she doubted this was possible. She'd stood on this ground before, only to unwittingly detonate one of the dozens of land mines that littered the emotional terrain of their marriage. Over the years she had learned the longer you were married, the more you had to deal with explosives.

Outside, crashing waves pummeled the shore with a ferocity that mirrored the emotional warfare being waged inside her head. Jeremy trusted her, he would never, ever believe her capable of cheating on him. For all their disagreements that much was certain. The truth of the matter was she had called him because he expected it, not because she wanted to, and she had discovered this week that despite his faith in her, she was highly capable of betraying him.

She wondered if she would see David again, it was difficult now that his family had returned. She told herself she just needed to talk to him one more time, sort things out, but in reality all she wanted was to be close to him again, relive the exquisite moment when he took her in his arms and kissed her on the beach. She *had* to see him again, once this vacation was over it would be impossible. He lived in Chicago, she lived in Philadelphia, cities eight hundred miles apart. There was no plausible reason for them ever to be in the same place. Their paths would not cross.

How on earth was she going to carry on with her life as a wife and mother now that she had tasted this kind of passion. *Had she fallen in love with him?* At first she had dismissed the "falling in love" notion as preposterous, this was raw physical attraction, nothing more, a force of nature that exists in abundance in a sex-driven culture. She told herself that this wasn't love because love took time and devotion and commitment and this was nothing of the sort. This theory had made her feel better for a while, but it had been exposed as a fraud when she saw him at the wildlife refuge. Yes, she felt a terrible guilt seeing him with his wife and family, but there he was comforting his little girl in a way only decent and good men did and this time the spark was not sexual, it was something else, and the something else was even worse.

She stared at her reflection in the mirrored wall opposite the sofa, her arms and legs echoing a bronze glint of the sun's rays, the humidity in the ocean air producing an abundance of curls in her hair. Assessing her appearance with a sharp eye for potential flaws, she found few. Even dressed in an old tank top and shorts, she looked great, people often thought she was in her thirties, and she did nothing to dissuade them. Her investment in a personal trainer and vigorous workout schedule had paid off. The mirror reflected a curvaceous body that was toned yet feminine, breasts perfectly apportioned to her frame, and height that gave her a regal air.

The wind blew harder and louder, the roar of the surf emanating a blaring and hissing upheaval like a person beset by howling demons. Saltwater spray splashed through the floor-to-ceiling screened lanai, a remarkable feat given she was on the fourth floor. Though the wind blasted through the lanai doors, she couldn't bring herself to close them yet because she was enthralled by the awesome sound of nature unleashed.

Exhilarated in the moody darkness, she stood on the lanai, gusts of sea spray blowing through her hair, wind whipping her clothes, the surf perfectly reflecting her emotional state of pure chaos.

Again she was reminded of her love for this island. Tomorrow would bring another resplendent sunrise, the iridescent violet rose hue stretching out across the horizon before the blinding light broke forth. At dawn's first light, the early risers would gather on the beach, some just watching, others in eager pursuit of the bounty of shells the tide had swept in overnight, others toting cameras to capture the glorious wonder that was sunrise.

Finally she closed the heavy sliding doors that led to the lanai, seeking refuge on the sofa in the living room. She picked up her book, *Pride and Prejudice*, and opened it to the first chapter. What she needed was a distraction. She had bought the book just for that reason today at Periwinkle Books, where she had been drawn to the romantic story of Miss Elizabeth and Mr. Darcy.

The last thing she expected to hear was a knock on the door.

L iz took a sip of her coffee and placed it on the coffee table, the ornate porcelain cup a souvenir from a trip she'd taken to Shanghai several years ago. Other souvenirs from that memorable journey—a beautifully painted Batik folding fan, a Chinese "lucky knot," and an intricately carved pagoda incense burner—were interspersed on shelves crowded with family pictures and assorted bric-a-brac. On a small card table squeezed into the corner of the dining room stood a half-painted canvas in water color, depicting a cabin on a picturesque lake. Liz never considered herself an artist, but a friend had suggested she give it a try, and she'd found it both a challenge and a satisfying pastime. She chose for her first work the cabin Edward's parents had owned on Star Lake in northern Wisconsin, a place that had given them all so much joy over the years. She had wonderful memories of camp fires, kids shrieking with delight as they played hide-and-go-seek at dusk, chasing lightning bugs, the screen door slamming with the breezy exuberance of youthful energy.

Life had been so different then, there was no denying it, yet the era had passed without a whimper of protest with the next generation. Today her grandchildren thought of fishing as only slightly more boring than watching paint dry. Her sons had tried to cultivate an interest in the outdoors with their children early on, only to arrive at a cabin in the woods to find their progeny

194

climbing the walls by Day Two. On one such occasion, Liz went fishing with her son and twelve-year-old grandson Patrick, who had insisted on plugging into his iPod and listening to rap music while they fished. It had been so different with her kids, she remembered how excited they always were to arrive at the lake, their sense of adventure, fighting over who would run the Evinrude 6-horsepower motor that they had named "Rudy", and how they never, ever would miss the opportunity to go to Grizzly Bob's Bait Shack, whose proprietor, a retired Chicago cop, was revered for his wisdom on all things fishing and knowing where the crappies were biting.

"Here's what I think," Liz said. "Mr. Foster isn't going to change his plans about building his house. But maybe with a little more pressure, he'd be willing to donate some of that vast fortune of his to help us move the chapel. I know it's a long shot, but I've been thinking about this and all of a sudden it occurred to me that just because we're being evicted doesn't mean we can't go on as a congregation somewhere else."

"But it won't be on the ocean with our beautiful views," Ronnie lamented. "It'll never be the same."

"No it won't be the same, but what are our options?" Liz replied. "We find another church, which means we'd join some other denomination. Now don't get me wrong, plenty of nice folks in those churches—but is that what we really want?"

"Abundant Life will never let us play bingo for money, that's a fact," Ruby declared adamantly, eyebrows raised, and Liz knew her well enough to know this was the nail-in-the-coffin regardless of any other salient theological considerations.

Liz seized the opportunity to make her case. "Look what we have here, our fellowship, our worship, the congregation we've built over the years. We shouldn't have to give that up."

"But wait a minute here," Ronnie said. "Liz, do you know what you're suggesting. Moving a building? How do we know the chapel is structurally sound enough to make a trip across town? And to where? And with what money? Makes me tired even thinking about it."

"If worry were currency Ronnie, you'd be a rich man," Liz replied, shaking her head. "The money we'll get from Mr. Foster and the community. Now Ronnie, think about it. Do you seriously see a shortage of money on this island? The last time I was at Over the Rainbow, they were selling five-hundred dollar designer sweaters like corn dogs at a carnival. Look around you. The money *is here*, we just need to tap into it. And who knows, the city owns all kinds of land, maybe we can convince them to donate some property. No it won't be on the ocean. And that's a terrible loss, I won't argue that for a minute. But we'll still be together. And that's what's important."

Pastor Roberts had been listening intently. The chatter in the room died down when the others saw he intended to speak.

"I agree with Liz," he said. "We are blessed with a vibrant community of faith and it's not about a building or beautiful ocean view. It's about the relationships we have with each other, the fellowship that has been nurtured over the years. On the surface, I admit, moving the chapel seems like a daunting task. But I'm reminded of what Jesus said to his first disciples: 'Follow me.' They had no special training, no special talents, yet they were chosen to lay the foundation for what was to become his church on earth. Now we're being chosen for a task, which by way of comparison is miniscule." Pausing, he smiled. "And I think we should embrace it."

Silence blanketed the room as the group considered this new vision of their ministry. Liz was elated. She hadn't been sure how Pastor Roberts would respond to taking on this challenge.

Ruby interrupted the stillness of the moment, "You know my sister Agnes loves the ocean but the poor thing lives in Phoenix— why I'll never know, it's like living in a blast furnace in the summer—anyway, she found a CD that has ocean sounds and plays it all the time. Maybe we can buy one of those ocean CDs and get a big boom box and crank it up during worship. WOOOSHHH . . . WOOOSHHH . . . WOOOSHHH," she said, arms raised above her head swooning back and forth, making the others laugh.

"Count me in," said Edward Campbell, who had been quiet

up to this point. "Life has become a little too comfy of late. I seem to recall, Pastor, your saying something on Sunday about getting out of the boat."

Margaret Campbell smiled and gave a nod that said "me too." Ruby was next, followed by the Stankes and Louise Stevenson, who said, "Oh, I don't know about this but, okay, I'll go along but if this doesn't work out I'll be the first one to say I told you so." Even Ronnie offered a begrudging nod of approval. By the time the last lemon bar was devoured, there wasn't a holdout in the room.

Ellen froze, and waited for another knock. Probably one of her neighbors had wandered down the white stucco corridor into the wrong doorway.

Within seconds it came, this time louder, more insistent. She heard her name. *Could it be . . .* Senses on high alert, she jumped up from the sofa, threw her book down and bounded across the living room to the foyer.

"Who is it," she asked tentatively.

"It's me. David," he said, his voice slicing through the thick metal door.

Elated and terrified, her fingers trembled as she turned the deadbolt lock to open the door. He stood at the threshold a mere twelve inches away from her. The fact that he was *here*, that they were *alone*, was so unexpected and overwhelming that she actually felt light-headed.

"David, well, what a surprise . . . come in," she said, wanting him out of the hallway quickly to avoid being seen.

"Are you sure it's okay? I mean, I know it's late but I was out walking on the beach, and I saw your lights on."

An unmistakable aura of vulnerability had replaced the Cary Grant bravado that he had emanated the other night at the pool. She felt a rush of anticipation but fought to show no outward sign. "It's fine, really. Come in," she said in her most nonchalant voice.

He crossed from the darkened doorway into the elegantly appointed foyer. A bamboo-framed mirror captured them on the far wall, and for the first time she saw the two of them together. Wearing a red polo shirt and blue jeans that accentuated his athletic build, he looked terrific. The reflection unnerved her, forcing her to think about the other man who had stood by her side for the past twenty years; she looked away. Still, her guilt was fleeting, deftly overcome by this man whose mere presence immobilized her defenses.

Stepping back from the door, the blood seemed to rush from her head, and she felt herself ever so slightly losing her balance. David attentively put his hand on her forearm to steady her.

"Are you okay?" he asked.

"This is so strange, but I think I'm a little faint. Maybe I got up too quickly . . . do you always have this impact on women you visit late at night?" she asked, in the flirtatious tone that commandeered her speech every time she spoke to him.

"Hard to say, since you're the only woman I've ever visited late at night." His dark eyes penetrated hers; there was something in his voice that made her nervousness more acute.

"Really," she said, unsure of what to say next.

"I had to see you."

"Let's go and sit down," she said.

She led him through the foyer and across the airy living room, where during the day, the windows offered a striking vista of sea and sky but at night only the ebony darkness. She sat down on the love seat while he scanned the room as if searching for something. Finding it, he walked back toward the hallway, found the master switch and dimmed the lights. The wall sconces cast the room in an amber glow, creating the unspoken intimacy they both desired.

He sat down close but not touching her. Outside the wind howled like semis roaring by on an expressway. The frenetic buzz of a thousand crickets reached a cacophonous crescendo.

Sitting next to him, it was as if everything she had ever done in her life had merely been a prelude to this moment. Panicked and exhilarated at the thought of what could happen now that they were alone, really alone, hidden from the rest of the world, she knew with certainty that if there were any stopping this train it would have to be right now. But she was tired of fighting, tired of always being the person who chose right over wrong, tired of denying herself this once-in-a-lifetime pleasure. *The hell with fidelity, who would ever know?*

Turning toward her, he spoke in a quiet, deliberate voice. "I feel like I'm in a parallel universe every time I see you. These last few days . . . it's been so hard . . . I think about you constantly. You're my last thought before I fall asleep at night and my first when I wake up in the morning. I felt so bad the other night, I needed to explain what happened, to tell you why I couldn't come back. Marianne came home with the kids just as I was leaving and I didn't have your cell or any way of letting you know . . . And then yesterday on the tour, well that was awful, I'm so sorry," he said, the torment in his voice evident. He looked tired.

"It's okay," she said. "There's nothing you could do about any of it."

"I could have never asked you to dinner."

"I could have declined your invitation."

"You're so beautiful."

Silence.

Their eyes locked again, but she had to look away. She needed something to calm her uproarious nerves.

"You know what I really need right now," she said. Realizing the double entendre she had not intended, blushing, she smiled. "A drink. Would you like to join me?"

"Do you have something here?"

"Yes there's some wine in the kitchen. I'll get it."

Getting up quickly, she walked through the dining room past the immense glass table into the kitchen. It was dark but she knew she had left an open bottle of merlot on the granite countertop. The long-stem crystal wine glasses were on a high shelf in the cabinet overhead. She tip-toed to reach one, aware that David had followed her. Seeing her reach for the glass, he moved swiftly behind her to reach it for her. As he brushed against her, she could feel his arousal through the soft cotton of his trousers. A blast of carnal electricity ricocheted between them. In one fluid motion, he put the glass down on the counter and turned her around, pressing his body into hers and kissing her hard on the mouth. It happened so fast, she surrendered without hesitation, clasping her arms around his neck she kissed him back, their mutual desire igniting like a lit match tossed into a bucket of gasoline.

Strong muscular arms lifted her, she wrapped her legs around him, they pivoted a step until her back was pressed against the rough stucco texture of the wall. There were no more formalities, not even the pretext of a struggle, just a man and a woman bound by a passion that was both ancient and universal. Her legs still tight around him, he kissed her again, and then carried her in a staggering fashion down the hallway into the bedroom. Gusts of wind from the lanai blowing around them, they fell into the king-size bed, taking ownership of each other's bodies in a symphony of erotic sensation.

She responded with a caliber of lovemaking she didn't know she possessed. He was hers, even if only for a few hours. Powerfully physical and sensual, he knew intuitively what she wanted. The only thing that mattered was to satiate this excruciating desire. Finally they came together in an exploding frenzy of thrusting motion and then collapsed into each other's arms.

An hour later, the wind had died down. Under the bedroom window, the cricket frenzy had quieted. The moon had emerged from behind billowing clouds, casting a thin beam of light over the bed. Spent, they lay entwined, her body cradled by his. For a long time, they did not speak.

The vanilla-scented candle on the bedside table flickered in the darkness. He nudged her to turn toward him, his face radiant from the afterglow of sex.

"I know at this particular moment you're going to find this a little hard to believe, but I don't want you to think this is just about sex," he murmured.

"Really, what's this about then?" she said dreamily.

"I think you know," he said.

"No, tell me."

"If this were just about sex I would have never let it get this far."

"So why don't you tell me what it *is* about," she coaxed him, wanting this moment to last forever because he looked as if he were in love with her, but she knew that had to be her imagination.

"Because you might laugh at me."

"I would never laugh at the man who just gave me one of the most unforgettable orgasms of my life."

"That sets the bar high for the next one," he teased, gently tracing the curve of her breast with his index finger.

"At the moment I don't think I would survive," she said.

"As you wish, Ms. Bennett."

"Yes Cary."

Each lost in their own thoughts, they didn't speak for a few minutes.

"I don't want to leave you tonight," David said, a shadow masking his eyes.

"I don't want to think about it."

"I won't go until after you fall asleep. Promise."

"You don't have to do that."

"But I want to. I want to see your eyes close and watch you dream," he said softly.

"I think I am dreaming."

"You *are* a dream," he said.

"Bet you say that to all the girls."

"I told you there are no other girls," he said tightening his grip. She felt secure and protected, and loved the feeling of being in his arms, the sound of his voice, soft and steady and warm.

"So I'm not just another notch on your bedpost," she said,

teasing.

"I'm not even going to dignify that with a response."

"That sounds like an excuse," she said. "So has there been anyone else, I mean, since you've been married?"

"No one. Not even close."

"So why me?" she said, with confidence that belied the question.

"Because you look spectacular in that swimsuit," he said, grinning, his eyes catching the glow from the candle.

"Hey, I thought you said this wasn't just about sex."

"Did I say that?" Smiling, he kissed her softly on the mouth. "It's not, but that's where it started. At the pool." He kissed her cheek, then her neck.

"I didn't even realize you had noticed me," she said.

"You were pretty intent on your book."

"Do you believe in fate?" she said.

"What do you mean?"

"Like there are unseen forces that control our destiny. Like the fact that I ran into you downstairs at the storage locker. What if that wouldn't have happened?" she said.

"I would have found you somewhere else." More silence. She thought about his having to leave. Then the words tumbled out.

"David what are we going to do about this?" Suddenly the giant wave she'd been surfing was crashing down.

"Shhh. No discussions. We'll talk tomorrow, I promise. Close your eyes and try to go to sleep."

She closed her eyes, but she doubted whether sleep would ever come.

The next morning brilliant sunlight streamed in through the pale blue sheers that covered the floor-to-ceiling bedroom windows. In her first moments of consciousness she was unaware of what had transpired last night, but suddenly the first snippet of memory emerged. No it wasn't a dream. She lay there remembering the evening in delicious detail, how he had carried her in here, made love to her and held her afterward, the tenderness in his embrace. The scent of his cologne remained on her and she loved it.

Slowly, she got up out of bed and walked across the bedroom into the bathroom, the marble floor cool under her bare feet. Standing in front of the ornate double-sink vanity, she studied herself in the mirror: disheveled hair, smudged eye makeup that had never been washed off, the tan lines on her naked body. She grabbed her robe from a nearby hook and wrapped it around her, tying it at the waist.

Every morning she had woken up here, it had been with a profound sense of appreciation for the day ahead. But today was different. As would every day that came after it. What she had done last night could never be undone. It was exhilarating and thrilling and morally despicable. The irreversibility of her actions reminded her of how she had felt on September 11 in the hours after the planes crashed into the World Trade Center: this changes everything, nothing will ever be the same.

As she left the room, she saw a note on the nightstand. *Missing you already, Love David.* Her sleepy eyes widened and she could feel her pulse quicken. *Love.* He signed it *Love.* Like a high school sophomore she pondered the word over and over again. Did he really think he was *in love* with her? Is that what he had been talking about last night? This isn't about sex, he'd said. Was it possible that she *loved* him as well? Or did Satan come wrapped in a package of "love" to gain the necessary foothold for infidelity? If she convinced herself she had "fallen in love" would that obviate her immoral behavior?

And what if they both were in love? Did it even matter? They belonged to other people and nothing they did last night was going to change that.

She wandered down the long hallway into the kitchen to make a strong pot of coffee. She had taken this vacation to be alone, sort things out, figure out what to do with the rest of her life. Never in a million years did she think that she would come here only to make matters far, far worse.

What could be the possible outcome of this affair, she thought, her mind racing ahead to assess the options. Would she, could she, ever leave Jeremy? She could barely imagine her life without him, yet clearly he had helped to lay the groundwork for this. She was trying to work at their marriage, he was not. She was a survivor, he had given up. Now she had slept with another man. Jeremy deserved it, she could argue. But deep down she knew that there was no justification for betraying her husband and marriage vows. And in spite of all that, there was the narcotic-like high she'd felt making love to David, who had been everything she could ever ask for in a lover—romantic, physical and unrestrained. His fervent passion engendered in her a sense of carnal empowerment that she could still have this effect on a man.

Like a giant teeter-totter, her rhapsodic ebullience balanced precariously against the weight of her guilt.

It would be so much easier if her parents hadn't been so vigilant in teaching her about right and wrong, morality and immorality. She had grown up on black and white, not shades of gray. She knew plenty of people who didn't lose any sleep over infidelity, who carried on affairs with people they worked with, or slept with strangers they met in bars on business trips in faraway cities. They went home to their wives and husbands who were none the wiser, showed up at their kids' soccer games and neighborhood picnics, the faux epitome of the happy family. But the problem was she could never be one of those people, despite the way she'd been acting for the past week.

She poured six cups of water into the Mr. Coffee. The first thing she would do was take a shower. She needed to get clean, wash away the outward stain of what she'd done. Then she would walk, it always helped to clear her head. But would she dare pray? What would she say now that she had broken her marriage vows, "*Sorry God, got a little carried away last night, hope you'll understand?*"

She desperately needed to talk to someone. Someone, but not David. She ticked through a mental checklist of close friends and family. There was absolutely no one she could share this with. Not her best friend Amy, not her sister, certainly not her mother. It was too explosive to share with anyone. Ellen had learned years ago the only way to keep a secret was to tell no one.

She sipped her coffee, the caffeine acting like jumper cables to her brain. Suddenly she had an idea. There was someone she could confide in. She scrambled through her purse to find her phone number. She would call Liz. Liz was someone she could talk to, it wasn't ideal but it was her only option.

Judy couldn't think of anything she liked to do more at the beach than watch her grandchildren play in the sand and chase the waves at the water's edge. It brought back memories of her childhood, vacationing at Indiana Dunes State Park on the shores of Lake Michigan. Although the Midwestern lake lacked the sheer magnificence of the ocean, it didn't matter to her and her brothers and sisters. Sixty years ago—how could it have been that long—since they had dashed up and down the sand foothills exploring the beach, racing toward the towering metal slide that shot them like cannonballs into the water.

On this glorious Thursday morning, Ethan was building a fort to protect his imaginary army from the diabolical Eye of Sauron, while Emma picked up shells and brought them over to Aunt "Gertwude" and "OOnice" for inspection. Gertrude loved children, and her "oohing and aahing" over the treasures Emma brought forth—calico scallops, periwinkles, whelks and conches—kept the little girl intent on finding more. Colin sat on Marianne's lap, his sun hat flopping over his forehead, almost hiding his baby-blue eyes, content with a bottle his mother had retrieved from her large straw beach bag.

Judy, George, Gertrude, Eunice, Marianne and Julia and her daughters Nicole and Rachel had met at ten o'clock to take their place in line for the highly acclaimed poolside brunch buffet. They were not disappointed as they filled their plates with eggs

Florentine, poached salmon, goat cheese omelets, lemon scones and the best orange juice they had ever tasted. Ethan, Emma and Colin devoured crème brulee French toast smothered in Vermont maple syrup. Nicole, a vegan, having been swayed to the philosophy by a charismatic professor at the prestigious Suffolk Academy, filled her plate with fresh strawberries, pineapple, honeydew melon and wheat bread sans butter. Gleaming silver serving pieces were placed on banquet tables on the large terrace that looked out over the diamond-blue waters of the Gulf of Mexico.

After breakfast, they settled into beach chairs and marveled at the extraordinary view.

"You know I think I've died and gone to heaven," said Gertrude, clad in a watermelon-print dress topped by a large straw hat. "Do ya think they'd mind if we stayed on? Wouldn't it be the cat's pajamas to spend the winter down here? Eunice, I think we oughtta find ourselves a couple of old geezers—you know, one foot in the grave and another on a banana peel—and settle down," she chuckled.

"Not for me thank you very much," replied her sister emphatically. "Too hot and too much sun. And can you imagine what Christmas is like here? Palm trees and no snow?"

"Where's David," asked Judy, as if her son's absence had just registered as an anomaly. "I'd think he'd be down here by now."

"He didn't get a lot of sleep last night," Marianne replied. "He was out pulling an all-nighter with his sisters."

"Not with me he wasn't," replied Julia, as she reapplied her lipstick, a perfect shade of vermilion that matched her eye-catching designer swimsuit. "I was back in my condo and in my PJs by eleven. Travel days are so exhausting. I'm pretty sure Maggie went back to her room as well. I think our all-nighter days are behind us. Well at least mine are."

Judy could see the muscles around Marianne's mouth tighten though her eyes were hidden behind sunglasses. "You left him at eleven?" Marianne said flatly. "I just assumed you were all at the bar. I woke up at one and he wasn't home."

"Oh, you know David," Judy interjected. "He probably stayed for a nightcap and wound up in a long conversation with some stranger who decided to tell him his life story. He's such a good listener, and he's too polite to get up and walk away."

"Let's go get him up," said Rachel with an evil glint in her eye. She would like nothing better than to jump on her favorite uncle's bed and wake him out of a deep sleep. "Mom, can I go wake him up?"

Julia looked at Marianne tentatively. The two women did not get along, their personalities as far apart as *Men are from Mars, Women are from Venus*. Each tread carefully on the other's turf. "Only if Aunt Marianne says it's okay," Julia said.

"Sure," said Marianne. "Just be sure to knock on the door before you go in. I'm pretty sure I left it unlocked."

Instinctively Judy could tell something was up with Marianne and David. She wondered where he'd been last night. She had the most bizarre thought, oh it was ridiculous even to speculate but earlier in the week, she'd seen him talking to that woman. She had been struck by how attractive the woman was and how engaged they were in conversation. Later that night, when George had wandered off, David had been out to dinner by himself, which now that she thought about it was a little odd.

"So Nicole," said Gertrude, looking over at Julia's sixteen-year-old daughter who was wearing a lime green barely-there bikini that revealed more cleavage than anyone in her extended family was comfortable with. A gleaming white iPod nano hung around her neck; her bleached blonde hair was pinned up with several hair clips, the effect messy but exactly what all the girls her age were wearing. "The only thing I saw you put on your plate was fruit. How'd you pass up all those other goodies? Don't tell me you're on a diet, you're as skinny as a rail."

"I'm a vegan, Aunt Gert. I don't eat animal products."

"Hmm. Vegan. Is that short for vegetarian? My neighbor Sally was a vegetarian, ate green beans and alfalfa for years," said Gertrude. "Didn't do much good though, poor thing, she dropped dead of a heart attack after church one Sunday morning right next to the vegetable garden. I always think of her when I'm having carrots . . . well anyway, she did have such a lovely funeral."

Glancing over at her sister, Gertrude continued. "Eunie, remember the time we went over to Sally's for Easter brunch, and she had all those vegetarian dishes on the buffet—spinach quiche, zucchini casserole, wild mushroom pie, all those things we'd never even heard of. Everything tasted so good, we kept going back for more. But the next day—jumpin' Jehoshaphat— we might as well have taken a bottle of ex-lax, that meal cleaned us out! We had the runs for two days and—"

"Gertrude!" Eunice exclaimed. "Where are your manners!"

"No, I'm not a vegetarian," interjected Nicole, her mirrored Ray Ban sunglasses reflecting the dance of a sailboat in the gulf. "A vegan is different. I don't eat anything that has been made from the exploitation of animals. That means milk from dairy cows, butter, eggs, a lot of stuff."

"Nicole was introduced to the vegan philosophy at school," said Julia. "This is one of the benefits of paying through the nose for a private-school education that they don't tell you about at Parent's Night. Her English literature professor is one of the founding members of Vegans International and is very vocal about his beliefs. I'm not a believer, but I'm trying to respect her views on it as long as she respects mine. The one plus is that she has learned to cook her own meals because Richard and I are meat eaters and always will be." She smiled at her daughter, who didn't return it.

"Vegan," mused Gertrude. "Hmm . . . rhymes with pagan."

Judy, eager to change the subject, jumped in before Gertrude started telling Old Testament Bible stories about Jews worshipping golden calves in the desert. "So what's the plan for today? I was thinking it might be nice to do a little shopping trip this afternoon to the outlet mall in Fort Myers."

"Did somebody say golf?" George said.

"No one said golf—shopping!" Judy smiled at George, thankful that his improved mood from last night had continued into today.

"How's the course here?" Julia asked. "Richard talked me into bringing my clubs at the last minute."

"Fantastic," George replied. "David and I played it. Not the easiest course in the world but I'm sure you're up for it. If Richard wants to go, we'll get David out there again and have a foursome. That is if he ever gets up."

"Oh he'll get up. Rachel will make sure of that," Julia said.

"Okay then. Gertrude and Eunice, are you up for some shopping?" Judy queried. They nodded in agreement. We'll meet in the lobby at two o'clock. Nicole, Marianne, you're welcome to come as well."

Nicole declined, saying she'd rather hang out on the beach and work on her tan. Marianne said she'd promised to take the kids to the Kid's Club for a scavenger hunt.

So the day's activities were settled. Still, Judy wished David would make an appearance. *Why wasn't he here?*

L iz had been surprised but pleased when Ellen called to invite her to lunch. She really liked the younger woman and was grateful for her help with the chapel. Sitting at her kitchen table, reading the *Fort Myers Herald* with the ever-affectionate Miss Kitty rubbing her feline head against her slipper-clad foot, she marveled at how the proposed demolition was now a front-page news story. The publicity was bringing in new offers for help every day.

Before accepting the invitation, she called Harold to see what time the hospice people were coming because she'd promised him that she'd be there when they arrived. He told her that they weren't coming until three, which would give her enough time for lunch. Plus, going later meant she could make sure Harold got a good supper. Physically and emotionally exhausted, Harold had finally agreed to call hospice. Lucille's condition had worsened; her defiant refusal to have "strangers" in her home had finally succumbed to the devastation of her cancer. She could barely speak and wasn't eating.

Liz felt terrible for Harold. Like an exhausted traveler on a dark wintry night, he had embarked on the inexorable journey from denial to sadness to the bleak acceptance that his wife would never get better. His present reality took her back to the anguished days that preceded Edward's death, the endless hours of waiting and unanswered prayers, the feverish hope for a miracle that never materialized. In the end there was nothing the doctors could do; Edward's cirrhotic liver gave out before a donor liver could be found. His death was the most difficult thing she had ever faced. But unlike Harold, at least she had been surrounded by her children, who in her darkest hours had comforted her and made sure she was never alone. Looking back, she saw their outpouring of love and support as one of the greatest blessings of her life, the grace of God wrapped around her like a warm blanket.

Even though Harold's marriage to Lucille had been less than perfect, Liz understood that there was no way to prepare for the loss of your life partner. In the months after Edward's death she'd found herself adrift in an ocean of loneliness, feeling as if nothing would ever be the same. She prayed and read the Bible, clinging to scripture as if it were a life raft from the Titanic. She found new meaning and much solace in the Apostle Paul's writings about suffering, especially in a passage from 2 Corinthians: "But we have this treasure in jars of clay to show that this all-surpassing power is from God and not from us. We are hard pressed on every side, but not crushed; perplexed, but not in despair; persecuted but not abandoned; struck down, but not destroyed." The passage became her mantra, giving her the strength to move forward down the road that led to her new life, as scary and uncertain as that prospect seemed at the time.

Today her loss seemed to have new purpose. She had endured and survived, and she knew what lie ahead for Harold. He would need someone to lean on, and she would be his pillar of support, just as her children were for her. She dared not think about the future without Lucille as much as she wanted to. That would have to wait.

LIZ AND ELLEN FOUND A SMALL TABLE shaded by a canopy of palms outside of Al's Diner, a perennial favorite of locals and tourists. Al, a native of Ypsilanti, Michigan, wowed patrons with two signature dishes: hot roast beef sandwiches and the best New

England clam chowder on the island. Located in The Palms Courtyard Shoppes, the diner, with its no-frills menu and Spartan ambience, offered a down-to-earth diversion from the tony shops and boutiques like Over the Rainbow and Eileen Fisher.

"Ellen, I've got to tell you, you've changed everything!" Liz said, her gray-blue eyes dancing with excitement. She was wearing a pink-and-white polka dot sun dress, the kind Ellen remembered seeing in Simplicity pattern books when she was a girl. "My phone is ringing off the hook with offers to help us move the chapel. Edgar Wilson, a retired artist in town, called me yesterday and said he'd donate five thousand dollars!"

"That's wonderful," Ellen said, trying to find an appropriate note of enthusiasm in the midst of her emotional meltdown. "I had a feeling this was the kind of story that would spark a chord."

"Spark a chord? You lit a fire!" said Liz. "I met with the congregation and they want to move forward, though a few members were worried about incurring the wrath of Foster," she said. "Now I wish someone would explain to me why his money makes him so darn special."

"Agreed." Ellen said. "My grandma used to say 'money changes people and not for the better.'"

"Amen," said Liz, nodding in agreement.

The waiter, tanned with flaxen hair as straight as a paint brush, took their orders.

"Liz, I know this is out of the blue, but the reason I called you today is because you're the only person in the world I can talk to about this . . . I'm not the kind of person who would normally do something like this," she said, exhaling deeply and averting her gaze. "It's very personal—"

"Whatever it is Ellen, I'm happy to listen." Liz inched her chair forward, and placed her hand on Ellen's wrist in a motherly gesture. "Really, let's hear it."

And with that gentle prod, the floodgates opened. At first it was awkward, but once Ellen found her voice the events of the past several days flowed.

"And last night, he came over . . . and we ended up . . . well," she lowered her voice to a whisper, "I slept with him. I'm *so ashamed* to even tell you this. What must you think of me?"

"That, my dear, is the least of your worries," Liz said evenly, taking a sip of her water. "Looks like what you think of yourself is enough for you to deal with at the moment."

"What I'm really upset about is that I've done something that I'll have to live with for the rest of my life. I broke my marriage vows. And for what, a fling with a guy with a wife and three kids? What on earth was I thinking? All of the things I know intellectually that should have stopped me just went right out the window." She thought but didn't add: *When I'm around him, it's like I'm in a hypnotic trance and all that matters is being close to him.* She continued: "I never thought this could happen to me, that I was capable of cheating on my husband. A little flirting, yes, but this, how can I ever face Jeremy when I get home?"

"Ellen, one thing at a time," said Liz, her concern evident. "Far be it for me to condone what you've done. It was wrong. Capital W wrong. What I find encouraging is that you seem to already know that. No you can't go back and rewrite history but you can learn from it," she said, her gaze resting intently on Ellen, "and make sure it doesn't happen again."

Her assurance met with skepticism.

"Even if I could, even if I turned my back on him and never saw or talked to him again, what about the feelings I have for him?" Ellen asked. "I think about him constantly. I can't believe how stupid I've been, letting myself think that I deserve this because I'm getting older and Jeremy doesn't seem to care . . ."

"Ellen, do you think you're the first woman on God's green earth to stumble? Yes, you opened a door that should have remained closed." She straightened the napkin on her lap. "We all fall short, some worse than others. But the good news is that God forgives us anyway."

"But how can I be forgiven after the way I behaved?" she asked, staring at a young couple seated at a nearby table who were engaged in intimate conversation. She wondered if they were married. "I was an active participant in this, I knew where this train was heading and I stayed on it and I'm still on it," Ellen said.

"Maybe you just took the first step in getting off of it," Liz countered.

"What do you mean?" Ellen asked.

"You called me. You had to tell someone. It's like confession. Not exactly your Catholic priest in the booth variety but confession all the same. Which, by the way, is the first step to repentance. First John, first chapter: 'If we confess our sins he who is faithful and just will forgive our sins and cleanse us from unrighteousness.' I'll bet you say that every week in church."

"Yes it's part of our liturgy."

"Do you believe it?"

"I don't know," Ellen replied. "It's just too easy to recite some words, for me to tell you and to think that everything will be okay."

"Are you sure you weren't raised Catholic?" Liz asked, with a wry smile.

"No I wasn't," said Ellen, smiling back. "Lutheran through and through. But it was back when they actually believed in hell—you know fire and brimstone. It stayed with me."

Surfer boy waiter brought over their entrees—a bowl of steaming clam chowder for Liz and a chicken Caesar salad for Ellen. Rafael, the wise-cracking South American parrot in front of Aunt Betty's Tasty Ice Cream Cones, could be heard in the distance entertaining a group of tourists by crackling out Paris Hilton's signature line "that's hot."

Liz took a roll from the basket and opened a packet of butter. "Do you know what the word "repentance" actually means? In Greek the word is *metanoia*, which means a change of mind. But for believers, it's actually much more than that. True repentance is a change in direction, a radical change of heart and behavior. It means letting the grace of God enter and change our lives."

"I want that to happen, but I'm scared because I'm so weak," Ellen said. "What happens when David calls me? What if despite my best intentions I hear his voice and go back into the trance."

"You're right, you don't have the strength to deal with this alone, you need to turn it over to God. It's the only way."

"I know that but—" her voice trailed off, wishing there was a magic pill she could take to jump-start her faith and curb her roller coaster emotions. "I know I need to rely on my faith, but here's what I don't understand. I *am* a believer. I go to church *every* week. I even used to teach Sunday school and despite all that—this still happened."

"Unfortunately, being a believer doesn't put an invisible shield around you to protect you from the world's trials and temptations and good looking men," she said, smiling. "Let me tell you something that you won't hear in church on Sunday morning. A lot of women think there's only one man in the world for them, and once they find their soul mate they'll never be attracted to anyone else. Now that's a big load of hooey but the myth lives on. The plain fact of the matter is that there are all kinds of men that we can fall in love with during our lifetimes. That doesn't mean we act on the desire, it just means that when it happens, we shouldn't be so darn surprised."

Liz couldn't have surprised her more if she had started speaking in tongues. Ellen couldn't believe she was hearing this from someone the age of her grandmother. Where on earth did this woman sitting across the table amass all this wisdom? She was like having a pastor, mother and best friend rolled up into one.

Liz continued, shaking her head, with a look of bemusement. "If I had a dollar for every woman I've ever known who had a serious crush on another man during her marriage, I'd have enough money to move the chapel to Naples!"

Ellen pushed away her salad bowl and reached for her iced tea. Was Liz right? Could she actually find her way out of this moral quagmire? Was she strong enough to walk away?

"Well maybe it's just that misery truly does love company, but hearing you say that, well it makes me feel a little better," Ellen said. Certainly her spiritual work was cut out for her. Trust

God. So easy to say, so hard to do.

"Here's what I think you should do. I'll open the chapel for you and you can spend some quiet time there this afternoon," Liz said. "That's where I go to find solace and peace."

"That would be great, assuming the walls don't cave in when the fallen woman walks in."

"You know," Liz said, smiling brightly, "it's refreshing to see so much guilt in a young person. Too often people today think that everything they do is right just because it's what they want."

For the first time that day, Ellen's inner turmoil dissipated like fog in the first shafts of morning light. She would go to the chapel, it was the perfect place to think and reflect. She looked at the abundance of life around her, people enjoying food, drink, shopping and conversation, birds flitting in and out of flowering shrubs, the midday light splashing the courtyard in golden rays amid pockets of restful shade.

Maybe this wasn't the end of the world after all.

Judy thought she heard a light tap on the door, but it was a false alarm. Her nerves on edge, this was not a visit she was looking forward to.

She had asked Maggie to join her and George for lunch, though the invitation really had nothing to do with food. More to the point it was an opportunity for George and his daughter to meet face-to-face for the first time in several months. Judy desperately wanted George to get over his anger and have a civil conversation with Maggie, but wasn't counting on it. Tumultuous was the best word to describe their relationship; George had decided a long time ago that his youngest daughter, who had been Daddy's Little Girl until she reached adolescence, was not a person he could trust or respect, though he did love her. In his mind, Maggie had skillfully manipulated that love and exploited it to the fullest. He hadn't always been like this, in the early chapters of Maggie's troubles he'd been there for her, talking to school principals, bailing her out from her various scrapes with the law and trying to do everything to get her to change her self-destructive behavior. There had been an unspoken cease-fire when she married Brian, but it didn't last. Maggie resumed her hard-partying ways after the children were born and George lost patience and interest in his daughter's escapades.

"George, she'll be here any minute. Now please, let's just try and get along. She came here to be with us, and I do think she's trying to turn her life around."

"Gee I never heard that one before," he said, his voice dripping with sarcasm.

This wasn't going to be easy.

"What I want to know is when does she stop turning her life around?" George said. "She'll still be raising hell when she's fifty and we'll still be saying—well you'll be saying because I'll be dead—'she's turning her life around.' Nothing ever changes, don't you see that? Oh wait, I've got an idea," he said, his tone mocking. "Let's tell Brian she's turning her life around. I'm sure that'll make all the difference in the world to him now that she's left him—and her sons—for another woman."

"I'm not condoning anything she's done," Judy said defensively, "you know that. It's just that we're all here, we're a family, she cared enough to come, and George, as angry as you are about this, sometimes you just have to let things go. I'm not happy about what's happened, but I don't want this unpleasantness to ruin our vacation."

"Unpleasantness?" George asked, rolling his eyes in reproach. "Our daughter ditches her family and you call it unpleasantness."

Before she could respond, there was a knock on the door. This time for real. Taking a deep breath, Judy went to open the door.

JUDY TRIED TO MAKE THE BEST of what obviously was a tense moment. "Hi honey," she said.

"Hi Mom," Maggie replied, looking a little apprehensive.

"Glad you could come for lunch. Your father is out on the lanai," Judy said, leading her out of the foyer.

"Wow, this is beautiful, you have a gorgeous view here," said Maggie as she entered the living room with its view of perpetual sky and platinum waves. She laughed nervously. "I'm in one of the so-called garden view rooms but what I'm looking at isn't much of a garden. There's a dumpster and a couple of bushes, but it was the only thing I could afford."

Judy's heart went out to Maggie who had spent most of her adult years not having enough money for the things that many people took for granted.

Maggie's hair was pulled back in a ponytail, accentuating her wide-set eyes and delicate features. The resemblance of mother and daughter was striking. It was a mystery, Judy thought, how a mother and daughter could resemble each other physically, but have such disparate personalities and character traits.

"George, Maggie's here," she said, feeling a little foolish because obviously he knew that the minute she knocked on the door. George said nothing, and did not turn to greet her. For the first time that day, Judy had the sinking feeling that this meeting could go worse than she feared.

"Hi Dad," Maggie said, the trepidation in her voice apparent. "I know you probably don't want to see me but I needed to be here."

"Did you? For us, or for you?" he said combatively.

Whatever composure Maggie had been able to muster for this encounter with her recalcitrant father was evaporating. Judy could see her daughter was visibly upset at her father's inability to even say "hello."

"Well you can be angry, you can stay angry at me for the rest of your life but I'm not sure what good it's going to do," Maggie said, standing with her thumbs tucked into the top of her low-rise denim jeans. "Listen if you want an apology, here it is. I'm sorry my life is screwed up. I'm sorry I'm a lesbian. I'm sorry I've disappointed you my entire frickin' life." Tears started to form at the corners of her eyes but she wiped them away in a defiant gesture.

"Oh here we go, the pity poor Maggie routine," said George, turning around to look directly at his daughter, beads of perspiration forming on his forehead. "The thing that you'll never understand is that sorry is only a word and it means nothing when it comes out of your mouth. You can be sorry the first time, maybe the second, but you've spent your entire life saying you're sorry, and where does it get you? If I thought for a minute this was the last time I was ever going to hear 'sorry' I would jump for joy. I would throw a party. But I've been down this road with you too many times. In a few months, you'll be kickin' out your new girlfriend for somebody else who happens to catch your fancy. And let's not forget about your sons that you've abandoned. I suppose you're sorry about that too."

"Great, bring the boys into it. That's a cheap shot." She paused to catch her breath. "This is a waste of time. Okay don't forgive me. Stay angry. That solves a lot of problems, doesn't it? Do you feel better? And by the way I didn't abandon my sons. They're just not with me right now."

"Maggie, George, both of you sit down and stop talking," Judy said in as stern a voice as she could muster to quell the battle. Father and daughter glared at each other, and for a long moment no one moved or spoke. Finally George took a chair at the end of the lanai. Maggie warily sat down in a chair at the patio table next to her mother as if the proximity would shield her from her father's animosity.

"George," Judy implored, "Maggie came here to celebrate our anniversary. It took a fair amount of courage for her to come here and face her family given the circumstances. I'm not in favor of punishing her for doing so."

"Maggie," she continued. "You've made some decisions we find difficult to accept. Your father loves you and if he didn't he wouldn't be so angry with you. I know it's hard but I want both of you to put all of this aside for now and try to be civil to one another. For our family. For me."

A long silence ensued. Down on the beach, a boy and his father threw a football, laughing. Along the shore the excited voices of happy children fluttered in the breeze. So much life out there, so much anger in here.

Finally, Maggie spoke.

"Mom, I don't want to ruin this trip for you. That's not why I came. I want to be part of this family and I want you both to love me," her voice cracked as she started to cry.

George sat stone-faced for a few moments that seemed an

eternity. If he took this opportunity to push Maggie away again, Judy didn't know what she would do. She looked first at her husband and then at her daughter. Life had so many good things to offer, certainly as a family they'd been abundantly blessed, yet when it came to their relationship with Maggie she couldn't help but think about how much they'd lost, and what might have been.

Maggie was silent, waiting for her father to speak. Finally he shifted his eyes upward to hers, and said gruffly, "You know I love you."

"I love you too Dad."

Anything beyond that could shatter the cessation of hostilities, both of them knew this. So they sat quietly for a moment, watching down below as the son lobbed a wild pass to his father, who took a flying leap to catch the football as his son cheered him on.

"Well then that's settled," Judy said, trying to lighten the mood. "Now let's have some lunch."

E llen got the check, paid it and took a sip of her iced tea, soaking up her lush surroundings. An influx of well-heeled shoppers driving expensive cars jockeyed for position in the parking lot, anxious for a spot to park their Lexuses or Escalade SUVs. Women sporting colorful Nicole Miller sundresses and Louis Vuitton handbags sauntered in front of the boutiques, trying to decide where to drop several hundred dollars on their afternoon shopping sprees.

"At least let me leave the tip," Liz implored. "I should be buying you lunch, after all you've done for us."

"No way. Not after what I've just put you through. You have no idea how much I appreciate your coming to lunch and listening to all this."

"Don't give it a second thought," Liz said. "Oh by the way, did I mention that I did an interview with the *National Tribune*?

"Really?"

"Yes ma'am. They sent a photographer to take a picture of me in front of the chapel."

"That's huge. Wait till Foster hears about that!"

"Louise and Ronnie are afraid he'll get angry. So I said to them, what's he going to do—dynamite the chapel instead of bulldozing it!" She laughed heartily.

Suddenly Ellen was blinded by the glare of something in the parking lot. Using her right hand to shield her eyes, she squinted to see the source of the beaming light. It appeared to be coming from the highly-polished chrome mirror on a motorcycle parked in front of Over the Rainbow. She recognized it immediately.

"Liz, speaking of Foster, do you see that motorcycle parked over there?"

"Yes, quite a machine, it belongs to Michael Thompson who owns Over the Rainbow. He's our resident Fabio, what you young people call a "hunk." A real playboy, but I hear that he's settled down since he moved in with his girlfriend Becca, who runs the boutique for him. You know they have dresses in there that sell for six hundred dollars!"

"Really," said Ellen, her excitement building. "Liz, this is very strange. Do you know where else I saw that motorcycle?"

"Where?" Liz replied, curious as to why this was worth mentioning.

"In the driveway of Gregory Foster's house."

"Really?"

"That bike, a Braxton Firestorm, sitting in the driveway of Foster's house the day the TV crew came to the chapel. That's a vintage custom bike, they're worth a small fortune. It's Jeremy's dream bike, and I seriously doubt there are two of them on this island. I was standing in front of Foster's house with the reporter when I saw it. It was odd, the windows of the house were wide open, it definitely looked like someone was home but no one answered the door. I really didn't give it another thought—until now."

"Do you think?—" Liz's eyes widened.

"You tell me. You live here, what do you think?"

"Hmm . . . could be," she said slowly, shaking her head. "Before he moved in with Becca, that man had a different woman every other week. Wealthy women. I heard that what he was really interested in—oh here I go gossiping again, do you know that one year I actually gave up gossiping for Lent which was way harder than giving up chocolate—anyway, I heard that he was dating those women so they would buy his art. He's an artist, post-modern, though I've heard mixed reviews of his work."

"Tell me about Foster's wife."

"She's young, beautiful and has a figure like one of those underwear models for Victoria's Closet or whatever the name of that store is with the half-naked women in the window," Liz said.

"Victoria's Secret," Ellen interjected, grinning.

"Whatever. I've only met her a few times, she seemed nice enough. Came to the chapel one Sunday, never came back. I wondered if she was there to worship or to scope out the new house."

"What if . . . can you think of any other reason why Michael would be there on a Tuesday afternoon?" Ellen asked.

"Not a one. Foster goes back to Chicago during the week when she's down here, so she's pretty much alone," Liz said.

"Foster is what, thirty years her senior. Fabio is a young stud. Interesting. Of course I have no room whatsoever to comment on this!" Ellen felt perversely giddy at the supreme irony of her discussing someone else's infidelity today of all days. She and Liz shared a good laugh.

"Ellen, I have an idea. A little far-fetched, and if it doesn't work I'll chalk it up to dementia. I'm seventy-six, I'm entitled to indulge in a little senility, right," she said with a look in her eye that was anything but confusion. "Here's what I think we should do."

Liz leaned over the table, and laid out her plan.

ELLEN HAD PICKED UP LIZ FOR LUNCH, so they drove to the chapel together in Ellen's rented Nissan Altima. They didn't expect to see a large red pickup truck from Conway Construction parked in the clearing. Ellen guided the car into the spot next to it.

"Well would you look at that," Liz said. Though she knew construction crews eventually were coming, seeing the truck was unnerving. Ellen turned off the car, and they sat there for a moment before getting out.

"I'm thinking this could be a divine intervention," Ellen said cheerily. "Should we execute our plan?"

"There's no time like the present," replied Liz. They got out of the car and started up the path, Liz walking briskly in front of her. Ellen marveled at the youthful energy of her elderly companion. Liz was a woman on a mission, the question was would it work.

As they turned the final bend of the walking path, the chapel came into view, its white walls awash in the dazzling afternoon sunlight, the flower beds ablaze in ebullient golds, fiery reds and splashes of orange. Ellen knew what Liz was thinking as she looked at this idyllic tableau of the ocean and all of its amaranthine wonders; even if they were somehow able to raise enough money to move the chapel it would never, ever be the same.

In the distance, a man and woman stood on the beach toward Foster's house, the man obviously explaining something, using his hands to gesture and point.

"Liz, is that Mrs. Foster?" Ellen said, not believing their luck of finding her outside.

"None other."

"Looks like Mrs. Foster is planning her dream house," Ellen remarked wryly. Ellen could only imagine the caliber of house Foster would build. Mega mansions were sprouting up all over the Gulf Coast, each one more palatial and ostentatious than the rest, making the modest homes of the 1970s and 1980s look dated and tired.

"Are you sure you're up for this?" Liz asked her.

"Oh yes."

They made their way across the beach, walking toward Jennifer and the construction man. Immersed in conversation, they did not notice Ellen and Liz until they were about twenty feet away. Ellen's low-heeled sandals kept sinking into the spongy sand, making it difficult to walk.

Jennifer, understandably, looked surprised.

"Mrs. Foster, Liz Taylor." said Liz, thrusting out her hand to Jennifer. "What a coincidence that we should meet. I was just thinking about you today."

Jennifer, looking like a reality TV show vixen, wore low-rise white denim shorts and a hot-pink tank top.

She greeted Liz with the kind of enthusiasm people have for door-to-door missionaries.

"Oh hello Liz," Jennifer said flatly. "This is Jeff Goldman of Conway Construction. He's going to be managing our building project for the new house."

"Nice to meet you," Liz said to Jeff, and then introduced Ellen as her friend. Goldman's cell phone rang, apparently an important call from another wealthy client, because he excused himself and walked away for privacy.

Ignoring the cool reception, Liz emanated goodwill. "Jennifer, I'm so glad I ran into you," she gushed. "I've been meaning to stop by. You know I feel so bad about all of this hullabaloo in the newspapers about the chapel. Seems the press just loves this story, my phone is ringing off the hook! Can't imagine why a little chapel would cause such a stir, well with all the terrible things going on in the world today."

"Yes it's rather amazing. I wonder how the papers even found out about it," Jennifer said, her tone one of suspicion.

"Well you know *those people* always have their ear to the ground," Liz said. "Or maybe one of our parishioners is Deep Throat." A pause. "That's assuming you're old enough to remember Watergate." Liz's smile appeared to be genuine.

"Well of course, I remember Watergate . . . well actually I remember learning about it in school." Jennifer said defensively.

"I just hope there's no hard feelings," Liz said genially. "This is your property and you and your husband have every right to do with it what you please. Oh, it's not easy to see all the change going on around here, but that's progress I suppose, just a little harder for us old folks to accept. But there is one thing . . . I have a *big* favor to ask. I had no idea Gregory was a Braxton man. Oh, the memories it brings back! My Edward, God rest his soul, how he loved that motorcycle! He used to take me out on it every weekend, I hung on for dear life when we were on those curvy country roads. Braxton Motorcycle Company was one of his clients and he traveled all over the country on their behalf. Anyway, I would be eternally grateful if you could persuade Gregory to take me out for a ride one Sunday afternoon. Tell him it would make an old lady very happy," she said, flashing Jennifer a magnanimous smile.

Jennifer's plastered-on smile faded and Ellen could see her visibly tense. Liz may have struck gold.

"I'm not sure I know what you're talking about," Jennifer said.

"I'm talking about Gregory's Braxton. His motorcycle," Liz said.

"You must be mistaken. He doesn't have a motorcycle. Why do you think he has a motorcycle?"

"I told her about it," Ellen said, seizing the moment. "My husband's a closet gearhead, and I couldn't help but notice that there was a seriously vintage pearl-white Braxton Firestorm in your driveway the day the TV crew came out here. That anchorwoman from Channel 14 insisted we go over to your house, well I didn't want her wandering around on your property alone so I walked over with her. That's when I saw the bike, of course I couldn't wait to tell Jeremy. He said there are only a dozen or so of those bikes on the road today. What a coup for Gregory to have gotten his hands on one. He must love it."

"I don't know what you're talking about. Gregory doesn't have a bike," she stammered. "What day was it? Probably a workman." Jennifer replied.

"Now that I think of it, this really is the oddest coincidence," Liz said, furrowing her brows. "Do you know who else has bike like that? Becca's boyfriend, the painter, the one who looks like Brad Pitt. Anyway I saw it one day when I was at Over the Rainbow, he'd just gotten it and Becca and I were laughing because he was as excited as a ten-year-old boy. Oh, but I couldn't ask him for a ride, he's too good looking to have an old lady like me on the back of his bike. That's why it would be so grand if you could ask Mr. Foster. Or if you'd rather not, I'll ask him myself the next time I see him. Bet he'll be surprised, I mean what are the odds that there are two of those bikes on the island! Hope he doesn't get upset, you know how men are with their toys."

Jennifer's cool demeanor snapped. "What's this all about?" she said icily.

"What on earth to you mean?" Liz said, seemingly mystified.

"What do you want?" Jennifer said.

"I'm not sure I know what you're talking about," said Liz, wide-eyed and innocent. She hesitated for a very long moment, sizing up her fifty-year-younger adversary, then shifted gears. "Well since you asked, one thing I do want so desperately is to save the chapel. The best way to do that would be a perpetual easement on your property. You could still build your house, just a little smaller."

Ellen, who had spent a fair amount of time dealing with egomaniacal CEOs and senior executives over her career couldn't remember when she'd seen anything so gutsy. She had to hand it to Liz, she was a pistol.

Jennifer said nothing, turned and walked a few steps away from them, as if unable to decide the best course of action. So far, the plan was working beautifully, they'd caught her off guard, and she couldn't be sure what they knew or what they would do with the information. She had to be thinking *what if they went to Gregory or Becca* for that matter. A volatile, jilted girlfriend could be dangerous. It was a fifty-fifty shot, and it all came down to how much of a risk taker Jennifer Foster was. Clearly she seemed guilty of cheating on her husband, her nervousness and lack of any plausible explanation for the motorcycle in the driveway were proof of that.

Ellen looked at her closely. Jennifer was pretty, but not beautiful, and though her makeup was perfectly applied, her features looked a little harsh in the glaring sunlight. Ellen had always wondered where women like Jennifer would be without pricey cosmetics, high heels and cleavage, not necessarily in that order.

Jennifer won a reprieve when the construction man clicked off his call and started walking toward them. "Sorry about that," he said apologetically, "we've got three other projects going right now, it's a little crazy. So are you ready to get started? I can show you some of the ideas I have for siting," he said. His aim-to-please demeanor was well suited to the wiles of wealthy trophy wives.

"Jeff—I'm so sorry. I just remembered something. I have an appointment this afternoon that I need to get to. Can we reschedule? I also think it would be good if I had more time to think about this before we go any further," said Jennifer. Then she turned to Liz and Ellen. "Sorry I've got to run, but I'll call you if I change my mind," she said, her voice brittle, betraying the indelible fear she was desperate to hide.

"Well I hope you talk to Gregory, I do so badly want a ride on that motorcycle," Liz said, her eyes sparkling with mischief.

Jennifer turned abruptly and started walking toward her house; Jeff the construction manager looked perplexed.

Ellen wanted to jump up and down and give Liz a high five, but knew it had to wait. They walked over to the chapel in giddy silence. Once inside, they burst out laughing, and reached out to hug each other, jumping up and down like teenagers. "Oh my gosh I cannot believe what just happened there! You were incredible!" Ellen exclaimed. "What an amazing actress you are Elizabeth Taylor!"

"That was something, wasn't it?" she said, a little breathless. "My heavens, who'd have thought I'd go to such extremes! I do hope the good Lord forgives me for a little bribery. I'm going to have a lot of explaining to do when I get up to those pearly gates! I just hope it works!"

A shriek pierced the silence in the living room of Julia's penthouse.

"Mom guess what?" exclaimed Nicole. "Alicia is HERE! Her dad didn't have to go to London, so they flew down this morning. They have a condo in Bonita, she says she's just a half hour away." The news had snapped Nicole out of an hour-long trance during which she'd been texting friends on her new cell phone.

"Really," said Julia, distracted by a message on her BlackBerry that required her immediate attention. Ever since Julia had been named senior vice president of supply chain operations, she frequently had to deal with pressing operational or management issues on weekends and vacations. She had surrendered to this onslaught of scud missiles into her personal life without resistance or complaining. It was simply the price one paid for a high-octane career, moreover, such diligence was required to shatter the pervasive myth that women with children weren't up to the rigors and demands of the executive suite. A black belt in time management, Julia juggled her personal and professional life with the stamina of an Olympic-hopeful figure skater. What she could barely acknowledge even to herself, though, was the gnawing irrational fear that one slipup, one crucial unreturned call during a soccer game or dance recital could sideline her relentless ambition.

"OH MY GOSH! I cannot believe this. Alicia says CrazyEx

Rampage is playing a show in Fort Myers tonight. Remember I told you about them, they're awesome. I just bought their CD and we can still get tickets!" Nicole beamed.

"Refresh my memory," Julia said, unwilling to hide her displeasure. "Is that the band with the lead singer who just had a baby with the porn star and then was arrested with the prostitute?" Appalled that her daughter could be so excited to see a band led by such a chauvinist Neanderthal she wondered once again *what's with this generation*? Nicole and her friends enjoyed freedoms and rights unknown to previous generations of women, yet dressed like pole dancers and worshipped misogynist rock stars. And sex, well she couldn't even think about the fact that blow jobs were as common as handshakes among her daughter's privileged Hollister-wearing BMW-driving friends. She had once thought a thirty-five thousand dollar-a-year private school education would shield her from these realities, but had learned instead that the wealth of her daughters' classmates merely fueled their desire for cultural trash.

"Mom" Nicole said. "Can I go?"

"Nicole, think about what you're asking," said Julia, her attention now fully diverted from the message-laden BlackBerry. "The luau is tonight and everyone is going, Grandma, Grandpa, Uncle David, Aunt Marianne—"

"But Mom, the real party is Saturday night. Grandma won't mind. Plus there are so many other people here she won't even miss me. Please Mom, Alicia says she and Justin can drive over and pick me up," she said. Justin was Alicia's eighteen-year-old brother.

Julia could feel the anger rising from her temples.

"Mom. *Please*," Nicole begged. "Can I go?"

"Tell me you're kidding. Do you really think I'm going to say yes?"

"Mom, I have to see this band. It would be *so cool*."

Julia didn't understand why she needed to explain to her daughter why she couldn't go see some depraved rocker, but didn't feeling like arguing.

"Where's your father? I haven't seen him since we got back."

"He's down at the pool bar. He said the pina coladas cost twelve dollars."

Julia said nothing, but was mildly annoyed. There would be plenty of time for cocktails at the luau tonight, and she didn't understand why Richard just couldn't wait until later. Lately, it seemed like his drinking had been exceeding the boundaries of what could be considered "social" and it was starting to worry her.

"Mom," her daughter said insistently. "What if I talk to Grandma and explain the situation?"

"Nicole, what do you think Grandma is going to say? Of course she'll say, 'whatever you want honey.' But she won't mean it, not for a minute. This is her anniversary. Do you have any concept of what a remarkable accomplishment it is to be married for fifty years? I know that's a little beyond the comprehension of an adolescent mind, but why don't you try to think about that for a minute. Tell you what. Why don't you invite Alicia to the luau? Then at least you'll have a friend to pal around with. I think that's a fair compromise."

"Mom," Nicole groaned. "Why would Alicia want to come hang around some dumb luau where a bunch of people are going to be stuffing their faces with a pig they burned and tortured all day? It's horrible, and I don't even want to be a part of it."

"Nicole, people have been eating animals for thousands of years. I don't understand why we're even discussing this. We're here for the anniversary, we're going to the luau tonight—end of discussion."

"No that's not the *end of discussion,*" she said, contemptuously mocking her mother's voice in the way that makes their parents momentarily wonder why they ever wanted children. "I'm going to be with Grandma all day tomorrow. So why can't I do something fun tonight? It's not fair."

Right, tell me about fair, Julia thought, looking at her daughter with her $120 designer top, $200 cell phone and salon manicure. Nicole's obliviousness to her good fortune, her sense of entitlement for anything she wanted as if that in and of itself were enough of a reason, troubled her. She also knew Nicole had no intention of giving up the fight, so she brought her focus back to her BlackBerry. "I have to make a call to the office, something's come up. If you want to continue to discuss this, I'd suggest you talk to your father."

"You know Daddy won't let me go, so don't pretend you're doing me a favor."

Julia picked up her BlackBerry, and headed toward the front door. Dealing with Nicole drained her emotionally, and she didn't understand why their relationship was punctuated with these ongoing battles. "I have to go outside because I can't get a good signal in here," she said. Just the excuse she needed. She shut the door firmly behind her, careful not to let it slam.

Taking a break from their bike ride, Maggie related her encounter with her father to David. They rested in the shade of a cedar gazebo several yards off the bike path that meandered past the quaint shops of downtown Sanibel. David had run into his sister after lunch, and knew she needed to blow off some steam. Marianne wasn't happy about it, but he was relieved to have an excuse to get away.

"What is it with him," Maggie said. "The older he gets the more of an asshole he becomes—is that it?"

"Try to think of it this way," he said, taking a generous swig from his water bottle. "If he didn't love you so much it wouldn't matter to him."

"Nice try," she said. "I know I can always count on you for a healthy dose of BS."

"It's not BS. You've always been Daddy's Little Girl, he just doesn't know how to deal with Daddy's Adult Lesbo Girl," he said, grinning. She hit him playfully on his arm in protest. "Seriously, give him some time, I think he'll come around."

"Do you really think so?" she asked. Maggie took off her sunglasses, her eyes reflecting a vulnerable promise of hope. Wearing very little makeup, she looked radiant and healthy.

"Well I'd say it's definitely within the realm of possibility," he reassured her. "But there are no guarantees, this is Dad we're talking about after all. Mom will work on him, and that'll help."

"Mom has been great," Maggie replied. "I wasn't sure what to expect from her. But she's been pretty accepting, all things considered."

A magnificent great blue heron executed a graceful landing along the edge of the bird sanctuary, not far from where they were sitting. Outside of the gazebo stood a prehistoric-looking saw palmetto with fan-like daggers. Jungle-green leaves from firebush and fiddlewood shrubs heaped over the brick path. In this tranquil setting, he was grateful to have some time alone with his sister.

"Think about it," he said. "Here's the best and worst thing about being a parent: You never stop being one."

Maggie offered a wry smile, shaking her head in agreement. "I know. The whole kid thing is overwhelming." She paused as if not sure whether to continue in this vein. David's attention shifted to the great blue heron as it slowly made its way along the grassy edge of the swamp.

"So here's my dirty little secret," she said, raising her eyes to him, "and it scares the hell out of me. Sometimes I just don't know if I can give that much. The boys, they're wonderful, I love them so much but I can't help thinking they deserve someone better than me for their mother. The everyday life of being a mom, it just sucks the life out of me. I really don't think I was cut out for this."

It was a piercing revelation, but David was not shocked. Truth be told, he felt the same way more than he cared to admit. In the child-centered culture he inhabited, it was blasphemy of the worst order. It also sounded incredibly selfish, for which he was ashamed.

He sighed deeply. "You're not going to get an argument from me," he said. "Ever since Colin was born, our house is bedlam twenty-four seven. Emma has tantrums—they're not getting better they're getting worse. Ethan is glued to video games and still wets the bed, and we have no idea why. We're constantly driving the kids to some activity, soccer, tai kwon do and now Marianne has Emma in a yoga class on Monday nights because she thinks it will help calm her. Our kids have every new tech gadget or toy but they still want more."

"You've taken on a lot David. Your career, the kids, Marianne, it's such a different world today."

"I remember being a kid and spending an entire day making a fort with my friends out of a refrigerator box we found in the garbage. My son hardly ever goes outside. I try to get him to catch a baseball and he's bored in five minutes. And I think about Mom and Dad raising us, it looked so simple, at least from my perspective. Was it this hard for them do you think?"

"Not until I came along," Maggie said, grinning. "At least you have Marianne. She loves being a mother."

"Yes, Marianne loves being a mother," said David, with an unintended trace of sarcasm.

Maggie didn't miss a trick. "Are you and Marianne okay?" she asked.

"Yeah we're fine," he replied.

"Cut the crap big brother. What's up?"

"It's just that . . . it's not Marianne, it's me, it's the whole situation," he said.

A few yards away, the stalwart heron drew up its prodigious wings and ascended in an awe-inspiring upward motion. How on earth could something that big lift itself into the atmosphere, he wondered.

He leaned forward, resting his forearms on his thighs, hands clasped. "In a nutshell, I'm not really cut out to be the kind of father Marianne wants and expects me to be. I'm like Dad . . . Provider Dad, come home from work and play with the kids for an hour and be done with it Dad. But instead, I come home, we grab dinner, go to Ethan's soccer game, take Emma to dance, start the two-hour bedtime ritual which may or may not produce results, try to keep Emma out of our bed because she's afraid of monsters . . . like I said, it's just exhausting. And I can't wait until the morning because I get to drink a cup of coffee and get the hell out of there. So how's that for an honest conversation about kids."

"I think you're brutally honest and that's a good thing. There's nothing here for you to be ashamed of," Maggie said. "Whoever said we're cut out for these lives? Society tells us to get married and have lots of babies and you'll live happily ever after. Look at the divorce rates, more than half of us can't make it. The other half drinks heavily. But marriage, this conventional life is foisted upon us by our culture, our families, our religion—"

"But I *chose* this life, Maggie," David said, sensing that Maggie was playing the victim card of which he would have no part. "I *chose* to get married and have three children. You know what I've turned into? A baby boom whiner." He grimaced at the thought. "Is there anything worse?"

"No you're not, you sound like a father who is a little overwhelmed with a young family. But you'll get through this, you and Marianne will get through this together."

His silence startled her.

"David, what aren't you telling me?"

Overhead a lone roseate spoonbill started to make its descent, its iridescent chiffon pink breastplate clearly visible. It reminded him of the tour in the wildlife refuge, when he'd seen Ellen standing in the distance, so lovely, in the midst of all the activity around the lake he could see no one else, only her. It was too hard to answer the question and too hard to lie.

"Listen big brother, if you can't talk to me about this, who can you talk to? Tell me what's going on."

He desperately wanted to confide in her, but realized there would be no taking back what he was going to say. Talking about these feelings could destroy what little control he seemed to have left over them.

He looked over at his sister, her eyes filled with genuine concern. "I'm not sure I'm in love with Marianne anymore."

This time it was Maggie's turn to be silent. He knew this would hit her hard. She had always put him and Marianne on a pedestal for their seemingly idyllic marriage and family. Amid the chaos of her life, they were an oasis of calm in a turbulent and unstable world.

"How long have you felt like this?" she asked quietly.

"I don't know. I don't know anything anymore. I think I've felt this way for a long time but I didn't want to admit it because it's just too horrible to even contemplate."

They sat in silence again, watching a cadre of white ibis circling the clearing. Occasionally riders passed by on the trail, fit-looking senior citizens, parents trailering young children in brightly colored traveling cocoons.

Finally Maggie spoke. Of course he had known she would get to this question. "Is there someone else," she said, her voice low, as if she didn't want to know the answer.

"Maggie, I really shouldn't say anymore... please understand," he said, anguished over the searing memory of last night.

"Just know this David, I'm here for you and I'm not going to judge you no matter what you tell me. That's the great thing about being a fuck-up most of your life. You learn not to judge. There are a whole lot of people who go through this life—Julia is one of them—whose goal is to have the perfect life," she continued. "Perfect children, perfect careers, perfect houses—and you know what, it's all bullshit. There's no such thing. Sooner or later, something or someone is going to come along and break the frickin' glass."

David felt it was an unfair assault on Julia, but nevertheless acknowledged the essential truth of what she was saying. Ten years ago, he might have disagreed with his sister. But the older he got, the more shattered glass he'd seen—divorce, drugs, alcohol, damaged careers that ruined people, serious illness that irrevocably changed people's lives. Like a motorist who looks away from a car wreck on the expressway, he tried not to dwell on such things. Yet this undercurrent of malaise was profoundly depressing, and certainly a radical departure from the boundless optimism of his youth.

"I don't know if this is going to help you but I'm going to tell you anyway," Maggie continued. "Sasha isn't the reason I quit drinking. The reason I quit drinking was because I tried to kill myself one night with a half dozen Xanax and bourbon chasers.

Sounded like a good idea at the time," she said ruefully. "I'd just left Brian, had a terrible conversation with him on the phone, I was overwhelmed with guilt, and I couldn't take the pain any more. I just wanted to stop hurting. Thank God Sasha came home and found me and took me to the emergency room."

"Maggie, I had no idea," David said, stunned. "Promise me you'll never, ever think about doing something like that again." He put his arm protectively around her shoulder.

"I didn't tell you to worry you," she said, her head on his shoulder. She paused a minute, then sat up and looked straight at him, her face aglow in afternoon sunlight. "I'm much, much better now, I think I finally hit the proverbial bottom and I never, ever want to go back to that dark place again. But my point is this: You can't keep all this stuff bottled up inside because eventually it'll kill you or make you seriously ill. You don't have to talk to me about it, but find someone you can trust to talk about it—I don't care if it's a shrink or a minister or someone at work. It's a toxic brew. You need to get it out."

David stretched out his tired legs in front of him. He wasn't a person who leaned on others, but right now he desperately needed a friend.

"Maggie . . . I don't even know where to start," he paused and exhaled deeply. "I met someone this week."

Her eyes widened and she placed her hand on his. David took another sip of his water, and told his sister everything that had happened. Under sapphire skies bathed in golden light, they talked there for a very long time.

All day long, preparations for the luau had unfolded at a frantic pace at the Paradise Resort & Spa as scores of hotel workers transformed the beach and outdoor terrace into a Polynesian Shangri-la. A huge pit had been dug in the sand for the day-long roast of the kulua pig. The buffet tables, painstakingly edged with raffia hula skirts, were topped with festive runners of ornamental fishnet sprinkled with seashells, glass baubles and scores of tea light candles. More than a dozen tiki bars had been hastily erected in the same way amusement park rides sprout out of the empty parking lots of shopping malls. In the kitchen, an army of Latino cooks tackled the preparation of the traditional Hawaiian menu of poi, huli-huli chicken, pineapple, haupia and other Polynesian favorites.

Strings of plastic lights were strung over the pavilion, the tags that said "Made in China" not visible. Sturdy boxes of carefully-packed white and lavender orchids sat in cavernous refrigerators in the resort's kitchens, the delicate flowers awaiting placement behind the ears of female guests. In keeping with tradition, a woman wore an orchid behind her right ear if available, behind the left if taken.

More than a dozen cases of Captain Morgan Rum were on hand for the hundreds of mai tais and pina coladas that would be served tonight. Several large Marshall speakers were stacked on the stage to pump out the music of the islands. Every detail, from the mangos to the flowers to the native Hawaiian hula dancers had been orchestrated with unerring attention to detail. More than 300 tiki torches had been brought in for the occasion.

At sunset, the festivities would begin.

JUDY PULLED THE EMERALD GREEN SARONG DRESS out of her closet and laid it on the bed. It was a gift from Julia. She couldn't believe how well the dress fit, it was as if it were made for her. She'd bought tiny matching palm tree stud earrings and a woven straw handbag with bamboo trim. Judy loved getting dressed up and going out as much now as she had as a young woman of seventeen, embracing wardrobe and accessories as one of her hobbies. Julia had definitely inherited her sense of style; Maggie, well, Maggie was a different matter.

"George, are you going to start getting ready?" she said, projecting her voice into the other room. George had been in a foul mood ever since Maggie had left, and she was worried it would spill into the evening.

He didn't answer; she assumed he was napping.

"George, are you awake?"

She went into the living room and found him sitting on the sofa, staring rigidly at a soap opera beaming from the flat panel television, which was on mute.

"George, did you hear me, you need to start getting ready." She walked in front of him and pushed the off button on the TV.

A confused look flashed over his face. "Ready for what?"

"The luau," she said.

"Where is it?" he asked.

"It's here, George. At the resort. Julia got you a new shirt for tonight," she said, trying to edge the fear out of her voice over his forgetting something this significant.

"All right. Just give me a few minutes," he said.

Why now, she agonized, her mood crushed again by the reminder that there was something very wrong with her husband. She looked at the dress. It wasn't that long ago she could have put it on and gone out for the evening without a care in the world. Now all she could do was worry.

BY EIGHT THIRTY, THE LUAU WAS IN FULL SWING. Partygoers talked, laughed and swayed to the gentle rhythms of Hawaiian music under a lattice of pineapple and coconut lights twinkling against the velvety night sky. People crowded around the tiki bars, ordering tropical drinks with names like lava flow, scorpion, Caribbean martini and blue Hawaii. Others patiently waited their turn to fill their plates at buffet tables heaving with huge platters of roasted pig, sweet potatoes, chicken, poke and other savory dishes.

Gertrude and Eunice, Julia and her family, Maggie, Judy and George and Judy's sister Maureen and her husband Frank were seated at a long table enjoying the feast, comparing notes on how delicious everything was. Nicole and Rachel wore orchids tucked behind their right ears, the other women had opted for fragrant orchid leis.

"Have you tried this yet?" Judy asked Julia, who was seated next to her at the long table. Julia looked amazing in an off-the-shoulder lavender dress that matched the orchid in her hair, which was swept off her neck in a French twist. Some women just had it all, people would often think of Julia, and it was for that very reason that most women didn't like her.

"That's the poke—it's delicious," said Julia, referring to the mixture of raw yellowfin tuna marinated in sea salt, soy sauce, sesame oil and chili pepper. "Richard and I always go to the luau when we're in Maui, and this is as good as anything you'll find there."

"Wait till I tell the ladies at bridge about this," said Gertrude, who was wearing an orange tropical-print shirt, a mirror of her sister's except Eunice's was bright turquoise. "Have you seen the hula dancers? They're wearing coconut bras!"

"I saw them," Richard said, feigning a dreamy stare. "They're gorgeous."

"What, the coconut bras or the hula dancers?" asked Julia.

"Both," Richard said, prompting a look of feigned reproach from his wife.

"Dad," said Nicole, with the special tone of disgust teenagers reserve for their parents. "Don't be a sexist pig. This isn't the seventies."

"Hush, little girl, you're insulting the main course!" said Uncle Frank, cherishing in equal parts his longstanding reputation as life of the party and his third scorpion, a rum drink known for packing a powerful intoxicating punch.

"I feel bad about eating without David and Marianne," said Judy. "I wonder what happened."

"I ran into them earlier, they were going to be late because they needed to get the kids settled in at the Kid's Club," said Maggie, trying to be nonchalant but still reeling from the conversation she had with her brother a few hours earlier.

"Rachel, you're not going up to the buffet again, you've already been up there twice," Julia said.

"Oh Mom, I just want one more slice of banana bread, please, it's so good." Julia relented, and took a sip of her strawberry daiquiri.

George pulled his chair back from the table. "All this good food and drink makes me want a cigar," he said, eliciting moans from the women around him. "Don't worry, I won't smoke it here."

"Hurry back, George, the entertainment is going to start in about twenty minutes," Judy said.

"I'll be back. Don't want to miss the hula dancers," he said, smiling.

"I'll go with you Grandpa," said Nicole. "I need to walk off some of this food."

And with that, the two of them started walking toward Judy and George's condo and its cache of Cuban cigars.

*　　*　　*

GEORGE AND NICOLE SAT DOWN AT A TABLE on a stone patio landscaped for privacy, the centerpiece of a large courtyard that was flanked by a quadrant of identical white stucco buildings. The sunset had vanished into the deepening shadows of nightfall, turning the rows of windows into a checkerboard of light. The sound of the surf, voices and laughter from the luau ebbed and flowed on the crest of gossamer breezes.

As much as Nicole hated cigars, she adored her grandfather. At least they were outside so she could avoid having to inhale the toxins. The bond between them had always been strong, and even the teenage years, a time when such relationships often grow distant, did not derail their mutual affection. In her eyes, Grandpa George was cool.

George had just taken the first puff of his cigar when they saw Marianne hurriedly walking toward them. Holding Colin on her right hip, a large leather bag slung haphazardly on her opposite shoulder, her hair breaking free from her messy ponytail, she looked frazzled.

"I cannot believe the day I'm having," she lamented, as Colin started to squirm out of her grasp. "Have you seen David? This is the second time today he's disappeared. Anyway, can I ask you both a big favor? I have to run into town to get some diapers for Colin. Ethan and Emma are at the Kid's Club. It'd be so much easier if I didn't have to take Colin. He's pretty rambunctious right now, I think he's on a sugar high and he missed his nap. Can you watch him? I won't be more than fifteen minutes, especially if I don't have to take him." While she was talking, Colin, his legs kicking as if riding an invisible bicycle, broke loose. Marianne immediately lunged for him and snatched him back.

"Sure Aunt Marianne. Grandpa and I will watch him, no problem. Hey Colin, come here by Auntie Nicole," she said, her arms beckoning him.

"Great," Marianne replied, relieved, as she transferred Colin onto Nicole's lap. "Thank you so much. I promise won't be long." Reaching into her bag, she found a bottle, container of fish crackers and a bright blue miniature cell phone and placed them on the table. She leaned over and kissed Colin, who was unfazed by this transfer from the mother ship to this young woman he barely knew. "Bye-bye sweetie, Mommy will be back in a few minutes," she said, then quickly walked away toward the parking lot.

"Hey there little guy," said George, smiling at Colin.

Nicole looked at George's cigar disapprovingly, and said to Colin as he squirmed on her lap, "Can you say stinky cigar?" Colin had decided that he didn't like being restrained by Nicole any more than he liked being held by his mother, and struggled to get away, squirming out of her lap. Once free, he started running from one end of the patio to another like a wild man.

"So much energy," George said. "Just like my brother Danny. Mother used to have me watch him when she was doing chores. He wore me out, running all over the neighborhood, he loved to pull Mrs. Shuster's sheets right off the clothesline, it made her so mad. One day he brought home a stray dog, a collie."

"Did you get to keep it?" asked Nicole, a staunch animal advocate and PETA member who had just completed a research paper on puppy mills for her honors English class. Colin came back by Nicole, who tried to put him on her lap and give him his bottle, but after a moment of repose he was on the go again.

"No, she took it to the pound because it chewed the leg off of one of her new end tables."

"That's so sad, I bet they put him to sleep," Nicole said as Colin wandered away with his bottle hanging out of his mouth by the nipple, swinging it back and forth like a pendulum. "Colin," Nicole said. "Come by Auntie Nicole." Colin, in the manner of all children having a sixth sense to ignore adult requests, ran in other direction. Nicole followed, picked him up and brought him back, his legs pumping in midair again. Suddenly the sound of rap music blared from her jeans; it was her cell phone. "Here Colin, you stay with Grandpa for a minute."

She walked to the other end of the patio, spoke for a few minutes, then flipped the phone shut.

"Grandpa, that was my friend Alicia. She just got dropped off, but she's at the other end of the resort. I need to go get her because she doesn't know her way around. Can you watch Colin while I'm gone?"

"Sure. I had three kids of my own," George said, taking a puff of his cigar. "Who'd ya think raised them?"

"Grandma," she said, smiling, prompting him to blow a thick ribbon of smoke in her face.

"Ew, that's horrible!" she said, wildly waving her hand in front of her face and moving away.

Nicole took Colin by the hand and brought him over to George. "Okay Colin, Auntie Nicole will be back in a little while. You stay with Grandpa," she said to Colin, who reached for his toy cell phone, put it to his ear and started speaking gibberish.

"Look," she said. "He wants to be just like his Auntie Nicole. Okay I'm gonna go. Bye Colin! Bye Grandpa!"

D avid had called several times during the day, leaving messages that he wanted to see her. Exhausted, Ellen had fallen asleep on the sofa after her long walk home from the chapel, where she had an unanticipated encounter with Pastor Roberts. She had been engaged in silent contemplation when the genial minister had entered the sanctuary. With instincts honed from a lifetime of ministry, he saw that she was troubled, and asked if he could help.

"That's very kind of you," she said, looking up from her seat in the third row of pews. "I'm just struggling with something and trying to find an answer, well I think I know the answer but it's just so hard."

Casually dressed in a polo shirt, shorts and sandals, he looked more like a tourist who had just wandered in from the golf course than a man of the cloth.

"Ellen, isn't it?" he asked, and she nodded. "Don't worry, it will come, it's all right there right before you. It always is," he said in a serene voice that calmed her raw nerves. The late afternoon sun bathed the altar in a brilliant amber light, the cross caught in its glow. He hesitated, waiting for her to speak, then moved down the well-trodden steps of the altar toward her. "Easy for me to say, right?" he smiled, "I'm not the one wrestling with God."

She smiled back. "All this wrestling is making me tired."

He took off his sunglasses, and hooked them on the pocket of his shirt. "Remember Sunday's Gospel? How Peter was afraid but Jesus stretched out his hand and saved him. The hand of Christ was there for Peter and it's there for us as well. All we have to do is take it, grab it, believe it." His words, spoken without knowledge of her personal moral dilemma, nonetheless penetrated the core of her being. It was inexplicable, this leap of faith required to trust God absolutely, yet breathtakingly simple in its clarity.

After leaving the chapel, she walked back barefoot along the water's edge, sandals loosely in hand. Watching the heaving waves, enjoying the splash of the surf, she immersed herself in the wonder of the day. A cascade of elation, regret and now, something on the edge of renewal came over her. Colonies of shorebirds flitted over crystal blue waters glistening in the golden light. She felt lifted, less burdened, having found a glimmer of a hope that anything was possible, and somehow she would get through this.

Her plans for the evening were to get something to eat at the luau, watch some of the entertainment and come back to go to bed early. This would be sufficient diversion until bedtime; she vowed earlier that no matter what, David would not set foot into her place tonight. That much she could control.

JUST AS ELLEN WAS READY TO WALK out the door, her cell phone rang. It was David, he wanted to come up. She told him that wasn't a good idea.

"Then meet me somewhere—just for a few minutes," he said. Reluctantly, she agreed to meet him at Oceanside Park, about a ten-minute walk down the beach. The trigger on her decision was that she had something to say to him and she wanted to do it before she lost her nerve.

The moon provided just enough light for her to see as she walked down the beach, seashells crunching under her Nikes. She arrived before he did at the park, a popular daytime spot for tourists, and sat down on a picnic table hidden behind a cluster of banyan trees. No one walking by on the beach could see them, a precaution she felt necessary despite the fact that she was sure his family would be at the luau and it was dark. The next ten minutes seemed like an hour; finally David came walking briskly toward her. She had just enough time to say the briefest of prayers before he pulled her tight to his chest and held her there. Clearly her battle for self-control would not be won easily, her longing for him as natural as the next breath.

"I'm so glad you came," he murmured into her windswept hair.

They sat down next to each other on the picnic table, their feet resting on the benches in a casual gesture that belied their mutual tension. Fine lines around his eyes reflected the stress of the past few days, but the anguish did not detract from the flawlessness of his facial features.

"I don't have long, but I had to see you," he said. "I could barely function today, last night was, well, what's the word I'm looking for . . . incredible . . . unbelievable . . . spectacular . . . stop me if I'm getting warm." He flashed a smile meant only for her.

"All of the above," she said, a glint of a smile in return but with a trace of hesitation so he could sense her discomfort. "David we need to—"

"Shhh." As if he knew what was coming, he put his index finger up to her lips, then took her hand in his, his almond-shaped eyes projecting the high-voltage intensity she found so damn seductive. "I know this is a little out of left field, but I think I'm in love with you Ellen."

The shutter in the camera of her mind's eye clicked to capture the ethereal wonder of the moment. *He was in love with her*, and although she knew it was terribly wrong and immoral she felt a powerful wave of triumph and elation sweep over her. In the distance the rhythmic strains of a steel drum ensemble wafted through the night air. Above, the stars glistened like a heavenly chandelier. If there were ever a more romantic setting, she had not seen it.

"I told you last night this isn't just about sex, even though you absolutely blew my mind on that front," he said softly. He reached over and lifted her hair off her face, his hand caressing her cheek.

"You did mention that though I'm not sure I believe you," she said, her brain reeling to reject the tantalizing possibilities that his being in love with her presented and instead convey the message she had rehearsed this afternoon.

"I need to know I'm going to see you again. After we leave here."

The "after we leave here" jolted her back to reality. She took a moment to gather her thoughts. "I don't know, David . . . I'm just so *overwhelmed* with all this," she said. "Do you know that I spent the afternoon in a church praying for forgiveness and guidance . . . I don't know what's happened to me, maybe I'm in love with you too, or maybe I'm just a bored and frustrated wife who needs to feel like a woman again, alive again, desired again. I'm overwhelmed and confused about everything except this: It's wrong David, it's *so wrong* what we're doing. We're married, we have children and you have a wife and I have a husband—"

"Yes, it's wrong," he said quietly. "It's also wrong to stay in a marriage with someone who's turned into a person you hardly know anymore." He looked as though he had just stumbled upon a profound cosmic reality. "People change, Ellen, I just wish someone would have told me earlier. Tell me you have a good marriage. You know damn well you wouldn't be here alone on this island if you did. Where's your husband? Why isn't he with you?"

His sharp tone and change in demeanor unnerved her.

"You're right, there *are* problems in my marriage," she said. "But this is all too fast, too sudden. Are you telling me you would even *contemplate* leaving your wife? For a woman you met a few days ago? That's crazy. Do you understand what you're saying?"

His eyes flashed with a conviction that was hard and relentless. "I know perfectly well what I'm saying. And you're right, it is crazy. Totally out of character for good old reliable do-the-right-thing David."

This was not the David she had encountered that first night on the beach. His cool composure had given way to an unrestrained passion, and though it flattered her to think she had sparked this torrent of emotion she also found it unsettling.

"We made a mistake, David. We let something happen that should have never happened. I don't like who I am right now. I don't like this guilt, and I don't like knowing that I cheated on my husband." She paused, and took a deep breath before she finished speaking. "This is very difficult for me . . . but I don't think we should see each other again."

"No." He shook his head resolutely.

"It's the right thing to do."

"Not acceptable. You're feeling guilty and scared right now so you want to turn your back on life and retreat to where it's safe. The feelings we have for each other are real, I don't care if it's a few days or six years. What we shared last night—my god most people will never experience that in their lifetime." His eyes were black canyons in the darkness, fixed on hers. Suddenly she felt transparent before him.

"I haven't been able to get you out of my mind since the first moment I saw you," he said, pulling her toward him. "Do you really just think we should just walk away, pretend like all of this never happened?"

Ellen sighed deeply. It would be so easy to give in to his insistence, to relent to his will and the ways of a morally tarnished world that would understand this and would not judge her too harshly for it.

"David, please don't make this any harder than it already is," she pleaded. "Of course I *want* to see you, do you think this is easy for me? Do you think I can walk away from you just like that?" she said, snapping her fingers to illustrate her point. She could feel the tears welling up in her eyes, she wished they would not come but there was no stopping them. The whole thing was just too hard, deep down she knew she had fallen in love with him, which is why her entire world seemed to be collapsing around her. Her earlier resolve was adrift in the force of a powerful tide, the waves pulling her down. This man standing next to her was a force of nature, she realized, one that she could not subdue or control.

He took her in his arms and moved to kiss her. Mustering all the strength she possessed she turned her head away but remained in his embrace, devastated at the thought it could be the last time.

"I'm not going to let you go just like that," he said, his face buried in her hair, arms tight around her. "We'll talk tomorrow, I have to get back now. I was supposed to be at the luau a half an hour ago and no one knows where I am." He kissed her gently on the forehead, the way a father kisses a little girl. She was so relieved he could not stay because in her current state of mind she could no longer fight him.

She walked alongside of him, though her intention was to break away as soon as they got closer to Paradise to avoid being seen together. They'd walked only a few yards when Ellen saw several small white beams of light dancing along the water's edge in the distance. "Look over there," she said, pointing them out. "What do you think those lights are?"

Looking down the shore, he shook his head. "I don't know. Looks like kids playing with flashlights."

As they got closer, they could see the beams frantically crisscrossing each other like a *Star Wars* light saber duel. They heard shouting. The sound of the wind and surf broke up the voices, so it was difficult to hear what was being said, but it did not sound like people partying on the beach. There was a definite cadence to the shouting. Ellen strained to hear, in a lull of the wind she made it out. Someone was yelling "Colin." An instant later, she heard it again. Her instincts as a mother instantly told her something was very wrong if someone was calling for a child at the edge of the ocean in the darkness. A jolt of fear raced up her spine. David had a son named Colin. It couldn't be . . . no . . . no . . .

"David—"

His attention riveted ahead, in the moonlight she saw a look of sheer panic sweep across his face. He had heard it too. "Oh my god, I've got to see what's going on." And without a second's hesitation he took off running in the direction of the lights.

When he got there, a sickening dread drenched his body. Walking back and forth on the beach with high-powered flashlights were Julia and Rachel, with Richard trailing them. They were shouting Colin's name. He thought he would pass out. He ran toward them, not caring about what they thought or what they would say, only thinking of his beautiful son, horrified to think that any harm had come to him, and if it had he would never forgive himself.

"Julia," he called out to them. "What happened?"

Rachel caught him in the beam of her flashlight.

"David—oh my god where have you been! Colin's wandered off and we can't find him! Marianne left him with Dad and Dad must have nodded off and now he's missing!" Julia said, her speech coming in torrents, the fear in her voice palpable.

"How long has he been gone?" he asked tersely.

"About ten, fifteen, minutes, we think," she said. "Nicole and Dad were watching him while Marianne went to the store but Nicole had to leave to meet up with her girlfriend. When she got back, Colin was gone."

"Where were they?"

"They were sitting in the courtyard by Mom and Dad's building. Everyone is searching for him, the hotel is sending out staff, they've called the police—David, we've got to find him!" He had never seen his sister so frightened. The fear immobilized him momentarily. He couldn't process the situation. Colin couldn't swim and there were swimming pools all over the resort let alone the ocean. The next few minutes could determine whether his son lived or died. *How could he have ever let this happen, he had been such a fool.*

"I've got to find Marianne," he said, while Julia and Rachel's flashlights continued to bounce off the water's edge and beyond. Leaving no stone unturned, Richard was carefully searching the dense tangle of sea grape bushes along the edge of the sand dunes.

David's mind raced to weigh the best course of action. *Where would Colin go?* His first guess was the main hotel swimming pool where he'd been almost every day since they arrived. Colin loved the pool and its tiny tot slide, where he floated around in his inner tube with his father at his side. The pool wasn't that far from where George and Nicole had been sitting. Surely that was one of the first places Marianne would think of, hopefully they already searched it.

Marianne. Just the thought of his wife sent another jolt of fear through him. Marianne would be a wreck. Again he cursed himself for his actions. If he had not left this would have never happened and Colin would be safe. Gripped with guilt, the thought occurred to him that perhaps this was the punishment for adultery.

He ran faster than he ever had in his life.

Alone, Maggie wandered through a dark jungle of trees and billowing shrubs in the heart of the resort's tropical gardens. The seemingly endless brick walkways curved and meandered, occasionally leading to an idyllic outdoor enclave with benches and tables for guests. A bank of clouds veiled the moon, making it hard to see, forcing her to rely on the glow from the constellation of solar lights staked along the path.

She had crossed a lawn the size of a small soccer field to get here. The others didn't think Colin would have come this way because it was too far and too dark so they were concentrating their search elsewhere, convinced he would have wandered down one of the main walkways that led to the luau, or heaven forbid one of the swimming pools. But Maggie felt otherwise. It was raw instinct, nothing more. Thank god she was sober.

Her racing heart felt like a stampede in her chest. *Where would I go if I were a little boy? Think think think.* She'd brought Colin and Emma back here to a secluded play area they'd found while exploring the lush grounds. Colin had been thrilled to discover the "caterpillar" slide. He had gone down it more than a dozen times and when it was time to go she could barely get him to leave. Problem was she couldn't remember where it was, and the darkness wasn't helping matters.

A fork in the path, left or right. She chose left. A few moments later, she came upon a familiar landmark, the mermaid fountain. Ethan and Emma and been delighted by the glittery gold fish darting to and fro in the pool of water encircling the mythic sea creature. She shouted his name. Again she had to choose between two paths. She chose the one that veered right. Walking a little further, she could see the faint outlines of a footbridge in the darkness. Yes! They had definitely come this way before. The footbridge crossed the lagoon that during the day was crowded with families in paddleboats. Emma had begged her to go on a ride but they couldn't because reservations were required.

"Colin," she shouted with renewed enthusiasm. "Colin, where are you? Come find Auntie Maggie."

Silence. The play area could not be far from here.

"Colin," she shouted again. She desperately wished her cell phone would ring and it would be Marianne telling her the search was off and everything was fine. Certainly someone would have called her if they'd found him. Her worries multiplied as she traversed the path that took her along the lagoon—surely he could drown in a lagoon as easily as he could drown in the ocean. Had the hotel even thought of this—shouldn't they be out here searching? She'd never been in a situation like this before, suddenly her thoughts careened to her own boys—*my god what if anything like this ever happened and I wasn't there to protect them.* She felt like she'd been hit in the head with a brick, the realization that she so implicitly trusted Brian with Tyler and Brad that she'd never really given any thought to the possibility of something bad happening to them while she was away.

"Colin!" she shouted louder, wishing she had a flashlight. Another horrible thought detonated in her mind—what if he didn't wander away? What if someone took him? Calm down, she told herself, trying to force the thought from her mind but instead pivoting to the memory of that best-selling book about the three-year-old who simply vanished from a busy Chicago hotel lobby. Kids disappeared every day in America—get a grip!

The sound of rushing water interrupted her thoughts as she approached the resort's garden of fountains. Above her dozens of silvery beams of water arched gracefully over the flagstone path. Emma and Colin had run back and forth under the volant streams, not understanding that unlike a sprinkler, they would never get wet because of the precision engineering that produced this visually stunning aquatic innovation. She knew she was close to her destination but that just produced even more dread. *What if he wasn't there? Then what?*

DAVID FOUND MARIANNE IN A HEATED DISCUSSION with the hotel manager near the main pool deck.

"We can't see, we need lights, we need the coast guard," she sobbed hysterically. "My little boy could be out there and we've got to find him now!"

"Mrs. Blakemore, as I explained, unfortunately that is not in my jurisdictional authority. But we have notified the police and I assure you they will be here shortly."

David came up behind Marianne and threw his arms around his wife.

"Where have you been?" she demanded angrily, pulling away. "I should have never left him. I thought you would be back and Nicole was there with your father—"

"I'm so sorry, I went for a walk, I needed to clear my head," he lied, knowing that any other story would not fly because Julia had seen him on the beach. He knew it was a weak lie, but it didn't matter because right now the only thing that mattered was finding his son. *Why did this have to happen?*

David turned toward the hotel manager. "Where haven't we looked yet?"

The manager, calm given the circumstances, extended his hand and introduced himself. "Grant Perkins. Let me assure you we're doing everything we can to find your son. We've notified our security team and they're checking the vicinity from where he disappeared and will work out from there. We're making announcements in the hotel and to the luau guests. The police have been called and are on their way. I know this doesn't make you feel any better, but we've had lost kids before, little guys just like Colin, and they always turn up. Usually somewhere on the grounds—not the beach. Too dark for most kids at night and it scares them. As you know, this is a big place with lots of nooks and crannies. Kind of like a corn maze on steroids," he said, his face twisted in a wry smile, odd considering the circumstances.

David didn't know whether to be angry at the manager's apparent nonchalance, or take it as a hopeful sign. This had happened before, the kids were found. That was good news. But until he had Colin back nothing would calm his worst fears. "Where's Mom and the others?"

"Your mom and dad and Uncle Frank are with the hotel staff checking the swimming pools," Marianne said. "Julia and Richard are on the beach, and Aunt Maureen and the others are searching the luau. Gertrude and Eunice went to stay with Emma and Ethan at the Kids Club—I just didn't want them there alone."

Anxiety gripped him like a vise. He had to find his son. *Where would he go?* Colin had an independent streak and had always been a wanderer, unlike his sister Emma who had been glued to her mother's side since she learned how to walk. He agreed with the hotel manager that it was unlikely that Colin would head toward the ocean, but you couldn't go on hunches where a child's life was concerned.

The look on his face must have frightened Marianne because she collapsed into his shoulder, sobbing. "We've got to find him."

"We'll find him, I promise you," he said to his wife, who was so upset that she didn't notice the subtle scent of another woman's fragrance on his shirt collar. "I want you to stay here and wait for the police. You can tell them what he was wearing, and fill them in on everything. I'm going down to the beach to look. I've got my cell on now, call me the minute the police get here."

He took his wife by the shoulders. "We'll find him. I promise," he repeated with conviction he wished he actually felt. And then he grabbed one of the high-powered flashlights the manager had offered and headed toward the beach.

ELLEN WATCHED THE NIGHTMARISH SEARCH SCENE unfold from a careful distance, terrified that they hadn't found Colin yet. She could only imagine how hysterical David's wife must be. She had walked past his family members on the beach, her heart pounding as they shouted his name. Torn between wanting to help and a deep apprehension about engaging in a rescue mission that could trigger a face-to-face encounter with Marianne, she convinced herself that many people were looking for Colin, and one more wouldn't make a difference. She wished the shouting would stop and that they would find the child safe and sound. Every time she heard them calling his name it was like a sharp knife being thrust into her heart. She couldn't shake from her mind the thought that somehow they were being punished for what they had done, all the while knowing that this was not right, that God didn't make children disappear because of their father's infidelity. Still, if David had been with his family where he belonged, this would have never happened and his son would be safe.

On the stage the steel drum ensemble and lead singer, a Jamaican with dreadlocks that fell below his shoulders, were cranking up the intensity of the music for an audience peeling off its inhibitions thanks to an endless supply of rum-fueled libations. After a burst of wildly enthusiastic applause, the lead singer got the audience to quiet down so someone from hotel security could speak.

"Sorry to interrupt the show, but I need to make an announcement," said the security officer, whose starched uniform and broad shoulders drew a stark contrast to the laid back reggae band members. "We have a little lost boy, his name is Colin and he's two-and-a-half years old. He's got dark curly hair and is wearing red overalls and a blue T-shirt. Please check around you and if you see him please bring him to the stage immediately."

The announcement punched a hole in the festive mood of the luau guests, who immediately started looking around them, in some cases lifting the grass table skirts to look underneath for the missing toddler. Many people put down their drinks and went to the stage and asked if they could help in the search. Watching them, Ellen realized how utterly wrong it was for her *not* to help, certainly there was *something* she could do, *someplace* she could search. Though it was completely unintentional, she shared the blame for what had happened and it was an extremely unsettling feeling. She prayed her worst fears would not be realized.

Liz had never seen Harold like this before. A veil of sadness hung over him like a shroud. His clothes looked like he'd slept in them, his eyes were bloodshot and he had two days of unshaven stubble on his jowls. She'd known this wasn't going to be easy for him, but had underestimated his emotional state and ability to cope with the arrival of hospice. A standard issue hospital bed, IV stands, oxygen and other medical equipment had been moved into Lucille's bedroom. A gray-haired nurse in her sixties and the noticeably younger hospice director were huddled in the dining room discussing a plan for round-the-clock medical care for Lucille. Down the hall in the bedroom his wife was dying and it was simply too much for him to bear.

Shoulders slumped, Harold walked slowly over to the kitchen sink, turning on the faucet to pour himself a glass of water. He came back and sat down at the table, his eyes blearily unfocused.

"Harold, listen to me," Liz said. "You need to go to bed and get some rest. I'm here now and I can handle anything that comes up."

"I don't think I should leave her alone right now," he said in an anguished voice. "Too much commotion."

"Please, I'm begging you, go upstairs and get some sleep. You're no good to Lucille or anyone else like this. I promise you I'll stay with Lucille and make sure she's comfortable and knows where you are."

"I don't know," he said. "She's going to be scared if she wakes up with everything that's going on around her. I didn't know it was going to be like this."

Liz did not see any need to tell him that Lucille was too sick and probably beyond the point of caring who was in her home or what they were doing. She already was heavily sedated from the first blast of pain meds administered by the hospice nurse.

"I'll sit right by her side," Liz promised. "Please just get some sleep. Tomorrow is another day, and a good night's rest is what you need."

"Well . . . all right, you win. You drive a tough bargain Liz Taylor," he said, a flicker of a tired smile crossing his lips. "I *am* tired, but I don't know if I'll be able to sleep."

"You try for a while, and if you can't, I'll give you a sleeping pill. I keep one in my purse for emergencies."

"Don't tell me you're pushing pills now," he said. "What would the ladies at bingo say?"

She grinned, pleased to see his sense of humor had not abandoned him. "Don't you tell them, especially Louise Stevenson," she warned. "She'd probably turn me in."

He pushed the upholstered chair back from the formica table, the table he had shared with Lucille for nearly fifty years of married life, the place where they had their breakfast, lunch and dinner, where they discussed the countless mundane things that couples talk about, where to go and who to see and how to spend their money. It was the table where Lucille paid bills and wrote out Christmas cards and had neighbors over for coffee. Liz imagined a much younger Lucille making a nice supper for Harold after he came home from work. The absence of children would have made it a quiet meal. Had they been in love, and when did that change? Was it the illness that had turned Lucille into a difficult and demanding woman? In the short span of years she had known Harold, he seemed more a devoted caregiver than a man deeply in love with his wife.

He walked slowly toward the stairs, then turned back to face her. "Goodnight Liz."

"Goodnight Harold."

"I'm so tired I almost forgot to say thank you for coming. I don't know what I'd do without you. You're a good friend, Liz. Probably the best friend I've ever had."

"You're a good friend too," she replied, the color rising to her cheeks. "Now get some sleep, and let me know if you need that pill."

Liz watched him make his way up the stairs. Friendship for him maybe, but not for her. Thinking back, she wondered when her "friendship" with Harold had metamorphosed into something else, something that was intense and real and exciting, a passion she had thought was forever in her past only to find it blossoming with the vigor and beauty of the first daffodils of spring. Under different circumstances this discovery would have been a time of great joy, but instead it was mired in the unquestionable immorality of falling in love with a married man, and worse, one whose wife was dying. Her emotional state hopscotched between guilty and grateful, and she could not reconcile these conflicting emotions. One thing was clear, right now she needed to put all these thoughts out of her head, take care of Lucille and help Harold through this difficult time. Everything else would have to wait.

Maggie turned the corner into the play area. Silence greeted her as her sandaled feet tread over wood chips designed to soften the landing in case a child fell from the elaborate kiddie play complex. Designed to delight children of all ages, it had swings, climbing bars, a rope walk, tree house and the caterpillar slide, a swirl of plastic tubing with yellow, black-and-white stripes and two shiny black antennae.

Scanning the darkness, she felt a surge of disappointment. If he wasn't here she was out of ideas and would go back to the hotel proper and search with the others.

"Colin!" she shouted.

She sprang up the ladder to the top of the slide. *Please, please be here baby boy.* She reached the top of the enclosed platform. Empty. Looking down the curved slide, she saw only darkness. It was a long shot but he could be in the slide somewhere below. She went down and landed at the bottom, no Colin. By now she started feeling ridiculous that she had followed her instincts to this place that was turning out to be a wild-goose chase.

She looked around for any other possible hiding place for a two-year-old. The tree house. She climbed up the rope walk that led to the tree house. Her foot slipped and she banged her knee hard. *Ouch, shit!*

On hands and knees, she crawled through the small doorway made for the bodies of five-year-olds. Inside the tree house, she had difficulty adjusting her eyes to the total darkness. Then much to her utter amazement she saw a shape on the floor. *Colin!* He was sleeping curled up on the hard plastic floor. She lunged forward and grabbed him. "Colin!" she exclaimed, and his eyes flickered open. She smothered him in a hug, almost light-headed with relief and overwhelming joy as his little body melted into hers. "Thank god, oh Colin I'm so glad I found you. Are you okay, little guy? I'm going to take you back to Mommy and Daddy right away, but first I'm going to call them."

He looked at her, rubbing his eyes and said "Mag-gee." Then a smile appeared on his sleepy face. "Mag-gee."

She fumbled for her cell phone with the one hand she had free. She punched in David's number. Five seconds later he answered.

"I've got him. He's okay," Maggie said breathlessly.

"Oh my god. Maggie—Thank god! You found him! Is he okay? Where are you?"

"He's fine. He was sleeping in the tree house at the playground. The one with the caterpillar slide."

"He was all the way over there, he walked all the way across that lawn at night?"

"I know, it's far, he was probably exhausted, poor thing. But he really seems okay, he's not even crying."

"Stay right where you are," David said. "We'll have management bring us over. They've got golf carts."

"Maggie?"

"What?"

"I can never, *ever* thank you enough for this. You're an absolute godsend."

AN HOUR LATER, THE ENTIRE FAMILY had reassembled at the luau except George, who'd gone to bed. Relieved but still shaken, everyone had something to say about the harrowing search as high-octane conversation ricocheted around the table. Inexplicably, no one questioned the fact that George had dozed off while watching Colin or why David had been out walking on the beach alone.

Judy did nothing to dispel the nap theory, though she knew in her heart of hearts it was more than that. She'd seen that stare before, usually when George was downstairs watching TV on mute as if in a trance. When this happened, she would say something to him and he'd usually snap out of it. But tonight— she shuddered at the thought of what could have happened, how tragedy had lurked in the shadow of her darling grandson. She vowed to never, ever let anything like this happen again, and that meant addressing the issue head-on and telling Julia and Maggie—but not on the eve of the anniversary party. Julia had worked so hard to make everything perfect, why should she drop this bombshell and ruin everything.

Uncle Frank, wearing two floral leis around his neck, brought over a tray of fruit-skewered daiquiris and passed them out to everyone at the table. Several were designated "virgin," for Maggie, Rachel, Nicole and her friend Alicia.

David stood up, interrupting the buzz of conversation. Sitting next to him was Marianne, who held a sleepy Colin on her lap as if she'd never put him down again.

"Hey everybody, I just want to take a minute," he said, "to thank you for everything you did tonight to help us find Colin. This little guy really gave us a scare tonight, and it's at times like these you realize how important family is. You all were there for us, you mobilized like an army to help us find him . . . and we'll never forget your love and concern."

A heartfelt sentiment of relief and goodwill imbued the moment. David's words rang true, the bonds of family had been strengthened and renewed by what had happened.

"But there's someone here I want to propose a special toast to, my terrific sister Maggie, who tonight again demonstrated that she occasionally marches to the beat of a different drummer," he said, pausing to flash Maggie an insider grin. "We're all very happy about that because she followed her instincts and found my son. Way to go Maggie!"

Glasses clinked and a chorus of voices said in unison "To Maggie." Then Nicole threw in, "Give it up for Maggie!" and everyone at the table started whooping and hollering and applauding. "Speech! Speech!" Aunt Maureen shouted over the din.

Maggie had not expected to be singled out for recognition. When the applause came, she found herself on the verge of tears, swept under a warm and wonderful waterfall of contentment and acceptance. She hadn't felt this happy in a long time, these were new emotions to her, having spent so many years chasing a high with booze and drugs and whatever else she could find to anesthetize herself from her demons. But none of that mattered right now. Even Julia was applauding and smiling. She had finally arrived at that place where she truly belonged with her family, there was no joy quite like it, and she savored the moment.

Ellen had considered getting up Saturday morning and catching a flight to go home. But that would raise a myriad of questions from Jeremy on why she'd abruptly terminated her vacation and paid a hefty change fee to fly home when she didn't have to. So she decided to schedule her last two days with activities away from the resort to avoid seeing David again. Marco Island this afternoon, perhaps a cruise to Boca Grande tomorrow.

After everything that happened last night, she wondered if David would try to get in touch with her today. Thank heavens they had found Colin unharmed; she shuddered again at the thought of what might have been. A wave of relief had poured over her after hearing the announcement over the hotel loudspeaker. All around her, the luau guests celebrated the news, but she had been too drained and exhausted to join in the revelry.

She had not slept well, the digital clock on the nightstand flashed 10 a.m. Last night's encounter with David produced another firestorm of emotions. The desire was still there, but tempered by the nascent realization that he didn't seem to be struggling with the same moral issues that she was. She had been stunned by his willingness to continue their affair and in doing so continue to betray his wife and children . . . what did that say about him, really? Then again wasn't she guilty of the same thing at the heart of it? Or was it one thing to sleep with someone, but quite another to contemplate leaving your spouse? Once you leave the morality playground, who makes the rules?

Groggy, feeling like her head was stuffed with wool socks, she shuffled down the hallway in her comfy slippers into the kitchen to start her coffee. She decided against taking her usual morning walk on the beach. Too risky, she could run into him or worse, his wife and kids. But that was silly as well, what was she going to do, imprison herself in her room? *This is ridiculous, I just have to put all this out of my head and go on with my life.* The reality was that even if she separated herself from him geographically, he still had her cell number and she was sure he would call.

She went out on the lanai to have her coffee. The languid parade of beach walkers was well underway, with the ever-present shell seekers crouching along the water's edge looking for treasure, beckoned by the recessing tide. Children built sand castles, their parents relaxing in lawn chairs enjoying another beautiful day. A middle-age woman struggled to push a younger woman in a wheelchair with huge inflated tires apparently made for beach travel. Ellen had seen them yesterday while walking and offered to help, but the woman politely refused. The daughter, obese and obviously disabled, did not speak. Ellen was deeply touched by this witness of maternal love, which also made her problems seem small and self-indulgent in comparison.

The strong coffee produced the desired kick-start to her brain, giving her the energy to take a shower and get dressed. She had just sat down to start the makeup ritual when she heard a knock at the door. Her stomach flipped. He couldn't be back already. She jumped up, went to the door. "Who is it?" she asked, praying it was housekeeping.

"It's a surprise," came the voice on the other side of the door.

It couldn't be. She had to be hearing things.

"Who is it?" she asked again, throttled by a tremor of nervousness.

"You've already forgotten, my feelings are hurt—it's me."

Oh my god—how could this be—was she dreaming—would

she wake up?

She flung open the door. Jeremy stood in the doorway with a huge grin on his face, and a suitcase parked next to him. "Surprise!"

"Jeremy —I can't believe you're here!"

"I thought that you might be lonely by now so I hopped on a plane," he said.

"I . . . I'm *so surprised,*" she stammered. There was a fleeting awkward moment before his arms went tight around her and they embraced. Her body responded on autopilot because she simply couldn't process the scene.

"Did you miss me?" he asked.

"Of course I did," she said, breathless. This time he pulled her toward him and kissed her, then held her close for a long moment.

"Come in, let's sit down. I'm in shock." she said, still trying to decide if she was going to wake up from this bizarre dream.

He wheeled the small black suitcase in behind him, and looked around the room approvingly, "Nice. What a view! I think I'll be quite comfy here."

"So do tell, what really made you decide to come?"

"I talked to Amy on Monday," he said. "I told her what I was thinking about doing, and she thought it was a great idea. So I decided to do something totally spontaneous for a change and come down here."

It was eerie having him in this room. Her mind raced down the infidelity checklist to see if there was anything that would give her secret away. Had David left anything here, some telltale sign? It was hard processing these thoughts while trying to give all her attention to her husband who had just flown a thousand miles to be with her. *Wait, there was something—where was the note he'd left her? Had she left it on the table?*

"Are you okay?" he asked. "You look a little out of sorts."

"No, I'm fine, just tired. I couldn't sleep last night for some reason so I'm a zombie."

"Hmm. Maybe I'll have to put you back to bed," he said.

She smiled, praying he wasn't serious and quickly changed the subject. "Where's Andrew?" she said.

"Amy took him."

"Was he okay with that?" she asked.

"He didn't have a choice," he said flatly. "I decided that it was more important for us to have some time together. I hope you don't mind my infringing on your vacation, but I thought by now you might want some company."

"I'm so glad you're here," she lied as convincingly as she could. What she couldn't tell him was how overwhelming it was to have him here in the room where David had been, like two spirits colliding in some weird science fiction time warp. It was as if Jeremy were an intruder on David's turf, the thought was ludicrous but indicative of the twisted reality that had become her life over the past few days. She remembered David sitting next to her on this sofa, where it had all started when suddenly she realized—oh my god—what if he called her! She had to find her cell phone and turn it off.

"You know what I'd like," she said. "Let's go get a real cup of coffee and take a walk on the beach. It's so gorgeous here, there are the most incredible shorebirds. I see snowy egrets and herons every day. And you remember the shells, they're everywhere!"

"Okay, I'm up for that. It *is* beautiful here, and this place certainly lives up to its name."

"Great." She looked at him, taking stock of his insouciant demeanor—a far cry from his melancholy self of late. "You seem to be in good spirits for someone who must have gotten up at the crack of dawn to catch a plane," she said.

"It just feels good to do something different for a change, something purely spontaneous and out of the ordinary," he said.

You have no idea, Ellen thought, keenly aware of the perverse irony of his observation.

"I confess that I've been stuck in a rut for a while, think it's time for a change." he said. "So are you *really* happy to see me?"

"Of course."

"Good, because I'm very happy to see you. I really missed

you Ellen, more than I thought."

"I missed you too, a lot. I'm just in a fog right now. C'mon, let's go get some coffee," she said. She really wanted to leave just in case he wanted to prove how much he missed her, which was inevitable now that he was here. What she needed now was time to adjust to this new reality.

"Just let me get something," she said, quickly rising from the sofa. She darted down the hallway into the bedroom to retrieve David's note from the nightstand. She only had a few seconds because she was sure he'd follow her down the hall.

"Come see the bedroom," she said, snatching the note off of the nightstand and shoving it into her makeup bag. She glanced around to make sure there was no other evidence of what had transpired in this room.

"This is great," he said, taking in the sumptuous king-size bed, wicker furniture and flat panel TV. "Had I known this place was this nice I would have been here Tuesday," he said. He put his suitcase on the unmade bed. "I'll get changed."

She left him alone, and went back into the living room. Fishing her cell phone out of her purse, she pressed the off button. Mission accomplished. But she still wasn't safe. If David couldn't get through on the cell he could show up on her doorstep.

Her nerves shattered, she desperately needed to tell him to stay away.

Twenty minutes later, walking on the beach with Jeremy, she ducked into the restroom at the public beach access. She dialed David's number, praying first that the call would go through and second that she would get voice mail. She won on both counts. She had rehearsed her lines. In the most nonchalant voice she could muster—just in case his wife got his messages—she said, "Hi David. I was at the luau last night and heard about your son, just wanted to let you know how glad I was to hear you found him safe and sound. Must have been a horrible ordeal for you and your family. Busy day for me, my husband arrived this morning, we're out and about on the island, he loves it here as much as I

273

do. Hope you enjoy the rest of your vacation."

The deed was done. She was as safe as she could be.

"Those ignorant sons of bitches!" Gregory yelled into his BlackBerry, a bluish vein bulging out of the side of his neck. The outburst startled Jennifer, who looked up from her *People* magazine. Wearing a pale pink silk robe and matching lingerie, she was ensconced on a sofa in the sunroom off the terrace, sipping her morning coffee and picking at a croissant. Her mind had wandered from the "Sexiest Man Alive" cover story to mulling her options on how to break the news to Gregory that she'd changed her mind about the new house without him getting suspicious. What she didn't know was that she was about to be handed a precious gift from the gods of serendipity.

She'd been obsessing about the problem since yesterday afternoon. The nerve of that woman to blackmail her! Her anger was mitigated by the very real danger she faced and the need to tread carefully. But the person she was really furious with was herself for being so stupid as to get into this situation in the first place. *What had she been thinking to have Michael in this house —in Gregory's bed no less!* She vowed that if she got through this, she would never, ever be this stupid again.

Gregory clicked off the call with his senior vice president and threw the phone on the chair. "Would they run this story if I were some Hollywood celebrity or some big democrat fund-raiser? They wouldn't give a shit if this was about one of their liberal elitist friends! The media is dominated by these leftist partisan hacks and they get away with it! Do you know what's in the *Tribune* today? A story about my bulldozing that god damn chapel! All of a sudden I'm the bad guy for wanting to build a new home. That chapel is on my god damn property and if I want to tear it down it's nobody's business but my own! I'm going to sue those sons of bitches I don't care what Christine says. Invasion of privacy. Defamation. I'll have my lawyers come up with something."

Jennifer's mind raced to assess this turn of events, which presented either a golden opportunity or a reason for Gregory to dig in his heels. She needed to think fast and act faster.

"When did it become a crime to make money in this country?" he muttered. "That's why they're after me, because I'm successful. God damn Stalinists—"

"Gregory"

"What sweetie?"

"I've been meaning to talk to you about this—I didn't know how to bring it up, but maybe now is a good time. Promise you won't get mad at me."

"If you promise me you'll stay in your nightie all day I promise I won't get mad," he said, leering at her in the way she knew all too well.

"Promise me," she coaxed.

"I promise," he replied. "Now what is it?"

"Okay. Well, I've been thinking about the house you're giving me for a wedding present, and it's such a wonderful and generous gift and gesture on your part . . . but there's something that's been bothering me and—"

"Tell me what's on your mind, honey." Gregory temporarily forgot his battle with the press.

"Well, it's this. This place actually. Gregory don't get me wrong, I want a house on the ocean and I can't wait to get to work on it, but I've been doing a lot of thinking and well—what I've realized is that I don't want it here. This place is so, well, *dead*, there's really nothing *here*, a few friends maybe, but darling, most of the *real money* is in Palm Beach and Boca. And that's where you and I belong. The parties, the social life, the charities, I'd love to be a part of all that, I think we could contribute in the most amazing ways. Here it's just a lot of people who want to save wildlife and land and really, I find that *so boring*. Think of the people we could get to know, we could have wonderful dinner parties and go to the best charity balls," she said. "So are you angry?"

"No but I'm confused. I thought you wanted to build a new house here. The plans—"

"I thought so too," she said, thrilled that her proposal wasn't immediately shot down. "I think I'm the one who was confused. Because when you look at who you are, your company, your reputation, Gregory, this place just isn't befitting a man of your caliber. You're the CEO of a global company, you should move in the circles of like people, people with influence, money and power. We can create a wonderful home for entertaining the right kind of people," she said.

"Well you do have a point," he interjected. "Evelyn loved it here, that's why we bought this place. She avoided the social scene like the plague. So if it's really important to you . . ."

"*It is,* darling."

"Well it's your wedding present, so if you want Palm Beach I'll get you Palm Beach. I know what I want," he said, in a clear signal of what was coming next.

"Whatever you want," she said demurely. "One more thing, though. And don't get mad at me. But since we're going to sell this place, and those people are so attached to their little chapel, can we let them stay? I met that woman, Liz, she's really a dear, she didn't have anything to do with those articles in the papers. She's a widow and the church is all she really has. She reminds me of my grandmother," Jennifer lied with ease.

Capitulation was not in Gregory's vocabulary. He didn't care one bit about the proselytizing poachers, and he certainly didn't want it to seem like the press made him cave.

"I don't know about that. Let me talk to Christine and see what she thinks." Gregory deferred to his vice president of communications on all matters concerning his public image. He picked up his BlackBerry and punched in Christine's number.

Back in Chicago, Christine's cell phone rang in the back seat of a $200-an-hour Hummer limousine filled with boisterous boys. "Shhh, quiet down," she pleaded. Christine had rented the limo to take her son and six of his best buddies to a Chicago Bulls game to celebrate her son's tenth birthday.

Gregory explained the situation.

"Gregory, here's what I think," Christine said. "If you can make those old folks happy and kill this ridiculous story I say go for it. We've got enough problems right now, you're becoming the poster child for all of the ills of the global economy, this China jobs thing is killing us in the press. We don't need any more bad headlines right now. Why don't we take this story and turn it to our advantage, make you look like Mr. Chivalry and defender of the faith."

"I just don't want it to look like I'm caving in. I haven't done anything wrong, it's my property for crying out loud," he said. He looked at Jennifer, and paused. "But it's probably not worth fighting over. Draft something and send it over."

"Don't worry, I'll take care of it as soon as I get done here. Check your email." She clicked off.

Gregory turned toward his wife. "Are you sure this is what you want?"

"Absolutely."

"Then it's done," he said.

Jennifer got up, dropped her shimmering silk robe on the sofa, and walked across the room and dutifully slid onto Gregory's lap. His attention elsewhere, he could not see the look of feverish relief on her face.

The festivities for the anniversary party were set to begin at six o'clock, just a few hours from now. Another splendid day in paradise—a balmy eighty-two degrees under a cloudless cerulean sky—with the evening forecast promising more of the same, just a few degrees cooler. You couldn't order better weather.

For all of them, but especially for Julia, a momentous day. Months of meticulous planning would soon come to fruition. David was awed by the boundless competency of his sister, who, in addition to juggling the relentless demands of her career and family, had in her virtually non-existent free time taken on the responsibility of orchestrating this lavish affair.

Ah, but he had his own talents, he thought ruefully, chief among them his being able to stand here and impersonate a *normal* person, the brother Julia had always known and loved, not the adulterous emotional train wreck he had become over the past several days. Ever since waking up this morning, he had waged a relentless struggle to silence the thoughts reverberating in his head.

He was furious at himself about last night, for what could have happened to Colin, thank god he had dodged that bullet, but now he was consumed by the excruciating thought of not seeing Ellen again. Clearly she made every excuse to pull away from him last night. It had really surprised him, so different from the way she had been the night they'd spent together when she hadn't held back at all. Whatever her reasons—guilt, morality, fear—he couldn't cope with losing her. But right now he needed to find the strength to put that all aside. This day belonged to his family, to his parents who somehow had managed to stay married for fifty years. Certainly he owed them that much.

He watched his sister move with swiftness of purpose as she oversaw the arrangements—deftly managing every detail: place settings, wine selection, lighting, flowers. Nothing escaped her attention. He wondered, had she ever confronted an uncontrollable passion that threatened her meticulously planned life? Julia was the most self-assured and confident woman he'd ever known, and an extremely private person as well. If there were turmoil under her cool and confident exterior, it surely was hidden.

A young Latino woman who worked on the hotel's catering staff carefully placed a huge crystal vase bursting with crimson-edged white stargazer lilies on the memories table, where Julia had just finished setting out a dozen silver-framed photographs. The pictorial assemblage spanned decades: a handsome young man and his pretty bride on their wedding day; a few years later the young couple, beaming, holding their infant son on the front steps of George's parents' bungalow; the family on the pier at Moon Lake on vacation; birthdays, Christmas and graduations; and David holding an enormous baseball trophy standing next to his proud father. A few hours from now these images would evoke a deluge of reminiscing and funny stories, and for many of the older guests, an unspoken melancholy for these cherished memories of days gone by, and youth that had vanished quietly when no one was looking.

Julia went over the itinerary again, while David mostly nodded in agreement. There would be cocktails, soft music, hors d'oeuvres, dinner, remembrances, and then dancing. She had hired a four-piece ensemble that featured the music of Frank Sinatra and Cole Porter, and had personally picked out every song, including many of George and Judy's favorites. The hotel staff had festooned the beachfront veranda with glittery ivory lights; in a few hours they would be dancing under the stars to some of the greatest music ever written. With the precision of a general planning for war, Julia had scheduled the hors d'oeuvres to commence with the setting of the sun, which according to her Google search would occur at 5:52 p.m.

"So David, I've been meaning to ask you, what do you think is up with Dad? Nicole was really kind of freaked out last night. She said Dad looked like he was kind of out of it when she came back and found Colin missing. That doesn't sound like Dad."

David desperately did not want to have this conversation now. He would have it tomorrow or any other time, but not on this day that Julia had planned for so long. An honest response could ruin it for her.

"I'm not sure, maybe he was just tired and nodded off. You know he *is* getting older, even though he doesn't look his age," he said.

"I hope that's all it is, I couldn't bear the thought of anything being wrong with him. I have so many friends who are coping with aging parents—we're so lucky, you know. I'll talk to Mom tomorrow." David knew that his highly capable sister would follow up until the issue was resolved, the question answered. He felt bad for her and for all of them for what might lie ahead. He couldn't for a minute imagine his father physically or mentally impaired, of being less than the larger-than-life figure he had always been.

"Now what do you think about gifts, should we have them open them before dancing?" she asked.

"You know I don't know anything about this stuff," David pleaded. "I'm a man, which when it comes to parties means I'm capable of ordering pizzas and buying booze."

"And *drinking* booze," she said, smiling at him, while the sun danced brilliantly on the silver pieces topping the white linen-clad banquet tables.

Suddenly David heard his name being called from a distance. Turning around, he saw Aunt Gertrude walking toward him, waving broadly, her jovial face shaded by a straw sunhat, its bright orange yellow scarf tied in a bow under her chin, a perfect match to her sundress.

"David, Julia," she greeted them, her plump cheeks a little flushed. Taking note of the tables, flowers and other preparations, she exclaimed breathlessly, "Oh isn't this nice, it's going to be a wonderful party! Eunice and I are so excited, we got new dresses from Don's Discount Bridal World on clearance, they're actually mother-of-the-bride dresses but no one will know. They even threw in matching handbags!"

"Matching handbags, I can't wait to see them!" David said, feigning excitement.

"Don't forget I used to change your diapers," she shot back, eyes narrowed.

"Enjoying yourself Auntie?" Julia asked.

"Am I ever! It's like I died and went to heaven. And you my dear," she said, looking at her niece, "I can't thank you enough for inviting us here. Eunice and I are having the time of our lives, well as much as Eunice ever has any fun because you know she's such a stick-in-the-mud and always has been! I just want you to know your generosity is very much appreciated by two old ladies on social security."

"It's my pleasure, we're just glad you could come," said Julia. "This is going to be a great party and it wouldn't be the same without you and Aunt Eunice."

"I can barely believe they've been married for fifty years! Where did all the time go? Poof and it's gone!" lamented Gertrude, shaking her head. "Remember when we used to come out on Sunday afternoons to visit and Eunice would take that big old mutt Daisy Dog out for a walk and we'd make brownies and then smother them with ice cream and chocolate syrup? Little did you kids know that was my secret plan to stay your favorite aunt. Of course, Eunice was never much competition in that department. The only thing she ever was good at was being cranky and they don't give out awards for that!"

David and his sister laughed, the sun dousing them in golden light.

"Oh I remember," said Julia, "I still use your recipe. It's the only thing I can bake that my family will actually eat."

In the distance, a battalion of sea gulls hovered over steely blue waters, the young children playing along the water's edge oblivious to their presence. The birds were so large it looked like they could easily swoop down and carry off a toddler.

"David, I have a favor to ask and if you don't want to do it just tell me, I'll find somebody else. Eunice and I were talking to the lady who runs the supermarket. She told us about this chapel on the island, it's right on the ocean, and they have services every Sunday . . . well, as long as we're here, we would love to attend. Would you be a dear and drive us there tomorrow morning?"

"I don't know—are you sure you're going to be up for church tomorrow morning after all the partying tonight?" he teased.

"Hate to burst your bubble but Eunice and I are slowin' down. A couple of vodka tonics and the old battle axes are in bed by ten," she chuckled heartily. "But don't you forget sonny boy that twenty years ago I could drink you under the table!"

"Funny that's not the way I remember it," he said, his grin wide and eyes filled with warmth. "But I'll be happy to escort you to church, ma'am. If Gertrude would ask him to drive her to Atlanta he'd probably say yes. He liked her the way people like hot fudge sundaes, always a happy thought, with wonderful memories of her doting over him as a young boy, taking him to buy him baseball cards at the local dime store, or just hanging out in her kitchen while she made delicious pies from the apples they picked in her backyard.

"You are a dear," Gertrude said. "I better go and leave you two to your work. Can't wait to see what you've got cooked up for tonight!"

It was getting close to three o'clock when Maggie, on her way to the hotel parking lot, spotted David and Julia talking on the pool deck. Quickly, before she was noticed, she made a sharp turn into the snack bar area. She simply couldn't see her brother right now, not after what Marianne had just told her.

Looking at him, his easy-going nature discernible even from a distance, his attentiveness to his sister apparent, she was overwhelmed with concern for him. He was thoughtful, dependable, so generous—he didn't deserve this. *And why on earth did Marianne have to confide in her?* Why not share her secret with her best friend or her own sister? Maggie couldn't help but think of Wile E. Coyote in the *Road Runner* cartoon holding a long fuse to a stick of dynamite for which Marianne had just lit the match. She didn't want to be around for the explosion, possess this knowledge of what fate had in store for her brother.

Just yesterday she'd been thunderstruck by his revelation about the state of his marriage. She couldn't have been more surprised if he'd told her he was gay. For years his devotion to Marianne was unquestionable, a fortress of certainty in an uncertain world. She could barely believe it had all been jeopardized by a chance encounter with a woman he'd just met. It was so out of character, so irrational, it made no sense whatsoever, and, yet, if anyone could understand it, she could. It had been that way with Sasha, so cliché, so romance-novel love at first sight, as if everything in the world ceased to exist except this intoxicating passion and the object of her desire. She wanted her, she needed her, and that was all that mattered. Leaving Brian wasn't a choice, she had told herself, it was necessary for her survival.

She wondered what David's future held, if this were just some weird blip on the middle-age radar screen or if his life was about to come as unglued as hers had. Shit, she realized for the first time, if that happened, it would kill her mother. Judy was used to one screwup for a child, but David was her pride and joy, and even the hint of divorce would devastate her. Though her father had never really gotten on well with Marianne, he would be shocked. Maybe this will all just blow over, she mused. But the agony infused on her brother's face yesterday told her otherwise. That woman, whoever she was, had turned his world upside down.

She reached for the key to David's rented SUV, which Marianne had let her borrow to go into town. Once inside, she turned on the air conditioning and reached for her cell phone to call Sasha. She missed her desperately. This was the first time they'd ever been apart for more than a night. She had a lot to talk to her about, the trip, how things were working out much better than expected, but most importantly, the future. Until now, they'd been coasting along in a euphoric romantic bubble detached from the wreckage of a failed marriage and two young sons who thought Mommy was working on a special project in a faraway city. Tyler and Brad deserved better. Things had to change.

Over the past few days, an uncomfortable truth had surfaced, the truth of how wrong it had been for her to leave the boys the way she had, and how selfish her actions had been. Last night, looking for Colin, it had really hit home, the need to protect them, to be with them, to somehow find a way to work it out. Until now she had been able to justify her actions by telling herself she was not to blame for rebelling against a society that doesn't embrace gays and lesbians, a culture that punishes nonconformity and a husband and family who didn't understand her. Fuck you had been her longstanding mantra. She had reason to walk out, to find herself, to give herself some breathing room to enjoy this fragile happiness that had eluded her for so many years. But those excuses detonated like a hand grenade when she found Colin asleep in the tree house, so young, innocent and vulnerable.

Life is filled with moments of clarity. You either seize them or let them slip by. You grow or you stagnate. The decisions that had been swimming in a murky pond of uncertainty were now in razor focus. It was time to leave all the baggage behind and build a new life with Sasha and her boys, time to stop making excuses and grow up. For the first time she could remember, she was not afraid and felt genuinely hopeful about the future. She couldn't wait to tell Sasha.

The dinner menu featured a choice of Black Angus filet mignon with port wine reduction sauce; fresh Chilean sea bass sautéed in extra virgin olive oil; and fettuccine with lobster medallions in white wine sauce. Julia had not even blinked at the cost of $300-a-head; she had long ago passed the point of having to worry about such things. It certainly didn't hurt that she'd received a substantial bonus for the year on top of her six-figure annual salary.

At half past eight, guests were finishing delectable chocolate ribbon mousse cake drizzled with caramel served on fine china. Some ordered brandy alexanders and golden cadillacs, David indulged in an espresso martini. Tuxedo-clad waiters unobtrusively removed empty bottles of Morgan Reserve cabernet sauvignon and Alexandre Estate chardonnay from the white-linen tabletops.

Aunts, uncles, cousins, grandchildren and longtime family friends sparked a cacophony of conversation. "I've never been to a party like this," gushed an incredulous Aunt Patty, Judy's youngest sister from Kansas City. Patty and her husband Virgil lived on a farm thirty miles south of the city in a small town, where kids still helped their parents with chores and the dominant social gathering was the church potluck supper. Around the table, threads of conversation ran the gamut from "isn't this the most wonderful place" to "my how the kids have grown" to "this must have cost a fortune."

Judy's sister Maureen was enthralled with the treasures she found on the beach. "We went out just as the sun was coming up, and there were shells *everywhere!*" Maureen exclaimed. "Conch and whelks and hundreds of pink scallops, we had to go back and get another bag because we couldn't carry 'em all!" Sitting beside her, Gertrude raised her eyebrows and shook her head. "I know what's comin' next," she bemoaned. "Looks like it's going to be another shell lamp Christmas!"

Maureen took the ribbing in stride. "All right then, if that's the way you feel, I'll take you off my list. But you'll be sorry because these are going to be the best lamps ever! I might even try to sell them on eBay."

A few tables away, Judy, wearing a glimmering ivory-beaded jacket and matching silk skirt stood talking to Maggie.

"This is all so lovely," Judy said, gesturing around her, eyes full of wonder. And it was. Mother Nature had cooperated beautifully. The heavens suspended a dazzling umbrella of stars against an ebony sky, the breezes were soft and the ocean calm. Closer to earth, hundreds of tiny white organza star lights sparkled overhead. "I wish this evening never had to end," she said wistfully.

Maggie, wearing a simple but attractive black cocktail dress, bore no resemblance to the grunge queen she'd been for most of her adult life. "I've got to hand it to my big sister, she certainly knows how to throw a party." Maggie paused, smiling at her mother. "Mom you look so beautiful tonight."

"Honey, you look terrific!" Judy said. "I can't believe you found a dress that perfect on such short notice. It really looks good on you." Maggie had ended up at the Fort Myers outlet mall hours before the party with David's charge card after realizing the dress she had brought was too casual for such an elegant party. "I hope I look as good as you do when I'm your age," Maggie said.

Judy reached over and squeezed her daughter's hand. "I'm so glad you're here honey."

Julia came up behind them, her stride purposeful. Wearing

an immaculately cut white Armani suite and silk trousers, she looked like she'd stepped out of a Bergdorf Goodman window. Tiny pearl earrings and a strand of pearls around her swan-like neck completed the visage of urbane sophistication. Julia's looks and innate sense of style had been a formidable asset in her ascent through the corporate stratosphere, though she never acknowledged it to anyone. To do so, in her way of thinking, would be a betrayal of her hard-fought fight to shatter the glass ceiling.

"Mom," Julia said, "you've got to get Dad away from Uncle Frank because he's going to get him drunk. Uncle Frank is ordering shots of Wild Turkey. And Dad is belting them down!"

Judy laughed. "I don't know Julia, I think he deserves to get drunk after fifty years of marriage. For that matter so do I."

Julia didn't take her mother seriously, because she could not ever recall a time she saw her mother drunk. Maybe a little tipsy on wine at dinner. Her father was a different story, however, especially when Uncle Frank was around. Uncle Frank never met a cocktail he didn't like, serving up lots of laughs to everyone except his long-suffering wife and keeper of the dirty little secret of his alcoholism.

"Mom, you know how Dad gets when he's around Uncle Frank," Julia admonished. "He's like a little kid listening to his big brother. You better go over there before he gets sloshed. The last thing we need is Dad falling into the swimming pool."

Judy started off toward the bar, leaving Julia and Maggie standing under the stars. All around them were family and friends, their voices from time to time ringing out in laughter, faces lit by the golden glow of tea light candles.

Finally Maggie spoke. "Julia, I just want to say," her voice quiet, "you've really outdone yourself on this party. Such a perfect evening, everyone is here . . . and Mom couldn't be happier."

Though her relationship with Julia had been thawing, she wasn't sure how her sister would respond. So she was relieved when Julia stepped toward her and put her arm around her shoulders.

"Thank you for saying that," Julia said. "It means a lot to me. I was looking at all those old pictures today, going up to Aunt Patty's cabin, sledding at Jefferson Park, the year we got Barnie the golden retriever for Christmas . . . all those great times we had growing up. And it made me realize how lucky we were to have each other. We're sisters, we're family, and somehow we've lost that . . . and I think about Nicole and Rachel, and I hope that when they get older that they'll always be there for each other."

Maggie's could feel the tears welling up. Despite their heated arguments the fact of the matter was that she loved her sister and missed the closeness they once shared. Many years had passed, but she could still remember hearing Julia's reassuring voice from the twin bed across from hers, calming her fears, telling her not to be afraid of the dark, that there were no such things as monsters that lived under the bed or in the closet. Most nights Julia would tell her long and elaborate stories, her lively imagination conjuring up tales about an enchanted fairy princess named Marigold, a lonely girl named Veronica who befriended a talking dinosaur and a nerdy boy named Alistair who discovered a space ship in his backyard that only he could see. The years had passed, but those memories were etched in her consciousness, where she wanted them to remain forever.

"I love you big sis," she said, repeating something she'd often said as a child, wiping away a tear perched in the corner of her eye.

Julia's eyes were warm. "I love you too, Maggie. And I'm really glad you're here."

Maggie reached over to embrace her sister, who responded in kind, the two of them hugging each other under the twinkling lights.

Nearby, some of the party guests looked on, thinking how wonderful it was that the two sisters got along so well.

*   *   *

A HOTEL STAFFER PINNED A SMALL MICROPHONE on Gertrude's sequined-edged jacket to make sure she could be heard by the fifty or so guests seated in the clusters of tables in front of the podium. Her rose-colored chiffon mother-of-the-bride dress billowed in the evening breeze.

"Good evening everyone," she said, waiting a minute for the conversations to ebb. "I'm going to say a few words about my two favorite people in the whole world, my brother George and his lovely wife Judy." Gertrude showed no sign of nervousness, quite the opposite, in front of an audience she possessed the glib demeanor of a politician at a Labor Day parade.

"Uh-oh," she said, looking straight at Eunice, seated at the table with Judy and George. "Looks like I'm already in trouble! I meant my favorite *three* people dear sister." Eunice shook her head, a hint of a smile on her perpetually pursed lips. Laughter rippled up from the guests, their heartfelt affection for Judy and George evident.

"When Julia asked me to share some memories the first thing I said was 'How much time do I have?' I'm eighty-two years old for cryin' out loud, and if there's one thing I've got it's stories and lots of 'em! Some I can't even tell!" she said, sporting an infectious grin. Again laughter wafted up from the crowd.

"But before all that, there's just one thing I want to say." She walked over toward Judy and George's table, her face lit in a loving smile. "Judy and George, I want to thank you for all the times you didn't have to call but you did, for all the times you didn't have to have us over for dinner but you did, for all the times you didn't have to take us on vacation but you did. I guess what I'm saying is thank you for making us part of your family. We love you from the bottom of our hearts, we love your children, you gave us a gift that we'll never forget as long as we live—and hopefully that will be a long time but at my age you never know! With that the crowd erupted in enthusiastic applause. While she waited for it to die down, Julia came over and handed her a glass of champagne for the toast.

"On behalf of everyone here tonight, I want to thank you for your love and friendship and for all the wonderful times we've had together all these years. You've inspired us with your love for each other and for your children. You make being married fifty years look like fun! A toast to my brother and his beautiful wife Judy. Happy fiftieth anniversary, and best wishes for many, many more!"

A tinkling of glasses and people saying "cheers!" were followed by another burst of spirited applause. Judy and George were beaming. Then George leaned over and kissed his wife. Gertrude waited patiently for the applause to subside.

"So, where were we? Ah yes, stories. Well, my dear brother ever since he was a little boy has had a problem remembering things," said Gertrude. "Mother used to say that he'd forget his head if it wasn't screwed on. And she was right. Eighty-two years I've been on God's green earth, and to this day, he doesn't have a clue when my birthday is!"

George protested loudly from his table. "That's not true! Judy tell her when her birthday is." More laughter.

"So one day George calls me up and he's beside himself. He says"—Gertrude dropped her pitch a couple of octaves in an exaggerated impersonation of George's husky voice—"'Gertie, I really screwed up because I just realized tomorrow is our twentieth wedding anniversary. I didn't make any plans, I don't even have a dinner reservation. Judy always drops me a hint but she didn't say anything and tomorrow's the day and I don't know what to do!'"

"Well I could barely keep my mouth shut," Gertrude said, "because I knew why Judy hadn't told him anything. She'd been planning a huge surprise for months; she was taking him to Las Vegas and had asked me and Eunice to stay with the kids. Judy had taken care of everything—the reservations, the tickets, she even got the time off work for him."

"But here he was on the phone, this poor tortured soul stumbling through life without a memory, he didn't have a clue as to what to do, so I told him, 'Listen Georgie, you're gonna have to go to Marshall Fields and buy her china because that's the symbol for the twentieth anniversary.' And he's real quiet for a minute, then he says, 'do I have to buy her an entire set of dishes?' Well that just cracked me up! I called him Mr. Romance because the first thing he thinks of is a set of dishes, not a keepsake or a beautiful figurine. He got so mad, he was yellin' at me, saying 'how can you laugh at a time like this, she'll never forgive me if I screw up our twentieth anniversary.'" Gertrude's impersonation of George was hilarious, and another round of laughter bubbled up from the guests.

Judy smiled at the memory, realizing she hadn't thought about that trip for years. They had stayed at The Dunes Hotel, gambled into the wee hours, slept until noon and seen Wayne Newton on the Strip. She looked at her husband, who was smiling, his arm loosely draped around the back of her chair. He looked very handsome tonight in his black dinner jacket and crisp white shirt, she marveled at the fact that in the moonlight, she could still see a shadow of the young man she'd married so many years ago.

Again she wished the night would never end.

It had been Jeremy's idea to go out to dinner, just as it was his idea to go down to the beach afterward. He'd been in good spirits all day, leaving Ellen to wonder if extraterrestrials had abducted her real husband and left this other specimen. It had been such an emotionally wrenching morning for her, just the idea that he was *here*, that he had walked into her deepest darkest secret with the air wreaking of her betrayal. It gave rise to an unsettling fear that if he were with her long enough he would *sense* it, much like an animal senses an unseen predator.

But then they had gone off together, first for a long walk on the beach, picking up shells scattered along the shore, then to lunch at the bar with the best grouper sandwiches that he'd remembered from their last visit. They took a nap during which he hadn't initiated sex but she could sense his desire, and now he was leading her down to the beach. "It's too beautiful of an evening to be inside," he said.

They came upon the village of cabanas that during the day cost sun worshippers twenty-five dollars-an-hour but now were deserted. Jeremy chose one with the royal blue canvas top rolled back with two chase lounges joined by a small wooden table. "How's this?" he asked.

A little buzzed from the wine at dinner that had blunted the jagged edge of her nervousness, Ellen marveled at the fact that she was actually enjoying this night out with her husband after all that had transpired. People say humans are amazingly resilient creatures, certainly this was evidence of that maxim. Their marriage had been so marred by conflict recently, they had not had an evening out like this in a long time.

"Perfect," she replied, looking over at her husband, whose sandy hair was tousled and eyes were intense. "Look at the stars."

"Wow," he said. "And I'll expand on that as soon as I go over there and get us a nightcap. Wine?"

"Yes, that would be nice," she said.

"Make sure no one takes my chair," he joked, as he disappeared behind the sprawling sea grape bushes.

Ellen stretched out on the chaise lounge and took in her surroundings. It *was* a gorgeous evening, the near-constant crash of the surf replaced by a calm, silky lapping of waves against the shore. Wearing a chambray floral print sundress, she was not chilled in the slightest. She could hear music from a party on the hotel pool deck, Frank Sinatra singing "Summer Wind."

She and Jeremy had danced to that song at their wedding.

Her thoughts lingered on that indelible memory when suddenly a light switch clicked on in her brain. Tonight was David's parents' anniversary party. That's where the music was coming from. *Oh my god*, he could be right over there, on the other side of the bushes. The realization jerked her out of her mellow wine buzz. The two of them, Jeremy and David, within a stone's throw of each other. Perhaps both standing at the bar ordering drinks. *Does life get any more weird?* Was it possible this entire week had been a dream from which she'd soon awaken? She wondered what David was doing, how handsome he must look in a suit.

"Here you go," Jeremy said, emerging from the dark path. He handed her a glass of wine. Sitting on the edge of the lounge chair next to hers, he proposed a toast.

"To new beginnings," he said. "Especially for me," he added. "Promise."

His quiet acknowledgment of the problems in their marriage

and his willingness to tackle them engendered in Ellen a tenderness that had been long absent. After so many months of bitterness and resentment, she was jolted by this wellspring of compassion; it was as if she had actually forgotten how much she loved him. He had given her so little reason to remember until now.

Their glasses clinked. She took a sip of her wine. Before them the moon cast a platinum ribbon of shimmering light on the Gulf of Mexico.

She savored the moment, unsure what to say, fearful of doing anything to spoil it. "You really surprised me this morning. I never in a million years expected you to show up on my doorstep."

"Good surprise?"

"Good surprise," she confirmed. "Why did you *really* come?"

"Because the third day you were gone I realized I couldn't live without you."

"Really."

"Yes."

"And this just occurred to you," she said with a glint of teasing.

"Well, yes—and no—I think I'm in trouble here," he said, smiling. A long pause ensued.

"Listen, I know things have been screwed up," he said. Reaching over, he took her hand gently in his. "I've been doing a lot of thinking over the past few weeks, even before you left, I knew that we couldn't go on like this. I know a lot of our problems are my fault. I think I've been depressed for a while now. Mom's death, my job, Andrew, it's just been a snowball that keeps getting bigger and bigger. I had a long talk with Bob the other day. When I told him we were having problems he looked me right in the eye and said that you were the best thing that ever happened to me and that I would be a fool to ever let you go. I don't know why I needed to hear that from him, but I did and it made me afraid that this trip might be the first step in your leaving me. I don't ever want you to leave me, Ellen. I cannot imagine my life without you. Promise me you won't leave me," he said, his eyes locked on hers.

Promise me you'll see me again. David's words last night.
Now this. Ellen's mind reeled to produce the correct response.
Despite her behavior of the past several days, normally she was a
scrupulously honest person. If she uttered the words he wanted
to hear right now she had to mean it. The question was did she?
Could she follow through, turn away from David and not look
back?

Again she found herself standing on the precipice of a
crevasse, this time from the vantage point of crossing over into
the arms of the man to whom she pledged her life, love and
faithfulness. *Isn't that what last night's speech to David was all
about?*

"Of course I'll never leave you," she said with forced
conviction. "I love you. She paused. "But I want things to get
better."

"I love you too," he said. He came over to embrace her,
kissing her softly on the lips. "You have no idea how much. I feel
terrible about the way things have been. And it will get better, I
promise."

For the next few seconds, neither spoke. The strains of Cole
Porter's "Night and Day" could be heard wafting on the breeze.
She sat back in her chair, closed her eyes, and breathed in the
night air. She could not deny that there was a part of her still
longing for David, but in a surprising twist of fate there was
distinct spark of desire for her husband as well.

"There's something else we need to talk about, Ellen."

The tone of his voice made her immediately paranoid. *Did
he know her secret? No, not possible, or else they wouldn't have
been just having the conversation they had.*

"I've been trying to find the right time to tell you." Another
long pause. "It's about Andrew."

"What? What about Andrew?" she asked, ripped by a flash
of fear.

"Well there's another reason I came here besides wanting to
be with you. I needed to see you and tell you in person. I didn't
want you to get home and find out."

"Find out what?" Now she was really scared. She put her glass of wine down and sat up in her chair.

He hesitated before speaking. "Andrew got busted for drugs at school. He's been snorting OxyContin. He's not the only one, the school has been watching a group of kids and he's one of them. He's also been selling it because he had seven hundred dollars in cash on him when they picked him up."

"What? OxyContin! He's been snorting OxyContin! Oh my god, why didn't you tell me!"

"I am telling you," he said calmly. "I've been trying to find the right time and there wasn't a right time, I couldn't just waltz in and tell you this morning . . . I knew I should but I wanted the day with you . . . I wanted some time to get things straightened out between us first."

"When did this happen?" she asked.

"Tuesday," he replied.

"You've known since Tuesday and kept it from me!" she exclaimed, incredulous.

"I didn't want to ruin your vacation. I didn't know what to do," he said.

"Oh my god." Ellen felt like someone kicked her in the stomach. The problems with Andrew had been ongoing, but OxyContin . . . and dealing! Anger and revulsion vied for supremacy in her turbulent mind. She could not fathom the reality of what he was telling her. *Okay this is a nightmare and I will wake up any minute.*

"Jeremy, are they sure, are they sure this wasn't a mistake? I know Andrew has his problems, but this, I can't believe he's capable of this, I've never seen any sign . . . OxyContin, isn't that a felony?"

"I'm so sorry I had to tell you this," he said, putting his arm around her trembling shoulders. He held her for a few moments before he spoke.

"Ellen, there's more."

"What do you mean there's more. I can't take any more," she said, anguished.

"He's in drug rehab."

"What! He's not with Amy—you said this morning—"

"He's not with Amy, Ellen. He's in a thirty-day program. He was high when the cops picked him up and he admitted snorting it whenever he can get his hands on it. He likes the way it makes him feel, he told me. I had no choice. I called Jeff," he said referring to a close friend who was a drug counselor, "and he agreed. Jeff said 'just get him into rehab so he can get the help he needs.' OxyContin is highly addictive, and snorting it can be more dangerous than taking it orally. The rehab will also look good when he goes to court, because you know, Ellen, this is a huge deal."

"Jeremy, I can't believe all this. I can't believe my son could be in this much trouble. OxyContin. Not pot, or booze, but this. How on earth did this happen?"

"I know, I know, it's a shock," he said, leaning over to gently brush her hair back from her cheek. "I've had several days to think things through. Do you want another glass of wine, maybe it'll help you calm down."

"No, I don't want anything except to wake up from this nightmare."

"I feel bad keeping this from you but you had so looked forward to this trip. When the police called I was devastated, I couldn't believe it. But now that I've had time to think, I'm actually glad he got caught. Now we know—thank god for that. He could have died, he could have accidentally OD'd, he could have sold it to someone who died. You never think this stuff is going to happen to your kid. I'm sorry I had to make the decision without you but it was crystal clear what needed to be done. He needs professional help. I've been so mired in my own bullshit I missed all this. I'm his father and I'm supposed to protect him and instead I looked the other way. Whatever happens, Ellen, I promise you, this will never happen again."

She was stunned by this unprecedented admission. Had the price of Jeremy's wake-up call not been so high she would have felt vindicated. Jeremy had been disengaged, always accusing her of worrying excessively, being too hard on Andrew. But even with all that, she could not let him take the blame alone. She'd been right there with him, missing all the signs. Until this moment, she'd lived on the periphery, listening to the accounts of kids selling Adderall at school and binge drinking at weekend parties but thinking it would never penetrate her family. Andrew just wasn't that kind of kid, she had told herself. She had been to all of the high school drug education nights. She knew what to look for. And somehow she'd missed it. All the wisdom she had tried to impart to Andrew about drugs and alcohol had gone unheeded; all the extracurricular activities, music lessons and sports activities she had orchestrated to provide an alternative to the lure of drugs had failed.

They sat on the beach and talked for a long time. They talked about past and the future, how they had trusted him and how he had abused that trust. They talked about how scared he must be right now, imprisoned in a facility full of strangers who wanted him to open up and share feelings and turn away from the drugs he thought were so cool. They talked about how disappointed they were at the way things had turned out, how was it possible that the son they had nurtured and protected had become addicted to drugs at the age of fifteen. It was a messed up world. All the while, the Cole Porter and Frank Sinatra songs played on, and the occasional sound of laughter could be heard from the party. Eventually the music and wine had their intended effect, and after a while she was able to calm down.

It wasn't until a few hours later, as she lie emotionally and physically exhausted in her husband's arms in the bed that she had shared with another man just a few nights ago that she realized Jeremy had done exactly the right thing for their son. And she loved him dearly for it.

This changes everything, she thought for the second time that week.

L iz realized soon after she arrived at the chapel on Sunday morning that the worship service would be overflowing. Awaiting her were more than a dozen voice mail messages. "Are you still having services, we want to see the chapel before the bulldozers come," said one caller. "We want to help, where do we send a check?" asked another. The TV crew from WBAY Fort Myers wanted to come out and talk to parishioners after the service. Liz was amazed at all the hoopla, she never imagined that so many people would care.

Well they were in for a big surprise, she thought, hardly able to contain her excitement. She couldn't wait to share the good news. Jennifer had called late last night to tell her that she and Gregory had decided that Palm Beach was a much more suitable location for their new home. Better yet, Gregory had agreed to create an easement to allow the chapel to remain on the property permanently. Mimicking her ten-year-old grandson, Liz, grinning ear to ear, made a fist, thumb outstretched, jerked her hand down and exclaimed "yesss!"

"Oh Miss Kitty we did it, we really did it!" she said, thrilled with the outcome.

In the midst of her triumph she had a fleeting moment of guilt; she knew her actions didn't meet the standards of honesty and integrity that she tried to live her life by—let alone the tenets of her faith. Call it what it is, she chided herself, blackmail, and that's not in the Beatitudes! She winced at the thought. Yet she didn't regret what she had done. And, she told herself with a wry smile, wasn't it Martin Luther who said "sin boldly?" Well she had certainly excelled on that score.

Everyone—Ruby, Myrtle and Ronnie, Millie and George, Betty Jo, Pastor Roberts—oh, she couldn't wait to tell Ellen— would be so happy to hear the news. Liz decided to wait until the end of the service to make the announcement so it wouldn't disrupt worship.

She walked up to the altar to make sure the appropriate Scripture readings were book-marked for the readers. The morning sunlight poured in through the windows, casting the room in an aquamarine glow. How she loved this place. She looked out over the empty pews that would soon be filled to capacity, filled with the faces of her dear friends and neighbors, people she had come to know and love over the years, people she would have never met had she stayed in Illinois after Edward died. She remembered those dark days after he passed away, and marveled at the new life she had been given and all of its blessings. Moving here was one of the best decisions she'd ever made, despite the fact that her children had fought her tooth and nail.

She heard a car pulling up. That must be Rev. Roberts. She headed into the back room to gather the bulletins for the service. People would be arriving soon, and there was still plenty of work to be done.

"So Mom, what's going on with Dad?" Julia asked, in between bites of a delicious portobello mushroom and spinach omelet.

Still basking in the glow of what had been a magical evening, Judy had invited her daughters to breakfast in the hotel's elegant dining room. She hardly ever saw Julia and Maggie and she wanted to spend some time with them, especially now that they were getting along. They were seated at a table in front of the signature floor-to-ceiling titanium-tinted windows overlooking the Gulf of Mexico.

"What do you mean?" she said, her eyebrows arched inquisitively as if she had no idea why this question was being put to her. Her response was designed to buy time—even if only a few more seconds—to decide whether to make excuses or tell the truth. The momentousness of her decision had not escaped her. If she were truthful, there would be no going back to "everything is fine" mode. Even though she desperately wanted to confide in them, she also wanted them to be able to enjoy the rest of their vacation and not worry about their father's bewildering behavior. She also was well aware that once they knew of the situation certain steps would have to be taken, and this was unsettling. Denial was easier, it prevented things and events from spiraling out of control.

"I didn't mention this the other day, but Nicole said that Dad was kind of out of it the night Colin disappeared," Julia said. "She said Dad didn't even remember Colin being there when she came back with Alicia. It really freaked her out. She feels terrible for leaving them alone, and blames herself for Colin wandering off."

Maggie, nibbling on a strawberry from her fruit platter, looked puzzled. "Are you sure Nicole isn't just being a drama queen?" she asked. "You know how girls are at her age."

"So what do you call it at your age," Julia replied, her tone affectionate to soften the sarcasm. "No, Nicole isn't like that, she's been known to embellish a bit but not on something like this. And I almost forgot. Aunt Eunice told me that Dad got confused when you were playing cards the other day."

Judy stared down at her half-eaten eggs Benedict, wanting the moment to pass but knowing it would not. Her silence prompted Julia to press on. "Mom, I'm headed out of here on a plane tomorrow night and after that I'm going to London. If there's something going on I need to know. This isn't a conversation to have on a cell phone at the airport."

Julia was right. It could be months before they would see each other again, and this wasn't something to discuss on the phone. Still, part of her resented the fact that this had to come up now, when she was so happy just to be having such a nice time with both of her daughters.

"Well, all right, to answer your question . . ." she said, then paused to inhale deeply. "I *am* worried about your father, and have been for a while. He can be very forgetful, moody and sometimes he just seems to lapse off into outer space. And the other night, he went for a walk to the store and got lost. David had to go out and look for him. He finally showed up when a limo driver from a hotel down the beach brought him home."

Heavy silence enveloped the table, as Maggie and Julia struggled to process what she was telling them. Their father didn't get lost, ever. The idea that their seventy-one-year-old father, a healthy, vibrant man, might be afflicted with something even remotely associated with dementia or Alzheimer's terrified them though they tried not to show it. Instinctively they knew how vulnerable and scared their mother must be right now, and their alarm would only worsen the situation.

"Mom, I know what you're thinking, but it could be a lot of other things. Is he taking any medication, maybe he's off schedule," Julia ventured.

"He doesn't take any medication, Julia," Judy said. "I don't want to worry you, but I have lived with this man for fifty years and I can tell something has changed."

"What happened the other night?" Maggie asked.

"I don't know. Apparently he took a wrong turn on the bike path. It was awful, he was gone for more than two hours and I had no idea where he was. Thank goodness that limo driver picked him up and brought him home. Apparently your father couldn't remember where he was staying, but when the driver ticked off a list of places, he recognized Paradise. By the time he got home he seemed normal, but tired. He went to bed and that was that."

"Mom I'm so sorry that you've had to deal with all this," Julia said. "You should have told me."

"I know honey, but it wasn't until we got here that I realized I couldn't keep making excuses. The night Colin got lost was a turning point, I just couldn't ignore it any more. But I didn't want to ruin the party."

They sat quietly for a moment amid the quiet symphony of conversation around them. Julia took a sip of coffee then gently placed the cup on the matching saucer. "Listen Mom, the first thing we need to do is find him the best doctors who deal with this. I know how Dad is, he's not going to want to go but I'll talk to him if you want me to. He's got to do this, for himself, for you, for all of us. Maybe it's not the worst. I'll help you find a doctor. I know a few people I can ask and then there's always Mayo. Maybe we should just get him in there."

In the midst of her unease, Judy couldn't help but smile upon hearing "Mayo" because she'd known that would be Julia's response. *Get the best, spend whatever it takes, don't waste any time* was her daughter's mantra for dealing with any crisis personal or professional. "I don't know Julia, I'm not sure your father will go along with this—"

"He's needs to see a doctor," Julia countered firmly. "And don't worry about money Mom. If you've got to travel I'll take care of the hotel and airfares. You can use my frequent flier miles and go first class," she added. In Julia's world if money couldn't solve life's problems, it could certainly make things more comfortable.

Maggie finished up the last of the blueberries on her plate, and reached over to touch her mother's arm gently. "Mom, we don't know what this is yet so there's no reason we should assume the worst. But even if it is something serious, we'll get through it," she said. There was a long pause before she continued. "If you need me to I'll come home and help you deal with this. You won't be alone. Promise."

Overwhelmed with the sincerity of her offer and genuine concern emanating from both her daughters, Judy felt tears welling up in her eyes.

"Maggie, that's so sweet of you to offer," she said, with the hint of a smile through a mist of tears. She took a tissue out of her purse and dabbed at the corner of her eyes.

It was the first time Maggie or Julia had ever seen their mother cry in public, and one of only a handful of times they'd ever seen her cry at all.

Judy reached across the table and grabbed both their hands. "I love you both so much," she said, squeezing the hands she held tightly.

The visage of their mother's face so poignantly expressing that love in the face of a deepening shadow of foreboding evoked a cloudburst of emotion that came to the sisters without warning. It was, for both of them, the profound realization that every child knows they will face some day—the inevitable changing of the guard, the juxtaposition of the roles of parent and child, mother and daughter. She who had protected them from the moment they had taken their first breath now needed them to protect her in the face of an unknown and uncertain future. Neither one of them hesitated, they knew what they had to do, their allegiance to their mother unflinching and as involuntary as breathing.

"We love you too Mom," said Julia, squeezing her mother's hand, while Maggie reached over and put her arm around her mother's shoulder. They stayed this way for a few more moments, oblivious to the people, conversation and activity around them. "It'll be okay Mom," Julia said. "I promise."

Judy knew her daughter could promise no such outcome, but nonetheless felt relieved. A heavy weight had been lifted. She had taken the first step on a journey into an uncertain future, but she was not alone.

Judy reached for another tissue as the waiter looked on curiously.

There was never a good time to start the conversation that would determine the course of one's life when you so desperately feared the outcome.

After dinner, Becca, who had put in a long day at Over the Rainbow, joined Michael outdoors on the patio, a rectangular slab of concrete shielded from view by a six-foot cedar fence draped with lavender wisteria. Michael, whose T-shirt bore splashes of vivid colors, a testimony to an afternoon of painting, was in a foul mood, but she had grown tired of waiting. Though she desperately wanted to tell him the truth—that she wanted a child, a commitment, a wedding—she knew in her heart of hearts he did not share her ambitions. True, she had the occasional fleeting fantasy that when Michael understood her innermost needs and desires he would magically transform into the man that she wanted him to be, but more often she felt like the hard edge of reality was closing in on her.

He had been distant and emotionally aloof. *Maybe I should wait,* she thought. But she couldn't stop herself. Like bile rising inexorably in her throat, the issue had to be purged. It was amazing to her how long she had kept it at bay. She felt like she'd suddenly been jerked out of a coma. Why was she so willing to accept the crumbs he was offering? Why was she afraid to speak up? So she did.

She cried for three hours after that fateful conversation. She had carefully presented her case, telling him that she wanted to have a baby, that time was passing her by, that she needed to know whether this was something he wanted as well or had even thought about. He never interrupted her; she felt like an actor in a play that had gone on too long, the audience restless and wanting to leave. They did not shout or argue. In the end it was seven words strung together in one heartbreaking sentence. "I can't deal with this right now," he said, the annoyance in his voice palpable. He didn't hold her hand or stroke her hair; all that followed was silence while he stared ahead at the creeping wisteria in the deepening twilight. She had no way of knowing that his dark mood was the result of being dumped by Jennifer Foster, the latest in a string of mistresses Becca knew nothing about.

But she did have her answer. The next morning, fueled by an explosive mix of anger and determination, she packed her bags. It was early; there wasn't much traffic on the causeway and bridge to the mainland. In the rear view mirror Sanibel was as beautiful as ever. But it was time to go home, time to start over. Life is too short to sacrifice your dreams, she told herself. There would be tears in the days ahead, but no regrets.

Ellen marveled at the throng of worshippers making their way into the chapel. So many that the ushers were putting out metal folding chairs to accommodate the overflow crowd. A boisterous cacophony of greetings reverberated inside the unadorned sanctuary with its blue green walls and old-fashioned casement windows. A buzz of excitement infused the air.

Ellen took a seat at the end of a pew near the back. She had woken up early, dressed quietly and slipped out, not wanting Jeremy to hear her. He probably would have wanted to come with her but she preferred to go alone, so she let him sleep. Still reeling from his unexpected arrival and the news about Andrew, she desperately sought refuge in the chapel in the hope she would find comfort here.

Replaying the events of the past week, she shook her head imperceptibly in amazement, letting a deep exhale escape the confines of her body. Twenty-four hours ago she'd been mired in guilt over an adulterous affair; now she faced the nightmare reality that her son had been busted for drugs. It was a terrible irony that it took a personal tragedy of this magnitude to push David off center stage of her emotional consciousness.

In her midst were many older couples, several with grandkids they probably only got to see once or twice a year when their children came to visit. Liz had been standing in a tight circle of parishioners when she arrived and Ellen didn't want to intrude.

She marveled at the woman's friendships and the life she had built for herself on the island, reading good books, tending to her garden and volunteering at the chapel. Ellen hoped it would be that way for her when she got older, and in that hope was the realization of how much she had changed over the years, that this so-called "simple life" would have so much appeal to her. Ellen in her twenties wanted a successful career more than anything in the world; now in her forties she could happily envision a life of putzing around in the kitchen, taking long walks and gardening.

There were three hymns in the bulletin, all favorites: "A Closer Walk with Thee," "Shall We Gather by the River" and "How Great Thou Art." Over the years she had come to cherish these old Gospel hymns, many she had first heard at her grandma's nursing home, where they held church services in the dining room on Sunday mornings. The elderly residents loved those hymns, they sang them loudly and with fervor, and although many of their memories were beaten away by the passage of time, remarkably most of them still knew the words. Her grandma had been a vivacious woman, full of life and laughter, a lot like Liz, she mused, as she lifted her head to see the organist. In that moment, her peripheral vision took in someone else, and her mind simply could not register the reality of what she saw.

It was David.

No it couldn't be.

It *was* David.

Sitting a few pews in front of her, his profile unmistakable, his head was turned attentively toward an elderly woman sitting next to him wearing a canary yellow hat with a spray of pink flowers on the brim. He must have said something amusing because the woman's eyes crinkled as her face lit up in a jovial smile. *Why was he here? Who was that woman?* Then she remembered him talking about his family on the beach that night, his favorite aunt with the old-fashioned name—*Bernice or Agnes—no, that wasn't it* . . . and then she remembered: Gertrude. The aunt who talked the mugger into giving her back her handbag. It had to be her.

Her heart pounding, she tried to absorb the situation. What on earth was he doing here? How was it possible that their paths should cross again on this Sunday morning in this holy place that was her fortress of protection against him?

Her eyes were still fixed on him when he leaned down to pick up something on the floor. As he turned to hand the bulletin to the man behind him, his eyes met hers. His surprise evident, he smiled at her.

Her first thought was to leave, but she quickly reconsidered. What good would it do? If her faith wasn't strong enough to keep her from running and hiding from him now, what hope was there for the future? She had never been a coward. Her panicked thoughts were interrupted by the first chords of the opening hymn. The congregation stood as the organist played the introduction to "A Closer Walk with Thee." The hymn reminded her of long ago summers and vacation Bible school, crosses made out of popsicle sticks and picnics on the church lawn.

The congregation sang loudly and with spirit, and Ellen joined in.

PASTOR ROBERTS TOOK HIS PLACE behind the pulpit to start the sermon.

"Matthew's Gospel begins with the story of John the Baptist crying out in the wilderness, 'repent for the kingdom of heaven is near.' And it is with this message that Jesus begins his ministry. Repentance is the cornerstone of our faith. This morning I want to talk about what it actually means to repent."

Ellen listened intently, he certainly had her attention. Liz. This had to be her doing. What were the odds of a missive on repentance on this particular Sunday after everything that happened this week? Serendipity? Divine intervention? An answer to prayer? All of the above?

"A lot of people think repentance means saying you're sorry. This is the prevailing view in our popular culture, especially when celebrities or politicians get in a jam," said Pastor Roberts, smiling. "No matter what the offense, they can't get to a microphone fast enough to tell the world how sorry they are."

"That may be what popular culture requires, but God wants more. It's not just about saying sorry and moving on. Genuine repentance is about a radical change in heart, a turning away from sin, and a renewed commitment to obedience through faith." He paused. "Obedience. People don't use that word much anymore, not even with their dogs." A murmur of amused agreement percolated through the congregation.

The sermon was excellent; it emboldened in Ellen the hope of a new beginning. She said a prayer of thanks for Liz, who had been such a godsend during the past week and so instrumental in helping embark on this journey of faith. She had never really believed in angels, but it seemed there was one in her midst.

AFTER THE PRAYERS, LIZ CAME FORWARD to do the announcements. "Good morning everyone," she said with enthusiasm. "We're so delighted to have you all here this morning for worship. You'd think it was Easter morning it's so crowded!

"Now I know there's been quite a lot of excitement around here lately. I'm sure some of you may have read about us in the newspaper or saw us on TV," she said.

An anticipatory silence hung over the congregation, who thought this representative of Grace Chapel looked to be in very good spirits for someone whose sanctuary stood in the path of a wrecking ball.

"You may recall that last week I told you that the owner of this property, Mr. Gregory Foster, informed us that he planned to tear down this building to make room for his new home. But yesterday, we received some good news—I mean very good news because I have a letter," she held it up, "from Mr. Foster saying he's changed his mind, that he's not going to build a house here after all. And here's the best part. He's granting us a perpetual easement on his property so we can stay here!"

An audible gasp of surprise came from the congregation,

followed by a burst of spontaneous applause. Ruby, seated in the front row, jumped to her feet, leading the way for others to stand and applaud. "Hallelujah! Praise the Lord!" she exclaimed, beaming.

Liz took off her reading glasses, looked out over the congregation. "I think this is what they call making a joyful noise unto the Lord," she said, straining to be heard over the din.

Ellen applauded loudly, almost dizzy at the thought of what they had accomplished, marveling at the sublime irony of how one vintage motorcycle and the infidelity of a gold-digging trophy wife had been the catalyst for this incredible turn of events.

After the congregation finally settled down, the organist played the introduction to "Shall We Gather By The River." The congregation sang loudly and with zeal. It was a wonderful hymn, an exuberant moment, one Ellen knew she would never forget. And in that sliver of time, she knew what she must do.

As if reading her mind, as soon as the hymn was over, he stood up quickly and left the chapel, giving her a look that said *follow me*. And she did.

They walked on the scruffy path that led to the small clearing where more than a dozen cars were parked. A fortress of Australian pines shielded them from view.

Wearing khaki pleated shorts and a vanilla-colored polo shirt that had the effect of deepening his golden tan, David was as attractive as ever.

"They say the Lord certainly works in mysterious ways," he said, grinning, as he fell into stride with her. She wanted to be serious, but found it hard to resist his cheerful demeanor.

"Mysterious yes, but not bizarre," she said, smiling back at him. "What on earth are you doing here?"

"Do you find it so hard to believe that I would be in church on Sunday morning? What do you take me for? A godless heathen?"

"Far be it for me to judge your religious habits, church-going or otherwise," she said. Again the flirtatious banter came as naturally as a spring rain. He made her feel smart and witty and beautiful, a lethal combination for a woman trying to do the right thing.

"Well, truth be told, Aunt Gertrude asked me to take her to church, and being her favorite nephew and all, I was happy to oblige," he replied, with the earnestness of a Boy Scout working on a merit badge.

He touched her elbow lightly, and turned in toward her as if to start their real conversation. "How are you? I couldn't believe your message yesterday." Quietly he added, as if he needed confirmation, "Your husband is here?"

She felt like a character on a soap opera.

"Yes. Jeremy is here."

He nodded, taking a moment to consider just what that meant. Tilting his head to look at her, he fixed his eyes on hers in that way he had of immobilizing her defenses. She remembered the old TV show *Lost in Space*; wouldn't it be wonderful if someone could invent an invisible force field to protect you not only from space aliens but from the seductive powers of another human being? Like a heat-seeking missile locking onto its target, his unflinching gaze penetrated not only her eyes but her being. But this time force field or not she had to mount a defense. *Think about what Pastor Roberts said, think about Jeremy, think about Andrew—*

On a wing and a prayer she spoke. "David, I'm really glad you're here because it gives us a chance to say goodbye. And that's what we have to do because . . ." she said, hesitating. "I told you why the other night, and nothing has changed. If anything it's more clear to me that I've made a huge mistake in judgment here."

He shook his head in disagreement, but before he could speak she continued.

"You know how I feel about you, nothing like this has ever happened to me . . . it was all so sudden and unexpected . . . and wonderful . . ." she said, her eyes meeting his as her words trailed off.

In the distance, they could hear the congregation singing the closing hymn. A diaphanous breeze floated around them, warm and inviting, while a squadron of gulls drifted nearby. She so wished things were different, that they were not married, that they had met twenty years ago when unencumbered by families and spouses and children, but thinking this would only prolong the agony.

An invisible curtain fell on his carefree demeanor. "Listen Ellen, do what you need to do today but understand this: I'm in love with you and I'm not going to just walk away. And nothing you do or say is going to change that. And you can tell yourself that this is a horrible sin that must be purged from your life but I believe in God too and I don't think God requires two people who fall in love to never see each other again." He hesitated, then took her in his arms and crushed her against him, so close she couldn't breathe.

Silence. A phalanx of battleship pelicans perched precariously on the lanky branches of the pine trees around them. A cadre of sea gulls circled overhead. The cadence of the gentle surf, constant and unceasing, beckoned.

Lifting her eyes to meet his, she summoned every fiber of willpower she possessed to break away from his embrace. "I'll never forget you David. But I think I really need to go now."

His compliance surprised her, but then again he had his aunt to worry about, the service would be over any minute. They walked back toward the chapel together, their sandals crunching in the gravel. Ellen had never liked saying goodbye to anyone—not family or colleagues or friends—and this one was excruciating in its finality. Yet from somewhere in the depths of her soul, a glimmer of resolve came over her.

They reached the chapel entrance, the ushers had opened wide the wooden doors for the end of the service. David reached for her hand. "I love you," he said, his voice a mixture of certainty and despair that was mirrored on his face. She replied with a smile tinged with regret and sympathy. Looking at him this one last time, she memorized with anxious scrutiny every detail of his face, piercing eyes, windswept hair, and then turned away, walking toward the beach, refusing to yield to the potent desire to go back. In the days and months ahead, she would look back on this moment and realize that she had not been the sole source of this strength, that it had to have been her faith that powered her on, kept her moving forward. Nothing else could explain it.

"I'll call you," he said, his voice trailing after her.

She didn't respond. The expanse of pristine white sand unfurled before her, hundreds of shorebirds flitting to and fro, azure skies over diamond-glistening waters. A faint breeze caressed her face, the sunlight dazzling in its brilliance.

It took a few moments, but then another feeling swept over her, this one euphoric and liberating. She was free. The spell was broken. For now.

The last place David expected to find himself after the heartrending anguish of saying goodbye to the woman he had fallen in love with was in a posh restaurant alone with his wife. But that's where he was, and he was utterly miserable.

After dropping off Aunt Gertrude, he had gone back to the condo. Much to his surprise, the place was eerily quiet, and Marianne was alone. "Where are the kids?" he asked.

"Your mother and Maggie are taking them to the pool and then to lunch. They wanted us to have some alone time."

Great. His thoughts heavy, he felt seriously depressed, and didn't know if he could pull off having lunch with his wife without the distraction of their children. She would have to sense something was wrong. He considered begging off with a headache, but rejected the idea. He would go along with her plans; he had no reason not to. The guilt that he'd been able to in large part ignore over the past several days was festering now that she was actually paying attention to *him* and not the children.

"Let's go to the hotel and have lunch at that restaurant with the beautiful view of the ocean," she said. "Julia says the food is wonderful."

He agreed, buying as much time as possible with changing his shirt and freshening up. Twenty minutes later they were on their way. Marianne wore a sleeveless sundress that showed off her tan, her long blonde tresses fell nicely on her bare shoulders, a definite improvement from her everyday Mommy persona.

It wasn't quite noon, so fortunately there wasn't a large crowd yet at Ocean View. They followed the maître d' to a table for two along the window wall. From there they had an incredible view of the silvery blue ocean, the midday sun fanning a constellation of twinkling stars on the water. They settled into comfortable leather chairs. At a nearby table, two older men clad in golf attire were drinking Heinekens, at another, two attractive women in their fifties were discussing the grilled tuna with their young waiter.

Marianne ordered a diet coke, David a rum and coke.

"Starting early today?" she quizzed.

"It's vacation," he said, smiling. "You should try one."

"Love to but can't. Which is why I wanted to bring you here. I have something to tell you. I just can't keep it a secret anymore," she said.

What? Her words hit him like a hammer. It took him a moment to comprehend the reality of what she was saying. *What would keep her from drinking?* It couldn't be an illness or medication or she wouldn't look so damn happy right now. In fact the only time she looked like this, no it couldn't be . . . not again.

"We're going to have a baby," she said brightly, her pale blue eyes brimming with happiness.

He tried to find his voice, but could not. He was literally and physically speechless. Another child. How could this be? They had decided not to have any more children; they had discussed it at length after Colin was born. Even Colin was a surprise. Marianne was supposed to be on the pill, but somehow she had forgotten to take it so along came his son. And that was okay, his son was an unexpected but wonderful blessing. But this. A tide of anger surged through him as he absorbed the full impact of her news. *Another baby.*

"David, you don't look happy," she said, her eyebrows knit together in a benevolent frown. "I know we didn't plan on this, but we're going to have another baby to love and nurture and be part of our family. I'm so excited and I know the children will be as well."

"Marianne," he said, trying to find the right words, struggling to be truthful while keeping the anger in check. "I'm sorry but this is a shock to me and my immediate reaction is not to jump for joy. We discussed this, we both agreed that we weren't going to have any more children. Once is a mistake. I don't think I need to tell you what twice is."

Angered by his assertion, she closed the menu abruptly and placed it on the table. "This is a child we're talking about, not a *decision*. I didn't ask for this to happen, but it has and this baby is a precious gift. I can't believe you don't see that. Are you really that selfish?"

It was too much, the co-mingling of his agony for the woman he loved and resentment for the woman he had married. He found himself losing control. "Selfish? *I'm selfish* for not wanting a limit on this three-ring circus we call a family. Don't talk to me about being selfish. You know what I really think? I think you're irresponsible. I think the reason you want all these babies is to fulfill your needs . . . because if you take an honest look at the situation we're not doing such a great job with the ones we already have. Do you really think we have a normal family life, with these spoiled rotten children we have created, whose whims are your sole reason for being?" He had difficulty keeping his voice at a low hiss so as to not attract attention.

"How dare you insult me for being a good mother! Are you that cruel? Don't you understand that when you have children they become the center of your life and that is *your precious normal!* So what if they act out? They're just being kids. They are a bundle of wants, that is what they are. So we deal with it the best we can. And that's just a small part of them, they give us so much love and joy and hope, how can you *not* see that?"

"Because I live in a house where chaos rules twenty-four seven. And don't give me that BS about hope and love. Of course I love them. But there's nothing wrong with discipline,

Marianne, and our children have none. The closest they get to punishment is a minute in the time-out chair."

The waiter came to take their order, halting David from continuing his unvarnished critique of their home life. They ordered their entrees, trying to hide the fact they were arguing, David having been taught his entire life never to air one's dirty linen in public. As soon as the waiter walked away, the argument resumed.

"Do you realize how awful you're being?" she said. "I bring you here to tell you I'm pregnant and you're lecturing me on discipline. You're my husband. I cannot believe you're this cold-hearted. I thought you might actually be happy."

"Oh come on Marianne. That's delusional. You knew this was going to be hard for me."

David took a gulp of his rum and coke, and promptly decided to have another. The image of Ellen exploded into his consciousness, her beautiful eyes, hair and body, the way she was obliviously unaware of the power of her own sexuality, which only ramped up the voltage and made him crazy. The entire time they were together this morning, he could not stop thinking about the night they spent together. He closed his eyes for a moment immersed in the memory before returning to the unwelcome present.

Another baby. He never thought he could feel like this. Dark thoughts swirled around him, rising flood waters of guilt, fear, anger, the overwhelming feeling of being trapped. This is not what he wanted. The question was, did Marianne even care? Apparently not.

All around him, people were talking, relaxing, enjoying the best that life had to offer. None of it was his. And maybe he was an unforgivable prick for what he'd done, for cheating on his wife, for not wanting a baby. Strange though, right now he didn't feel guilty. He felt used, like he no longer mattered, as long as he was there to create more babies and means to support them.

In the midst of his despair, he had a moment of clarity. It was not the first time the thought had crossed his mind, but this time it was more real, urgent, a life raft in stormy seas. He could not stop his wife's insatiable maternal desires and obsession with their children. But there was a way out—divorce—yes it was ugly and would kill his mother and potentially hurt his children but right now, the thought, elusive and far away as it was, gave him comfort. Would it ever come to that? He did not know. It wasn't until much later did he fully understand that something in him changed that day, and his feelings for his wife had been irrevocably altered.

"Liz, I just had to see you before I leave," said a breathless Ellen, who had just pedaled her bicycle across the island to see her friend. "So glad you're home!"

"I had a feeling you'd be coming by. Especially after you hightailed it out of church this morning. Was that—"

"Yes," Ellen said. "That was him."

"Handsome," Liz said, giving her a knowing smile. "Come in and have a cup of coffee. I'm going over to Harold's but we can have a little chat before I go."

Ellen followed Liz through the tidy but crowded living room into the kitchen, where the afternoon light gave the room a lemony glow. Miss Kitty, who looked blissfully content, napped in a triangle of sunlight spilling in through the screened door.

"Does she have the life or what?" Liz said, smiling. "If I did believe in reincarnation—and mind you I don't—I'd come back as a cat!"

"I'm not sure I'd come back at all," said Ellen, making Liz laugh.

"Oh you don't mean that, you're so young. You've got so much life ahead of you. You've just been through a rough patch."

The automatic drip coffee pot belched out the last gust of steam, signaling that the coffee was done brewing. Liz took out the cream and sugar, placed it on the table, and poured the coffee into two ceramic cups.

"Liz, where do I start?" Ellen said. "First of all, thank you for everything you've done for me. You've been a wonderful friend to me when I needed one and I will never forget it. And the sermon today," she said, smiling wryly, "why do I think you had a hand in that?"

"Well, from time to time I do offer suggestions," Liz said, feigning modesty.

"It was a wonderful sermon. And when I think about this week, well it's almost like you've been a guardian angel to me," Ellen said.

"I'm glad I was able to help you out dear. No angel here, just a mere earthling. But enough of this—look what you accomplished for us! We'd probably be planning a demolition potluck if you hadn't have come along. We're indebted to you, and to show our gratitude we've decided to make you an honorary member of Grace Chapel," said Liz, her eyes bright.

"I'm honored," Ellen said. "And don't worry, this won't be goodbye forever. But I have to tell you what happened. I had a surprise visitor yesterday. My husband."

Liz's grin turned into a wide-eyed look of surprise. "Heavens to Betsy! Do tell."

"I heard a knock on my door yesterday morning, opened it, and there was Jeremy! I was so shocked to see him, that he would care that much to fly here to be with me. It's a long story but he said he wants to try to get our marriage back on track." Ellen decided not to mention the situation with Andrew; she just didn't want to deal with that now.

"That's wonderful news, obviously he loves you very much."

Ellen took a sip of her coffee. "It's the first time in a long time I feel hopeful about things between us. I was so confused at first, actually panicked, but now I'm actually happy he's here. It's like a big meteor of reality landed from the sky," she said. "So tell me about Harold. Is he a friend, or something more?" she teased.

Much to her surprise, Liz blushed. Intrigued, Ellen continued. "Well, you know all my secrets, out with it!"

"Harold is a dear friend," she said. "His wife has cancer and

I've been going over there to help out. She's in hospice now and he's a wreck."

"I'm so sorry to hear that," Ellen said. "It must be so hard for him."

"It is, and it's to the point where I wish the good Lord would just take her home. But that's not in our hands. In the meantime, I'm there to help out any way I can."

"He's fortunate to have you as a *friend*," Ellen said, the emphasis on the last word deliberate. The scarlet hue that colored Liz's face confirmed her suspicions.

"So more than friends?"

Liz's eyes met hers; her smile was wistful. "Yes, at least for me, but he doesn't have a clue as to how I really feel. Promise me you'll never breathe a word of this to any other living soul."

"Your secret is safe with me," Ellen promised. "As mine is with you."

So that is why Liz understood, Ellen realized. That day at lunch when she talked about women and soul mates and being attracted to other men—now it all made sense. The entire time she was listening to me go on about David, she had these feelings for another man, a *married* man.

"I never thought there would be anyone else after Edward," Liz said. "Then Harold came along and everything changed. If someone would have ever told me I'd fall in love at my age I'd have thought they were crazy! But sometimes I feel like the one who's crazy." Her voice was hushed as she continued. "I think about him all the time, I can't wait to see him . . . I feel like a young woman again, like I did when I was nineteen. So don't go beating yourself up too much over what happened with that handsome man in church this morning, because well, these things just happen. That's what keeps us going, I guess," she said, smiling, "even for old ladies like me."

"Lady yes, old—heck no! If they measured age in attitude instead of years you'd be younger than me. Seriously, though, I think it's so wonderful that you found someone. I hope that someday you can be together."

"I hope so too," Liz replied quietly. She looked faraway in thought for a moment, then regained her usual cheery disposition. "And I hope you work things out with your husband. Now listen, Ellen, I want you to promise me that you'll keep in touch, and that you'll come back here again for a visit."

Ellen promised, even though she felt a twinge of anxiety that returning here would somehow place her in harm's way again. She dismissed the thought, knowing it wasn't rationale and certainly not a good reason to stay away from a place that she loved and meant so much to her. More importantly, how could she refuse this delightful woman sitting across from her, no longer a stranger, but a dear friend.

Judy slipped off her sandals, and stretched out her tanned legs in front of her, relaxing into the soft cushions of the chaise lounge, the royal blue canvas of the cabana shading her from the late afternoon sun.

In the distance near the water's edge, Ethan, Emma and Maggie were building an elaborate sand castle replete with moats, turrets and shell-encrusted walls. Overseeing the construction and offering advice when needed, Gertrude and George sat side-by-side in low-rise beach chairs, the kind you take to summer concerts in the park, letting the frothy waves splash over their bare feet. George must have said something funny, because she could hear Gertrude's hearty laughter carried on the velvet breeze.

Judy sighed contentedly at the sight of the two siblings, and marveled at the longevity of their relationship. Despite their occasional bickering, they were devoted to one another and had been their entire lives. George had always hoped Gertrude would marry, but the years went by and that fate eluded her. He loved Eunice as well, but that relationship was more perfunctory given her cantankerous temperament. He'd often joked she'd been born an old maid. It was Gertrude who made him laugh, Gertrude who could light up a room with the sheer force of her charismatic personality.

For the moment, an aura of harmony had descended on her

family and Judy welcomed it with joy. The fact that George was even in close physical proximity to Maggie indicated a thawing in father-daughter relations. Her grandchildren were having the time of their lives, squealing with delight as they raced away from the waves, thrilled at the discovery of a giant clamshell to adorn the castle's main turret. Taking in the mélange of sun-drenched beach, father and daughter finally reunited, her grandchildren happily carrying buckets of sand, she wished the moment could last forever.

A lifetime of experience had taught her the rarity of times like these and need to cherish them. Looking back over the tapestry of her life, she realized with heartfelt longing that it had all gone too fast. Kind of like the way fall comes every year, with barely a whisper of warning and then suddenly one night it's dark at seven o'clock and there's a chill in the air. There is no going back. One day your children are building sand castles, the next they're going off to college, leaving you to wonder how on earth it was possible that eighteen years could pass so quickly. Time is the enemy of mothers and fathers, they know it intellectually but the frenzied pace of busy lives keeps it at bay until the day of reckoning arrives, and the infants you once cradled in your arms give you a kiss and a hug and walk out the front door. They come home for visits but it will never be the same. There is a great sadness in the silence that blankets the rooms once filled with so much joy and laughter. Life goes on, but the void remains.

A handsome man who looked to be in his fifties walked by and she had the distinct and pleasurable feeling she was getting the once-over. He smiled at her in an approving way. With her sunglasses on and petite figure, she could easily pass for a younger woman, which ironically is what she felt like. She wondered why no one had ever told her that one of the strangest things about getting older was that you never felt "old" no matter how many candles were on the cake. True, she'd learned a lot on life's journey, yes, wisdom had been gained, but despite all that she still felt like the same person she'd been fifty years ago. And most of her friends did too. They chafed at the fact they were now identified as senior citizens. Hell, those were *old people*, not them. Sure their children were grown and their grandchildren were teenagers, in some cases married and producing great-grandchildren, but they weren't *old*.

When she was younger, Judy mistakenly believed that at some point in the aging process a mystical transformation would take place and one day she'd wake up knowing she was old. But this had not happened. Instead, she woke up every morning, the mirror reflecting an attractive but older woman with laugh lines around her eyes and mouth. It is a cruel trick of time, she thought, this being old but feeling young.

A dark thought fired in her subconscious and her thoughts returned to George. It took an extraordinary effort, but she made a silent vow not to let the anxiety return or it would ruin the rest of the precious time she had left with her family. She would deal with all this when they got home. In the meantime, she let the scene of happy grandkids etch itself into her consciousness so she would remember it long after she left this place and put away her photo albums.

DEEP IN THOUGHT, SHE DIDN'T REALIZE David had come up behind the cabana.

"Hi Mom."

"Oh, you startled me," she said.

"Got room for me?"

"Sure, honey, I always have room for you," she said, looking up and smiling at him. "Let me move my bag."

"That's okay, I'll get it."

David moved the beach bag, and stretched out on the chair. Judy sensed there was something wrong; it was odd that he was here without Marianne. She wondered if they'd had an argument.

"This is beautiful," he said, taking in the ocean vista. "Do we have to go home?"

"I could stay here forever," she said, "Not just because we're in one of the most beautiful places on earth but because my children are all here and that's the best gift a mother can have. I know that sounds corny but it's true." She looked at him affectionately.

David forced a smile, and wondered how it was possible to be having this conversation with his mother at this moment when he was so miserable in his own marriage and conflicted about his family. He looked over at Ethan and Emma happily shoveling sand into buckets, plopping them over upside down to build another tower, and chided himself for being so selfish. They were his children. He loved them with all his heart. Yet he somehow had grown to resent them because of their mother, who created the world she thought best for them without letting him have any say at all about that world. She had driven a wedge between him and his children and he had let her. For his sake and the sake of his children, it had to stop.

"David, are you okay?" said his mother, jolting him out of his thoughts.

"I'm fine. Just a little tired," he said, in an attempt to deflect any further scrutiny.

"Where's Marianne?" she asked.

"Something at lunch didn't agree with her so she's lying down for a while. Nothing serious."

"It's too bad she's missing such a gorgeous afternoon."

They watched as Emma brought over a bucket to George, who got up from his chair. He went down to the water and filled it up. "Grandpa, give the water to Aunt Maggie for the swimming pool," Ethan shouted. George did as he was told, and though they were fifty feet away, Judy could see the hostilities had fallen away as Maggie looked up at her father who for the first time did not look away.

"Look David, I think they're actually getting along. I'm so relieved. Isn't it wonderful?"

David smiled at his mother, touched by her joyful sentimentality, his love for her deep and true. His respect for her had intensified since he had his own children. Looking back, he realized how much she had given them over the years:

love, laughter, encouragement, values, home-cooked meals, bedtime stories, and when needed, discipline. She devoted her life to raising a family and had never complained or regretted her decision. He wondered how the corresponding maternal desires of his wife had metamorphosed into such a dysfunctional environment for his own family.

He reached over, took her hand in his and held it there, watching his children run back and forth to the water's edge as the sun sparkled brilliantly over the iris blue waters.

"Happy anniversary Mom," he said, turning to her. "I love you."

She squeezed his hand, lifted her eyes to his and smiled. "I love you too, honey. And I'm so proud of the person you've become."

She had no way of knowing that was the last thing he needed to hear today.

One Year Later

The Spartan interior of Grace Chapel had been beautifully transformed by bouquets of flowers, satin ribbons and a pristine white runner that led to the altar. Ivory-rose nosegays and cloudbursts of tulle streamers adorned every pew. The sun streamed in through the large windows behind the altar, bathing a vase of stargazer lilies in a prism of golden light, their sweet fragrance filling the sanctuary.

Ever since Ellen had opened the creamy vellum envelope containing the invitation, she knew she could not miss the wedding. She was thrilled for Liz, and knew how happy she must be.

The bride wore a lavender chiffon dress under an elegant brocade jacket, the groom a charcoal suit. The couple stood facing the minister on the altar, reciting the words that would establish the covenant of marriage. They could not help but think of the last time they had spoken these vows, so many years ago, their hearts then full of love and anticipation for all that lie ahead, the future stretching out before them with the immensity of the Grand Canyon. "Till death do us part" had little meaning for two young people barely in their twenties. Yet today in the midst of this celebratory gathering lurked the unspoken recognition of a future together not of decades but of years, God willing. This awareness did not deter them, though, on the contrary it inspired them to live life to the fullest, making the best of the time they had each and every day. There was so much to celebrate. Neither one of them had ever thought they would fall in love again, and yet it had happened. At a time in life when people needed each other more than ever, they would not be alone.

"I now pronounce you man and wife." said Pastor Roberts. Harold took a step toward Liz, kissing her gently on the lips. Turning to face the congregation, Liz flashed a beatific smile to the throng of family members and friends crowded into the pews, who burst into hearty applause. Harold turned to look at his bride, his eyes sparkling with happiness. A renewed vitality had replaced the shroud he had worn throughout Lucille's illness. In the first row, two little girls wearing taffeta dresses smiled excitedly and waved to their grandmother. The organist hit the first notes of the traditional bridal march, and the couple took their first steps together as man and wife.

As the newlyweds made their way past them, Jeremy looked over at Ellen with tenderness in his eyes and squeezed her hand. Ellen squeezed it back, and felt her eyes fill with tears. Jeremy had no way of knowing her tears were not of joy, but of a memory. Ellen took a deep breath, and once again banished the thought of him from her mind.

Author's Note

Denizens and visitors to Sanibel will likely notice a few liberties have been taken with places and geography. The inspiration for Grace Chapel comes from Captiva's storied Chapel By The Sea but the name, history and location were changed to advance a fictional narrative. The Paradise Resort and Spa is a product of my imagination but is very loosely based on a wonderful beachfront hotel and condo complex on Middle Gulf Drive, where the first chapters of this novel were written.

What is not fictional in any aspect is the extraordinary beauty of Sanibel Island. It is my favorite place in the world to visit. Sanibel never fails to renew my spirits and belief in all that is possible. Walking on the beach, listening to the surf, watching the shorebird ballet at the water's edge, I'm overwhelmed by a deep and abiding connection to all of creation.

Thank you to everyone who has worked so hard to protect this exceptional natural sanctuary.

Book Club Discussion

1. What do you think about the portrayal of family issues and relationships in this novel?

2. What characters resonated with you the most and why? Least?

3. What do you think about the way infidelity is addressed in this novel? Does someone have to be unhappy in a marriage to be attracted to another person?

4. How does the character of Ellen evolve during the course of the story? David? Others?

5. Describe the role of setting in this novel.

6. What do you think about the way this book tackled issues of faith?

7. What kind of mother is Judy? What kind of father is George? What do you think about his treatment of Maggie?

8. In your view, who has the upper hand in the ongoing debate between Julia and Maggie? What role does society and culture play in assigning status, success or failure to these characters?

9. Do you think Ellen will be happy in her marriage going forward?

10. Were there any scenes that were especially interesting or memorable to you and why?

11. What are your thoughts on the differences between Marianne and David's parenting beliefs?

12. What are some of the major themes in this book and which ones, if any, are relevant to your life?

Thank You!

Thank you for reading *Ten Days In Paradise.* I hope you enjoyed it. I welcome your thoughts on my novel and reviews on Amazon and Goodreads.

If you're in a book club, I hope you will consider reading *Ten Days In Paradise* for one of your selections. This novel touches on many areas of contemporary life that are likely to stimulate a robust discussion. The book club discussion questions on the prior page can also be found at www.TenDaysInParadise.com.

If you enjoyed this book and want to spread the word on or offline, please know that your efforts are greatly appreciated!

— Linda Abbott, Nov. 18, 2014

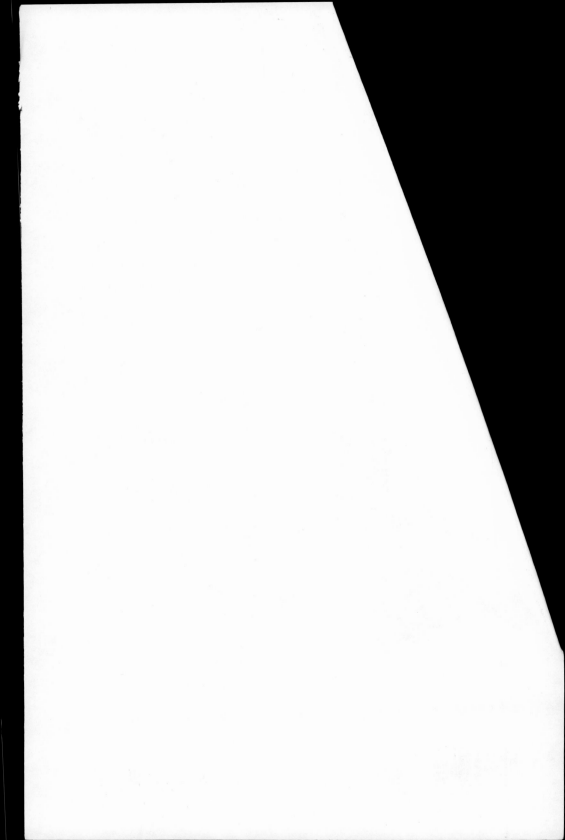

Made in the USA
Charleston, SC
30 January 2015